A Date With Teeth

by Kirk Thomas

Different Kinds Of Hurt

The boy had always wanted his father to love him. But his father had no love to give. And that hurt. It hurt him deeply. Deeper than any cut or bruise ever could.

But it was a hurt you couldn't see, unless you knew to look. Unless you knew what the hurt looked like. Unless you'd felt it yourself, that hole in the soul. It was a feeling of something missing, deep inside. It was a feeling of not belonging, no matter how hard you tried.

The boy had friends. But even when the boy was with his friends, the feeling never left him. He felt an apartness. As happy the circumstance, as strong the camaraderie, there was always something. Something holding him back, preventing him from connecting.

And they didn't understand it, his friends, but why would they? They were loved, by the only people a child really needs to be loved by, its parents. Real love that is, not its imitation.

Merely professing a thing does not make it so, and the love between a parent and a child should not be conditional, on any one thing or another, on the right choice of calling, the right choice of friend, or the right choice of thought or expression.

Worries that bothered his friends not, for his friends knew care, kindness and the kinship of family. They were nurtured and urged to flower. They knew nothing of coldness, disdain and wrath. And even less of the suppression of self, in the preservation of self.

Sometimes his friends would make jests and call him 'Little Storm Cloud'. This just hurt him more, as he was small for his age and sensitive about it. It made him feel insecure and uncertain.

He knew it shouldn't bother him, he knew it was just the jests boys make with one another. But whereas the words rolled off his friends backs like water, they hung over him like clouds, and his mood would darken.

He'd become quiet and introspective, or his face would flush, and his fists would bunch. He hadn't learned how to deal with these things from his father, as boys do. He didn't know how to deal with the jests and the jibes. The jokes and the horseplay. No one spoke to his father like this. And so he'd learned to keep his mouth shut, and his 'eccentricities' to himself. It wasn't worth the wrath.

So where he should have been testing boundaries and learning limits, he was feeling fear and sowing suppression. The thought of his father lashing him with his tongue made his stomach twist in knots. He'd tried of course, after he'd made friends with his little group of 'des voyous', as his mother scathingly called them. But it did not go well.

And as for the wrestling and the boisterous play his friends sometimes engaged in, he daren't not try with father. And so, he continued, unsure, upset, and growing further apart from his friends, as they grew together, and their bond of brotherhood strengthened.

It was funny. He'd fallen and twisted his ankle once in the summer, breaking it badly. The pain was excruciating, for the still young boy. He'd cried his eyes red raw and wailed for his mother. But Louis, his friend, had said nothing.

He remembered he found this strange. He'd expected to be ridiculed, had feared it, even in the midst of the pain, but the ridicule never came. Louis had simply thrown his arm around him and carried him home, like a comrade in arms from one of the old tales the boy was so fond of.

His mother had rebuked him sharply of course, and admonished him for being foolish. His father simply shook his head and returned to his work. There was no rage, for which he was thankful, but the look in his eyes cut him. It was dismissive and cold, and a look that said, you disappoint me.

Some nights, when the hurt was heavy upon him, the hurt inside, he thought he'd endure a lifetime of twisted ankles if it meant he could feel like he belonged. If he could somehow make sense of this life, and what he needed to do to know happiness.

What he would give to know the same camaraderie with his father, Louis had with his. To know the loving admiration his friend Edouard knew from his mother. She was so warm and so playful.

He envied them. Sometimes he wished he'd wake up and find his life thus far had all been a dream. That he was brother to Edouard, or Louis, or Noël.

He didn't understand why he couldn't be like them, or what he had done to warrant such scorn from his own parents. Perhaps he'd been born into the wrong family by some unfortunate happenstance.

Things hadn't always been bad. He could vaguely remember becoming aware of his father's growing dislike of him. It was around the time he learned he was no longer a boy and had begun down that path toward manhood.

As he had grown in confidence and maturity, he had felt a rift grow between them, that soon became an uncrossable chasm. It had begun with his curiosity. You see, his father didn't mind when he asked questions, as long as he accepted his answers without question. To question his answers was to err on the wrong side of caution.

Unfortunately, his questions had come in droves, as his young mind exploded with new energy and ideas, like a supernova of excitement and curiosity, and eccentricities took root in the garden of his mind. And as his eccentricities bloomed, and his newly garnered opinions blossomed, his father's tolerance withered and waned.

His father did not like to be wrong, and he did not tolerate a difference of opinion. To disagree with him was a mortal sin, punishable by banishment, until one learned the error of their ways, and came back obeisant to his feet, newly enlightened as to the error of their thinking and the rightness of his.

To repent for one's sins was the only path to salvation. And to repent, one must worship at the steeple of superiority, and profane the gospel of he, he who is right, and always shall be.

He feared his father, was the truth of it. It was a fact he had become painfully aware of, and in a much more sudden fashion, than his recognition of his father's creeping dislike.

He had been playing with Marie-Jeanne one morning, play-fighting as brother and sister often do, when she had cried out loudly and started crying, as if he had hurt her. He panicked, for he knew his father was only in the next room, and the bottom of his stomach fell from him. He had barely touched her, but he knew his father was prone to believe Marie-Jeanne, for she was his favourite, and could do no wrong.

His father came upon him furiously, grabbing him by the neck and throwing him hard against the wall. He would never forget his snarling face, nor the threatening words he spoke. It shamed him that he wet his new trousers, but his father cared not, for he wrenched open the door and threw him from the house. Marie-Jeanne had followed him and feigned sympathy for a short while, but her self-satisfied smirk told him everything he needed to know.

It was the beginning of the end for them, little did he know it, but his father's goal had always been to create discord between them, ever since he realised Marie-Jeanne was more pliant than he and was happy to worship at his steeple.

In return, he ordained her as worthy to carry his gospel. He praised her, and she began to rely upon it, and over time, to rely on him completely. He had created in her a self-sustaining economy of praise and admiration, that he so desperately needed to function, to keep his baser self at bay.

In her, he had an echo chamber of stale ideas and untested, unchallenged authority. She feared him, of course, as the boy did, but she chose not to fight him, choosing instead to recite his gospel and live in his delusion.

Part of this delusion was that the boy was bad. The boy wasn't bad, he was simply a boy, but the boy **had** to be bad for the charade to continue, and for the father to remain safe in the castle of glass he had enshrined himself in. It was safer for the girl to support this fallacy, so that she did not become the one to draw his wrath, the wrath reserved for nonbelievers. It was safer, for her perhaps, but what of the boy?

Whereas his sister Marie-Jeanne was serious and presentable, the boy was eccentric and a source of constant embarrassment to the family. You might in fact go so far as to say he was queer, odd, or fae. And this certainly did him no favours.

In a house of blacks and whites, he was a hastily painted canvas of colours, splashed too many hues, of too many vibrant colours, one across the other in quick youthful strokes in even quicker succession. There were hues of tangerine, merigold and cider apple sweet. There were magenta and mauve, grape and periwinkle, emerald, and olive soothing as the spring orchards. There were greys that went as grey as shadow, and reds as deep as blood. There were blacks as black as onyx that absorbed all light, and other blacks that were dark like the midnight sky with a little twinkle to them. And there were whites, some pure as snow, and some like the coat of an albino stallion with a little kick to them.

Where he should have been monochrome, he was a cacophony of colour. Where he should have been of one mind, he was of many. The brighter he shone, the darker his father grew, and for their own self-preservation, his mother and sister darkened too, and so things for the boy grew dark indeed.

His light hurt his father, you see, though he would not realise it, for many a moon, and many more tears yet. And as his light hurt his father, so his father hurt him. It was his only choice, to extinguish that light, as quickly as possible, lest it shine upon him too brightly, and show him his true self. A self he had hid from, for years incalculable.

To hide behind his imagined facade, was his father's only choice. His self-imposed purgatory, for his inability to be his true self, to wear his true colours, to confront himself and his past.

And as his father before him, he took his hurt, and threw it at his son. It hit the boy with the force of a hurricane, knocking the wind from him and spinning him wildly, so that he may never keep his feet on solid ground, instead doomed to blow with the winds of his father's pathos, that seldom knew stillness.

It can change a boy, living in the eye of a storm. It is tempestuous, and when living in a tempest, one can take on the tempest and become tempestuous one's self. There is little time for self-reflection in the storm, little time for the quiet stillness one needs to form a sense of self, a confidence in oneself and most importantly, a love for oneself.

Deprived of this love of self, there is only chaos and uncertainty, a vortex of doubt and precariousness ensues, and one can easily succumb to the baser nature of the tempest. Unpredictability, instability, anger and violence can all take hold in one's heart and colour one solely with shades of red and grey. Violent brush strokes splashing over what was once a complete palette of colour and emotion but is now nothing but a hollow revenant of its former self.

And how does one remember colours so mercilessly stripped away from one? How does one remember the majesty of the snow dappled mountain top, when one can no longer see white? How can one remember the camaraderie of brotherhood, when one's light has been extinguished, and one can no longer see orange, the warming colour of kinship. One cannot be a kindred flame, burning brightly in a band of brothers, bound by spirit and seen by soul, when one's flame burns so low as to barely flicker, extinguishable by the slightest gust or gale, dimmable by the merest pall or pale.

This person can only live a cursed life, a half existence, watching through monotone lens, colours and feelings unjustly robbed from them, forever yearning for them, reaching for them, yet always unable to grasp them, cursed to only feel them tickle the tips of their fingers, to know the merest brush of them, the smallest drink, the most inconsequential sip, for them to slip away once more before that thirst can truly be quenched. The real curse is having known the colours in the first place.

The mercy would be to have never allowed the boy to learn the warmth of the summer sun, or the thoughtful melancholy of the winter moon. To know the fulfilling feeling of kinship and brotherhood. The mercy would be to hide the colours away, to later be discovered, in a time of stillness, far, far away from the tempest.

But mercy is not often forthcoming from a tempest. The tempest deals in absolutes, and mercy is born of contemplation, of forgiveness and ultimately of compromise, the compromise of values, conflicting ideals of right and wrong. But most importantly, mercy is born of maturity, maturity born from wisdom, long sought, and hard acquired. Without wisdom, there can be no maturity. And without maturity, there can be no mercy. There can be no consideration, and there can be no selflessness, for selflessness is gained through contemplation. And the merciless man is not contemplative. He is a tempest. Unpredictable and unforgiving. He knows only the storm raging in his own heart, and can see no further than it, for he refuses to.

And so the merciless, tempestuous man rages, darkening the sky for all those unfortunate enough to be sucked into his path, and turning it black forever, for those unfortunate to live in his tempest.

For those unable to escape him, the tempest rages forever, passed down from father to son, the gift of storm, the gift of grey, the gift of apartness, the gift of self-doubt. These are gifts given to any child fortunate enough to shine as their true authentic self in the eye of the storm. Fortunate enough to see the world for what it is, to see people for who they are, to see things as they are.

The fortune of the child of the tempest is to know hurt. The hurt of longing. The hurt of rejection. The hurt of self-loathing, the hurt of aloneness and the hurt of a premature maturity. An incomplete maturity, not gained through the natural passing of time, and the natural gaining of wisdom, but through the unnatural need for self-preservation, to keep oneself safe from the storm, to keep oneself on the right side of the tempest, to keep oneself from spiralling evermore in its vortex, in the hopes that one day, the child can laugh and run free once more, free from its shackles, free from its pain.

And so this is where our story begins, with a child of the tempest. A child become a man before his time. A man attempting to find his stillness, his belonging, his peace...in a world raging around him all the while.

Born of the tempest, he is a different kind of man, how could he not be?

He is a man of extremes, for he carries the volatility of the storm within him. Capable of lightest light, or darkest dark, which path shall he walk? Light or dark. Good or evil. Is it ever so simple?

This is not a man of simple strokes. I shall remind you of his vivid hues.

His canvas of colours. Are they lost forever? Or do they lie mute, under a cloak of greys and reds. It may not be as simple as you think. Only time will tell.

But the tale is not his alone.

Prologue

It hadn't always been like this.

There used to be a time when it meant something to be of the Tableau Haute. A time of higher ideals, a time of purpose, a time of meaning.

What would they think, if they could see us now? Reduced to our baser instincts, like common moindre.

Tis for the best that they are not alive to see it, for it would only hurt them, to see how far we have fallen.

It would surely hurt them, for it hurts me. And...I am powerless to stop it.

A chair scraped sadly across the floor, as a tall man in a black cloak dragged himself to his feet.

He stepped back from a grand wooden table, slick with blood, and walked toward an ornate wooden door.

"Not to your taste?" a voice called.

The cloaked man paused for a moment, as if considering his response. "I indulged myself previously, monseigneur", he said, bowing.

A man sat at the table watched him closely, his look coldly calculating.

After a moment, he broke into a malevolent smile and inclined his head, returning his attention to the table.

The cloaked man pulled the door open gently, so as not to disturb those at the table.

He stepped swiftly through, closing the door on the other side with a click.

Hidden under the hood of his cloak, a single tear slid slowly down his face.

A Chance Encounter

Lucien was a man who liked order and efficiency in all things, especially when it came to his business affairs. Chief amongst those was, of course, DuPassé.

So it should come as no surprise that it is where we find Lucien on this day, and that it is where our story begins.

"Did you complete the inventory as I requested, Duphan?" Lucien asked.

"Of course. And more importantly...your café", Duphan replied, handing Lucien a small mug.

"Ah, excellent. What would I do without you, Duphan?"

"I shudder to think".

"But what about th-".

"You needn't worry, I responded to The Marquis as requested, letting him know you will attend him this evening".

Lucien rubbed his chin and grinned.

"Well, it sounds like everything is in order..." he trailed off, his eyes and attention now on something at the back of the store.

"Monsieur?" Duphan asked.

He furrowed his brow, watching Lucien intently for a moment, before following his eyes, and realising what he was looking at.

"I see..." Duphan muttered to himself.

He shook his head and shuffled away from Lucien, toward a rather comfortable looking chair behind the counter at the front of the store.

The counter was awash with parchment and old books, but Duphan seemed more interested in a well-thumbed newspaper sitting atop a stack of books.

Lucien walked slowly toward the back of the store, his eyes on a man with his back to him.

The man did not appear to hear Lucien's approach, perhaps due to how intently he was looking at a glass display cabinet full of rings, of all shapes, sizes and persuasions.

Lucien stood for a while, watching the man, his face thoughtful.

"An interesting piece", Lucien ventured quietly.

The man jumped, startled by Lucien's sudden appearance.

"What? Oh, I am sorry, you startled me... I was so engrossed in the beauty of it", the man replied.

"Yes, it is certainly beautiful", Lucien agreed, staring intently at the man.

A small blush blossomed on the man's face.

"There are many beautiful things here", the man said, looking at Lucien, before gesturing around the store. "But of them all, I was most drawn to this". He pointed at an ordinary looking silver ring sat upon a bed of red velvet.

"Why this?" Lucien nodded at the ring.

"I do not know", the man replied lamely. "A feeling, perhaps".

Lucien took a moment before responding. "There are many beautiful rings in this store, but you are the first to recognise the beauty of this one".

"Really?"

Lucien nodded. "It is beautiful. Though most do not see it, distracted as they are by the sparkle and shine of its gaudier companions". He gestured to the other rings in the display cabinet.

The man nodded in agreement.

A pause grew between them, then Lucien extended his hand. "Lucien", Lucien said.

"Gabriel", the man replied with a warm smile. Lucien could not help but smile back.

"A pleasure to meet you, Gabriel", Lucien said, still holding his hand, sounding his name slowly, as if seeking some meaning in it.

"The pleasure is all mine". Gabriel took a moment to study his new acquaintance more closely. He had the most peculiar brown eyes, and an intriguing smile.

"Thank you for taking the time to find such beautiful things, it is the best part of my day coming here to look at them", Gabriel said suddenly, aware that he'd been staring.

Lucien frowned. "Do you come here often? It is the first time I've seen you in DuPassé, though admittedly I am not here as often as I like".

"As often as I am able, though I usually visit in the evenings. I love that you are open at night, not a lot of the other shops are...in fact, I think you are the only one". Gabriel looked around the shop as if pondering this piece of information.

"Yes, well, some of our clients are very particular, and shall we say the evenings are more to their taste", Lucien said.

"I see..." Gabriel said, unsure what to make of this. "Well, I am grateful either way, I have always been something of a night owl. I love exploring Paris by night. That, and it's often the only time I can find to explore after work". He grinned sheepishly.

"Well, perhaps a more accommodating line of work may be of interest to you then? Duphan is always impressing upon me how terrible the help I find him is". Lucien gestured to the man sitting behind the desk at the front of the store. "And how quite uninterested they are in the history of our merchandise".

"What do you mean?"

"Well, you could work here, of course".

Gabriel flushed softly, averting his eyes. "But I have no

formal training, or recommendation. I'm really not qualified".

"Maybe not, but I have a feeling you have a knack for this, and I am something of a good judge of character", Lucien replied, intrigue playing across his face.

"I, I don't know… thank you so much for the offer, I don't want to seem ungrateful…" Gabriel said.

Lucien watched Gabriel, a smile dancing at the corners of his mouth.

"Can I think about it?" Gabriel asked.

Lucien's face darkened, and he swung away from Gabriel dramatically, turning his back to him.

"Wait, I-", Gabriel started to speak.

But Lucien swung quickly back to face him, a mischievous smile on his face. "I suppose that would be acceptable", he said imperiously.

Gabriel snorted. "You are a rogue, monsieur".

"Somewhat", Lucien admitted. "You know where to find me when you have made your decision. Unfortunately, I am needed elsewhere presently. It has been…a pleasure". He stared at Gabriel for a long moment, before tilting his head respectfully and moving away to the front of the shop.

"I may have finally found you some worthy help", Lucien muttered to Duphan, watching Gabriel from the corner of his eye.

"Really, monsieur? You managed to ascertain the gentleman's suitability to work here from just that chance encounter?" Duphan said dryly.

Lucien looked up sharply from the stack of parchment he had been pretending to read, fixing Duphan with a piercing stare.

Duphan looked back at him balefully, down the bottom of his glasses. After a moment Lucien relaxed and laughed.

"You really are incorrigible", he said.

"Whatever do you mean, monsieur?" Duphan replied

impetuously, studiously keeping a straight face.

Lucien shook his head. "I must be going now".

Fastening his black coat, he paused, gave Gabriel one last look, then left.

From the back of the shop, safely nestled between the myriad bookcases and display cabinets, Gabriel watched as the mysterious owner of DuPassé left the shop.

He was too distracted now, to enjoy DuPassé, and to lose himself in the history within.

Sighing, he shook his head, and walked toward the front of the store.

Catching Duphan's eye upon him, he smiled shyly. Duphan tipped his head politely and returned his attention to his newspaper.

Did the man ever do any work? He'd scarcely seen him move from that chair since he'd arrived. Quite the comfortable calling, this antiquing, perhaps he would give it some real thought.

He stopped for a moment as if searching for something to say, but finding no words, he stepped out into the street, closing the door behind him.

Catching another figure with a purposeful walk from the corner of his eye, he smiled, then went on his way.

In DuPassé, the ring that Gabriel was so enamoured with seemed to glow for a moment, though perhaps it was simply the afternoon sun, shining prettily down upon it.

It's Best Not To Keep Him Waiting

Lucien shut his apartment door behind him and leant back against the door, eyes closed, taking a moment to relax in the peace and solitude of his home.

He was tired. Tired from his work, and tired from the human contact that went along with it. He enjoyed human contact, but the problem was that he tended to loath most humans, which was quite the predicament.

Many of them made him despair and made him want to lock himself away and never venture forth again. Or perhaps hop on a boat and sail far, far away somewhere.

Though he loathed not all of them. Some of them energised him and lifted him, giving him cause for hope and joy.

A beautiful face ran through his mind, and he smiled.

He took off his coat, and almost immediately a slender, impeccably dressed figure appeared in the hallway, hand outstretched to take it from him.

"Thank you Alonze", Lucien said.

"You are welcome, monsieur", Alonze replied dutifully.

"I am going to my study", Lucien said stiffly.

"Monsieur", Alonze bobbed his head in acknowledgement. He knew what that meant. He knew his master well and recognised his need for solitude.

He would respect his wishes. Lucien was a good master to

him, and he cared for him, and more, respected him. Not out of duty, but from knowing. Knowing he was a good man, who was worthy of his respect, and more, had earned it in his treatment of him.

Alonze disappeared into the depths of the apartment. A quiet clinking sound rang out soon after.

Lucien smiled, then followed him into his apartment, across the beautifully waxed parquet floor. He stopped to admire it. He truly loved these old buildings, and he felt blessed to live in a place like this. He felt like he walked on history. He walked through into the living area, and a few rays of sunlight hit his face through the large ornate windows. He crossed the room and drew the curtains.

The living area was sparsely furnished, but stylishly so, as if every choice was carefully considered. He didn't like clutter, apart from in his study, where it seemed to accumulate against his wishes.

The centrepiece of the room was a gilded fireplace and a fire laid ready, waiting for him. He loved to stare into the flames in the evening, watching them flicker, listening to the cracks of the wood, as it burned to give him warmth. He was grateful for its gift.

He considered his chair and his fire. Not yet, he thought. He felt drained, stifled, stiff. He needed to relax. He eyed a regal looking door with a golden handle that sat at the end of a hallway to the right of the living area. Rolling his lips, he made up his mind, and went to his study, closing the door behind him with a satisfying snap.

He relaxed almost immediately. Bookshelves spanned the walls of this small, square shaped room. They were lined top to bottom with books of all sorts. New ones, old ones. Fictions and stories, histories and accounts. Serious tales and comedic adventures.

He felt happy here.

But he was not in the mood to read. He needed to create. His work had tired him, drained him, and he felt grey and without colour. He loved antiques, and he loved history, but he was not sure he loved business. In fact, he rather suspected he hated it.

He had many business interests, having developed something of a knack for it, but DuPassé was his favourite amongst them. Perhaps because there was a certain romance to it. Antiquing, that is.

He saw the pursuit not as the collecting of 'things' for the purpose of sale, but as the collection of memories, the collection of history.

He loved the smell of the old books, and the feel of their pages. Every book smelt the same, yet somehow different. He felt that when he smelled them, he could picture days long past, and often found himself wondering, what was life like back then.

Were things better, or were they worse? Were people nicer, were people kinder? He doubted it. But he was a natural cynic. And his cynicism always seemed to rear its ugly head most after a long day's work. And that was why he was not sure if it was the path for him. He had thought it was. He'd wanted to prove himself adept at it. To prove he could make it on his own, to make something of himself. To become a man to be proud of. Lucien, man of commerce, titan of industry!

He'd lay awake dreaming of it at night, picturing himself as the strong, self-assured businessmen he saw in the city, walking with head high, back straight.

His mother had scoffed at him and assured him he would do no such thing. He would work for The Tableau, as his father before him. His father of course found the whole thing laughable. And so, he'd grit his teeth, set his jaw, and dug his heels. He would prove them wrong. Little Lucien would make his own way.

And make his own way he did, and his little follies bore fruit, and the fruit bore seed. He'd reaped what he'd sown, and he'd lived a good life.

Things were good. For a while. But he was not happy. Though his coffers were full, his heart was empty.

He cleared his throat, and shook himself from his maudlin thoughts, turning his attention to the parchment and quill in front of him. He knew he could easily afford paper and pen, but he preferred the parchment. There was just something about it that he liked.

A knock at the door distracted him, and he frowned, turning in his chair as Alonze entered, bearing a tray with a squat, ridged glass. In it was a dark liquid and some ice.

Seeing the glass, Lucien smiled.

"I thought the master might like some rum", Alonze said, his eyes twinkling.

"That would be nice, actually", Lucien admitted.

"Arr", Alonze said playfully, his face painfully serious.

Lucien snorted into his glass.

"Arr, indeed", he agreed, with a nod and a smile.

Alonze inclined his head, then left, tray in hand.

"Arr", Lucien repeated wistfully, shaking his head. "I do not know why I have such a proclivity for employing such colourful characters".

He turned his attention back to the parchment in front of him and wrote.

*

After a while, he looked up from his writing, and pulled a brass pocket watch from the desk. Checking the time, his face fell.

"Well, it's best not to keep him waiting, twilight approaches". He sighed resignedly.

He'd realised of late that he was beginning to loathe his work, and with it his lot in life. He knew he had chosen this lot, picked it himself from all other lots, but it made it none the easier.

Part of him wondered if he was still just trying subconsciously to prove himself to parents he would never please.

He hated to be pulled from his writing, pulled back to the world, with its relentless relentlessness, and its distinct lack of romance. It had become worse of late, and he had found himself lashing out in impatience, and sometimes, in anger.

What had started as an exciting adventure in pursuit of freedom, had fast become a prison of his own making. A prison of the mind, and a prison of the heart. Each interaction had lessened him, chipped into him, scratching deeper and deeper at his spirit.

Perhaps he was just a hopeless romantic, but the world saddened him to no end, and as of late he had been looking at things differently, thinking of days gone by.

Nostalgia? Perhaps. Almost certainly there was some of that. But he felt there was more to it than that.

He found himself pondering the politicians, and the factory owners, and the bankers. Their sole pursuit in life was the accrual of power and wealth, seemingly at any cost. And for what?

A small slither of bloated, grey men, taking far more than their due.

Depriving others of necessities, draining them and reducing them to grey men too. But the greyness of poverty, the greyness of despair, and the greyness of servitude that knows no end. Rather than the greyness of the corrupted, bloated spirit, that has bled all its colour to the ledger book.

He'd watched as men who'd honed their craft their entire lives fell to the wayside, swallowed by the inevitable march of industrialisation and the howling groans of the factories.

Watched as they dragged themselves to work, day in day out, breaking their hands and their spirits, so that the factory owner might extract his pound of flesh from them. So that he might drive a bigger motor car, sleep in a bigger bed, dine on finer food. The problem was, the factory owner already had the biggest car, already slept in the biggest bed, and already dined on the finest food. His burgeoning waistline was as much a testament to this as anything. His greed knew no bounds, as his workers' misery.

There were no more hunters and there were no more gatherers. No more smiths, no more fletchers. And soon there'd be no more tailors, or fishermen, or butchers. The day would not dawn for many moons yet, but he could see it.

It was inevitable. The factories, and the factory owners would consume them all. Maybe the factories would look different. Maybe they'd come in different shapes and sizes. Maybe they'd have friendly sounding names, and maybe they'd be heralded by convincing sounding politicians, with smiles and handshakes and promises of wealth for all. But come they would.

Human greed was inevitable. Like a slow building tsunami, stirring restlessly in the ocean, hungrily hitting out and lapping at the shore again and again. Searching for the slightest shift or crack in the tectonic plates of civilization, to give it the momentum needed to burst from its cold captivity. And then, it would strike, as it always did, rolling in with dark waves hundreds of feet high that blacken the sky, washing away everything in its path, uprooting homes, lives and livelihoods.

The people would scramble to rebuild, as they always did. And rebuild they would, helping one another, uplifting one another and reassuring one another that the waves were done. Things would be well once more. But then, the next wave would come. The next factory. The next tax. The next rule from on high.

It sickened him. Where did it end? Did it have an end? He'd read of his ancestors, and how they had lived in small communities. Towns and villages. Everyone had a purpose. A craft. A trade. Everyone contributed, helped, loved and nurtured. He loved these stories, and had pursued them in his leisure, reading of heroes and heroines from days gone by, ages lost.

Hunters and gatherers. Farmers and shepherds. Tailors and fletchers. Not a factory in sight. Just people. Living amongst people. No greed, no waste.

He thought it sounded wonderful. There were poets of course. And writers. And artists. Travelling troubadours. Travelling merchants as well, and tinkers, who made it their living plying their trade on the open road, travelling from town to town, fixing and mending things. He found it awfully romantic. Inspiring even.

He knew nostalgia wasn't the answer, and that the past wasn't all romance and high ideals. The cynic in him made sure of that. But when compared with modern day? He wasn't so sure things were better. Things were supposed to get better. **We** were supposed to get better.

He knew there was much evil in the past, and much injustice. Greedy men. Warmongering men. Their innumerable victims strewn across the pages of history.

Well, there were still greedy men, there always would be. And still men intent on conquest and death. But it seemed to him there was less romance. Less idealism. Less freedom. Both of the mind, and of the spirit. Perhaps it was just his own conflicted state of mind, and his growing lack of passion in life. Sometimes he hated himself, as much as he hated others.

If only he could bury himself in his writing and make it his life. To never have to contend with another ledger, another greedy businessman, or another corrupt politician. That would be a life of romance. That would be a life worth living.

Pushing himself wearily to his feet, he opened the door at the back of his study into a larger room. His bedroom. It was supposed to be a place of quiet comfort. But it had become a place he dreaded visiting. Sleep had always eluded him, ever since he was a child. He supposed there must have been a time when he looked forward to its quiet, healing darkness. But more often than not, it danced tantalisingly ever outside his reach, taunting him.

He'd lay awake much of the night and try as he might to keep his eyes closed and to find that place of peace and rest that so eluded him, he could not. And as the night wore thin, and the sun's delicate fingers stretched languidly across sky, he would toss and turn, and fret some more, and his anxiety would deepen to a fever pitch, and his despair would grow with it. Eventually, mercifully, the sun would rise, and end his misery.

Often when he did sleep, he would awake tired and irritable, as if he'd slept not at all. These were dark days. Days for commerce and work which required labour of the mind, rather than labour of the spirit. He dared not write on these days. Could not. It was all he could do to make it through the day in a caffeine fuelled haze. He would certainly write nothing romantic on days such as these, when his thoughts were bleak and grey, and his mind full of sand and sharp edges.

Sitting on the edge of his bed, he ran his hand absentmindedly across the satin sheets. It was a lovingly made four poster bed with skilfully carved wooden bed posts. He loved wood and could not tolerate it when it was over engineered or painted unnecessarily. It had been stripped from a forest somewhere so that he might sleep and know comfort. It was perfect as it was, and he was grateful for it.

The room was sparsely furnished, as the rest of the

apartment, the few items of furniture were wood and beautifully simple. Lucien liked this much about the room at least.

Grinning fondly, he leant across the bed, and lit a candle, sat atop a hastily stacked pile of books on a wooden side table.

Light from the candle swept forth, illuminating the room, and with it, a small picture sitting on the other side table.

Lucien looked at it for a moment, then turned away, his eyes clouding over, their usual twinkle hidden by the grey film that had come over them.

He sat for some time thinking, then rose to his feet and threw open the door to a large armoire opposite the bed. Taking a shirt and jacket from the wardrobe, he closed the door with a snap and began to dress himself, his mind elsewhere.

I don't know why I think of you so, Lucien thought to himself.

I do not think that you deserve it.

Do you think of me?

As I think of you?

I doubt it...

Raising his head, he looked at himself in the mirrored reflection of the armoire door and liked not what he saw.

Maybe you deserve it.

He screwed his eyes shut, his thoughts overwhelming him for a moment.

Why couldn't you just be normal?

Maybe it was your fault.

Maybe you were the problem all along.

Why couldn't you have just been like Marie-Jeanne?

Or Tomas?

They liked Tomas.

Nice, quiet Tomas.

Why couldn't you have just shut up and indulged him?

Even a little.

It's your own fault.

You brought this on yourself.

He shook his head violently and his eyes flew open.

Punching the hard wood of the armoire, he snarled back at his reflection and its accusing eyes.

"Fuck off!" he growled.

Turning aggressively, he stormed from the room, slamming the door shut behind him.

Alonze was waiting for him in the hall.

Lucien stood before the door, uncertain. He felt vulnerable, he'd not meant for Alonze to see him like this.

Caught up as he was in his thoughts and his memories, he'd let fall his shield, his cloak, and had opened himself to his sadness. It panicked him, no one was meant to see him like this.

Alonze said nothing for a moment, then walked slowly forward, stopping just before him. Still saying nothing, he placed a hand on Lucien's shoulder, and looked deep into his eyes.

Lucien struggled to meet his gaze and looked away. He felt so uncomfortable, it was overwhelming, he wanted to be anywhere but here, but for some reason he could not move.

Part of him wanted the contact, desperately wanted Alonze to comfort him, to tell him everything would be alright. The other part screamed at him to break the contact, to push Alonze from him, to deny, to protest, to lie, anything to detract from this intrusion into his feelings.

He stood still, rigid as a plank, as Alonze squeezed his shoulder softly.

He felt his feelings rising fast within him, throbbing painfully, straining to break their dam of repression, yet he could not allow them. Could not touch them. Could not release them. Could not engage with them.

He clenched his jaw again and again as he pushed against them, suppressed them, and finally buried them deep. Back where they belonged.

Eventually the pressure in his chest subsided, and he turned to Alonze, smiling falsely.

"Thank you, my friend", he said quietly.

"Are you well, monsieur?" Alonze asked.

"I am well. Just tired...and stressed", Lucien replied.

Alonze nodded knowingly but said nothing. He gave Lucien's shoulder another squeeze. He hoped one day his master would confide in him, so that he may comfort him.

He knew he was a troubled man, but he refused to ever speak of it.

Perhaps one day he would. Perhaps one day he would realise he didn't have to battle his demons alone, and that there were others in his life who would gladly battle them with him. Alonze prayed for such a day.

"Well...you must look your best, young lord, if you are to dine with the devil", he said.

A disbelieving expression appeared on Lucien's face, as his eyes widened, and his mouth dropped open. He looked for a moment as if might rebuke Alonze, but instead, he laughed, the tension leaving him, as his shoulders fell from where they sat tightly scrunched under his ears.

"Damnit man, are you trying to kill me?" Lucien replied weakly.

"Arr, my lord, perhaps", Alonze replied in a poor affectation of a pirate, winking.

Lucien snorted and his eyes regained a little of their usual twinkle.

"Fool!" he exclaimed, aiming a kick at Alonze, as he shooed him away down the hall.

"Tis not foolish, tis the pirate's life, monsieur", Alonze

replied from the doorway to the kitchen, before disappearing quickly from view with a parting wink.

Lucien shook his head and smiled. It was a nice smile.

*

"Ah", Lucien looked up apprehensively at the gate of a rather intimidating looking manor house. "Here already".

He paused to straighten his jacket, then approached the gate of the manor where a sallow faced man stood in a crisply fitting suit.

The man nodded at Lucien robotically. Lucien nodded back.

With a creak, the gate swung open by itself behind the man.

The sun sunk behind the towering height of the house, so that it was barely visible.

Stepping aside to let him pass, the man at the gate bowed to Lucien. Lucien approached the house, walking resolutely up the curved gravel driveway. It was adorned on either side by immaculately kept grass, and majestic looking shrubbery that looked as if it had its own barber rather than gardener, such was the finish of the cuts and trims.

The house was even more intimidating up close. Made from ancient stone, carved or quarried god knows when, it stretched expansively around the grounds upon which it stood.

How many rooms does such a place contain, Lucien thought to himself, as he marvelled at the three majestically carved wings of the house. The thing was damn near as grand as some of the palaces!

If you didn't know who lived there, you'd guess some manner of king.

Which wouldn't have been a bad guess.

The door, a daunting looking thing, solid as the stone of the house, sat recessed into the entrance of the place, hung in shadow.

Lucien approached it with trepidation, his face set. After

taking a moment to compose himself, he knocked once, the last of the sun catching his face as he stepped into the shadow of the archway.

It was a firm knock. A resolute knock.

And then, he waited. At first for seconds, then long moments, then longer, ponderous, tense minutes. His mouth dried, and his palms grew slick with sweat.

Finally, after what felt like an age, the door opened.

It swung open slowly, with a creak and a groan, the weight of the thing pressuring further moans from the ancient door frame.

A man stood there in the doorway; his face only partially illuminated.

Though only of average height, he was firmly built.

He radiated power and something...else.

Something more sinister, something more dangerous.

His dark eyes bored into Lucien's own, as he smiled sardonically. "Lucien, so glad you could make it", he said. "Do come in...we are all waiting". He gestured languidly behind him, as if he were king of the world and everything in it, and Lucien but another of his subjects.

Lucien stepped dutifully past the man, as the sun finally disappeared behind the house, and darkness claimed the land.

As the door began to close, and the last remaining ray of sunlight flitted over the man's face, it seemed for a moment, as if his eyes flickered red.

A Change Of Pace

As we leave Lucien to fates unknown, a bright and beautiful day is dawning elsewhere in Paris.

We find ourselves in the company of a man, a beautiful man. He is stylishly dressed, and he is familiar to us, as he should be.

On this day, as before, his face is set in concentration, his soft lines tense in imitation of sharper edges.

He sits atop a small wooden stool, but he is not alone, as he rarely is.

He is warm and inviting, and draws others to him, like a candle in the night, or a refreshing spring on a warm summer's day. It is not a conscious thing, it is simply his way.

His companion, a woman in late middle age, is focused intensely on a chessboard sitting on a small table between the two of them.

As the man pondered the board, the woman pondered the man, gazing fondly at him, the corners of her eyes creased with love.

She has the look and bearing of someone who was once a great beauty but has since settled for ageing gracefully.

Hers is a regal beauty, tempered by deep lines of caring and wisdom, etched into her face as though hard fought, and hard earned.

They sit before a large open window.

The sun shines sublimely into the kitchen they occupy, the glare of it dimmed by a pretty net curtain that flutters gently in the morning breeze beside them. It is a beautiful spot, and they both know peace here.

"Check...I think?" the man ventured, his eyes darting across the board for confirmation.

The woman smiled fondly, watching him.

He is so beautiful.

And yet so unaware of it.

So unaware of his effect on others.

That is true beauty.

Beauty that shines without shining.

Without glaring, without blinding.

Softly, yet surely.

"La Meme?" the man enquired.

"Hmm?" the woman replied.

"Uh...check?" the man said.

"What's that?" the woman asked.

The woman's eyes flashed from the man back to the chessboard, and her demeanour changed in an instant, from that of a caring, loving woman, to the attack readiness of a cat.

Her eyes narrowed tensely, the pupils dilating rapidly.

Her back straightened ramrod straight as she leant back sharply on her stool.

Her eyes locked to the figurines on the board as she took stock of the situation immediately.

She snapped forward toward the table, her back arching low, bringing her face closer to the board to better assess the battlefield.

"Zut", she muttered grumpily.

"What was that?" the man asked.

"Nothing, nothing", she grumbled, running a hand across her chin.

She pursed her lips at the chessboard and began tilting her head from side to side as if taking in every angle, every line of attack.

The man smiled. He had got her! Finally! Justice!

She caught his smile and thinned her eyes threateningly at

him.

He couldn't help but let out a small chuckle. La Meme was so funny sometimes. He gazed back fondly at her, his grin ill contained.

"Not quite", she interjected sweetly, eyes still on the board.

"What?" the man shot back, the smile gone from his face.

"I said not quite, Gabriel, my love", the woman replied, a small smile now curving the corners of her mouth.

Gabriel frowned and leant forward; his expression serious as he studied the board.

La Meme watched him with arms crossed, love in her eyes.

So beautiful.

"Merde!" Gabriel exclaimed with a flourish.

He leapt to his feet and spun away from the chessboard.

"Gabriel!" La Meme admonished. "Such language! You are worse than a sailor".

"I said curd", Gabriel protested shyly.

"You said no such thing!" La Meme pressed.

"I said curd, I know what I said!" he replied, flustered.

Turning his back to her, he paced up and down in front of the window, his frustration evident.

A giggle from behind him made him turn back to La Meme.

His face was set and angry. He was ready to storm out, until he saw her giggling into her hands trying to conceal her laughter.

"Grrrr", Gabriel growled. Though his voice was full of frustration, his eyes had begun to shine with humour.

La Meme knew his anger was always quick lived, and he could never stay mad for long. It was one of the things she loved about him. He was actually quite a good loser, as much as he pretended otherwise.

Gabriel knew she enjoyed their little dramas, and that she loved to win, and he was always willing to indulge her in a little theatre.

"What have I told you about leaving yourself too exposed?"

La Meme asked, after managing to get her giggling under control.

Gabriel smiled ruefully at her, then turned to look out of the window, a far away look on his face.

Who this time, I wonder? La Meme thought.

"Are you well, mon petit soleil?" she asked softly.

She rose gracefully from her stool, and moved behind him, running a hand lovingly across his face.

Gabriel appeared to wake from whatever reverie held him. "Hmm? Yes, I am well, no need to fret".

"It is nothing, honestly", he continued, as La Meme stared at him expectantly.

Silence.

"Ah, fine. I met someone", he admitted after a few moments.

She smiled knowingly. "Someone".

"Yes. And he offered me a job".

"He? Job? You have a job, petit soleil".

"Yes...but this is a good one".

La Meme watched him, waiting. She knew there was more.

"It's at DuPassé", Gabriel confessed finally.

"DuPassé", La Meme repeated.

"Yes", Gabriel confirmed.

La Meme returned to her stool. She leant back against the kitchen counter behind her, her face falling into shade as she slipped outside of the sun's reach.

She looked thoughtful now, and concerned, somewhere between the cat and the carer.

Gabriel bit his lip. He wasn't sure how she would take the news.

"And what is the job?" La Meme asked.

"Well...I don't know", Gabriel replied dumbly, his face reddening a little.

"You don't know?" La Meme asked incredulously.

"Well...I do...but I don't know the particulars... the details",

Gabriel said.

"Ah the details", La Meme replied, raising her eyebrows.

"Oh hush", Gabriel said. "I would get to work with antiques...things with history...a past".

La Meme shifted on her stool. "And your current job?"

"Well, I don't need two jobs, goodness knows one is enough", Gabriel replied.

"But they have treated you well, my love", La Meme pressed.

"I know, I know..." Gabriel trailed off. "But this is a chance to do something I love...something I truly enjoy. Who knows where it will take me, what doors it will open?" he continued excitedly.

La Meme pursed her lips to prevent a smile escaping them.

She had to play the concerned parental figure here, but it was hard sometimes when he smiled so infectiously and with such youthful exuberance.

Ah, to be young again, she mused.

"I haven't decided anything yet", Gabriel announced suddenly. "I'm still considering it".

La Meme nodded and smiled. "I just want you to be happy, my love...it warms my heart to see you so excited".

Gabriel crossed the room and sat opposite her, taking her hand across the table and rubbing it lovingly. "I know you worry about me. But you needn't. I can take care of myself".

"I know", she smiled weakly. "But it is my job to worry. And worry I will".

They sat in silence together for a while, both lost in their thoughts. Gabriel ran his hands gently over La Meme's, as he looked out of the window and romanced in the view of the city he so loved.

La Meme's thoughts were not so romantic.

"I hear things about that place", she said, breaking the silence.

Gabriel turned to her, his eyes dreamlike and faraway.

"Things?"

She pursed her lips as if considering her words. She breathed out deeply as if making up her mind. Never one to sugar the medicine, she leant forward on her stool, her face catching the light.

"It is not a good place, my love", she remarked.

Gabriel frowned and leant back.

"And why is that?" he asked.

Drat, she thought.

I have already irritated him.

I must play this carefully.

How to put this?

It sounds foolish, even to me.

He will never believe me.

"People do not last long there", she said.

"They do not last long?" Gabrielle replied. "Whatever do you mean? Their employment is terminated?"

"Not quite", La Meme observed.

"Then what?" Gabrielle pressed, growing impatient.

"They disappear", La Meme replied lamely.

"They **disappear?**" Gabriel scoffed. "Oh, come now, surely you don't believe that nonsense".

La Meme rose suddenly from her stool, and walked deeper into the kitchen, busying herself in some pots on the counter.

"Tea, petit soleil?" she called.

"Yes, please, but what about this disappearing business", he replied distractedly, fidgeting with his hands as he watched her closely.

It seemed for a while that La Meme would not respond at all, intent as she was upon her tea.

Is she ignoring me? Gabriel thought.

La Meme picked a cube of sugar from a small, cream porcelain pot. She dropped it gently, with a little **clink**, into a small teacup adorned with yellow flowers. It was very pretty. La

Meme liked flowers.

Stirring gently, with her back to Gabriel, she allowed her worry to show, the gentle clinking of her spoon against the sides of the china cup providing some relief to the silence permeating the room behind her.

There is no deterring him from this.

I can feel it.

Best not make this forbidden fruit.

If I cannot keep him from the orchard, perhaps I can rub the shine from the apple.

"Well?" Gabriel demanded.

Realising this was not something she could leave unresolved, she turned to face him.

"It is probably nothing", she said, as she set down a finely polished silver tea tray on the table.

Gabriel watched her closely as she poured the tea.

"Nothing? I thought people were disappearing?" he asked, confused.

She waved her hand dismissively. "As you say, it is probably just rumour mongering...you know how the girls can be".

"You heard this from the women in the building?" Gabriel asked, still playing with his hands in his lap.

He took a sip of tea, but his eyes never left her.

"Oh yes...you know how we love to gossip...there is seldom anything interesting to do when you are old and grey, certainly no men to while away the day with in the summer sun". She grinned impishly.

"La Meme! I do not want to hear this!" Gabriel moaned.

She chuckled throatily, her affectation changing in a way that made Gabriel acutely uncomfortable.

He placed his head in his hands and moaned. "Too...much...information", he protested.

"Oh behave". She whacked him lightly on the back of the head.

He lifted his head and shot her a dazzling smile.

"I was a great beauty once, you know", she informed him, shifting in her seat as if to get up.

"Oh no", he muttered. "Not the painting".

Her face fell, and realising his mistake, he grabbed her hand quickly. "You are **still** a great beauty", he said, staring earnestly into her eyes.

She placed her hand on his. She was touched. She did not like to show it, but she was conscious of her slowly fading beauty, and as any woman, wanted to feel beautiful in herself. Regardless of how many moons she had watched rise and hold court in the sky.

"Thank you", she said thickly, turning from him to look out of the window.

He watched her, thoughtful. He wanted more for her. This was no life for her, sat in this little apartment, whiling away the days with the stool sitters.

A sadness came on him then, and he rose quickly from his chair, walking to the kitchen counter so that she would not see his eyes moist with tears.

"My love, are you well?" La Meme called.

"I am well", Gabriel called back, wiping his eyes on his shirt sleeve.

He turned and flashed her a winning smile from the kitchen. "But I must go", he chimed with exaggerated exuberance. "Things to do!"

She watched him intently. "Are you sure?"

"Of course!" he said. "Do not worry about me, worry about those stool sitters, I have a feeling Gisèle plots for your cake". He gestured at an elderly woman sitting in the window of the apartment directly across the street.

"She would be most foolish to try", La Meme replied icily, turning her cold blue eyes on the woman across the street.

Gabriel's eyebrows rose in surprise at this chilling threat.

Then, he laughed and bounded over to her. Throwing his arms around her, he leant forward to place a big kiss on her cheek. His thick golden hair fell forward into her eyes, obscuring her line of sight on her prey.

She closed her eyes, and wrapped her arms about his own, revelling in the contact and the peace she felt.

He kissed her again, then straightened and walked toward the door. "I love you", he said seriously, stopping and turning back to face her.

She felt tears gather in her eyes and brought her hand to her mouth, as was her way. "And I you. Now go". She shooed him with her hand.

"I must move this cake, before Gisèle falls from her window to the street below". She nodded her head at the freshly baked lemon cake on the window sill.

"She best not touch it. Or I shall have to pull her from the window myself", Gabriel threatened.

La Meme snorted, her mouth twitching as some of the sadness left her face.

"I shall be back for my cake later", he said seriously.

"Go now, little pig", she said with a smile and a shoo.

He grinned, and closed the door behind him

She turned back to the window, and the smile left her face.

Dangerous Liaisons

Gabriel was sad as his feet beat a path through the streets of Paris. His thoughts were of La Meme and her life upon the 'stool'. He wished he could do more for her, but he was not a man of means and was still young, just beginning to make his way in the world.

La Meme's little apartment was not the worst, but it was certainly not the best. She seemed content, though Gabriel was not. He knew that she had a life of her own before taking him in, but she had given it all up, closing the door to it. Though she professed that he was all she needed, he did not believe it, could not believe it, stirred as he was by the discontent of youth.

He watched her, sunbathing on her little stool, in front of her little window, and saw not a woman basking appreciatively under the sun's warm touch. He saw a woman wilting under its harsh glare, unable to fully enjoy its warmth.

One day he would pluck her from that stool and set her upon a bed of roses by the sea. She had always dreamt of the riviera, and he meant to give it to her. She told him he was foolish to dream of such a thing, and that she was perfectly happy where she was, but he knew Paris held painful memories for her, though she would not speak of them.

He'd take her away some day and give her the life she deserved. And what a life it would be. Tanning brown as leather in the sun, growing round as a barrel on sweet treats and wine.

He smiled ruefully. The hopeless dreams of the common man. "I need a drink", he said to himself, as his thoughts turned maudlin once more.

"Where in the blazes am I?" he muttered, looking up and down the rue in an attempt to make sense of his location. "I must have walked a way".

A man in a suit strolled past holding the hand of a small boy. The boy, who had been watching Gabriel talking to himself, looked back over his shoulder and stuck his tongue out at Gabriel as he passed.

"Jean-Baptiste!" the man admonished sternly, giving the boy's hand a little jerk, having caught his child's rudeness from the corner of his eye.

"Sorry, papa", the boy said sheepishly, as the father and son continued on their way.

Gabriel smiled and watched them disappear into the distance. Perhaps one day he would have a little rogue of his own, and walk hand in hand with him in the summer sun.

"J'adore", he purred, cherishing the day.

He returned his attention to the task at hand, finding out where in the blazes he was.

He stood upon a cobbled street. There were restaurants, cafes and bars. But he recognised none of them. He could ask someone for directions, he supposed.

He glanced at the Seine, glittering magnificently in the distance. "What do you think?" he asked. "Am I to be sensible? Or am I for adventure?"

He placed his fist under his chin, and stood, pondering, as if awaiting the river's answer.

The river seemed to glisten at him mischievously, or at least, it seemed that way to him.

Taking it for an answer, he held his hand above his brow, like a debonair pirate spying a merchant vessel ripe for plunder.

"To adventure!" he exclaimed, throwing his hand out and pointing to the horizon.

He chuckled to himself, as a passing couple eyed him like a plague carrying pigeon and crossed to the other side of the street.

Let them look. Life was for living. Live it he shall.

He would not give in to melancholy. He strolled purposefully down the street, looking hungrily up and down the buildings for some kind of sign or portent, some call to adventure.

It was a beautiful street, wherever it was, and there were plentiful people sitting outside eating pastries and delicious meals at little round tables, in gorgeously upholstered chairs.

They looked so glamorous, he thought, in their dresses and jewels, some of them even wore furs. They must be roasting!

He did not think he could tolerate the thought of gallivanting about in furs in this weather. And besides, it would prevent his skin from bronzing the way he liked.

The men as well, looked equally impressive, in their summer suits, and their summer shirts, with their summer hats. One man had a colourful turquoise cravat nestled comfortably under the collar of his shirt. Gabriel thought it looked very stylish indeed.

"Quite the place", he mused, as he drank in the sights and sounds.

As he walked, the sights continued, and so did the sounds. But soon the sights changed, and so did the sounds.

The furs became dresses, threadbare and roughly woven, and the laughs became growls and barks, coarse and harsh.

"Perhaps it is time to abandon ship..." he muttered.

At that moment, a tavern door was thrown loudly open to his left and the roar of raucous laughter exploded into the street.

The sound startled him, and he stepped back quickly, which was fortunate, for at that moment a roughly garbed fellow with greasy shoulder length hair came hurtling out of the door.

He clattered painfully to the floor in front of Gabriel,

landing on his face with a pitiful groan.

"Goodness gracious!" Gabriel shouted. "Monsieur, are you well?" He fell to his knees beside the man and turned him over quickly to see if he was conscious.

The man moaned, and closed his eyes, lying back on the cobbles.

A group of ladies swept past, tutting, hitching their dresses from the floor so as not to dirty them by any contact with the fellow.

Gabriel looked up and reddened. Some people were completely devoid of humanity. Whatever it was that coloured a person beyond the flush of their face, these women lacked.

He looked down at the man.

His eyes were glazed and rolling back in his head, as he ran his hands over his face and through his hair in an attempt to check his injuries. Or perhaps just in an attempt to soothe himself as a mother might.

"S-sorree", the man wailed from the floor suddenly.

"S-sorryy?" Gabriel repeated softly. "There is no need to apologise. You have taken quite the fall. Rest and gather your wits".

The man said nothing for a moment, breathing slowly and rubbing at his temple.

Gabriel knelt by his side, his hand upon the man's shoulder, his eyes searching the man's face, watching carefully his condition.

"Urts", the man said after a while.

Gabriel smiled sympathetically, his eyes shining with empathy. "I am sure that it does. What were you drinking to bring about such a tumble?"

Gabriel was eager to keep the man talking.

The man said nothing for a moment. His face creased in thought, and a large frown appeared on his face.

Then, he smiled dumbly. "Rum!" he purred, punch-drunk

as a lover remembering their first kiss.

"Rum", Gabriel repeated. "Remind me never to try it, for I do not think I have the constitution".

The man smiled wider.

Gabriel had never seen someone so happy to have kissed the cobbles. He was certainly a resilient fellow.

As they smiled at one another on the cobbles, a shadow darkened the doorway that hung open, leaking light and loquaciousness.

A stern looking woman in an apron stood there.

She looked as if she'd seen everything there was to see in this world, and need not see it again. Haggard bags hung from her eyes, but they had not yet managed to dim the fire burning within them.

She leaned in the doorway, watching Gabriel and the man upon the cobbles. They had not yet noticed her.

As she took in the scene, her eyes narrowed, and it seemed as if she might speak, and might admonish them for this roguelike behaviour outside of her establishment.

Instead, she crossed her arms and watched them quietly a while more. "Bring him inside", she sighed finally.

Gabriel looked up in surprise.

"I..." he glanced apprehensively at the fellow on the floor.

"He'll be fine", the woman said gruffly. "Won't yeh Voyou?" she asked the man still lying flat on the cobbles.

"Rum?" he inquired hopefully from the floor.

The woman started muttering under her breath and walked back into the bar. Gabriel could only hear snatches of what she muttered as she walked away, but what he did hear caused him to blush profusely.

"Come on then, up with you!" Gabriel encouraged his new acquaintance.

"Ugh", the man groaned loudly, as Gabriel threw his arm under him and levered him ungainly to his feet.

"Merde", the man spat.

This isn't quite what I had in mind, Gabriel thought to himself, as he inspected the bar the man had fallen out of.

"L'ancre", he mouthed, observing a grimy wooden sign hanging above the door.

I'm starting to wish I was home.

"Ohh, my head", the man groaned.

"Yes, yes, let's get you inside", Gabriel said.

And so, his call to adventure apparently found, he helped his unlikely companion hobble into L'ancre.

Intent as he was on the safe passage of his cargo, he did not notice the peculiar marking at the bottom of the sign above the door, which was partially obscured by the top of the door frame.

If he had, he might have found it a little strange. The little dot, in the little red circle. It almost looked like an eye of sorts. A red eye.

*

"You're a good man", Berthe declared, thumping a large mug of beer down on the counter in front of Gabriel.

"Thank you", he said, blushing. "I was just doing what I felt right...it was quite the fall he took".

"Maybe, but there's not many in these parts who'd stop twice to piss on a man like Voyou, let alone take time out of their day to help him", Berthe replied bitterly.

Gabriel said nothing. Her blunt speech unsettled him a little. She was so sure of herself and spoke so frankly. He was not used to such frankness.

He realised that although Berthe was without affectation, and spoke, in the words of La Meme, 'Like a sailor home to whore and claw', she was a good person, and refreshingly honest.

He decided he liked her, though he would endeavour to remain in her good graces, for she also frightened him a little.

Realising he had been lost in his thoughts, and ignoring Berthe, he nodded quickly.

"I am not familiar with this part of Paris", Gabriel ventured in an effort to change the subject, uncomfortable with the praise.

"Well, it's not Montmartre my boy, that's for sure", Berthe chortled, flashing a telling smile at a wiry man, who was cleaning a jug at the other end of the bar.

She stopped laughing and gave him an appraising look. "I don't mean to be rude, but you might try your luck back down a ways", she said, pointing back the way he had come.

"Don't misunderstand me, me and Ernie are grateful to yeh, and you'll always be welcome in our little home", she continued, spreading her hands out and encompassing the bar. "But, this is no place for yeh".

"And why is that?" Gabriel retorted, raising his chin, his face flushed a redder red this time.

"It's choppy, boy. A home for pirates and rogues". She smiled a little to take the sting from her slight to his toughness.

"Rogues bother me not", Gabriel replied, a quiet strength on his face.

Berthe examined him, her head tilted to one side, as if drawing upon her years of experience in reading people to reassess him, to ensure she had not missed some hidden facet of his character.

Straightening her head on her thick neck, she grunted. "Hmph. Maybe there's more to you yet, jeune homme".

"Maybe, indeed", Gabriel conceded, gracefully inclining his head.

"Go on over". Berthe gestured to a choice table near the fireplace, with a clear view of the street outside through the window. "Enjoy yer drink, I've to see to this pirate".

She nodded her head in the direction of the little room upstairs, where they'd laid Voyou to sleep off his rum. She strode away then, up a set of stairs to the left of the bar.

Gabriel took his drink and walked to the table by the

window. He sank gratefully into the firm wooden chair, enjoying the relief its sturdy back provided his aching muscles.

It had been no simple task, carrying Voyou up the stairs. He was still without his wits and had fallen backward down the stairs twice, dragging Gabriel and Berthe down with him.

Thankfully they had not made it far up the stairs at the time, and managed to hop frantically back down the stairs under his weight, sweating and cursing all the while, Gabriel beginning to pick up and regurgitate some of the choicer phrases Berthe had been muttering earlier.

He had looked like a child, when they left him, curled up on the bed, his legs drawn up under him, arms wrapped about himself.

I am glad he is safe. For the moment at least.

Gabriel pondered his drink apprehensively.

So this is a distingué.

It was a rather large glass mug, with rather a lot of beer in it. A litre, if he recalled correctly. He would have preferred wine, but he did not want to appear ungrateful.

Taking a large swig, he nodded his head appreciatively, holding the mug up to the light and admiring the colours swirling in the glass. There were shades of amber, ruby and gold. It was pleasing to look at. And pleasing to the tongue. He could see how one could develop a taste for it.

He sat, enjoying his drink, turning it in his hands, and smacking his lips from time to time. L'ancre filled around him with thirsty mouths and eager ears.

It was still early, and the sun hung happily in the sky, though red and orange blemishes already stained the horizon, heralding the coming darkness.

Watching the faces pass him to familiar seats and stools, he realised the beer had gone to his head. His cheeks had turned flush and warm.

He did not make a habit of frequenting the cafes or the bars.

For him, it was usually a glass of wine if he did imbibe.

I should drink no more.

Lest I become truly maudlin.

Would that be such a bad thing?

Before he could make up his mind, a swarthy man in a tattered jacket threw himself into a chair behind Gabriel by the fireplace.

The man cleared his throat loudly, stuttering and starting like a phlegm powered steam engine struggling to gather steam. He finally released his spit into a small tin pot that must have been on the table when he arrived.

Or perhaps the fellow carried his own...spit pot. Gabriel grimaced. What a thought.

The phlegmy man was joined shortly after by a scared looking woman in a maroon dress that looked as though it had seen better days.

The couple intrigued him. They had a different look to the rest of the patrons, a certain agitation to them.

As disgusting and irritating as he found the spitting stranger, he was a slave to his curiosity, and remained in his seat, in the hopes of hearing something interesting.

The strike of a match loudly catching against a matchbox jarred him, intent as he was on his eavesdropping.

"That's better", the man said appreciatively, as his cigarette lit, and he inhaled deeply.

"Would you?" the woman asked.

"Mmhmm", the man obliged, leaning across and lighting the end of her cigarette with his own.

"Mmm, thanks", the woman said, sucking hard on her own cigarette, breathing a sigh of relief as the nicotine entered her body.

"I cannot believe that spineless worm!" the man spat suddenly, aggressively tapping the end of his cigarette.

Gabriel watched enthralled, as a small hailstorm of ash fell into the spit pot.

This certainly was a choice table, he thought, as he stared raptly at a large bronze plaque hanging from the wall in front of him.

In it, he could see the reflection of the man and woman behind him, and everything they were doing.

"Garlon!" the woman admonished him in a conspiratorial hush.

"Pardon, pardon", the man said apologetically, puffing on his cigarette. "But, you know I'm right". He glanced furtively around the bar. "You mean to tell me that a man as powerful as Marceau cannot find a few lost lambs? That he couldn't scour the city, turn it upside down if he wanted to?"

"Did you not see his speech? He is looking, Gar!" the woman replied. "Speech?" Garlon scoffed. "I saw just another opportunity for the man to listen to his own voice".

The woman frowned, the look of worry on her face becoming more pronounced.

"You mustn't say that!" she implored.

"And why not? Les enfants de Paris are snatched from the streets, from their homes, and I must spare the feelings of the colverd responsible for finding them, as he speaks his pretty speeches while sitting on his hands?" Garlon seethed.

Les enfants de Paris? Gabriel thought, his interest well and truly piqued.

Missing children?

What is he speaking of?

"He is a true politician and would promise you the moon on a platter if it served his purpose. It is the way of the man, the way of them all, him and his slippery kin. They will say anything, promise anything, it means nothing to them. Words are just...tools to them, like a hammer and nail to me, or needle and thread to you. Tools...to make you worry, to make you happy, to make you sad, or angry", Garlon said.

"Angry?"

Garlon waved his hand dismissively.

"Why'd they wanna make us angry, Gar?"

"Angry people make bad decisions, they're easy to manipulate".

"Manipulate to what?"

"To vote, to fight, to go to war...it dun't matter".

"Go to war?" The woman looked scared now. "We just had a war, I don't want another war Gar, I don't think I could stand it".

"There won't be...I hope...but that's not the point. Point is. Politicians can rile yeh up to do just about anything they want, if they tell you the right lies".

"Right lies? I don't know Gar, what's this got to do with the missing wee'ns".

"It's got everything to do with it, Nise. Marceau stood out there and gave his pretty speech, and told his pretty lies, and you come in here invigorated, excited even. Marceau the great man will save the day! The ween's'll be fine and all's the happy ending", Garlon said.

He tapped the butt of his cigarette into the spit pot, though the cigarette had long since burned out.

"So you don't think we'll find the wee'ns?" Nise's face fell.

"I think there's as much chance of that happening, as there is of me being elected president of France", Garlon said.

"Oh..." Nise quietly.

Merde, he thought to himself.

You and that mouth.

"I'm sorry my dear", Garlon said suddenly, throwing his arm around Nise and pulling her to him. "I'm talkin silly. You know what I'm like. I'm sure the pretty boy will find em".

He plopped a kiss on her forehead.

"N if he don't", he lit a new cigarette and took a large pull on it before continuing. "He'll have me n Clet to answer to".

Nise giggled. "What'll get him first, the fists or the smell".

"Fel!" he exclaimed, mouth twitching with humour. "I'll have you know I washed just this week. Clet...aaaah, I'm not so sure. I think it was this month. Certainly this year sometime. He's not sproutin no mushrooms no more anyway".

He frowned and rubbed his chin while looking thoughtfully at the ceiling.

"Bricon", she punched him lightly on the arm as she continued giggling.

At the table in front, Gabriel smiled.

The interaction warmed him. Suddenly, the worries of the world did not feel so heavy upon him, and he decided that he'd had enough adventure for one day.

At that moment, the door to L'ancre banged open loudly, rattling in its hinges, and a gaunt man with sweaty hair stuck to his neck stood there.

He looked a little like Voyou, but less friendly. He did not look like someone Gabriel wanted to be confronted by alone on a dark night.

The stranger walked into L'ancre, ignoring the bar, instead walking swiftly toward Gabriel.

Does he come for me? Gabriel thought nervously. He was no coward, but the man was making him anxious.

As the stranger approached the seating at the side of the bar, he altered his course, moving toward the back of the room.

As he passed Gabriel, he paused a few feet away, and stood, statue still.

Gabriel tensed.

What is he doing?

A noise. A strange noise.

Is that... sniffing? Is he...sniffing me?

Gabriel leant back in his chair, eyes wide with trepidation, trying to create a little more distance between himself and the odd stranger.

The stranger turned his head to the sky, and appeared to be sniffing, breathing, something, quickly, like some sort of animal.

It was the most bizarre behaviour, and Gabriel was beginning to consider whether Berthe had been right in warning him away from L'ancre.

Just as he was considering leaving, the stranger stopped and exhaled, slouching down, apparently relaxed.

What now?

And then, as if nothing had happened, the man walked briskly past Gabriel and threw himself into a chair at the very back of the room.

Mon dieu.

What type of establishment do you run here, Berthe.

Perhaps I should leave.

It grows late.

Should you?

Why should you?

It is your day of rest.

Enjoy it.

Lest you later regret it.

"One more won't hurt", Gabriel muttered to himself. "Besides, the rogue seems to have settled himself".

He glanced back over his shoulder, at the man who was now sitting quietly watching the patrons of the bar.

"It did rather hit the spot". He pondered his now empty mug, and spied Berthe back at the bar.

She caught his eye and grinned. She must have seen the searching look on his face, for she walked across to the table, muttering.

"Another, rogue?" she asked, sweeping his mug from the table before he had the chance to respond. "I know, I know. I seen it on yer face. You've a taste for my beer!"

"Well..." he began, but she had already begun walking back to the bar, her pace brisk, her arms swinging confidently at her side.

"Beer!" a gruff voice shouted, from a stool at the end of the bar seating in a secluded corner.

"Wait yer damn turn, pig face", Berthe barked back.

"Pig face", Gabriel chuckled.

"Here yer go, boy, drink up!" Berthe instructed, plonking another distingué in front of him.

"Funny, I had you for a wine man", she mused, watching him thoughtfully.

"Merci, Madame Berthe", Gabriel replied graciously, raising the mug to his lips.

Berthe blushed a deep, maroon red, her cheeks turning red as cherries.

"Madame Berthe, I never, never in all my days", she muttered, retreating from Gabriels disarming charm, back to the safety of her bar.

It pleased him to see this softer, more vulnerable Berthe.

A haunting voice shook him from his contemplation, and he turned to locate the source of the noise. The owner of the voice was a small, round shouldered, old man with a wispy white halo of hair around the back of his head.

He'd begun singing on a stool in front of the fireplace. How quaint. How romantic!

The man saw Gabriel looking and winked.

Perhaps I shall stay a while longer.

Tis not everyday I am serenaded, so, Gabriel thought wryly.

Another sound joined in, accompanying the man's voice.

Perhaps he had a companion with an instrument!

Snatching another glance at the singer, Gabriel frowned in disappointment. There was no companion, so where was the noise coming from?

Thud. Thud. Thud.

Again and again. It was not loud, but irritating. It sounded like the dull thudding of wood on wood. What was that blasted thudding?

Thud. Thud. Thud.

He swung around agitated.

The rogue at the back of the room was tapping the heel of his boot against the ground again and again, in some mad frenzy.

He felt churlish, it was not loud, and it was not hurting him, or the other patrons, but it was grating, and distracting from the theatre of the singer's song.

And why did he have a coat on, on a day so warm, and why was it pulled so tightly about his face? It was very odd.

Gabriel shook his head to express his irritation and turned back to his drink.

Deciding he would not let the man irritate him, he swivelled in his chair to watch the singer on his stool, nodding his head encouragingly, and smiling here and there, to encourage him and show his appreciation for his music.

He soon forgot about the thudding, and clapped loudly as the singer finished his song. He raised his mug in salute, sloshing a mouthful of beer over himself in the process, as he slammed the mug back down onto the table.

Zut!

I hope no one saw, he thought, glancing around suspiciously.

Phew.

I could not stomach such a hit to my reputation so soon.

Just as Berthe is warming to me.

Snorting at his own silliness, he took a gulp of beer, and awaited the next song eagerly.

The second mug went the way of the first, and third the way of the second, and before long Gabriel's head spun and his senses swam.

Now, it was definitely time to leave.

He'd had his fill of adventure, and beer, and no doubt the morrow would give him his fill of headache and hangover.

Rising to his feet, he headed for the door.

"Goodnight, Berthe, my love", he called, sketching a courtly bow with his arm thrown out low to one side.

"Goodnight, drunken oaf", Berthe shot back dryly, her eyes smiling.

Gabriel feigned outrage and stepped back as if struck.

Berthe waved the rag she was using to clean a glass affectionately at him, and he stepped out into the night.

Did I stay so long?

The sun had set, and the sky was dark.

Excellent.

Drunk, and still lost.

As lost as he'd been when he arrived, but now also, unhelpfully inebriated.

He began walking. Better than sleeping on the street, he supposed.

La Meme's face popped into his head, aghast at the thought of her petit soleil, drunk, and asleep on the street, a jacket for a pillow. It was an amusing thought.

And it will become more than just an amusing thought, if you do not do something about it.

And so, he walked, his feet crunching painfully loudly on the uneven ground of the street. Each crunch echoed loudly between the large buildings, standing towering over him from either side.

It was dark, the only light coming from the moon, a grey crescent in the sky above, and a few scant stars twinkling timidly.

Turning a corner, he found himself at the bottom of a long, narrow street on a hill. Angled such as it was, in the shadow of a particularly tall and imposing tenement building, there was no relief to be had from the moonlight.

He couldn't see more than a few feet in front of him. It was oppressive, and he wanted to be free of it as soon as possible.

Increasing his pace, he began trudging up the hill, his eyes set on the crest.

Crunch.

He jumped, as his stomach fluttered uncontrollably.

His heart crescendoed loud enough for the entire street to hear.

This was a different crunch. He knew the sound of his shoe on the ground, and this was different. It was heavier, like a boot of some sort.

Perhaps you are imagining it. You are drunk, after all.

Reassuring himself somewhat, he put his head down resolutely and continued up the hill, as fast as his legs would permit.

Unfortunately, it was a rather steep hill, and a rather long street, as if it were placed there, and designed in such a way, to torment him on this night.

He was alert now, and on edge, his eyes darting around suspiciously, side to side, and over his shoulder behind him.

Merde! he exclaimed, as he stumbled and almost lost his footing.

A crossroads.

There are side streets!

And more tenement buildings.

Who would choose to live at the top of such a torturous hill.

It must be ghoulish to bring groceries home, climbing this macabre mountain every time.

His feeling of unease grew, and he hurried past the crossroads which made him feel exposed on all sides.

Almost there.

Not long now.

The crest of the hill was in sight, and he increased his pace, spurring himself on, eager to reach the top.

Whoosh.

Scrape.

A noise from behind, like a steel chair dragged over a hardwood floor, caused him to spin around wildly.

He stumbled and fell to the floor roughly, scraping his legs and knees.

"Zut alors!" he grunted.

He lay still for a moment, rubbing his injured legs. He'd ripped his trousers and was bleeding.

What is that? he thought to himself, as a new noise punctuated the foreboding silence of the night.

Breathing?

It sounds like breathing. Heavy breathing.

But unlike any I've heard before.

"Argh", he groaned, as he tried to push himself to his feet and pain flared in his leg. "What a night".

He brushed dirt from his jacket and trousers, his eyes flitting around the street nervously.

He stared back down the hill, licking his lips.

I can't see anything. Maybe it is the drink.

Perhaps I have no stomach for pirate swill.

But I certainly heard something.

It is probably just a cat, you fool.

Some alleycat, out for a night of adventure, while you lie a spectacle in its street.

A cat breathing so deeply? Perhaps it is laughing.

Laughing at you, and your foolishness.

Smiling weakly, he gave himself another cursory inspection, and shook his head.

Time to go.

He turned, and before him, stood a nightmare.

Eyes, floating like glowing red coals, burning hungrily into his own.

Hair, slick with sweat, plastered to a porcelain pale skull, sharp and gaunt.

Long, gangling arms, rising and falling in unnatural harmony with deep, disturbing breaths.

Gabriel stepped back quickly, his chest constricting tightly.

He opened his mouth to scream, but could find no words, his mouth had become dry, his tongue stuck to the roof of his mouth.

A low growl issued forth from the...man...and Gabriel scrambled backwards.

This can't be real. I am hallucinating.

They have drugged me with some sordid spirit.

"Wh-what do you want?" Gabriel asked, surprised that his voice showed his fear only a little.

The man growled, deeper this time, more insistently, and lowered himself into a weird crouch.

What is he doing?

He looks as if he means to...pounce at me...like some sort of animal.

Perhaps he has come from one of those...opium dens.

Yes that must be it.

"Do you need help?" Gabriel asked, extending his hand toward the man, exposing the cut on his leg in the process.

Something about this seemed to agitate the man, for he became quiet, and his breathing stopped.

A feeling of dread consumed Gabriel, swamping what remained of his reason.

He began to creep, ever so slowly, away from the man.

All he knew was he had to flee this man.

And now.

But gently.

Softly.

Do not startle him.

The man tensed, and Gabriel screamed.

Marceau

Marceau was a short, finely featured man of middle age, and though his features were fine, his morals, unfortunately were not.

Marceau's sole concern in life was the pursuit of power. And accrue it he had, rising quickly through the ranks of the political world in which he lived. His single mindedness served him well, you see, in this murky world of seductive smiles and lurid lies, but it was most certainly a detriment to the countless citizens who relied on him to be otherwise.

But what did they know?

He was a politician, you see, and a good one, very good. A born politician, you might go so far as to say. Perhaps it was his presidential manner, or his classic good looks. But people liked Marceau, they warmed to him, trusted him, and **believed in him**.

And that, really, was the crux of it, and the reason for his prodigal rise to prime minister at such a young age. Marceau could make people believe him. And in this, lay his power. It is the power that all politicians crave, but thankfully, only few truly possess.

It is the power of oratory, combined with the lure of charisma. It is the power to turn others to one's will, to make them sway, like a sunflower in the wind, to the music of one's words.

And for this, his colleagues despised him, loathed him, but envied him, most of all. For they could not create the music, as Marceau could.

Marceau could inspire vivid colours, you see. Raging reds and yearning yellows that would make the people take up arms against their neighbour if he so willed. Make them take to the streets and storm the Élysée itself if he so decried.

But his fellows? Why, they were relegated to painting their shades of grey, and shades of grey alone. Pallid increments, and pale inches, were all they could incite from the people.

Marceau? Well Marceau could make them dance.

It certainly did not hurt that he was so fine to look upon, something that he capitalised on, in both his professional, and private life. And why shouldn't he? He was the prime minister after all. Didn't that afford him certain privileges, certain rights?

His job was not from the common lot. There were certain burdens, certain responsibilities, certain stresses that came along with it. Things that the common man simply wouldn't understand.

And they did not have to. What did it matter to them, if he indulged himself, now and again?

"Carmen", Marceau called from his desk.

A pretty young woman with red hair appeared at his door, which was ajar.

"Yes?" she asked eagerly.

Marceau grinned.

"I just wanted to see you", he admitted.

The woman flushed, her skin turning as red as her hair.

"You shouldn't..." she protested.

"And why not?" Marceau quipped back at her.

"You know why..." the woman replied meekly.

Marceau rose to his feet and swaggered over to her, his eyes drunk, his mind a million miles from music.

He pulled her to him hard, his hand low in the valley of her back, his fingers spread possessively across the top of her buttocks.

"Tell me why", he breathed huskily, his face inches from her own.

"Marce, the door…" the woman whispered, gesturing at the open door behind them.

Marceau reached over her shoulder with his free hand, his face brushing hers and filling her nostrils with the scent of his cologne.

He pushed the door shut.

"And now?" he breathed in her ear.

She turned her mouth to his.

*

"You are a revelation", Marceau proclaimed as he buttoned his shirt.

"Stop it", the woman chided.

"I mean it, Carmen", Marceau insisted, repinning his cufflinks.

Carmen said nothing. She could not resist him, though she knew she should.

"I mean to leave her", Marceau declared, suddenly.

"What?" Carmen shot back, surprise causing a lapse in her normally perfect manners.

"Armandine, I mean to leave her for you", Marceau confirmed. "I think of you day and night, I cannot be apart from you", he gushed, crossing the room and pulling her to him, his natural proclivity for storytelling charging his words with energy.

"But, you can't!" Carmen cried. "What of your children?"

"They will understand", Marceau said with unwavering certainty. "They want their father to be happy".

He fixed her with a compelling stare. "And I am not happy!" he exclaimed suddenly, waving his hand dramatically. "Nor have I been for some time".

"But it will be a scandal, and such a scandal!" Carmen said, excitement now on her face.

"I will bear it", Marceau replied manfully. "For you". He

kissed her deeply. "I would bear a thousand scandals, to hold you in my arms, to hold you in front of the people, to show them our love".

Carmen's red brown eyes lit up. "Do you mean it?"

"I do", Marceau replied, his voice husky again.

She kissed him passionately, running her delicate fingers through his lustrous brown hair, enjoying the feel of it in her hands.

"Mmm", she murmured. "All mine".

He returned her kiss, his vigour increasing as his hands roamed under her blouse.

"No, stop", she muttered.

"I cannot", he protested.

"You must", she said more firmly, placing her finger on his lips and pushing him back gently.

He moaned, turning his attention to her neck, kissing the soft curves, running his tongue over the milky white skin, nibbling gently, insistently.

She smiled, enjoying the sense of power she felt.

"You have an appointment", she said sadly, knowing this would quell their passion.

"Appointment?" he muttered; his face still buried in her neck. "Ah, yes", he said suddenly, stepping back from her, his face tight.

"Who is he?" Carmen asked innocently.

"You needn't worry", Marceau said jovially.

Carmen thought his voice sounded forced.

"I'm not worried", she said.

Marceau waved his hand dismissively. "It's nothing really, it would only bore you, I assure you".

Carmen crossed her arms. "Fine".

"Don't be like that", Marceau pleaded.

"Monsieur". Carmen inclined her head and walked out of the office, pulling the door closed behind her.

Marceau muttered to himself grumpily, as he pulled his suit jacket around his shoulders. Carmen could be flighty. He had upset her, and he knew he'd pay for it later. She would make him earn his way back into her good graces. He was happy to pay the price.

Returning to his desk, he looked out of the window.

"Not long now..." he said quietly.

He picked up his favourite fountain pen and turned his attention to a stack of papers on the desk, his attention resolute.

Not long came quicker than expected, and he looked up in surprise, as a confident knock rang out from the other side of the door.

"Is it time already?" he mumbled, snatching up a gold wristwatch and frantically checking the time. "Yes, yes...well...yes".

"Send him in please, Carmen", Marceau called authoritatively.

The door opened, and Carmen stepped through first, her face impassive.

She stood quietly beside the door, as two people entered the room, a man and a woman.

Marceau licked his lips, and jumped to his feet, his chair scraping backward loudly.

"That will be all, thank you Carmen". Marceau dismissed her.

Carmen bobbed her head politely and left the room, giving Marceau a little look as she went. Intent as he was on his guests, he did not see it.

Marceau addressed the man the moment the door clicked shut. "Monseigneur", Marceau said sombrely, bowing from the waist.

The man smiled, accepting it as his due. "Marceau, a pleasure", he said lazily.

Marceau rose from his bow, and smiled nervously at the man,

his eyes darting back and forth between the man and the woman beside him.

"Ah, yes", the man said, turning his eyes upon the woman. "Where are my manners?" He smirked. "Allow me to introduce my companion, Madame Dagger".

"Madame", Marceau purred, leaning forward and reaching for her hand.

The woman hesitated for a fraction of a second, tensing slightly, then offered her hand to Marceau. She smiled as he placed a courtly kiss upon it.

"Ahem", the man said, interrupting them.

"Ah, yes, my apologies, please, take a seat", Marceau said quickly, offering them seats in front of his desk. "And for Madame".

He ran around the desk and pulled her chair out for her, pushing it gently under her as she sat. Then he made an odd hop back around the desk to his own chair.

He straightened the papers on his desk, averting his eyes, a small blush on his face.

The man smiled, enjoying the effect his companion was having on Marceau.

"We were pleased with the last...delivery...very pleased", the man ventured after a while, breaking the tension.

Immediately, the atmosphere in the room changed.

"Monseigneur", Marceau bowed his head briefly. "I am honoured...as you may have seen, it has not been without incident".

The man's wintery blue eyes penetrated Marceau's own with ease, ripping through his defences and laying him bare.

"But it is nothing I cannot handle", Marceau added quickly. "I am committed...completely".

A bead of sweat shone brightly on his forehead.

The man held Marceau in his gaze a few moments longer, before relaxing in his chair, the blizzard in his eyes subsiding.

"Excellent", he said.

He nodded his head slowly, watching Marceau, the way an eagle might hold a worm in its fierce glare, before sending its attention somewhere more worthy of it.

"I hope this proves my commitment to you, and your cause, monseigneur", Marceau suggested.

The man said nothing, but rose to his feet and approached the window, turning his back on Marceau.

Marceau looked to Madame Dagger questioningly, but she stared back at him impassively, her face betraying no feeling.

"We have a date for you", the man said after a while, his back still turned.

"What do you mean, monseigneur?" Marceau asked, rubbing his hands absentmindedly atop his desk.

The man walked across to Marceau's desk and stopped right in front of him. He stood looming over him, his shadow smothering Marceau.

Marceau averted his eyes uncomfortably.

The last of the sunshine that had been shining weakly through the window disappeared, and the room turned dark.

"A date with teeth", the man said.

Liaisons

The two men sat in companionable silence, both taking stock of each other, snatching curious glances at one another every now and then.

The morning sun shone down upon them, as a little bird sang his morning song for all the street to hear.

Toutes Sortes, shone prettily in black cursive script on a white banner above them.

Lucien sat back in his chair, shadowed by the overhang of the cafe terrace, protecting him from the sun's kiss.

He looked pensive. His hands were clasped atop the delicate white metal table, and he was running his thumb along the edge of his hand. His eyes roamed back and forth from the busy street to Gabriel.

"Bonjour, what can I get you messieurs?" a waitress asked, a small menu clasped neatly in her hands behind her back.

"Un café, s'il vous plaît", Gabriel asked.

"And for you, monsieur", the waitress addressed Lucien.

"Wine. Red. Vintage". A look passed between them, and the waitress nodded, before disappearing into the back of the cafe.

A silence grew. Comfortable at first.

"So-".

"I-".

They both started talking at once.

Lucien grinned wolfishly. "After you". He inclined his head politely.

"I feel embarrassed. About the other night", Gabriel said.

"Don't be. It is completely understandable", Lucien replied, settling his hands on the table in front of him.

"It was foolish of me", Gabriel continued.

"Braver men than you, have been caught unawares by a vagrant at night", Lucien reassured him.

"Yes…" Gabriel looked off into the distance for a moment, as if thinking.

But was it a vagrant?

*I wasn't **that** drunk, was I?*

Maybe you were just tired…

Maybe it was a trick of the light…

"Something on your mind?" Lucien asked, staring intently at Gabriel.

Gabriel opened his mouth as if to speak, then shut it, as if thinking better of it.

"No. I'm just glad nothing came of it. And lucky you were there. I think the man was crazed, and I did not fancy getting into it with him", Gabriel admitted.

"Think nothing of it". Lucien smiled.

Silence. A more comfortable one this time, as they both enjoyed their drinks and continued surreptitiously snatching glances at each other, as if trying to appraise one another without it appearing obvious.

"So, have you thought about my offer?" Lucien asked, gently breaking the silence.

"Your offer?" Gabriel asked.

He frowned for a moment, before realisation dawned on his face.

"Yes of course. I have given it some thought". He leant back in his chair, rubbing his finger over his bottom lip, his eyes thoughtfully watching the street.

After a moment, he dropped his hand and fixed his attention on Lucien.

His back straightened and his bearing became serious.

"I'd like to take you up on your offer", he declared.

Lucien grinned with the air of one who is used to getting his own way, a twinkle in his eye.

"On one condition", Gabriel appended.

"Oh?" Lucien's grin faltered.

He leant forward in his chair, uncrossing his legs.

"There's someone you have to meet", Gabriel declared, smiling widely.

Happily Ever After

Henré was just about as happy as a newlywed man could be. He loved his wife, he loved their little home and he loved their baby girl. He couldn't wait to meet her.

He'd fallen for his wife, Amerie, almost instantly. Poleaxed as he was by her alluring blue eyes, figure hugging dress, and shock of strawberry blonde hair, he didn't stand a chance.

They were married within the year.

Not everyone approved, namely Henré's mother, who thought it was scandalous the way the woman dressed and carried herself. And besides, she wasn't even Parisian.

But Henré didn't care. They were happy, and that was all that mattered.

Their little apartment comprised a small living area, a kitchen, and a bedroom. The living area had a sofa, a fireplace for the winter that they fed boulets, or whatever they could find, and some old wooden furniture.

The kitchen was tiny, with just enough room for a small table, a worktop for preparing food and a compartment under the floor for storing perishables that kept food cold.

And at the back, past the kitchen, was their bedroom. It was small, but it had a generously sized bed, two small bedside tables and pictures of the two of them dotted around the walls. In the corner of the room by the bed stood an old crib. It looked rather worn, as if it had been used before.

Amerie's mother did not approve and had taken many opportunities to voice her displeasure at the 'unsavoury little hole' Henré had moved her daughter into. Amerie didn't mind though, so Henré paid it no mind.

He supposed it was **little**, so she wasn't **entirely wrong**, he thought.

"I will look upon you later, mon coeur", Henré said gently, leaning over the back of the sofa to kiss his pregnant wife as she lounged.

He let the kiss linger a moment, then pulled back from it, gazing down fondly at his wife.

He smiled suddenly.

"Why do you smile like that? If it grows much wider, you'll look like a grinning cat", Amerie teased. "And do not mon coeur me, you promised me there would be no more of this".

She stared at Henré accusingly.

"I know, I know". Henré shifted guiltily. "But the baby".

His eyes lit up with childlike enthusiasm. "I want her to have everything I could not have...everything we cannot have...and if I work hard..."

He trailed off, a determined glint in his eyes.

Amerie pondered this. "She'll have you, and she'll have me. It's enough".

He frowned, as he digested his wife's wisdom.

After a moment, he smiled, the smile lifting his cheeks high on his face.

It was a Henré grin. A pure grin. And a little bit of a grinning cat grin.

"If you say so, mon coeur", he agreed dutifully.

Amerie's mouth twisted. She was unsure as if her husband was simply humouring her, and it showed. Her mouth was gyrating between irritation and affection, twitching up and down at the corners. Affection eventually won the day.

Henré smiled back. "I should not be late. Maybe I will bring you something", he teased.

"You better", Amerie ordered, her eyes sparkling.

Henré gave her a peck on the check, then straightened himself proudly. "Au revoir, mon coeur", he said softly from the door, snatching one last love drunk look at his wife.

He took the stairs to the bottom of the building quickly, jumping down them with purpose. He did not want to be late; it simply would not do.

Henré worked as a porter at one of the most exclusive member clubs in Paris, Au-delà Du Clair De Lune, a fact he was very proud of.

The pay was poor, and the work was hard, often for long hours. But he loved it anyway. Demanding patrons aside.

The glamour of the place wore on him, filling his head with dreams above his station, of extravagant parties, dangerous liaisons, and rubbing shoulders with the high society of Paris.

Someday, he wanted to open a club of his own. Perhaps he would call it *Henré's*.

No, that sounds terrible, he thought, stopping and frowning, exasperated at himself.

It is supposed to be an exclusive members club, not a pirate hideout, bursting at the seams with vagabonds and rogues.

Henré's sounds like a place for poivrotte's.

Marceau would not be seen dead in such a place.

I am sure of it.

I will have to work on the name.

Amerie will help me. She is very creative, and good at this sort of thing.

Yes of course! I remember now, she helped Eugénie with her cafe.

Or was it a patisserie? A cafe that sells pastries? Maybe best not to mention Eugénie after all...

Anyway, I remember she helped her come up with the most wonderful name for the place. Was it Cafe Flower? Or de Flore?

Something like that. And the furnishings. They were beautiful. It really was a very beautiful cafe. Amerie had helped her with all of it.

She could help me too.

He smiled happily, his dilemma resolved for the time being, and continued on his way.

For now, his duty was to De Lune, and he felt that the connections he could make there would be invaluable.

Besides, how else could someone such as he, with no formal education, and no friends in high places, succeed in such an ambitious undertaking as opening his own exclusive members club?

Things would be easier, if he had such friends.

He rounded the corner onto the street where Au-delà Du Clair De Lune stood. The contrast to where he lived was immediately apparent.

Large, imposing buildings towered over Henré from all sides, their magnificent windows reflecting the fast-waning sunlight at sharp angles across the street like mirrors.

The people were different too. No patches on suits or worn-out shoes here.

The women were intimidating, in a way that Henré was unused to, with their expensive dresses, their furs and their jewels.

He looked up at an intimidating set of wooden doors that stood guard like castle gates.

These were the doors that decided if you were worthy. Worthy of entrance. Entrance to this hidden world. This hidden world of mystery, intrigue and renown, that many sought, but few found.

It wasn't just the wealthy who frequented De Lune, whiling away their nights in its secluded corners and secret rooms.

There were poets, artists, even politicians. If you were somebody in Paris, chances are, you were a part of De Lune.

"One day I too shall be a member", he promised, walking down the street to the porter's entrance at the back of the building.

Knock, knock.

The moment his knuckle connected with the door for its second knock, the door whipped open.

A waspish looking man with a receding hairline appeared, looming over him.

"You're late", the man hissed.

"Monsieur, it is only-" Henré stammered.

"I don't want to hear it", the man snapped, interrupting him. "Get back there and start laying the tables, they'll be here soon".

He pulled a white porter's towel from his shoulder and snapped it impatiently at his side.

Henré looked as if he might say something, then nodded in assent. "Monsieur", he replied dutifully, moving past the waspish man into the club.

That is the second time he has accused me of being late.

*I am **not** late.*

The man has it in for me.

"Hairpiece give you a hard time?" a musical voice chimed.

Henré looked up quickly from the table he had been working on, a panicked expression on his face as his eyes flashed around the room.

He spotted the culprit. A set of perfect white teeth and an impish grin, smiling wickedly at him two tables over.

"No more than usual". Henré smiled back sheepishly, his heart rate returning to something close to normal.

"He's got a real bee in his bonnet today. Must be that small patch of hair he is so fond of finally disappearing from the top of his head", the man mused mischievously.

The mischief came from an unexpected source. Pierre was a small wiry man that should have retired years ago. He'd been a fixture at De Lune for as long as anyone could remember, and he was one of Henré's closest friends.

Pierre's eyes always swam with humour, whether it was good intentioned or mischievous, and a smile was never far from his face.

He had the kind of smile that demanded repayment in kind, no matter the circumstance.

"Are you trying to get us both fired, old man?" Henré exclaimed in a hushed voice, his eyes following Hairpiece around the room.

"Pah. Hairpiece doesn't scare me". Pierre grinned cheekily. "Besides, I imagine he is more concerned with our guests, especially tonight".

The smile faded from his face, as all the humour in the room seemed to evaporate.

"What do you mean?" Henré asked seriously.

A mixture of emotions crossed Pierre's face, though not in the way they might across a young man's face, wild and unrestrained.

"Nothing, just be careful boy, it's a serious bunch in here tonight", Pierre said, smiling reassuringly as he gripped Henré's shoulder. He gave it a little squeeze.

Henré looked uncertain but returned the smile.

They worked in companionable silence together, laying pristinely white napkins across the expensive chairs, buffering and polishing the ornate wooden tables, and helping to prepare silver trays of snacks and refreshments in the kitchen.

The main hall was an impressive affair, not that the rest of De Lune was not, of course, but it was reserved for the biggest events, and the most impressive guests, and tonight was both big and impressive.

The parquet floors were gleaming, freshly waxed. Henré had never seen them waxed before and his unease grew.

The grand chandelier was not lit, which was also strange, but the torches on the walls had been lit.

Why they still even had torches he did not know. It was eerie.

"Showtime", Pierre whispered, thumping him on the back.

Henré jumped. The old coot had startled him, and Henré glared at him, as Pierre chuckled quietly.

Rubbing his hands nervously on his waistcoat, Henré turned his attention to the entrance.

A flurry of activity was underway, and elegantly dressed men and women had begun to enter the main hall.

He smiled. It was so exciting; he was blessed to work here.

He watched, as a trickle of people filed into the hall, past the greeters who were taking their coats and greeting them graciously.

He wondered who he'd see on this night. A famous artist or musician? Perhaps a politician? Perhaps several.

Pierre had hinted that this would be an important evening, though annoyingly he had been rather tight lipped about the details.

His theorising was cut short by the entrance of two women. They waltzed into the room arm in arm.

What women, he thought, his mouth agape.

Both wore midnight black dresses, cut scandalously high to just above the knee, and long stylish gloves up to the elbow.

His eyes followed their legs, as they swayed hypnotically.

He found the woman on the right particularly enchanting, and his eyes kept returning to her muscular legs, tracing them from ankle to knee, his imagination attempting to fill in the details. He had never seen women like this.

"If your mouth drops much further, you'll be kissing the floor, rather than Hairpiece's ass", a voice murmured vulgarly from behind.

"Mer-". Henré stopped himself from cursing as Hairpiece threw him a filthy look from across the room. "Zut!" he grumbled, pushing Pierre away. "Do some work you incorrigible old pautener".

Pierre giggled with glee and swept past Henré toward the guests, flashing him a wink over his shoulder as he went.

Hairpiece watched Pierre, scowling.

Pierre set his face seriously, and bobbed his head insolently to Hairpiece as he passed him, causing Hairpiece's face to moulder to murderous levels.

Pierre did not care. He was beyond reproach; the owner of De Lune loved him. And besides, he was already overdue retirement, what could they do to him?

Henré did not share the same carefree nonchalance. He fretted, as the young do, and saw his job as the beginning and end of his little world.

He had not learned the studied indifference to the stress of the workplace that comes with age, with the realisation that there are many things in life more important than work. That there are many men like Hairpiece, drunk on their miniscule pittance of power, and that there is always another job, somewhere around the corner.

"Merde", Henré muttered quietly, his eyes searching. He had lost sight of the enchantress.

Where is she?

With a jolt, his eyes met hers.

Mon dieu.

She cannot be real.

Is she human?

Or goddess.

She was sitting a few tables away, and she was looking at **him.**

She held his gaze for a moment, the shadow of a smile curving her lips, before turning away.

He watched her. as he clumsily laid cutlery at a table at the back of the room.

She was the most beautiful thing he had ever seen.

What about Amerie?

Your wife?

His stomach churned guiltily, and he looked away. But his eyes soon returned to her, drawn like magnets.

She wore only a little makeup, compared to the other women in the room, but the effect was mesmerising.

Her eyes were heavily lidded and green as emeralds, flecked with brown. Her lashes were purest black and curled sharp and tight.

Her eyes prowled the room, flashing dangerously now and then, as if challenging those who held her gaze for longer than she deemed prudent. As if daring them to continue their uninvited stare, if they had the stomach for it.

They were the most alluring eyes he had ever seen, and his stomach clenched as he remembered the effect of them meeting his own.

Her skin was caramel gold, and the shadows cast by the torch above her seemed to worship it, clinging to it desperately, smothering its soft curves and its sharp edges, so that no matter how she turned, her face was always in perfect harmony with the darkness that courted her.

The effect was strengthened by the panther black hair that framed her face and hung dangerously down her back. It swayed with menace as she turned her head haughtily from side to side.

Her bearing was regal, but untamed, wild almost, like an exiled princess.

He watched as she extended her hand to a passing waiter, who levitated toward her, his hand reaching for her own, as if by magic.

The boy stopped himself just in time from taking her hand and blushed.

He dropped his hand quickly to his tray and pressed a glass of champagne into her open hand.

She took the glass and dismissed him with a turn of her head.

The boy scurried away from her to his position in front of the wall, shamefaced, and crossed his arms, casting his eyes down to the ground.

"Boy, come on!" Pierre whispered anxiously, pulling at the sleeve of Henré's shirt. "That's one lady you don't want to get caught staring at". He had no trace of humour in his voice now.

Henré turned, confused, and irritated that Pierre had interrupted his admiration of the lady from afar. "Who is she?" he asked breathlessly.

"Trouble, for the likes of us", Pierre responded, pulling at him more insistently this time. "C'mon, if I've noticed you watchin her, Hairpiece certainly will have".

Henré brushed his arm away, and shook his head, still irritated, but let Pierre lead him away.

"Good boy", Pierre said, patting him on the back, as they settled against the wall to await the call of any guests who may require them.

Pierre watched Henré, who was still glancing across the room, trying to catch a glimpse of the mysterious beauty. "The honey is undoubtedly sweet, my boy, but is it worth the sting?"

Henré looked at him, confused.

Sting?

What did he mean?

What was he talking about?

He didn't know, but right then, he didn't care about any sting. He felt he would suffer any pain, if it meant a moment in her arms.

"Henré", a waspish voice whispered aggressively. "Kitchen, now!"

He sighed and slouched away in the direction of the kitchen.

Across the room, the beautiful woman tracked Henré with her eyes until he was out of sight, a look of interest on her face, and perhaps, something else.

Wrong Place, Wrong Time

Henré stepped out into the cold night air and breathed deeply, enjoying the crisp feel of it as it chilled his lungs.

The evening had been stressful. He loved his work, but on evenings such as this, it could be tense.

His every move was being scrutinised, both by the guests, and by Denis (Hairpiece's given name).

He didn't have it in him to muster a smile or mutter a quiet curse at Denis right then, tired as he was. He just wanted to go home.

He couldn't believe Marceau had been there, at his club, where **he** worked. What an honour. He couldn't wait to tell Amerie. His stomach tightened guiltily.

He had spotted Marceau, after he'd managed to detach his eyes from the mysterious beauty, and had even shaken his hand, after gushing out a jumble of compliments and praise. Marceau had taken pity on him.

What a man. What a great man. And such a presidential figure he cut, in his suave suit and handsomely styled hair. It was no wonder the people loved him, who wouldn't vote for such a man?

He looked as if someone had dreamt up what a president should look like, drawn it on a page, and Marceau was what had jumped out from the page and taken form.

He wasn't the president, **yet**, but Henré could see it.

And he wasn't the only one. His colleagues from De Lune all spoke about it in the bar after work sometimes, placing their bets on how and when he would take the presidency.

There was a running joke that he would have Renard assassinated, and his colleagues from work took great joy in dreaming up elaborate methods of assassination, and then loudly acting them out over their demi's.

Once Denis had gone home, of course.

Henré thought it was in bad taste but laughed along anyway. They were very funny after all, his work friends, and he wanted to fit in, so he kept his opinion to himself, and overlooked their roguish behaviour.

Not only was Marceau there, but he had brought with him a table-full of prominent Parisian politicians, and for some reason, the mysterious beauty was later sat next to him, at his request.

She must be very important to dine with Marceau. And to sit at his right hand no less, much to the displeasure of his colleague who sat to his left, who had curled his lip at regular intervals throughout the night at the usurping beauty, but was careful to never let her see it.

His thoughts turned to the woman once more and a dreamlike expression came over face.

If anything, she was more impressive than Marceau. There was something about her. But he did not know what. It was not simply her beauty; she had a certain power about her.

Marceau was a powerful man, a man of presence, a man of charisma, but when watching him talk with her, he seemed almost...childlike, in comparison.

What a treacherous thing to think.

And you have a wife!

Tear your mind from this other woman.

His guilt struck him with renewed vigour.

He hadn't thought of Amerie all evening, consumed as he'd

been with his adulterous fantasising.

He felt sinful, as if he'd wronged her somehow. He would make it up to her.

All I did was look.

I didn't lay a hand upon her.

No, but you wanted to.

Would you have?

It was an uncomfortable thought, and one he did not want to consider too deeply.

As he walked, his guilt grew, and he became depressed.

He was a married man. Happily married. And he loved his wife. Loved her deeply. He knew why he felt so guilty, and he hated himself for it.

Hated the power the woman had held over him. How she'd held him with her eyes like a puppet on a string, spinning him in pirouettes of desire, with each toss of her hair, each flutter of those perfectly perfect lashes.

He cursed and stopped.

Consumed as he'd been by his lecherous thoughts, he'd taken the wrong way home. He didn't like to come this way because it was poorly lit, and his work friends said it was not a safe place to be alone at night.

Well, they were characteristically more colourful in their depiction of the place, actually, but that didn't bear thinking about right now.

As he took stock of his surroundings, he was inclined to agree with his colleagues. It didn't seem very safe to him either.

Pulling his coat more closely about him, he increased his pace.

As he walked, he became aware of...something. Something moving at the edge of his vision.

He wasn't entirely sure how he became aware of this fact, as he could barely see anything, but the hairs on his arms and neck were raised and something felt wrong.

He started walking faster, and faster, until he was almost running, glancing behind, and around, every few steps, to see who, or what, was following him.

Turning the corner at the end of the street, he came onto a narrow path that was more of an alleyway than a street.

There were small shops on the ground floor of some of the buildings, and some apartments above them, but no lights to be seen. Many of them appeared to be abandoned, with no sign of habitation.

There were faint lights glowing hopefully at the end of the alleyway and he hurried toward them. "Almost there", he muttered.

He felt elated as he reached the middle of the alley, and the glow from the streetlights fell stronger upon him.

Almost free of this darkness. Almost home.

He hurried forward, a spring in his step.

Suddenly, a figure emerged to his left, seemingly gliding across the cobbles toward him.

He jumped back, his heart hammering in his chest.

As the figure came closer, he scrunched his eyes, trying desperately to see who, or what, it was.

"Who...Madame?!" he stuttered, as the figure was brought into focus by the light above. "You were... De Lune".

She ran a hand lovingly down the side of his face.

He felt as if he were dreaming.

I must have fallen and cracked my skull.

Fallen, and lost my wits.

This is my punishment, my penance, for my sinful soliloquising.

Now I am seeing things, things that are not there.

"Why are you...what are you..." Henre stammered. She was so close now, and he struggled to think clearly.

"Henré", she whispered.

"How do...how do you know my name?" he replied huskily,

collecting himself enough to utter a sentence.

She smiled, and he melted.

"I asked", she whispered.

"Why?" he replied hoarsely.

"I was...interested in you. Weren't you interested in me?" She fluttered her eyes prettily, a hint of sadness in them.

He did not want to upset her, he couldn't bear the idea of making those sad eyes sadder.

"Why...ah...yes...of course", he replied lamely. "I couldn't take my eyes off you", he said, his baser instinct taking hold.

She inched closer to him, and her cloak fell away revealing her soft neck.

He could not breathe, such was the effect on him, and he stood still, ensnared, as she closed the remaining distance between them, until they were only inches apart.

His breath caught tight in his chest.

The smell of her filled his nostrils like an explosion of violets, and he became drunk on her intoxicating scent. It was sweet and inviting and made him think of nothing rational.

He feasted on her glistening lips. Shining wet, slick with lipstick. Shaped as cupid's bow, darkly red as a rose. But they put him in mind of other things.

He studied her cat-like eyes, like a scientist came upon his greatest discovery, his most novel finding.

Enthralled, bewitched, ensorcelled, desperate to take in every line of her, every curve, every inch, so that he might capture the discovery and make it his, lest it flee from him, a fleeting thing, never to be found again.

He could hear his heart beating loudly in his chest.

Her every breath came sharp in his ear, the sound magnified.

It was maddening.

He could bear it no longer, and pulled her to him, his hands grasping desperately at her waist.

And she came to him. Allowed herself to be pulled, to be

possessed, to be grasped, her exotic mouth opening seductively. Invitingly. Tantalisingly.

He closed his eyes, and felt his lips meet hers.

His tongue entered her mouth, probing, searching, hungering. It was bliss, ecstasy, such consuming mania such as he'd never felt. He gave himself to it, lost himself in it, threw himself to oblivion.

Her arm encircled his neck, and her fingers trailed his neck, fondling it, playing with it, delicately, softly, at first, then more insistently.

She ran her hand through his hair. Gripping it tightly, she pulled him out of her mouth, and held him steady a few inches from her face, looking upon his face and neck.

Her eyes flashed wildly, and she drew him to her hungrily, her passion now primal and fierce.

Shrouded in darkness, in various nooks and crannies, several watchers watched in silence, as the lovers flailed madly in the starlight, entangled in one another, lost to the night, and to their passions.

He's Never Late

Amerie paced back and forth restlessly, her face wracked with worry.

Where was he? This is not like him.

He is never this late.

Even after drinking with that villain Pierre.

"Zut alors!" She slammed her dishcloth down on the kitchen counter. She snatched it up again immediately, along with a mug to polish.

She had already cleaned all of the mugs, and the plates, and the glasses, and polished them several times, but it was all she had to distract herself from worrying.

And so, she continued polishing, furtively striding to the window and parting the curtain every so often for an anxious glance down at the street below, hoping she might see her husband bounding down the road, a tired smile on his face.

And she would smile back. And her worry would cease, and her stomach would unclench, and she would relax, at last.

Until he climbed the stairs that is, and she would be waiting, with her best serious stare, to admonish him, and reprimand him, and harry him with her dishcloth to the tub.

She wouldn't mean it, well, not entirely, but it was a wife's prerogative to scold her husband from time to time, when he exhibited roguish behaviour, lest he start scanning the horizon too much, and his swagger grow too great.

"What is taking him so long! I will flay the skin from his bony behind when he returns! And that Pierre!" she growled.

She trudged wearily from the kitchen to the bedroom and

stood in front of the mirror.

I look deathly.

How ghastly!

She had made a special effort with her hair today. She knew how much Henré loved her hair, so she had risen early and pulled it into an elaborate arrangement that he always complimented her on.

But all she could see were the morbid bags hanging sadly under her eyes, and the tiny lines at their corners.

"Ohhh", she moaned, pulling at her cheeks, pinching and prodding the skin of her face. "I look like a faded oil painting".

She turned her attention to her stomach, which was still small, but noticeably rounder than it would usually be.

Her face fell, and she felt tears well in her eyes.

"No! No, I won't". She angrily dabbed at her eyes and rubbed the tears away. "I won't stay here and cry, like some helpless little girl".

She looked up at the mirror, and met her gaze in the glass with intensity, watching it turn from helpless to resolved.

"I will find this loutish husband of mine, and drag him here by his ear, through the street in his underwear if need be".

She smiled at the image of Henré flailing and crying as she pulled him through the street in his caleçon.

But first.

I must do something about this.

I don't want to go out like this...

She frowned at her reflection in the mirror, her confidence wavering.

She did not see a beautiful woman; she saw a tired mother-to-be with bags under her eyes and stretch marks already beginning to sink their teeth into her sides.

No.

You are beautiful.

Think of how many hands you have spurned.

How many eyes, full of heady hopes, you have felt upon you.

How many you turned away from, before you took his hand, your Henré's hand.

I need remind my husband what he is neglecting, and leaving cold, at home, alone, while he drinks till the early hours with villainous old men who should know better.

This is no behaviour of a father-to-be.

Placing her hair brush down on the table in front of her, she looked up at her reflection once more and smiled.

"It shall suffice. Now, to Pierre's, for the rogue shall surely be there, curled up on the sofa, or in the bed with his old lover".

But where was Pierre's?

I haven't the faintest idea.

I don't know if I can do this!

"Nonsense woman! It is simply a walk. You know that he lives not far from De Lune…Henré has spoken of it before, told you the rue, the building even".

She searched her memory, her face screwed up in concentration.

Aha.

Yes, I have it.

I think.

I think?

Her cheeks bunched high like a grinning marsupial, and she rubbed her lip and tried to remember.

"Ahhh. Rats! I have no choice. Off I go". She forced a light-heartedness that she did not feel into her voice.

The sun was shining, that was something at least, and she smiled, as she set off toward De Lune, and her wayward husband.

Pierre lived in a small apartment above a shop, she knew that much, and she knew it was not far from De Lune, as he had told her he did not like to have to walk too far to work in his old age.

What he meant to say was, he did not like to have to **stumble**

too far home after drinking the bar dry every evening after work.

She did not know where he put it all, the alcohol that is, as he was such a small and wiry man, with no hint of a stomach.

Henré had told her that some people are blessed with good fortune, others with good looks, Pierre, why Pierre, was blessed with a horse like tolerance for alcohol.

But he also said that Pierre rarely ate, subsisting mostly on café and cigarettes, which she expected had something to do with it.

As she walked through the streets, pondering her husband's choice in friends, she noticed a change in her surroundings, subtle at first, and then more pronounced, as she came closer to De Lune.

The modest little bakeries, cafes and patisseries disappeared, in place of grand buildings and grander people.

There were even motor cars, and finely dressed drivers in crisp new suits letting people in and out of them, holding the door open dutifully for them to get in or out, and then closing it softly behind them.

This area always made her feel uncomfortable, and out of place. She had come from a good enough family, and had known no real hardship growing up, but her family were not wealthy like this.

This was different. This was intimidating.

The women were bedecked in jewellery, their fingers dripping with rings, their wrists groaning with bangles, their necks straining under gold and silver and pearl.

And the men.

The looks from the men made her uncomfortable. She was acutely aware of what those looks meant.

A family brushed past her, a little boy eating an ice cream and loudly bawling at his mother, gesturing impatiently at something in the shop window next to them.

"But mama, mama, mama!" he screamed, stamping his foot like a little piston, again and again, yanking his mother's arm insistently all the while.

Goodness gracious, Amerie thought, as she stepped to the side, narrowly avoiding the child's petulant foot as it struck down hard on the pavement.

Enfant gâté.

I hope I do not raise such a child.

She ran her hand over her stomach, frowning disapprovingly at the little boy, as the family disappeared into the shop, the boy having succeeded in his tantrum.

They paid her no mind; she did not think they even noticed her. Perhaps she was invisible, clothed as she was, in a modest dress, and a distinct absence of precious metal on her person.

She slunk back into the shadows of the overhanging shop awnings, studying the people in the street, watching them, observing.

She liked to 'people-watch' and took great joy in thinking up backstories for the people she saw who caught her interest.

There was an elderly lady who lived near them, who walked the street alone, every night, in the dead of night.

She would walk, arms clasped peacefully behind her back, hair bunched tightly atop her head, without a care in the world.

She wore a beautiful, brightly coloured silk robe. Amerie knew it was called a kimono, for she had asked about it in the quarter, intrigued as she was.

The lady would walk their street, then round the corner and disappear, every night, without fail.

She wondered where the lady went. What she did. When did she return? Why did she not fear for her safety?

Paris was a wonderful city, but there were rogues afoot always, and everyone knew the night was the refuge of the rogue.

The woman was not Parisian, Amerie knew that much. She had the most exquisite almond shaped eyes, and her hair was uncommonly black and shiny.

She thought of the lady often, and wondered what adventures she sought each night.

The people near De Lune, however, were different.

The lady in the kimono had a quiet grace to her. These people had something, but it was sour in some way. It did not sit right, upon their faces, and it rode high up their backs, and sat visibly on their shoulders.

She wasn't sure she'd call it a grace.

They did not smile. Well, they smiled, but it was more a smirk or a sneer, or a lazy thing. A half thing, an imitation, a lip service. It was not a happy thing. It was a reflex, but a reflex born of smugness, rather than joy.

The more she watched, the more she disliked what she saw. It reeked of discontent here, of greed, of **wantonness**. How could people who had so much, who had everything, who wanted for nothing, be discontent? How could they be unhappy?

Yet that was what she observed on every face, in every sneer, and in every scoff. She did not see people who were happy with their life, she saw people fat with discontent.

Grown fat with gluttony, as if they were desperately trying to fill a hole in their life, in their soul. A hole somewhere deep inside their heart. Fill it with money, and clothes, and lavish gifts, and expensive motorcars, and precious stones.

They trod, shop to shop, bored looks on their faces, their bags growing larger, and heavier, as they bought, and spent, and acquired, and accrued. Their children, watching, learning, absorbing the behaviour of their parents, their role models, their teachers.

And they learned, the children. They learned greed, and wantonness, and from it, they learned discontent, and unhappiness. And finally, they learned callousness, and coldness and careless disregard.

And so, the next litter of petulant pups mewled and pawed and grew fat and bold and entitled, ready to assert their place in the pack. To dominate their lessers, and pay lip service to their betters, circling them, nipping at them. Waiting like jackals, scheming like hyenas, to take what was theirs, and grow their pile of treasure even bigger, even fatter, so their scoffs and sneers might come faster and sharper, for years to come.

She shook her head. She had seen the same thing with her own parents, though on a smaller scale, their ambitions hindered by their means. They had been obsessed with things and the opinions of others. The right clothes, the right profession, the right company.

Everything had to be right, lest they appear less than perfect. Lest someone in the quarter say something. Lest the lady down the street say something, which would of course bring about the end of days.

The lady down the street was blind, with cataracts in both eyes, and spent her days feeding the pigeons in the park. It was maddening. And she had been glad to be free of it.

She found in Henré a refreshingly humble and uninhibited companion, to her mind and her heart, to her childhood of stifling repression and judgement, of everyone and everything.

Henré didn't care what anyone thought, about anything, and she adored that about him. He only cared for her.

"They're not all bad, you know", a voice said from right beside her.

Amerie jumped, cursing coarsely, like one of the rogues she so disdained.

The speaker, a woman, giggled mischievously, and placed a hand gently on Amerie's arm. "I'm sorry, my dear, that was rude of me, a bad habit of mine".

"Bad habit? What are you talking about?" Amerie shot back gruffly, still startled by the woman's sudden intrusion.

"Sneaking up on people", the woman replied apologetically.

"I've always been rather sneaky, you see, ever since I was a girl. Sneaking here, sneaking there. Rather a good way to listen in on conversations one should not be privy to".

Amerie looked at her blankly.

"Eavesdropping", the woman clarified matter of factly. "You know-".

"Yes, I know what eavesdropping is, thank you", Amerie interrupted her curtly.

"Yes, of course, and now I am being patronising. You must wish to be rid of me, so I shall leave you be, and once again, I am sorry my dear. In my old age I have become rather lonely and find myself yearning for company now and then, unfortunately it has led me to become rather too curious for my own good", the woman explained.

"No, wait, I'm sorry", Amerie said suddenly, her hand shooting out to grab the woman's arm.

She released it quickly, surprised, feeling she had overstepped herself. "I didn't mean to be so rude, you just...scared me".

"It's quite alright", the woman said amiably. "I can be a nosy old crow".

Amerie giggled. "No, really, I'm sorry", she said, touching the woman's arm, gently this time.

"Are you well, dear?" the woman enquired suddenly, placing her hand atop Amerie's and watching her closely.

"Yes, yes I'm-" Amerie began, but she could not continue, for her words would not come. And suddenly, she was sobbing.

Softly at first, covering her mouth her hand, and then in great heaves as she struggled to draw breath.

"Whatever is the matter?" the woman exclaimed, pulling Amerie to her and wrapping her in her arms. "There, there, dear, shh, shh".

The woman cooed as she petted Amerie's back in a practised manner, as if by instinct. As if Amerie were yet another child, and she a mother.

"This quarter brings me to tears too, dear, I don't think anyone would forgive you a little cry", the woman said.

Amerie snorted into the woman's chest, the laughter welling in her chest interrupting the flow of tears for a moment.

But they came right back, and she cried some more, and the woman comforted her, as one of her own.

When she was done, she felt lighter, as if through her tears, she had shed some of the burden she felt, and some of the worry.

Sniffing, she wiped her nose with the back of her hand, and shook her head desolately.

"I am pathetic", Amerie said quietly.

"No, no, none of that now dear", the woman replied, lifting Amerie's chin and fixing her with a fierce stare.

It was the first time Amerie had seen the woman's face clearly, shadowed as she'd been by the shop awnings.

It was a strong face, a beautiful face, with a perfect symmetry to it. The cheeks were high and well formed, not too sharp, not too soft, sat atop a finely set mouth, with perfectly thick lips. Not too thick, and not too thin.

The nose was small, with but the slightest aquiline sharpness to it, so that it curved harmoniously downward, drawing the attention to the lips.

The eyes were truly striking, a shocking mix of blues, as if someone had taken a brush, and splashed together their interpretation of a choppy sea on a warm summer's day.

Her brow was high, but not large, her golden blonde hair was parted to one side, resting playfully beneath her ears.

It wasn't just the features that were finely formed. There was an inner beauty to the face, a certain virtue to it, a nobility of sorts. It was a caring face, but it had a humour to it, a mischievousness.

Amerie stared back at the woman, marvelling at her eyes. They made her think of crashing waves.

The woman stared back, expectantly, and Amerie blinked.

"I'm sorry", Amerie said shamefaced. "What must you think of me?"

"I must think that I am very scary indeed, to elicit such a reaction", the woman said seriously.

Amerie stared blankly for a moment, her mind still foggy from her crying, before her mouth dropped open in comprehension.

"No, it's not-" she began explaining.

"Hush, now", the woman said imperiously. "I shan't hear it".

Amerie closed her mouth, unsure of what to say or do.

"You were upset. There is nothing wrong with that. It is quite natural. And quite healthy. There is sometimes no greater remedy for a heavy heart, than a good cry".

Amerie stood quietly, intrigued.

"I'm sorry, dear, please, tell me, why do you cry?"

Amerie bit her lip and turned away.

"What is it, dear?"

Maybe she can help, Amerie thought.

You could surely use a friend.

"It is my husband", Amerie confessed. "He did not come home last night, nor this morning, it is...not like him".

The woman waited expectantly, as if she knew there was more to it.

"In fact, he has never done this, he would always tell me if he planned to stay late and drink with his colleagues, or with Pierre. Pierre is his friend, an old man, a roguish old man actually", Amerie gushed, the words flowing fast from her.

The woman listened, and nodded encouragingly here and there as Amerie told her tale.

"And so here I am, come to find my husband, but I cannot remember exactly where Pierre lives, so I thought I would come, and wander, and see if I could find the street where he lives. Maybe I am worrying unnecessarily, and maybe he is just drunk, sleeping it off, but... I couldn't just sit and do nothing", Amerie finished lamely, as if worried her plan would be judged harshly by this dynamic woman.

The woman smiled understandingly. "I understand, completely, of course. It is a horrible thing to worry about the one you love, it can make you sick, in your heart, in your stomach, and in your mind". She spoke in soft, gentle tones, understanding apparent in every syllable.

Amerie nodded.

"The uncertainty is the worst of it", the woman said.

"Yes", Amerie agreed.

"Well, let us find him then". The woman slapped her hands down against her legs, brimming with energy.

The suddenness of her decisiveness shocked Amerie, and she stood uncomprehending for a moment. "But I don't even know your name, why would you help me?"

"Call me La Meme, dear, everybody does". The woman gripped Amerie's hand, as she introduced herself with a warm smile.

Amerie frowned.

"Now that you know my name, will you accept my help?" La Meme asked.

"Why would you help me?" Amerie repeated.

This was not what she was used to. Everything had a price, everyone had a motive, no one did something for nothing, at least not in the world she grew up in.

"Because you need it", La Meme said simply.

"Thank you", Amerie choked, holding back tears.

"Now, now", La Meme chided. "Your husband needs you, let us find him. How else will you scold him otherwise?" There was a mischievous twinkle in her eyes.

Amerie giggled. "True".

"Where does he work, this roguish husband of yours?" La Meme enquired.

"It's a place called De Lune, do you know it?" Amerie asked.

"De Lune?" the woman replied sharply, all traces of maternal affection gone.

In fact, she seemed a little scary to Amerie, the twinkle had gone from her eyes which were now intense and rather piercing.

"Yes", Amerie confirmed.

"Your husband works there?" La Meme pressed, her tone authoritative.

"Yes", Amerie replied. "Yes, Pierre, his friend, also works there. He's always trying to involve Henré in his after-work debauchery, drinking in the bar, or trying to lure him to that other awful place in the city".

"Which place?" La Meme asked.

"Le Bateau, Le Marin, L'ancre, something like that", Amerie mused.

"L'ancre?" La Meme repeated, the same hard edge to her voice.

"L'ancre, that's it", Amerie agreed. "What is it? Tell me, is it a truly villainous place?"

La Meme smiled. "Do not worry, my dear. We shall find him, wherever he may be, and we shall scold him, together. He shall think twice before such a dalliance again".

"Are you sure?" Amerie asked, chewing her lip. "I do not want to trouble you".

"Nonsense. We Dames de Paris must stick together", La Meme said.

Smiling warmly, the older woman took her by the arm and led her away, chatting animatedly, about this and that, and lighter things, unrelated to roguish husbands, and their roguish ways.

La Meme, Lucien, Lucien, La Meme

She grinned in spite of herself.

Well, I cannot fault his taste, she thought, as she watched them approach.

As they drew nearer, she composed herself, a veil of neutrality falling over her face.

He moved with grace, but it was an uncertain thing, an undecided thing.

"La Meme", Gabriel purred, as he bounded over to her and leant down to give her a hug and a kiss.

"My Gabriel", La Meme murmured, pulling him down to her bosom.

She smiled fondly up at him, before turning her eyes on his guest.

He was tall, and well formed, but lean. It irritated her that he cut an impressive figure, she had wanted to dislike him.

He wore a tailored suit and waistcoat that fit snugly, accentuating the curvature of his torso.

His face was handsome in a serious fashion, but his eyes had an enigmatic shine and a humour to them. It was a face of contradictions, and she found herself studying it, intrigued.

His thick, dark brows suggested a serious nature, but his wide mouth, full lips, and the laughter lines under his flat, low cheeks spoke of a playfulness.

He had a masculine nose and was clean shaven, as was the

fashion. His hair was soft and black, cut short. His skin was brown, like black coffee with a splash of milk.

She stared into his eyes. There was pain there. Behind the shine.

He returned her stare, and she watched his face tighten, as his eyes searched her own, and performed their own assessment.

Interesting, she thought.

"Lucien", he said suddenly, extending his hand.

She gave him her own, and he raised it to his lips, kissing it softly.

"La Meme", she replied, smiling cooly.

"La Meme?" he enquired, frowning.

She waved her hand dismissively. "Don't ask".

Lucien smiled politely.

"Gabriel has told me a lot about you, too much, in fact", La Meme said.

"La Meme!" Gabriel grumbled, embarrassed.

"Only so much as is pertinent to your employment of him, I am sure", she assured Lucien dryly.

Gabriel blushed, covering his face with his hand.

Lucien smiled, amused, and La Meme found herself smiling back.

It was a different thing entirely, this smile, to that shadow of a smile he first used.

"Come, let us sit, and enjoy what remains of the sun, as we get to know one another". She gestured at the little iron table she was sitting at.

They took their seats, Lucien taking the seat directly under the terrace, La Meme to his left, and Gabriel to his right, forming a triangle of sorts.

The Seine glittered prettily at them in the distance, sending a few rogue rays of sunshine at them every now and then. They sat quietly pondering one another, in wait for the waitress.

A few couples sat in happy silence around them, quietly

sipping wine, and enjoying each other's company.

"Bonjour, madame, messieurs", an enthusiastic voice chirped at them.

The speaker was a young girl with a bob, cut severely to the middle of her cheeks, and a splatter of freckles on her nose.

"Madame?" Lucien gestured to La Meme, grateful for the arrival of the waitress and an end to the silence.

"How kind of you, Lucien, however I am more than satisfied with my tea for now". She tapped her saucer gently with her spoon, flashing the waitress an endearing smile as she did so.

The waitress grinned toothily back at her.

"Messieurs?" she enquired, turning to Lucien and Gabriel.

Gabriel looked to Lucien.

Taking the cue, he responded.

"Wine please, red", Lucien said.

"Something, vintage", Gabriel added, smiling mischievously.

"Yes, indeed", Lucien confirmed, smirking impishly, and a little sheepishly, back at Gabriel.

La Meme pouted. She leant back in her chair and crossed her arms, watching the two of them speculatively.

As the waitress smiled and turned to Gabriel to take his order, Lucien interjected: "And un café, for my thoughtful friend here".

There was a hint of impishness to Gabriel's grin now also.

La Meme's mouth twitched.

"Of course, messieurs", she said, her eyes darting amusedly between the two men. She turned and left with an efficient flourish.

"So, Lucien", La Meme mused. "Gabriel tells me you have a love for antiques, or beautiful things, as he calls them".

Gabriel shifted in his seat.

"I seek beauty, wherever I can find it", Lucien replied seriously, seemingly unfazed by her remark. "Sometimes I stumble upon it, and sometimes, it finds me".

"And have you always been in this line of work?" La Meme asked, undeterred.

"Well yes, for the most part", Lucien responded.

"For the most part?" Her eyes were glittering keenly.

"Yes", Lucien replied, shifting ever so slightly in his chair, but still holding her gaze.

"And do you have any other talents I should know of?" La Meme pressed.

Lucien frowned at this. "Talents?"

What does she know?

"Talents", she replied, narrowing her eyes.

"I feel remiss, it seems you are privy to something I am not. Madame, what have you heard of me?" Lucien asked, grinning wolfishly.

"This and that", she replied coolly. "Some of it good, some of it not so good".

"La Meme!" Gabriel exclaimed. "What has he done to warrant this?"

"No, no, it's fine Gabriel, I know there are... rumours about me. Some of

them unfounded, some of them". Lucien paused as if deciding whether to continue.

"All I can say is, my intentions are pure. Gabriel is a fine man, and I think he will make a valuable addition to DuPassé, that is why I seek to employ him", Lucien said sombrely.

La Meme watched him intently. She looked like a cat deciding whether or not to pounce upon its prey, or let it live to see another day.

"That will do, for now", she said, glancing at Gabriel fondly, before returning her attention to Lucien. "But look after him, he is all I have, and I love him dearly".

Look after me? Gabriel thought.

*Perhaps she **does** believe that nonsense about disappearing antiquers?*

"And I you", Gabriel replied, "But I am quite capable of taking care of myself, and Lucien has been nothing but forthright with me so far. Besides, I think we are unlikely to come under enemy fire in DuPassé".

She looked unsure at this, for the first time in their interaction.

"But thank you for worrying about me", he said, sensing that she may be hurt. As if considering his words insufficient, he leant forward and gave her a quick peck on the check.

At this, she brightened.

"You are of course welcome to come and visit Gabriel, anytime", Lucien said softly.

"How kind of you". She beamed.

"As long as you do not interfere with his work, and pull him into any mischief, that is", Lucien qualified.

"Mischief? You forget your manners. Why, I never..."

She bristled, as Gabriel laughed loudly and infectiously.

She turned her bristles on him, then back to Lucien, then back to Gabriel, her mouth open, aghast at the nerve of them both.

Lucien started laughing then too, his chest shaking with each deep, soulful laugh.

After a while, La Meme started to laugh too, slowly at first, in little snorts, and then little giggles, then tears began at the corners of her eyes, and they glistened wet with whimsy.

Why even the Seine seemed to laugh along with them. Gabriel really did have quite the infectious laugh, you see.

A Most Unfortunate Turn Of Events

Infectious as Gabriel's laugh was, unfortunately it could not cure all woes. Least of all, those of the poor soul lying cold and catatonic before us.

Poorly concealed in the stairwell of a bakery, lies a man, shivering, wrapped in his own arms against the chill of the early morning air.

It is early, still too early for most.

As if on cue, a sturdy wooden door to the left of the man groaned open with a jarring creak, and a burly man stepped out into the stairwell, yawning loudly.

Blinking blearily in the grey blue of the predawn, he reached a hand down his pants, and stood, scratching at himself sleepily under his longs.

Seemingly content with his scratching, the scratching slowed, then stopped, and the man went still, his head lolling forward onto his chest and bouncing gently up and down a few times.

After a moment, a snore escaped his nose, or perhaps it was his mouth. It was hard to tell given the sound, which sounded a little like an automobile with a pig's snout exhaust backfiring.

The sound was loud, so loud that it woke the man from his

standing slumber, and he jerked awake, cursing and muttering in a heavy voice.

He took a deep breath, filling his lungs slowly, and ponderously, then let loose a deep sigh, a sigh so deep it seemed it would go on forever.

When the sigh was done, the man sniffed, then began pawing at his torso and legs, as if engaged in a ritual as old as time itself.

Finally, his hands found what they sought, and he whipped a cigarette from the lining of his johns into his mouth.

A matchbox soon joined the cigarette in the man's hands, and he artfully struck a match against the edge of the box, even though his fingers were thick and calloused, and looked large and ungainly compared to the tiny match.

He brought the wavering redly orange flame to his mouth and held it against the cigarette, creating a shield against the wind with his other hand.

With the cigarette lit, the man discarded the match with a flick of his finger into a little corner of matches on the floor, and took a long pull on the cigarette.

Removing it from his mouth, he eyed the cigarette speculatively, then took three quick pulls in succession, before releasing a massive cloud of smoke, and a slightly more satiated sigh.

More sighs followed, as the man pulled on his cigarette, and returned to his scratching. After a time, he finished his cigarette, and looking at it, disappointed. He flicked it into the same corner as the matches.

He turned briskly to go back inside, then stopped, his hand on the door. "What the-" he grumbled, turning back in the direction of his cigarette.

"Who the-".

His face soured like old milk.

"Oi", the man said, addressing a figure sleeping on the floor of his stairwell.

"Oi", the man repeated, sticking his foot into the side of the figure. The figure groaned and pulled his arms tightly about himself.

"I said oi", the man said, more insistently this time. "What you doin ere? Get out of it! I'm sick of you wretches thinkin my stairwell some sorta hotel for the likes of yous".

He kicked the figure, a man, in the side.

When the figure did not stir, the aggrieved man roared, "Get up!"

"Please...stop", the man on the floor moaned, throwing his arm up to shield his eyes from the growing morning light.

His face was grey as the floor on which he lay, and his hair was flecked with dust and debris from the floor. His clothes were badly ripped and torn. He looked every inch the vagrant.

"No I won't be stoppin!" the man shouted. "I've had it up to ere with you lot". He raised his hand above his head.

"Every mornin I come out ere, another villainous vagrant sleepin on my porch", the man complained, spitting as he griped. "What ave I gotta do to be able to smoke me cigarette n wake up in peace?"

"I'm sorry", the vagrant rasped, as he attempted to pull himself up using the wall of the stairwell. "Where am I?" He looked around confused.

"Where am I?" the aggrieved baker repeated, amazed. "Don even know where he is", he continued under his breath. "You're where you shudn' be, that's where!"

"Water, please, water", the vagrant rasped painfully.

"Water". The baker shook his head. "You'll be gettin no water from me, now get outta here, before I break yer head", he roared, his rage returning.

A window cracked open above, and a disgruntled looking woman in frilly white pyjamas thrust her head and shoulders out aggressively.

"Will you shut up you stinkin English dog?" she screamed.

"Every morning, you and your damn shoutin! Just give the boy some water and send him on his way, I'm sick of hearin it!"

The baker turned to shout back, but the woman threw herself back into her apartment, snapping the window shut with so much force that it rattled violently in its frame.

"I'll give you English dog, French bitch", the baker spat.

Turning, he grit his teeth, and glared down at the vagrant, slumped down against the wall, and quickly falling back asleep.

"Oh no you don't", the baker said, before disappearing inside.

The door slammed shut behind him, and muffled shouting rang out from above. It must have been loud shouting indeed, for the window remained shut.

The shouting did not have long to marinade, before the door whipped open once more, and the baker appeared, looming madly in the door, a large wooden pail hanging from one thick arm.

Splash!

"Aghhh!" the vagrant screamed, jolting upright against the wall, now slick with water.

He scrambled frantically to his feet, pushing and scratching at the floor in his haste to rise.

The baker grinned grimly. "That'll teach yeh".

The vagrant panted heavily, fear in his eyes.

The baker stood, uncertain, watching him malevolently. "Well go then!" he shouted, rattling his pail.

"Please..." the vagrant pleaded between pants, still breathing heavily. "Water".

Unsettled, the baker considered his options.

Part of him yearned to fill his pail and douse this cheeky sod once more.

Another part of him, a smaller, but more powerful part of him, was scared, though he was loath to show it.

This wasn't how it usually went.

Usually he gave them the pail, and they woke, screaming and cursing, and fled quickly, or stumbled off, depending on the state of them.

This man wasn't acting right.

"Fine", the baker spat. "But then off with yeh! I haven't the time for this, I've bread to bake!"

He stomped back inside muttering hatefully under his breath.

The vagrant twitched, and turned, strangely, as if listening. As if tracking the man's voice through the door.

He watched as he passed in front of a small window shaded by little net curtains, which were savagely ripped to the side as the baker reached them. "You don wanna see an angry Frenchman deprived o his baguette boy, I can assure you", the baker grumbled, pushing the heavy wooden door back open as if it were weightless.

"Now take this, then be off with ye!" he thrust a mug of water at the vagrant, who took it gratefully in shaking hands.

The vagrant sipped at the water, then drank deeply, draining the mug, which was not small, in a matter of seconds.

"Th-thank you", the vagrant stammered, his breathing slightly calmer now.

The baker grunted. "Be off with ye". He gestured to the street above the stairwell.

"Y-yes, of course, thanks again", the vagrant said, approaching the baker with hand outstretched.

The baker hesitated, then walked forward, extending his own hand.

Before he could take the hand of the vagrant, he stopped, his eyes widening, a look of fear on his face.

"I gotta go, don't come round here again, or it'll be the cudgel next time for yeh", he said quickly. He disappeared into his bakery and slammed the door shut behind him, which shook heavily in its frame.

"Fils a putain!" a woman screamed from above.

The vagrant jumped, startled at the noise. He could have sworn it was right beside him, but he could see no one, and there were no windows open or people in the street beside him.

His head ached abominably, and the water had left a metallic, acrid taste in his mouth. Perhaps the baker had poisoned him.

Don't be stupid.

It is likely just old and stale.

Or has been left outside and lapped at by the dogs.

The vagrant's mouth twisted distastefully.

Wonderful, dog water.

Smacking his lips, he closed his eyes, his head thumping like a drum.

It really did taste rather foul, the water. But it had replenished him, at least partially, and his head felt marginally better. But he knew not where he was, or how he had got there.

Come on man, find your wits.

A jarring knocking noise distracted him, like a heavy spoon on glass.

From the corner of his vision he saw the baker, knocking aggressively on his window with one of his oversized knuckles.

He stared at the baker, and the same look of fear appeared on the baker's face. The baker gestured rudely at him, suggesting that he should leave immediately, then the curtains snapped shut and he was gone.

Charming.

A pain lanced through his neck, then his stomach, and he fell to his knees, moaning loudly and gripping his stomach tightly, as if to squash the pain out of existence.

My god, what was that pain?

I have never felt the like.

"Don't make me get my cudgel boy!" the baker shouted through the window.

Putain.

This baker.

Will he cease his prattle!

The vagrant lashed out, swinging his arm wildly toward the window, making an angry, guttural sound. A sound of pure frustration and rage.

He stormed toward the window scowling and snarling. The curtains closed rapidly.

The vagrant breathed a sigh of relief, and closed his eyes, enjoying the return to silence. The pain in his head had dulled a little and he opened his eyes.

Time to go.

Before I kill this wretch.

He frowned, surprised at himself. He was not a violent man, nor prone to such thoughts.

Where did that come from?

It must be the pain.

I must leave this place.

Now.

Casting a murderous glance back at the window, he slowly climbed the stairs to the street above.

It was getting brighter, and there were hints of orange and red on the horizon. For some reason, this panicked him, and he started to sweat.

Must get out of sight. Can't be seen like this.

He clawed at his clothes, covered in dust, and debris, and cuts, and blood.

Blood?!

Why is there blood?!

He clawed more frantically in an effort to clean himself of the mess.

Glancing around wildly for something to clean himself with, he spotted a round tin of water atop a small bench, sitting in front of a door that was slightly ajar.

Without thinking, he ran to the water, and stuck his head

into it, submerging it completely.

As the water closed over his face and head, he closed his eyes, the cold water shocked him from his panic, and bit into him pleasantly.

Pulling his head from the water with a satisfying **slosh,** he whipped his hair back out of his face. He ran his hands thoroughly over his face, trying to clean it as best he could.

Spotting a wash rag, he snatched it up and rubbed it roughly across his forehead, then his nose, and his mouth and chin.

Satisfied, and feeling slightly better, he tore his shirt off and dropped it onto the bench, then brought the rag down across his chest, wincing as water reached his neck.

He closed his mind to the pain and anxious thoughts in his mind.

He continued to sponge himself with the rag, washing himself clean under his arms and back, paying special care to avoid coming anywhere near his neck.

When he was done, he whipped his shirt from the bench, and submerged it in the water, beating it ineffectually with the rag, twisting and stretching it in an attempt to get the blood out.

It was no use though, and he felt the panic start to well up inside once more.

Looking around, he spied a washing line down the street, hung with clothes. There were men's shirts, women's dresses, and what looked like children's clothes, little socks and shorts.

Snatching a clean shirt from the line, he threw it loosely around his shoulders, and returned to the tin of water.

The water was still now, and he could see himself reflected in it.

Curious.

My face looks strange.

And my eyes...

His head snapped back, and he felt a deep dread go through him.

Why are my eyes red?

He pushed his face back down to the water and stared as hard as he could at his reflection.

His head swung back, quickly, mechanically, as if on a metal arm.

Why are my eyes red?

Why are they red?

Why are they red?

Red.

Red.

Red.

"Hey! What are you doin with my tin!" a shrill voice exploded in his ear.

A hand grabbed his arm, and he spun ferociously, viciously wrenching his arm out of the grip.

"Ahhh", the voice wailed, as its owner, a woman, fell backwards onto the hard cobbles of the street.

As she fell, she hit the back of her head on the hard wooden exterior of the building behind with a jarring **smack.**

The vagrant stared down at the woman, aghast, and still breathing deeply from the shock she had given him.

What have I done?

"Ma..madame?" he ventured quietly.

"Madame?" he repeated, unsure of what to do.

Oh no.

Oh no oh no.

The woman lay still, her head tilted at a strange angle. A trickle of blood had appeared beneath her ear, and was winding its way slowly down to her neck.

Her soft, beautiful neck.

He shuddered, as a different kind of shock ran through him.

"OIIIII!" a coarse voice yelled loudly from the other end of the street. "What are you doin! I warned you, it'd be the cudgel for you if you pushed yer luck".

It was the baker, and he was climbing his stairwell, his face set and angry.

A window clicked open somewhere above, and the vagrant spun on his feet, wildly seeking the sound with his eyes, like a feral cat.

"What is all this noise!" a disgruntled old woman wailed. "Harry, if that's you makin all that racket, I swear I'll never buy yer bread again. I'll walk to that Pole, every day, even if it kills me". She brandished her fist out of the window to drive the threat home.

She caught sight of the vagrant below in the street, and looked surprised. "Who're you!" she demanded. "N what are you doin here at this time makin all this noise? You another Englishman like that good for nothin baker?"

She pointed at Harry.

Then, she peered down at the vagrant, who was backing slowly away from the window, his eyes darting between her and Harry.

Picking up a thick pair of very round glasses, she settled them onto her face to better inspect the shenanigans taking place below. As they settled onto the rim of her nose, she frowned and squinted.

"You don't look English", she stated.

"But what's..." She leant out of the window, following the vagrant's eyes, to see what he kept staring at.

"What's..." she repeated, her face growing still.

"What's...that's...what ave you done!" she shouted suddenly. "Harry, Harry, he's killed her! Oh my god, he's killed her!" she screamed, gesturing at the woman lying still beneath her window.

"Harry, Harry, get him Harry!" She frantically waved her hand toward the vagrant.

Killed her?

The vagrant stood, dumb, the words struggling to register.

I can't have killed her.

Pounding feet.

Run.

He turned and ran, as fast as he could.

He ran, and he ran, and he ran, his feet burning the earth beneath him, as he twisted, and turned, and scrambled, and slid.

He ran, the sky growing ever lighter above him, the light on the horizon inexorably pushing back the grey, and the blue, and the purple. Higher the light rose, and thicker it became in the sky, as if it was chasing him, closing in on him like the hangman with his noose.

His blood thumped in his ears, and his nerves burned.

He had to run, had to hide.

Somewhere.

Dark.

Safe.

He skidded to a halt.

I know this place.

I know this.

The Catacombs!

Yes.

I will be safe there.

Safe.

Quiet.

He had run himself ragged, and in his panic and his fear, had brought himself close to an old, unused entrance to the catacombs.

Perhaps something in him had been drawn to it.

There!

The entrance.

Surrounded by trees, and overgrown by shrubs and bushes, but it was there, nonetheless. He knew it was there, hidden, at the end of the street, and out of sight, for he had visited it as a child, against the wishes of his mother.

He sprinted across the road, his shirt whipping wildly around him, his face a panicked blur in the glass windows of the shop fronts that he passed.

Yes.

I have made it.

Darkness.

Blissful darkness.

He felt an immediate calm as he entered the protective shade of the trees.

The entrance was concealed in an old wooden building, that was more of a shack than anything else. He stumbled to the back of the building and forced open the door with his shoulder. The door was slowly rotting and offered no resistance.

As he entered, he spied it. There, the entrance. A manhole, with a ladder down.

He squatted, placing both hands on the cover, and heaved it clear to one side, then lowered himself gingerly onto the ladder below.

He paused and looked up, uncertain.

Just for a while.

Until I can collect my thoughts.

Making up his mind, he reached for the stone cover plate, and pulled it back into place above him with an ominous grinding sound.

As the plate slid into place, and the last of the light was smothered, he let out a small sigh of relief.

At least, he was here now.

He was tired.

He was hurt.

He was Henré, and he was scared beyond words.

The Ramblings
Of A Mad Man

The fire crackled comfortably, as a particularly ripe log split in the fireplace.

Garlon smiled, enjoying the sound.

He watched the eager young faces staring at him expectantly. He loved a good debate. And he loved to talk, or 'yap like a dog', as some put it. He guessed it depended on which way you looked at it.

"What do you mean Gar?" a young boy asked, his face confused, and a little scared, at what he was hearing.

The other boys leaned forward on their stools to hear better, their faces set and serious.

"What do you think I mean?" Garlon replied, sipping his demi.

The boys watched silently, and the barmaid, who had been wiping out a jug, now watched too from the corner of her eye, half-heartedly rubbing the inside of the jug.

The silence continued, and the room waited expectantly.

Garlon sighed.

Couldn't keep your fat mouth shut, could you?

"Those that seek power, shouldn't find it", Garlon said, knowing he would have to explain himself now.

The boys stared blankly.

"Well, think about it", Garlon leant forward on his stool. "The game of politics. The game that Marceau and them play.

What do you think they're playin for?"

"Playin? Ain't nobody playin Gar", one of the boys cut in.

"No, that's...that's not what I meant". Garlon shook his head.

"Why become a politician?" Garlon asked, earnestly.

"To help the people", a serious looking boy guessed.

"To **serve** the people", a naive looking boy retorted.

"To serve **France**", a confident looking boy corrected the naive boy.

Garlon nodded. "Yeah, yeah, maybe".

"What do you mean maybe?" the serious boy asked. "Marceau is a great man, my pa said so, said he's great for France".

"And maybe your pa's right, Horace", Garlon addressed the serious boy.

"But you don't think he is?" the naive boy quipped.

"Now that's not what I said, Gabin, don't put words in my mouth", Garlon admonished the naive boy, watching Horace's face flush from the corner of his eye.

"Then what are you saying!" the confident boy demanded.

Garlon bristled. "Now Ariste, if you quiet down and let me speak, I'll tell you", he said shortly, giving his head a little shake.

He pulled a copper cigarette case from the inside of his jacket.

The boys quietened, and settled themselves back in their seats, waiting patiently as Garlon lit his cigarette.

"Now", Garlon said, taking a long drag on his cigarette. "Why become a politician". He nodded his head, as if in thought, or in appreciation of his cigarette. Or perhaps both.

"Those were good answers". He nodded again, slower this time. "But why become a politician to do that?"

The boys said nothing, recognising that he wasn't looking for an answer. "Why not a baker, like your da, Ariste?" he asked the confident boy.

"Or a nurse, like your ma, Horace?" he continued, before

Ariste could reply.

"Or a volunteer at one of them orphan houses, like your ma, Gabin?" he said to the youngest boy.

"I don't understand you, Gar", Ariste replied first, fingering the shadow of a moustache above his lip. "We're talkin about politicians here, not bakers and nurses".

"We're talkin about servin France, I thought", Garlon interjected, taking a short pull from his cigarette.

Ariste shifted uncomfortably on his seat, and the grin left Gabin's face.

"The politicians do serve France", Ariste replied defensively. "They swear to it".

"Do they?" Garlon asked.

"Of course they do", Ariste scoffed a little. "And more so than bakers and nurses".

"Is that what you think?" Garlon asked, staring at them all in turn.

"My da makes bread, Marceau will soon be president of France!" Ariste said.

"And who do you think is more valuable to France?" Garlon asked.

"Marceau, of course", Ariste answered, frowning incredulously.

Garlon paused, and ashed his cigarette, saying nothing. Ariste quietened, wondering if he had been too brazen.

Garlon sniffed and turned to watch the fire for a moment.

The boys looked at one another, raising their eyebrows. Garlon could be like this sometimes.

Finally, after an uneasy silence, Garlon pawed at his jacket, his eyes still on the fire. Finding his cigarette case, he pulled it out, flicked the clasp open, and jabbed another cigarette into his mouth.

With his other hand, he reached for his lighter, checking his jacket pockets, then his trousers.

Horace, who was closest to him and desiring an end to this silence, struck a match from his own matchbox, and held it to the cigarette in Garlon's mouth.

Garlon smiled politely at Horace, and puffed quickly on his cigarette, helping it catch light. When it was burning sufficiently, he pulled it from his mouth, and exhaled deeply, turning his eyes back to Ariste.

"And if your da...say he woke tomorrow, and he decided, you know what Ariste, I don't wanna bake my bread no more, I don't wanna bake no more...would he still be less important than...than your Marceau". Garlon spoke slowly and quietly, his eyes fixed on Ariste.

Ariste frowned.

"Yes..." he said uncertainly after a moment. "He's to be president of France!"

Garlon nodded.

"And what if the baker down the street, he wakes up, and he too thinks the same thing. He thinks, you know what? I don't wanna bake my bread no more either. And his friend, he's a baker too, and he thinks the same, and he boards up his oven, and there's no more bread to be had. Would Marceau still be more important?" Garlon pressed.

"I...I don't know", Ariste admitted.

"And your ma, Horace, what if she decide she don't care too much for bein a nurse anymore?" Garlon asked. "You think your man Marceau will come nurse you when you get sick?"

Horace said nothing, his face thoughtful.

"You think Marceau would roll up his sleeves and put on that gown like your ma?" Garlon grinned.

"And a right pretty sort he'll look", a stout woman boomed, chortling madly as she thumped across the hardwood floor, to snatch up the boys' mugs that lay empty on the table by the fire.

Garlon chuckled as the boys jumped in their seats, though he didn't blame them. Berthe could be scary, and though only short in stature, he personally felt she was more formidable than most men twice her size.

Gabin shooed at his trousers where a puddle of beer had appeared, glancing around sheepishly to see if his friends had noticed him spilling the remainder of his drink down himself.

Garlon, a veteran of Berthe's antics and slightly more hardened to her jokes, saw his predicament, and tilted his head knowingly toward the bar, where a washcloth lay.

Gabin licked his lips, and jumped up, scurrying across the floor to snatch up the washcloth while the boys were distracted laughing at Berthe. Hopping back into his seat undetected, he flashed Garlon a thankful smile, and hurriedly rubbed his trousers clear of beer, before chucking the washcloth into a corner by the fireplace.

"Where is my thumpin washcloth", Berthe mumbled, as she stomped across the room and out of sight behind the bar.

Gabin's eyes widened as he forced himself to laugh and woop with his friends.

Garlon smiled.

The boy's laughter dimmed, then faded away, gratefully replete, as a quiet settled on their little nook of L'ancre once more.

"But seriously, my boys, do you think Marceau would rise with the dawn to put food in your bellies, like your da Ariste?" Garlon asked.

Ariste considered this, then shook his head.

"You think he'd stay up late changin bedpans, and riskin his life, riskin influenza, or lord knows what else, night after night, for folk like us, like your ma do Horace?" Garlon raised his eyebrows at Horace questioningly.

Horace didn't have to consider; he shook his head.

"And you, Gabin, can you see Marceau at the orphan house, ladlin out soup with your ma?" Garlon watched the smallest and youngest of the group expectantly for his answer.

"No", Gabin said quietly.

"No...not so glamorous that...no glory in that", Garlon affirmed. "There's nothin glamorous bout bakin bread, or bein a nurse, or helpin orphans...and for that reason you'll not find Marceau, or a man like him, within a mile of a poor house, or a hospital, or a bakery...unless it's to fill his stomach mind".

"Now you might think that Marceau is more important than you, or you da, or your ma, but your da and ma, they're for France. They serve France. They are France. And he wouldn't be a damn thing without em, no matter how loud he shout, or how pretty he talk. Same goes for the rest of them politicians. And let me tell you something else. Without your ma and da, there'd be no France", he said passionately, a gleam in his eye.

"Nothin", he continued. "No baker's, no bread. No builders, no houses. No nurses, no hospitals. No railways or roads. No soldiers to keep us safe. Strong men, of heart and arm, willin to give their life, so that you and I can drink our drink, and have another story to tell. Hell, even them stools you boys sit on night after night, you think a man like Marceau made em, or a man like your da, Gabin?" Garlon inclined his head at the boy.

The boys listened, understanding dawning on their faces. Perhaps he had reached them. Perhaps not. But he liked to think he had made them think. And he liked to think that was enough.

Perhaps he'd planted a seed in their minds. A seed that might grow into something bigger.

He couldn't tolerate folk that didn't think for themselves. Folk that listened, but didn't hear, didn't think, and recited whatever gospel was considered holy. Whether it be at the bar, in the church, or in the paper. Folk picked up gospel all sorts of places, and took it forth, unthinking, like preachers with blind faith.

Was easier with the young, to make them think. Before they'd sung their hymns, sung em over and over. Until the words was ingrained so deep in their minds that they didn't even have to think em anymore. Till they just come, unbidden, as easy as breathin.

"So don't tell me Marceau's more important", Garlon said fiercely. "Cause he ain't. Your ma works harder than Marceau could ever **dream** of, she does the lord's work, thinkin only of others, never of herself, and for what?" He raised his hand angrily at Horace. "You livin good boy, in a big house like Marceau? You eatin the best food? Suppin at the best bistros?"

Horace reddened.

"No, I didn't think so". Garlon shook his head. "That's cause your ma is selfless. She don't care a damn about herself, or no glory for that matter. And that's why she should be president. Not that damn Marceau".

"You think...my ma should be president...president of France?" Horace asked, bewildered.

"I do", Garlon said, his face gravely serious.

"But...she's just a nurse...she don't know nothin about politics", Horace said lamely.

"That's exactly why I'd vote for her", Garlon said quietly, his cigarette long ago burnt out, hanging forgotten between his thumb and forefinger. "And she ain't, **just a nurse**, boy".

"She's caring, hard a worker as any I know, and spends her life looking after others, the people of France, France itself. What other qualities would you want in a president, boy? Fancy hair and limitless ambition?" Garlon mused. "You don't want a politician for your president, boy, you want someone who don't want the job. Anyone who wants the job, has failed already".

Garlon reached for his cigarette case again, this time, Gabin was ready, and scrabbled at the table, scooping it up from behind a little tin pot, and palming it into Garlon's hand.

Garlon inclined his head gratefully and pulled another cigarette out from the case with his mouth. Finding a match in his trouser pocket, he struck it against the matchbox that Gabin eagerly pulled from his own pocket and held out for him.

He brought the lit flame to the cigarette hanging in his mouth and shielded it with his hand as it began to smoke.

Winking at Gabin, he took a couple of quick puffs to get the cigarette going as he liked. The boys watched carefully now; certain they were witness to something beyond their youth.

"Power should be thrust upon yeh...duty that is...bad word power... don't like that word", Garlon muttered. He pulled deeply on his cigarette, letting out a large cloud of smoke. It hung lazily in front of him, drifting slowly toward the fire.

"See most people they don't want...power...duty...they care more for givin, and lookin after their own. That's a good man. Or woman", he added, nodding at Ariste and Gabin.

"Most people, it don't take much for em to be happy. Find somethin they're good at, make a livin doin it. Find a good woman...or man. Start a family. Find some good folk to drink wine and beer with", Garlon said.

"Or rum", he added, grimacing and sticking out his tongue. "Takes all sorts", he mumbled, surreptitiously glancing over his shoulder to check for sailors.

The boys laughed quietly, making their own checks for sailors.

"That's life. Find a trade. Start a family. Make some friends. Put down roots. Build a home. That's good folk does that. Politicians? They ain't like that, see, different dreams", Garlon said sadly.

"Berthe!" he shouted suddenly, raising his glass mug above his head and shaking it, the remains of his drink sloshing about in the bottom.

"Pig! Where's your manners!" she shouted back.

"Where was I?" he continued thoughtfully. "Ah, yes, politicians. You know what politicians dream of, boy?" he asked, singling out Ariste.

"Rum", the boy replied cheekily.

"Gah", Garlon stuck his tongue out again, a nasty look

contorting his face. "Horse piss".

"No, boy, they dream of power. Power, and fame, and glory. They're emperors without the balls". Garlon's lip curled. "And they don't care how they get it, or how many people like your ma or da they got to step over to do it".

The boys laughed, enjoying the imagery of an emperor without appendage.

"Why are they like an emperor without balls, Gar?" Ariste said loudly, brandishing his distingué, his face flushed.

"Cause they want glory, boy, but they ain't got the balls to get it themselves. They'll send your da out to get it for em, while they hide in their mansions, and their palaces. They'll hunger for war, for conflict, for conquest, but you'll not see them anywhere near it. Emperor from an armchair. That's your Marceau. Least them emperors of old, they'd fight for it boy, fight for their glory. They'd see it with their own eyes, lot of em. They'd sweat for it. Bleed for it. Die for it. These politicians... they'll have you do the dyin", he said sombrely, staring into the depths of his drink.

The boys sat quietly.

Garlon's sombreness was catching. The war was still fresh in their minds.

"Right, enough of that", a gruff voice said from behind them. "No more drink for you Garlon, you're cut off!"

They turned to see Berthe cross both arms in front of her chest, then throw them outward in a cutting motion.

"The hell I am", Garlon mumbled.

"What was that?" Berthe snapped, swivelling sharply on her feet toward Garlon and the boys.

"Nothin", Garlon said moodily.

"I thought not!" Berthe stomped off toward the bar.

"Women". Garlon grinned toothily at the boys.

They nodded, understanding, yet not, their learning on this matter still to come.

"Well, bitchin about politicians ain't half as fun without a demi in my hand". Garlon pondered his drink, then turned to stare yearningly at the bar and the barrels behind it.

"I said no!" Berthe thundered across at him.

"Zut alors, woman", Garlon seethed.

The boys sniggered. It was always entertaining watching Garlon meet his match in Berthe, and they still had their drinks.

"I dunno what you're all laughin at, it was my round next!" Garlon laughed loudly, the sound bursting out of him suddenly. His mischievous cackles filled the room, as he realised the situation was not entirely to his detriment.

"Merde", Ariste spat.

"Shut it, you drunken oaf!" Berthe shouted.

"I'll give you oaf", Garlon said quietly.

"What was that?" Berthe asked sharply, her barmaids hearing razor keen.

"I'm goin", Garlon said, accepting defeat and pushing himself to his feet. "You boys, have a good night".

"Where's my..." he began patting himself down, when a youthful fist shot forward and opened in front of him.

"Ah, thanks Gab", he smiled fondly at the boy, taking his cigarette case and matchbox from the boy's hand.

"Adieu", Garlon said, doffing an imaginary cap at the boys.

"Get out!" Berthe shouted good naturedly, waving him away.

Garlon grinned and left.

The boys smiled and returned to their beer and their conversation.

"And just **what**, was all that about?" a grumpy looking old man rasped, from his stool at the bar.

"Oh, nothin, just the ramblings of a madman", Berthe replied, smiling widely.

Sometimes, Angry Is All That I Am

"Gabriel...I was wondering if I might speak with you for a moment", Lucien asked, approaching Gabriel where he sat comfortably at the front desk in Duphan's favourite chair.

I wonder if Duphan knows Gabriel has molded himself to his chair, Lucien thought.

I sometimes think he cares more for that chair than this job.

He was certainly not best pleased when he caught me in it.

Yes, well, Gabriel is not napping in it with a bottle of rum cradled like a babe in his arms.

He's working.

And not snoring.

Like a pig in a storm.

What on earth?

Pay attention!

Now is not the time for foolishness.

Gabriel looked up, surprised.

*Why he almost looks **uncertain.***

I've never seen him uncertain before.

He is always so...self-assured.

"Yes?" Gabriel replied, unsure as to the nature of this intrusion.

"I was wondering…if we could talk privately", Lucien murmured.

Gabriel frowned and looked around the store. "We are in private", he confirmed.

Lucien looked around the store too. "Ah, yes", he said, reddening. "Of course".

"What do you need, **monsieur**", Gabriel asked with exaggerated seriousness.

Lucien smiled, the impishness of his smile robbing him of some of his previous uncertainty.

"Yes, well", he began, before taking a deep breath. "I require your help with something, actually".

"Oh?" Gabriel leant back in his chair.

Not his chair, Lucien thought, his mouth twitching.

"Is everything alright?" Gabriel arched his eyebrows.

"Yes, sorry", Lucien said, more businesslike now.

Gabriel smiled, though Lucien saw it not, intent now as he was on his objective, whatever that may be.

"Well, I need your help with something, something rather important actually", Lucien explained.

Gabriel nodded, waiting.

"It's a ring…a rather rare ring, you see. A ring that I have been trying to acquire for quite some time, to no avail. Well, the ring is now in Paris, tonight, actually…and I'd like you to help me acquire it", Lucien said.

"It's valuable, I take it?" Gabriel ventured.

"Somewhat, yes", Lucien replied.

Somewhat, Gabriel mused.

I see.

A game of shadow and shade, is it?

"Somewhat", Gabriel repeated, crossing his arms, one eyebrow raised so high it was at risk of disappearing.

"Yes", Lucien said.

"Right", Gabriel said slowly. "And why do you need me,

pray tell?"

Lucien folded his arms, and turned away from Gabriel, casting an uncertain, searching look out of the front window.

"The owner of the ring is not...particularly fond of me", Lucien admitted. "We have a history. Not a pleasant one".

Gabriel grinned happily, snapping sharply to his feet. "Oh, **do tell**, what did you do? I do love a scandal".

Lucien's mouth fell open.

Gabriel paced behind him slowly, hands clasped together at the bottom of his back. "What did you do to the fellow? Is he a rival antique's dealer?" He rubbed his chin thoughtfully as he walked toward the front of the store.

He swivelled suddenly to face Lucien.

"Or perhaps, a personal acquaintance?" Gabriel fished.

"Yes, well, suffice to say, he is not best disposed toward me", Lucien said stiffly.

"Oh, rubbish", Gabriel tutted, twirling away to look out of the window. "And what if I say, I won't help, unless you tell me", he said quietly, turning back to look Lucien in the eye.

"I..." Lucien started. "I don't know...but I'd really rather not speak of it. I'm sorry".

Gabriel cocked his head, fixing Lucien with a scrutinising stare.

Why does he arouse such uncertainty in me? Lucien thought.
I don't owe him any explanation. I hardly know him.
And he is my employee. It wouldn't be proper.
Nor is it proper to involve him in this, out of hours.
Oh, shut up.

"I'm sorry", Lucien said again, unsure why he said it.

Gabriel's eyebrow arched inquisitively, then he shrugged. "It's fine, I will help you, I was only jesting".

"Well...good", Lucien said.

"Besides, I take it this little dalliance will result in some amount of coin joining me and my pocket?" Gabriel ventured cheekily.

A large grin appeared on Lucien's face. "Rogue", he scoffed, as he turned to take his coat from a hook on the wall.

"I **do hope** that is Lucien for yes", Gabriel pressed, imitating the accent of a rich dandy.

"Come, or we'll be late", Lucien grumbled, pushing him gently toward the door.

"Really rather rude", Gabriel mumbled, still as a dandy. "I do hope this other antique owner has better manners".

*

As it turned out, the other antique owner did have better manners, and a better choice of business residence, at least in Gabriel's estimation.

"Au-delà Du Clair De Lune", Gabriel repeated, enunciating the words, savouring his demi.

"Yes, quite", a foppish looking man agreed smugly, watching Gabriel with great interest.

Lucien watched quietly as Pavo had his fun with Gabriel. He was not good at this, at this...flattery. This subtlety. He liked plain speech. Direct. Decisive. These were qualities Lucien possessed and prized. They served him well in his business endeavours but were of no use when it came to men like Pavo.

Some men liked to be flattered. Needed to be flattered. He didn't understand it. It was a business transaction, and a simple one. What need for flattery? Why did the man's ego come into it? Or who he liked, or disliked?

Though perhaps, he was the problem. He was not exactly **normal**, or so he'd been told all of his life. Perhaps he was rough and abrasive, a sharp edge, in a soft world, chafing his way through.

He found it hard to relate to others, to engage in their simple talk, their **small talk.** It often bored him to tears, was the truth of it. The same conversation had over and over. It felt like reciting the words of a play, with no audience, and no accolade.

What was the point?

And sometimes he just wanted to be quiet, still. To be. To enjoy. Whatever it was, that he was doing. Why always the need to fill every silence with pointless prattle?

Perhaps Gabriel knew something he didn't.

He could talk about certain things, of course. Certain things, he could talk of until there were no more words, or breath to breathe them. Antiques, for example, he could happily speak of for hours.

But he didn't like **things**. Well, not entirely true. He didn't like things, for the sake of things. Antiques, they had history, and there was nobility in preserving them, and their fine craftsmanship, so that another might enjoy it. Someone had worked hard to craft them, well most of them, crafted lovingly, with quality materials.

But, fancy clothes. Shiny baubles. Extravagant affectations. They felt wasteful.

Automobiles. The gliding metal wagons were the new thing. The new symbol. The new status. The new want of the dandies and the privileged. He really couldn't muster a care for them. They were functional, and practical, yes, but what was wrong with horse and cart, or wagon? Or walking. He walked everywhere. And always had. He liked walking. It soothed his mind, and the crickets in his stomach.

These automobiles...they would soon blight the streets, and belch their smog, thickening the skies. And why? So the dandies could grow fat and lazy, driving their metal chariots, instead of walking the beautiful cobbled streets.

And soon they would say, but the cobbles, my they look fine, but they are awfully impractical for our metal wagons. Wouldn't it be more prudent to pave over them, with something more **modern.** Something more fitting. And pave they would. With what he knew not. But he suspected it would not be beautiful like the cobbles.

Of course, it wouldn't be just the dandies, but that was just how it started, these things. No common man would step where a dandy hadn't already trod. And before long the sky would hang grey and comatose, drugged, on a concoction of metal mist and smug sighs.

Perhaps he was just a damned, miserable cynic, incapable of embracing progress. Incapable of subscribing to the designs and desires of his peers.

I can surely be a miserable bastard, he mulled, pondering his wine, a sour look on his face.

It is no wonder you have so few friends, Lucien, when you are so warm and devoid of melancholy.

Bonjour, je m'appelle Lucien.

*Let me tell you, how everything you believe is a **lie**.*

How all is misery, how everything old was good, how everything new is bad.

How there is no point to any of it. To any of your pretty things. To any of your pointless prattle.

How everything you love, will soon burn, and you shall surely burn too. And what exactly makes you so informed?

What unique perspective do you possess that others do not?

Perhaps the only thing you possess is a dark mind, a dark mind shrouded in shadows, locked behind dreary doors, devoid of colour.

*And a darker perspective. A perspective grown too dark. Too dark to see the colours where they lie... Too dark to **scry** them out, even, as you must, for you surely cannot see them.*

How is one supposed to like you...love...you...with such a perspective?

When your mind is such a barren warren, full of wonky walls, and sourly shaped rooms.

Scathing slants and crooked corners. Why is everything grey?

Grey, and loathe.

He snorted into his glass.

Gabriel looked at him strangely, before returning his gaze to

Pavo.

At least he could laugh. What else?

"So, as I was saying", Gabriel said. "It would mean a lot to me, if you could see it in you to part with it". His eyes were on a silver ring, sitting awkwardly on Pavo's finger.

Pavo pouted smugly.

"Well, I suppose I could consider it, if it means so much to you" he said, holding his hand up to admire the ring. "It is not particularly pleasing to look at, rather a dull thing, if I'm honest with you. And I have plenty more. If Lucien is so desirous of it...I am not uncharitable", he jabbed, smirking at Lucien.

"Yes, well", Gabriel said, gripping Lucien by the arm to stop him responding. "It really would be rather grand of you. Rather grand indeed".

"Oh, fine, take the thing", Pavo scoffed, pulling the ring from his finger and tossing it to Gabriel.

"What..wh", Gabriel stammered, as he caught the ring. "But, what about the price?" he breathed.

Pavo waved his hand magnanimously. "My gift to you, and perhaps, a lesson for you, Lucien, in manners", he drawled. "Not everyone wants to listen to you drone on about antiques, you know? History this, history that. Some of us have better things to do, than indulge in such prattle. Not all of us are so **enthralled** with such **boring** antiquity. Why, I can scarce trace my own family line, a rather important line mind you, back further than a few hundred years, but I'm expected to care about some dreadfully dull **peasant ring** from lord knows when? But he does go on, you know?" he said in a bored tone, turning to Gabriel.

Gabriels's grip tightened on Lucien's arm, as his face turned stormy.

"Just a joke, my boy", Pavo added quickly, after seeing the look on Lucien's face.

"Thank you, Pavo, I mean it", Gabriel said, smiling warmly.

"It's nothing". Pavo waved a hand airily, sipping his drink. "I am a generous man".

Lucien turned and stormed away, unable to bear the barb.

Pavo chuckled. "He is rather easy to rile, isn't he? Rather takes the fun out of it".

Gabriel smiled sympathetically.

"Do tell him I am only having sport with him though, won't you", Pavo added as an afterthought, grabbing Gabriel's arm as he turned to leave.

"Of course", Gabriel agreed, patting Pavo's hand sympathetically.

Gabriel pocketed the ring, then hurried out of the bar in search of Lucien.

Where is he? he thought frantically.

I have his blasted ring.

There.

In the distance.

That rather angry stride.

"Lucien!" Gabriel called.

But Lucien did not stop. Perhaps he did not hear. Perhaps he was angry.

Gabriel suspected the latter and strode after him.

"Lucien! Will you stop!" he called, as he followed Lucien away from De Lune. It was dark, and he did not want a repeat of his experience at L'ancre, so he was wary of becoming lost.

Lucien was his beacon. So, follow him, he must.

"Zut!" he panted, after a minute's sprint to catch up. "Will you stop?" He yanked at Lucien's arm, pulling him to a halt. "What is the matter with you?"

"Get off me!" Lucien snarled, ripping his arm away.

Gabriel stopped, shocked, the colour leaving his face.

"Who does he think he is?" Lucien roared. "To talk to me so!" he seethed, pacing up and down.

"Lucien...what..." Gabriel asked, lost for words. "What is the matter?"

"You heard him!" Lucien raged. "He insulted me! Mocked me! Belittled me!"

"No...well...yes...maybe a little", Gabriel admitted. "But why are you so angry?"

"I should rip his head from his shoulders", Lucien seethed.

Gabriel said nothing. He could feel the anger coming from Lucien. He was shocked by it, frightened by it. Frightened that he did not understand it, frightened that it existed. Frightened that it could exist, and frightened at what it could do, if released unchecked.

"Lucien...why are you so angry?" Gabriel repeated, after he could watch Lucien pace agitatedly no longer.

"Why do you think?" Lucien rounded on him aggressively.

"I do not know, but I am trying to understand", Gabriel said firmly. "But if you do not want to tell me, I shall leave you". He turned to leave.

"No, wait", Lucien said quickly, grabbing his arm.

Gabriel tensed, his eyes falling to Lucien's arm.

Lucien quickly released him, and took a deep breath, filling his lungs and exhaling purposefully.

"I'm sorry, please, stay", he pleaded.

Gabriel inclined his head tightly. "Why don't we walk?" he suggested after a moment. "It always helps clear my head".

Lucien took another deep calming breath, then beckoned that Gabriel should go first. "Yes, let's".

They began walking, slowly, quietly, both keenly aware of one another.

Gabriel was at a loss. The evening had been a mystery to him. An entertaining mystery, but a mystery no less.

Lucien had taken him to this mysterious members club...De Lune...in the wealthiest part of town. Then, he'd bid that he charm this...man, Pavo.

Who this Pavo was to Lucien, Gabriel knew not. That there

was some enmity between them was obvious, but this reaction, and this anger?

Lucien was closed to him. If he would not speak, how could he understand?

As they walked, the river came into sight, and Lucien walked quicker toward it. Gabriel followed, matching his pace.

Arriving in front of the river, Lucien stopped, and stood, silently, watching the water. It seemed to roll softly, ever forward, or was it backward?

"I love the river", he said suddenly. "I love the sea, too, though it does not love me".

"And why is that?" Gabriel asked cautiously.

"Sea sick", Lucien replied shortly.

He turned then, miming sickness, poking his fingers down his throat and pulling a foul face.

Gabriel grinned. "Charming".

Lucien turned back to the river. "I'm sorry", he said suddenly, spinning back to face Gabriel. "I did not mean to bite at you, so".

"Accepted", Gabriel said graciously. "Will you tell me now, why you were so angry?"

Once more, Lucien closed himself to him, turning his face to the river and his back to Gabriel.

Am I wasting my time? Gabriel thought sadly.

I felt...a likeness with you.

Perhaps I was wrong.

Gabriel sighed.

"I...don't know", Lucien said quietly, shifting uncomfortably.

"You don't know?" Gabriel repeated.

"I do not know", Lucien said, firmer this time as he turned to face him. The moonlight from above struck the side of his face sharply. "I do not know".

"I do not think of myself as an...angry man, yet sometimes,

angry is all that I am", Lucien confessed. "Sometimes, I feel it quickly, the anger... boiling inside me, it is...overwhelming. It feels like...someone is heating me, from the inside. Sometimes, the heat is bearable. Sometimes, it feels as if the fire is cold, dormant, extinguished, even. But it must surely be there, laid, ready and waiting to burn, for how else could it flare so, at the slightest spark? My heart, my chest. My head, my face. My cheeks", he trailed off. "I feel it everywhere. I am consumed".

"And then I burn", he said softly. "And I am lost".

"I cannot control it, perhaps I am a beast", he finished sadly.

"I do not think so", Gabriel said.

"And how would you know? You do not know me", Lucien said, tense now. "I am not a good man".

"I see no beast", Gabriel said.

"And what do you see?" Lucien asked.

"A man. No more. No less", Gabriel replied.

Lucien shook his head, as if he could not believe this.

"I was ready to..." Lucien said.

"But you did not", Gabriel explained.

"No, because you stopped me", Lucien replied.

"Perhaps", Gabriel conceded.

"I do not know why I am like this", Lucien railed.

Gabriel frowned.

Lucien was agitated, but more, he was stressed, pained, upset. He did not seem like a tall, self-assured man at that moment, but as a boy. Uncertain, confused and lost.

It saddened him. He thought of La Meme, and what she would do, were she to see him like this.

"Lucien", Gabriel said softly, extending his arms invitingly.

Lucien stared back with the frightened eyes of a child.

"Come", Gabriel beckoned.

Lucien went to him, hesitantly, slowly.

Gabriel encircled him with his arms. Softly, not too hard as to startle him and drive him away, from his arms, and from his comfort.

It felt as though this was difficult for him, and he did not want to make it more so. He just wanted to give him comfort.

They stood, in the dark, Gabriel with his arms about Lucien, Lucien with his arms ramrod stiff by his sides.

He is so tense, Gabriel thought sadly.

I have never felt such a tenseness.

If I squeeze too tight, will he turn and flee, like a deer from the hunter's horn?

He smiled.

Lucien? A deer?

No.

A stag.

A stag is more...fitting.

Noble, gentle, but...strong.

Strong if pushed. If prodded.

If threatened.

Will you run, stag?

After a while, Lucien twitched, some of the tenseness leaving him, and Gabriel smiled.

Perhaps not.

After a while more, Lucien squirmed under Gabriel's arms, and pulled one of his arms free. He wrapped it gently around Gabriel's back.

And then, slowly, softly, Lucien's other arm slipped free and joined the other, both of them wrapped comfortably around Gabriel.

Gabriel's smile widened, and he closed his eyes, as he listened to the water gently kiss the shore.

And they stood quietly, in comfort and in caring, the two of them together, under the moonlight.

Oh, That's Nice

The boy was excited.

Ecstatic, even.

Madame had tasked him with a story. And a story he had given her.

He had furrowed his brow and frowned his hardest, his face keenly focused, his concentration complete upon his story.

And he had written. A simple story, with a sing-song style. A little ditty of a thing. But it read prettily, and it sounded pleasant to the ear. So he thought.

And surprisingly, so Madame thought. For she had smiled brightly when he brought it to her.

"And what is this, Lucien?" she asked, curiously examining his story from the bottom of her rounded glasses.

"My story, madame", he mumbled.

It is too wordy…I'm sure of it.

Too…verbose, he thought, searching for the word, and feeling proud that he found it.

He did not know why Madame had asked them for a story. But he had been excited to write one, feeling an unfamiliar thrill and focus, as he tasked his mind to it.

"Mmm", Madame hummed, as she read the story from top to bottom.

"There is more, Madame", he chimed, as she reached the bottom of the page and blinked, confused.

"Ahah…yes". She smiled at him and turned the page, raising her eyebrows in surprise.

Lucien blushed as his friends sniggered. Only one page had

been required, but he had gotten carried away, his pen scratching furiously at the page in an effort to expel the jumble of thoughts tumbling through his mind.

Madame smiled warmly, as she read the tale to its close. "My, my", she said thoughtfully. "How very interesting".

"Did you like it?" Lucien asked hopefully.

"Very much", she admitted. "Though there were some errors", she chided.

"Yes, sorry", he mumbled. "I was in a rush".

"A rush?"

"To write my story".

"What do you mean?"

"I don't know…I had so much story in my head…and so little time to tell it".

Madame watched him strangely. "Finish it at home", she soothed.

He looked down uncomfortably. "Yes, perhaps".

"Now back to your seat". She shooed him away from her desk, and he ambled back to his friends, smiling sheepishly.

"Little Lucien and his stooory", Luca teased.

Lucien frowned, his face darkening.

"I am only jesting". Luca nudged him.

Hugues, the other side of Luca, as always, snorted, grinning mischievously, with his eyes down at the desk so that Madame would not see him.

Lucien's face grew darker, and clouds gathered above him. Luca nudged him once more, and he forced a smile.

But the clouds were above him now, and his day was grey.

He sighed, and looked out of the window dreamily, as Madame began speaking, about something or other.

The words were lost on him, for his brain was a fog.

The clouds dogged him, until they met the sun, as he and his friends kicked and chased one another in the field at lunch.

It made him happy, and he thought of it no more, though he

did think of his story, and he thought fondly of Madame's praise.

It was strange to receive praise for something so...hobbylike. Writing was a hobby, a diversion, a pursuit of the creative. It was not a serious thing, and one did not pursue it seriously.

His father scoffed at such things, and his mother dutifully scoffed along with him.

If he had been thinking clearly, he would not have brought his story to his mother. But his excitement had burned through his usual cautious reticence when it came to seeking praise or encouragement from his parents.

And so he bounced home, and he approached his mother smiling, his enthusiasm radiating from him.

"Look at this", he said, excitedly, as he passed his story to his mother.

She looked up, distracted. She had glasses too, like Madame, though they were thicker and more square.

"Bonjour", she said, her irritation poorly concealed. "What is it?"

"It's a story", he explained. "I wrote it today! Look at it!"

"A story?" she asked, grimacing slightly. "Why are you writing stories?" "Madame asked us to. She liked it, what do you think?" he asked quickly, his enthusiasm slightly chilled.

"Oh, Lucien, I have just returned home, and I am tired", she complained, exasperated. "Give me a moment".

"Alright", Lucien said quietly, fidgeting.

His mother sighed and placed her newspaper down on the chaise longue. She took his story gingerly, and began to read it down her glasses, her face twitching slightly.

Reaching the bottom of the page, she frowned, and looked at him questioningly.

"Turn it over", Lucien instructed.

"Ah", she mumbled.

She nodded perfunctorily as she read it.

He waited, quietly, as she approached the end of the story. His stomach was tight now.

"What?" she exclaimed loudly, arching her eyebrows. "What is this?"

"It's a story", he explained dully.

"Yes, but about what, I do not understand it", she said stubbornly.

"Magic", he said quietly.

"Magic?" she asked, her face pitying. "It is rather...far-fetched".

"Madame liked it", Lucien justified. "Look at what she wrote".

He pointed to a carefully penned review written in red ink.

His mother glanced at it. "Oh, yes. Oh, that's nice. Well done for pleasing, Madame. I am pleased to hear you are receiving praise from your teachers for a change". There was an edge to her voice.

"It is good, is it not?" Lucien asked, desperate for her praise.

"Yes, I suppose", his mother admitted.

He stood dejected, watching his mother.

"I'm not sure what you want from me, Lucien". His mother sighed. "It is not really my thing...this magic...this fantasy". She rolled the words distastefully around her mouth.

He waited, his passion bone cold now.

"I was thinking...I might finish my story", he ventured.

"Finish it?" his mother asked impatiently. "Is that not all of it?"

"No..." Lucien said.

"Whatever for, was that not the task?" She snatched up the story once more, searching for the feedback. "It says here...'very...encouraging Lucien'". His mother slowly read the words of praise, as if to say them too quickly would make them real.

"Yes, but it's not all of it", Lucien explained, feeling as if he was on trial.

"Oh", his mother said.

"I was thinking…maybe I could be a writer".

"As a profession?"

"Yes".

"Oh, do not be so foolish", his mother scoffed. "You cannot make a living from this".

"And why not?" Lucien asked defensively.

It felt as if the walls were closing in around him. Everything suddenly felt so heavy, so cramped, so sad. An ache began in his heart, and he felt it creeping up into his throat, making it harder to talk.

"Because it's a…a…**hobby**", his mother said, searching for, and finding, the appropriate disparagement.

"Other people are writers", Lucien said, agitated now. "They make their living from it".

"Who? Who is a writer?" his mother asked, disbelieving.

"Well…there's…" Lucien searched his mind, which had turned frustratingly blank. It was always so when his mother or father tried him like this.

"Dickens", he said suddenly, producing the first name that came to mind.

"Dickens?" his mother said, incredulous. "You think you will be Dickens? Lucien, you are dreaming", she continued, seemingly taking great joy in his delusion.

"Zephirin", she called suddenly, seemingly energised. "Zephirin!" She was eager to share her amusement with her husband.

"Yes?" a voice, dripping, with barely contained condescension, oozed from the doorway.

Lucien's stomach knotted. He wished he'd never told her. Wished he'd kept his mouth shut.

"Lucien thinks he is to be a **writer**", she scoffed, eager for the praise of her king.

"A writer?" Zephirin asked haltingly.

He needn't say a thing. He didn't have to. It was in his father's eyes, a mocking twinkle. And it was on his face, a cruel curl at the corners of his mouth, as he pouted in an effort to contain it.

It was a subtle thing, his father's mockery, his derision, it never had to be more. It hit as intended, every time. He would paint the target and let fly the arrow.

His mother would drive it home, and his sister would twist it in the wound, and his humiliation would be complete.

"Yes, why not?" Lucien asked, a little more strongly this time. "I am good at it".

"What do you know of writing?" his father asked softly.

"Exactly", his mother chimed, on cue. "I was just telling him the same thing".

"I don't know...I am good at it...I could learn", he justified, throwing his defences in quick succession.

"Lucien, you don't know anything about writing", his father said, ignoring him.

"I just told you that I could learn", Lucien seethed, angry now.

"Lucien, there is no coin in writing", his father explained, as if to a dullard, smirking smugly.

"Plenty of authors make it their living!" Lucien exploded.

"Like who", his father asked.

His mother watched giddily, proud that she had not fumbled her opening lines in this play of derision.

"There's Dickens", Lucien started.

"Dickens". His father nodded patronisingly.

"And Austen...and Bronte..." Lucien continued, thinking.

"They were women, were they not? And English" his father interrupted him.

"Yes...so? What in the blazes is the relevance of that?" Lucien fired back, his face hot.

"Lucien!" his mother scolded. "And how can you write about **women's** things?"

"What?" Lucien asked incredulously. "That's not..." He sighed, trying to calm himself and compose his argument.

It seemed the more frustrated he became, the more enthused they became, as if they were somehow feeding on his misery.

"I'm good at it". Lucien tried stubbornly to marshal his defence.

"Good at it, how?" his father asked.

"Madame told him", his mother interjected.

In the hall, a door slammed, and Lucien paled.

"Bonjour", a merry voice called from the hall. "Bonjour", his sister repeated, as she strode into the room confidently.

"And what is going on here?" she asked inquisitively, taking in his mother's merry expression, and his father's mockingly despairing one.

"Your brother thinks he is to become a writer", his mother answered helpfully.

"I see", his sister replied, her eyes meeting his fathers and adopting the same mocking twinkle.

"Yes", Lucien said, dejectedly.

He was defeated, and he knew it. There was no point. No point speaking, no point fighting. He could not bear the three of him mocking him in turn. It was hard enough standing strong and not quailing under his mother and fathers' eyes.

But now, the trifecta of torture had assembled, and they would lay waste to him if he let them.

Well, he would not lay at their torturers table. He would not lay as they tried their tools and sharpened their instruments. As they assuaged their twisted need to cut and peel away the layers of his mind, so that they might cut and salt and stitch the wounds, to be later ripped open and inspected at their pleasure.

Lucien shook his head and tried to leave the room.

His sister blocked his path, standing challengingly in the doorway.

"Move", he said gruffly, pushing past her.

"Lucien!" his sister exclaimed. "Did you see that?" she cried to Zephirin.

"Do not push your sister", Zephirin growled menacingly, a hint of violence bubbling quickly to the surface. "Or else. Now begone with you, if you are going to be such a sour sport".

"Unnecessary", his mother agreed sadly, her eyes a little frightened now.

Lucien stomped angrily up the stairs, and slammed the door of his room closed, throwing himself down on the bed.

It was not dark, but he felt dark, and he had nowhere else to go.

He heard his family laughing, the sound echoing jarringly up the stairs, and he snatched up the book from beside his bed.

I hate you so much, he seethed.

*

The man awoke suddenly, violently thrown from sleep and jolting upright quickly in his bed.

He was bathed in sweat, and breathing heavily, a current firing through his veins.

It was like this, sometimes, when his dreams were dark.

It felt as though he were fighting for his life, for a few terrifying moments.

He did not understand it, and he did not like it.

He glanced at the picture staring at him from his side table and slammed it down aggressively.

Throwing himself from the bed, he strode brashly into his ensuite, and stared at the reflection in the mirror.

He did not like what he saw. At that moment, he did not see a confident man. He saw a frightened child.

He breathed slowly, trying to calm himself, as the sneering sounds faded from his mind, back to the recesses of his mind in which he thought he had imprisoned them.

Everything felt so grey, so black.

Suddenly, his fist shot forward, and the mirror shattered, the pieces clattering and shattering as they fell haphazardly into the sink, and onto the floor.

His hand had started to bleed, but he did not notice.

It hung dejectedly at his side, as he gazed, loathe, at his reflection in the mirror.

If Not Us, Then Who?

The fire crackled, and the people listened.

Garlon was on his stool in L'ancre, in front of the fire as always. His mug was empty.

"Then why have none been found?" he asked Whitebeard.

Whitebeard waved his hand at Garlon. "What's to say they haven't?" he replied defensively.

"Then where are they?" Garlon asked. "Do you see them?" He singled out a young boy from the crowd gathered around the fire.

The boy shook his head.

"Do **you** see them?" he asked Berthe, as she nudged her way through the mass of bodies to collect his empty mug.

"Leave me out of your politicking", she said gruffly.

"Do you not care?" Garlon challenged.

Berthe stopped and placed both hands on her ample hips.

Garlon threw his hands up apologetically and the crowd laughed.

"Do not ask **me,** if I care", Berthe warned, unperturbed by the crowd, her eyes as hard as her voice.

"I know, I know", Garlon apologised embarrassed. "Désolé, it was the drink talking".

Berthe snorted and left with his mug.

"Close one, Gar", Ariste leant forward from behind where he stood, and mumbled close to his ear.

Garlon gave him a thankful pat over his shoulder, and he took his place once more, standing watchfully behind Garlon's stool.

From time-to-time Ariste turned his eyes challengingly at any face in the crowd looking a little too displeased for his liking with Garlon's sermonising.

Ariste and his little rogues had taken it upon themselves to stand as impromptu bodyguards of their older companion, and they stood behind him in a semi circle.

"You've no balls, boy", Whitebeard growled, and the crowd roared with laughter.

Garlon grimaced and rubbed his chin.

"Not when it comes to Berthe, perhaps", he admitted.

"Not when it comes to nothin", a thickset man with a dirty face cruelly scoffed. He'd pushed his way to the front of the crowd to say his piece. "You're nothin but a drunk, Garlon, and you know nothin about nothin same as the rest of us".

Garlon's face hardened, and he stood, facing the man.

"A drunk and a rogue I may be, but I've balls a plenty, boy, and any man that thinks otherwise is welcome to step outside and find out". He spoke quietly, walking forward so that he stood directly in front of his accuser.

The crowd went quiet, as the two men stared at one another tensely. Ariste and his friends moved forward slowly, ready.

The man stood, quiet now, inches from Garlon.

Suddenly, the man scoffed, and shook his head, before walking away into the crowd.

Garlon nodded, as if an understanding had transpired.

"You told him, Gar", the youngest looking boy said, in awe.

"Thanks, Gabin", Garlon accepted the compliment humbly. "But I didn' do nothin but show him himself".

"What do you mean?" Horace asked frowning

"Don' matter". Garlon waved his hand.

"I was talkin about the children, with ol Whitebeard here",

he said, thumping an old man on the back.

Though old, Whitebeard still looked formidable, and he had a spirit to match.

"Less of the old, jeune homme", Whitebeard rumbled. He tipped his mug back and downed its contents.

There was still a significant amount of beer in the mug, and the boys gasped, nudging each other appreciatively.

"Tell your tale", Whitebeard demanded. "Let's hear it".

"Marceau could find those children". Garlon sprang into action, resuming his speech immediately. "Like that". He snapped his fingers.

"He's a father his self", Whitebeard commented, beckoning imperiously for a distingué as Berthe scowled at him.

"He's no father", Garlon disagreed.

"I seen em, his kids!" Whitebeard shouted, rising to his feet.

"Keep your voice down, you old coot!" Berthe boomed back.

"That's not what I meant", Garlon explained.

"Splain yourself then and stop speaking riddles man!" Whitebeard demanded.

"You said it yourself", Garlon said tiredly. "The man has children".

Whitebeard stared blankly, then opened his mouth angrily.

Garlon placed a calming hand on his arm.

He quietened, but his eyes were still narrowed.

"You got children, if they was lost, would you rest a wink till you found em?" Garlon asked.

"We ain't talkin bout me-" Whitebeard argued.

"Answer the question", Garlon pressed.

Whitebeard scowled, as though it pained him to be caught in the web of Garlon's logic.

"No. Course I wouldn'...I'd kick down doors man!" Whitebeard shouted, rising to his feet once more.

The boys chuckled loudly.

"QUIETLY!" Berthe roared.

Whitebeard muttered something less than choice under his breath, glaring venomously at Berthe.

Garlon laughed. "There, there old man". He thumped Whitebeard on the back.

Whitebeard turned his viper like glare upon Garlon, who snorted.

"Like I was sayin, the man is no father", Garlon continued. "He don' care a damn about his own, they're for show".

"For show?" Whitebeard asked suspiciously.

"Yeah, what you mean by that Gar", another man asked from the crowd.

"The man's a politician. Everything he does is for show", Garlon explained quickly, as if this was obvious.

A mass of faces regarded him blankly, and he sighed.

"It's all curated", Garlon pointed out.

"Curated?" Ariste asked quizzically.

Garlon raised a hand gently to stop him.

"Everything he does, is carefully considered, carefully chosen, carefully curated. The man's no fool, he's terrible shrewd, or he wouldn' be where is he so young". Garlon beckoned for Berthe, slightly more politely than Whitebeard had, and she nodded tiredly.

In the wait for his drink, he palmed his cigarette case, and stared down at it appreciatively, as he flicked the clasp, exposing his cigarettes.

Gabin stepped forward importantly, a match at the ready.

Garlon grinned, and leaned back, cigarette hanging devilishly from his mouth, so that Gabin could light it.

He smiled thankfully, as the cigarette caught, and a cloud of smoke obscured his face.

All that they could hear was his appreciative sucking, as he drew on the cigarette, two, three, four times, before gratefully exhaling.

Berthe hipped her way through the crowd, and placed a large

jug overflowing with beer, down on the table in front of him.

"Berthe, I love ye", Garlon confessed dreamily.

"You love nothin but beer, ye glos", she said, and though she chided him sternly, her eyes smiled fondly down at him.

"Is it such a wasted love?" Garlon asked, more to himself than anyone else.

"No Gar, I love it too", Horace replied seriously.

The men laughed at this, and Horace blushed, unsure of why.

"We all love beer", Garlon agreed amiably.

"Certain'y do", Whitebeard growled, grabbing the jug and filling his mug, before taking a deep swig and slamming it back down on the table.

"Careful man! For the love of god..." Berthe grumbled.

They all smiled. Whitebeard was something.

"Carry on, boy", Whitebeard instructed, content now that his mug was no longer empty. "And give me one of them". He pointed at Garlon's cigarette.

Garlon obliged, and Gabin lurched forward uncertainly. Whitebeard nodded and beckoned him forward. As his cigarette caught, he nodded once more, curtly, in thanks, and Gabin scurried back into place at Garlon's back.

The room had grown dark, and Berthe stoked the fire to their side with a metal poker. She chucked another log into its depths, where it shook up ash and the flames licked at it.

Garlon watched the fire thoughtfully, ashing his cigarette now and then.

"It's a play, a performance", he said slowly. "Marceau...I'd be surprised if that was even his wife".

"What?" Whitebeard asked, outraged. "You go too far, man. Armandine is a treasure!"

The boys chuckled.

"You got somin to say?" He turned his eyes on them challengingly. "Didn' think so", he grumbled, as they quietened.

"I'm not sayin she's not", Garlon responded carefully. "I'm sayin, I'm not sure she's his wife".

"And just what do you mean by **that?**" Whitebeard demanded, his eyes angry as he clenched his fists. "That's Armandine you're speakin of! Careful how you speak of her in front of me, Garlon".

Armandine was well loved in Paris, particularly by the poor. She was responsible for the funding of many of the poor houses, and regularly worked in them herself. Without her, many would go hungry, and without shelter.

She was a charitable woman, and seemingly modest. She was also beautiful, in an understated way.

She was loved. Seemingly most of all, by Whitebeard.

Garlon nodded. "She's a fine woman", he agreed. "No question".

Whitebeard's anger abated somewhat.

Garlon chose his words carefully. "I am saying that...Marceau probably knows she's fine, and that she comes across fine, and that's why he chose her".

"And what's wrong with that?" Whitebeard asked suspiciously.

"Nothin...on the face of it", Garlon mused, drawing his cigarette down to the butt and looking at it wistfully. "But he should'n have chose her cause she looks fine, and acts fine, he shoulda chose her cause he loved her, and loves her".

"He does love her", Whitebeard said certainly. "How could he not?"

"I've seen love", Garlon said. "It don't look like any love I ever saw".

"What do you know about love!" Whitebeard thundered, half rising from his stool.

Berthe clenched her jaw and turned her eyes to the heavens.

"I just told you", Garlon said coolly, his eyes cold.

Whitebeard ran his tongue over his teeth, a sour look on his face, then snorted, baying his head like a horse.

"And why do you think he don't love her, let's have it", Whitebeard demanded.

"Well for one, he loves his secretary, or at least thinks he does", Garlon said.

Whitebeard gasped, but Garlon cut him off.

"For two, it's not in his nature to love anyone, anyone but his self", Garlon continued, unabated.

"I've had about enough of this", Whitebeard exclaimed. He made to rise from his stool, but Garlon grabbed his arm, and held him steady.

"Trust me", Garlon said quietly, but intensely.

Whitebeard was mad, but there was something in Garlon's eyes that made him unsure, and he wouldn't fight on an uncertainty. He was old enough to know better.

"I ain't happy with what you said, Garlon, I want you to know that". He wrenched his arm out of Garlon's grip. "I ain't happy at all". He shook his head and rose to his feet, then made to leave.

Spying drink still in his mug, he thought better of it, and turned to raise the mug to his mouth. It was still near full, but he drained it, in four large, loud swallows, smacking his lips when he was done.

Then, without another word, he ambled out of L'ancre.

"You upset him, Gar", Ariste stated.

"Really?" Garlon replied drily.

Ariste blushed.

Gabin grinned and sniggered, and Ariste turned to thump him in the arm.

Garlon couldn't help but laugh.

The crowd dispersed then, slowly. The life had gone out of Garlon, and his eyes were hollow and tired.

"Magical as always", Berthe muttered to him, as she shuffled over to take Whitebeard's mug and clean up a little.

He shook his head sadly.

A cigarette appeared in front of his face, sandwiched between a youthful finger and thumb.

He closed his eyes and snorted, as a cynical grin spread across his face.

Eyes still closed, he shook his head, and took the cigarette, plonking it into his mouth, unthinking.

The sound of a match striking rang out, and an acrid smell hit his nostrils.

The Tableau Haute

The great hall was as grand as any named before it. The floor was stone, cold and unwelcoming. The ceiling was high, domed and imposing.

On this night, in this grandest of halls, the room was dimly lit, the only light coming from a series of torches hung in golden braziers from the walls.

The walls were cast from stone, as the floor. The torches crackled menacingly now and then, as they expelled embers and shadows.

Embers that fell and shadows that fled. Fled the table, and the man at the table. Fled to hide in safety, in the darkness of the dome above.

Works of fine art aplenty littered the walls, but our eyes are drawn to one particular piece. It depicts a handsomely dressed man, looming magnanimously over another.

The submissive rests on hands and knees, head bowed. The dominant stands, foot firmly on the back of the submissive. The dominant drinks from some kind of chalice, head thrown back deeply, both hands cupped greedily about the base of the chalice.

The room is dominated by a long table, carved from wood so dark as to be black. The wood is as uncommon and unsettling in nature as the artwork.

Seated at the table are six figures, five in red robes, and one in white. Behind each of the figures, kneels a man, or woman, in grey robes.

It is an eerie and sinister scene, and we find our attention drawn to the figure in white, who is sweating profusely.

His face is flushed, though not from the warmth provided by the torches, and from time to time, he rubs his hands on his robe to cleanse them of sweat.

In between his sweat, and his trepidation, he glances around the room, his eyes flitting left and right nervously.

A silence hangs heavy in the air.

It appears as though the figures at the table are waiting for something, as their heads are bowed, and their eyes are closed.

After a time, a heavy groaning noise issues forth from the western end of the room.

The man in white looks up, panicked, to see a hole appear in the wall.

The wall was opening!

And apparently of its own volition, the stone rumbling ominously, as it slowly slid apart to create an opening. An opening from which a void appeared, a void of black.

From it, stepped a man.

A man dressed in a black robe.

The stone doorway closed behind him.

He looked upon the hall. His hall, and his subjects before him. He looked like a man accustomed to power.

Even through the shadows that coiled symbiotically about his face, a sardonic grin could be seen, building tensely at the corners of his mouth, as he chewed on the tenseness of the room.

After seemingly taking his fill of the scene before him, he walked confidently forward into the room, and approached a gilded chair at the head of the table.

But he did not sit.

First, he languidly cast his eyes about the table.

It was a slow, scrutinising undressing, an impalement.

For some, an impetuous smile was their reward, others, perhaps out of favour, were punished with a dark glare.

Finally, the figure in white was poleaxed by the dark eyes of the dark man, as they lanced through him.

"Marceau, so nice of you to join us", the man in black dripped, the words rolling off his tongue, as if every syllable was a treat to be savoured.

The handsome man in white blushed red as a maiden. He licked his lips, grinning sheepishly, exposing his teeth like a dog.

"Monseigneur, it is an honour", he breathed excitedly, jumping to his feet and bowing so quickly, and so deeply, that his forehead hit the hard wood of the table with an embarrassing **thunk**.

A couple of the others sniggered quietly at this, their heads still bowed.

The man in black smiled. "Yes I am sure it is", he drawled. "For you know much of honour, do you not Marceau?"

Marceau remained standing silently and bowed his head like the rest.

"An honour indeed", the man in black said softly, still watching Marceau, amusement in his eyes.

Gratified with the respect that was his due, and replete with the humiliation that he had extracted as his appetiser, the man in black moved to seat himself.

The servant kneeling behind his chair jumped to her feet immediately.

She pulled the chair back for him and pushed it back into place in perfect timing, before returning to her position behind his chair.

She sat back on her haunches, hands resting obediently on her legs.

"Be seated", the man in black instructed Marceau.

Marceau scrambled into his seat, as the manservant behind it clumsily tried to push it under him, failing miserably due to

Marceau's overexcitement.

The man in black watched, amused.

After allowing his subjects their sniggers, his eyes narrowed dangerously, and the room fell silent.

"In sanguine serviunt nobis", the man in black intoned gravely.

"In sanguine serviunt nobis", his subjects responded dutifully, raising their eyes as the last word was spoken.

An exquisitely beautiful woman began to fidget restlessly, extending her arms above her head and locking her fingers into place, provocatively pressing her bosom forward inside her robe.

The firelight clung to her, exposing her toned arms, and hugging the curves of her neck tenderly.

Marceau could not take his eyes from her, and sat, jaw agape, like a sucking camel.

She felt it. Felt his lust keenly. Felt its intrusion, and she pouted, flicking her lustrous panther black hair impetuously behind her shoulder.

"I'm hungry", she purred innocently to the man in black, watching Marceau from the corner of her eyes. She fluttered prettily, making full use of her full lashes to keep her admirer admiring.

"Patience, **Madame Dagger**", the man in black chided, seemingly amused, as his eyes flicked lazily from Marceau to his darkly beautiful companion. "We have matters to discuss, first".

She turned her head away sharply.

A delicate waif of a woman, sat to her right, took her hand and gave it a squeeze, smiling brightly at her.

The waif looked positively childlike compared to the tempestuous beauty of the woman at her side.

Two wisps of vanilla blonde hair framed an oval face, from which, two round, wide blue eyes shone forth luminously. They glittered incandescently like little puddles of innocence.

"Marquis, why have you brought us here tonight?" the waif

asked softly, bobbing her head respectfully at the man in black.

"Yes, pray tell, for I grow bored of the theatrics", answered a well-spoken young man.

The Marquis snapped his attention toward the man, who wilted under his icy glare and seemed to immediately reconsider his words.

The man managed to hold The Marquis' gaze bravely for a few moments, before smartly lowering his eyes in obeisance, like a dog faced with a wolf.

The Marquis continued to hold his hound in his vicelike stare, until satisfied the hound had remembered its place.

"There are matters to attend to", The Marquis continued as if nothing had happened, his tone now curt and serious. "The first, pertains to our new friend here". He grinned ever so slightly, a flash of malevolence fleetingly crossing his face. "I am sure you all know, Marceau".

The table muttered their assent, as if on cue.

"What you do not know...is why he is here", The Marquis informed them.

The table watched Marceau curiously, but cautiously.

"For the past year, Marceau has been...serving us". The Marquis rolled the last words around his mouth, as if tasting them, savouring them, deciding how many of them to share with his guests. "He has served us, and served us well...so well, in fact, that I have made a decision". He paused, waiting to see the effect of this on his subjects.

The cautious curiosity of his subjects had shed its veil now, and glared naked and brazen from their faces.

"Due to his service...to us...and to our cause, I have made a decision", The Marquis repeated, watching the table closely.

The dark beauty turned angrily from the waif, who was idly playing her hair. Her chin jutted aggressively. "Decision?"

It seemed as if it pained her to pass the word from her luscious lips.

The Marquis grinned at her suggestively.

"You cannot be serious, man!" growled a grizzled looking older man, slamming down his block like fist down on the table, causing it to shake dangerously.

The waif jumped in her seat, both hands moving protectively to her abdomen.

The dark beauty turned back to her quickly, pulling her close and nuzzling her. She shot the old man a truly lethal look, felt by all.

"But I am", The Marquis said quietly, drawing the attention of his insubordinate back upon him. He locked eyes with the older man.

The old bull quailed under The Marquis' gaze and turned away. He turned back after allowing a moment's subservience.

"This is madness, he is not of us. You would entrust all of our knowledge, all of our secrets to a... a... politician?" He spat the last word, shooting Marceau a withering look across the table.

Marceau squirmed uncomfortably in his seat, watching the faces eyeing him angrily. He decided to focus his gaze on his hands, which he ran slowly across one another to try and soothe his nerves.

The Marquis' eyes boiled at the old bull, who had the good sense to lower his gaze.

"What service has he performed for us, monseigneur". The interjection came from a gruff looking mountain of a man, sat to the right of The Marquis.

"Yes, well, as I was saying before I was... interrupted", The Marquis said quietly, shooting deadly looks at the dark beauty and the old bull. "Marceau has been instrumental in helping us procure something of a rare...delicacy".

"I am sure, that once you understand what I speak of". He shot another venomous glare at both of his subjects, as if daring them to interrupt him. "You will agree that this service demonstrates his commitment to our cause...and renouncement of his own".

The man mountain nodded simply, as Marceau continued squirming in his chair, unable to lift his eyes from his hands.

"It is through his service...through his allegiance to us, and to our cause, that we have been able to acquire this...rare delicacy. And quite the delicacy it is", The Marquis teased.

"Delicacy?" The question came from a familiar face that seemed somewhat out of place with the foreboding feel of the table. The voice sounded marginally too laissez-faire to be natural.

"That's right...Lucien, a delicacy". The Marquis smiled hungrily at the man to his left.

"A delicacy previously forbidden to us, by the powers that be". He laughed derisively at Marceau. "Well, it just so happens that the powers that be, want a little more power...a little more power than the people of France are capable of providing".

Lucien watched intently as The Marquis rose and strode over to Marceau sat at the opposite end of the table. He draped his hand lazily on Marceau's shoulder.

Marceau looked up and caught Lucien's eye, his expression unreadable, before lowering his gaze once more.

"But no matter. For the powers that be are cunning. And they are resourceful. And that led them to us. And to a power beyond anything the common men and women of France have ever known, or ever will...ah, a corrupt politician...can you believe it?" The Marquis laughed coldly, looking around expectantly at his subjects.

The others laughed merrily, with wicked smiles and merciless eyes.

Marceau licked his lips and smiled toothily, playing the subservient hound well.

Releasing his hound, The Marquis clasped his hands behind his back, and began to walk slowly around the table, pacing ominously behind each of them in turn.

"It is for this service", he said slowly. "This service, that none of his **noble brethren** have previously had the gall to offer to us". He stopped behind his throne. "That he is to be welcomed into our ranks. He is to become one of the Tableau Haute".

Marceau looked a little more confident at this, straightening in his seat, daring to meet the eyes of some of his soon to be brethren now, though thinking better of holding the gaze of The Marquis or Madame Dagger for too long.

A silence filled the room, contemplative this time, as each of the tableau sat quietly, digesting their own thoughts and feelings at this proclamation.

Of them all, only Lucien showed any sign of concern. His hands pressed down hard on the table, the whites of his fingernails showing.

Please don't let this be what I think it is, he thought.

"It is due to the efforts of our friend...our **brethren**, Marceau, that the liberi are now to serve us, as their makers", The Marquis declared.

Lucien gripped the table so hard that a crack appeared in the wood under his hand.

Thankfully, an excited murmuring began at the same moment. He ripped his hands from atop the table, and leant back in his chair, enveloped by shadow.

Please no, Lucien thought.

Please god, no.

How can we sink so low?

Eventually the murmuring subsided, and the tableau fell silent. "In sanguine serviunt nobis", they uttered as one.

Marceau was now beaming smugly and self-importantly, waggling happily around the table like the obedient, happy hound that he was.

Lucien stared at him incredulously, his face, thankfully, hidden from view.

They say the man has children of his own. Is he bereft of soul?

"Magnificent news, monseigneur". Lucien tore the words from himself. "I will make sure to bear it in mind when-". He made to rise from his chair, but was interrupted by a firm hand on his forearm, holding him in a vice- like grip.

"Where do you think you are going?" The Marquis enquired, his voice as cool as his eyes. "The evening is not yet over".

What now? Lucien thought frantically.

After pulling Lucien back into his seat, The Marquis grinned around the room at them all in turn, glee, or something perversely close to it, shining from his face.

He directed his eyes to a servant, standing guard in front of a door. A door at the opposite end of the room to the stone gateway.

This door was made of wood, rather than stone, and usually opened to opulence, rather than darkness.

He raised his hand, and clicked his fingers, the sound echoing sharply from the stone of the hall.

The servant turned, and opened the door, stepping through it and disappearing momentarily.

He returned, leading a hooded figure. The figure was small, a boy, from the looks of it, who couldn't have been much older than twelve or thirteen. A boy on the cusp of adolescence.

The boy's hands were bound, and he stood silently, his head slumped to one side.

At another click of The Marquis' fingers, the servant removed the boy's hood, and the tableau gasped collectively.

Though the gasps were collective, they did not all sound the same. Upon seeing the boy, Lucien went numb.

This is...abhorrent.

To bring him here like this.

To parade him so.

The boy was in shock.

His eyes were seeing, yet sightless, and he appeared unaware of his surroundings.

Marceau's newfound confidence appeared to have subsided, for he sat quietly, hands in his lap, eyes wide and staring.

"Dinner is served". The Marquis smirked wolfishly, his teeth glittering sharply.

You fucking monster, Lucien thought.

He could feel it bubbling inside, the hatred and the rage. It was as if someone had set his blood to boil.

It hissed virulently, so hot that it spat inside his veins. First his face, then his neck.

Red, everything was red.

"Good, for I am famished", Madame Dagger drawled from the other side of the table.

"Come Ivy". She pulled the waif up by her hand, and started walking quickly toward the boy, her eyes watching him greedily.

"Oh, finally, why didn't you just say so and save all the theatrics for the peasants", the well-spoken dandy said, also rising from the table.

At a look from Madame Dagger, he sat back down promptly.

As she reached the boy, standing alone by the door, she grabbed him roughly by the arm, pulling him to her.

"Disgusting thing", she hissed, as her eyes popped madly.

A calming hand appeared at her back, as Ivy whispered in her ear.

"Just a boy", Madame Dagger said, her eyes unseeing. "Yes...yes, you're right".

She appeared to relax, whatever madness had gripped her dissipating, along with its tempestuous energy.

Do something! Lucian thought.

What can I do?

What can I do against the full tableau?

You could do something.

Anything.

I'll die.

Better to die than live with this.

To live as a coward.

Cold, cold fear slithered through his stomach, chilling his boiling blood with a hiss.

Coward.

You'll do nothing as you always do.

"And what makes you think you get the first pick?" the dandy interjected, having had a change of heart.

"Because I deign it to be so!" Madame Dagger screamed across the room, a tempest erupting from her, seemingly from nowhere. "Now be silent, disgusting manling!"

"How dare you!" he shouted back, jumping to his feet. "I'll not be spoken to like that by a common who-".

He did not manage to utter another word.

Madame Dagger materialised before him, and pinned him viciously to the wall with one beautiful hand, driving a dagger into his side with the other.

He groaned weakly, and coughed, spraying blood over her shoulder to the floor.

"You **dare** to call me that", she hissed violently, leaning her weight on the dagger.

The dandy beat at her ineffectually, but his strength was no match for her.

"Enough", The Marquis drawled lazily, as if this were nothing more than the play time of children. "Pavo, do not antagonise her", he said, addressing the dandy. "Dagger, learn to share, my darling".

Such was the anger in her eyes, it looked like she would sooner kill Pavo rather than do anything of the sort.

"Have you forgotten your manners, **Madame** Dagger?" The Marquis teased, stressing her honorific.

Her jaw clenched like a vice, and she turned her wrath upon The Marquis.

Ivy's calming hand, seemingly never far away, appeared again, slipping through her arm to wrap around her waist.

The Marquis grinned a moment more, then turned to address the tableau, undeterred. "We have a guest with us. And as he has brought us this... delicacy...it is only fitting that he should have the first **bite**". He grinned at Marceau.

"Isn't that so, Marceau?" he asked, the smile fading, as his face took on a more calculating look.

Marceau swallowed. "Why yes, of course, monseigneur", he said quietly. "If that is your will..."

"My will", The Marquis repeated dreamily. "Yes, indeed, it is...but...for now, I do not think it would be quite...to your taste". His mouth curled.

"I am hungry damnit!" The man mountain smashed his fist down frustratedly. "Ah, enough of this!"

He sprang up from his seat, unnaturally fast for such a giant. His heavy chair flew backwards, screeching across the floor toward the wall.

His manservant, by instinct, or perhaps just luck, somehow managed to avoid the destructive path of the chair, and threw himself to one side, stumbling to his feet in time to watch as the chair smashed into pieces.

The servant stood still in shock, trembling.

Before he could collect himself, a huge paw of a hand appeared at his throat and lifted him from his feet.

He began to choke and gag.

He looked about frantically, as he dangled helplessly.

His eyes cried, begged, pleaded. Help.

They fell on Lucien, and he turned away.

The giant pulled savagely, with a beast-like roar, and the servant's head left his shoulders.

Blood burst from the servant's neck like a hydrant, spraying and spurting in all directions, showering the giant and the rest of the tableau in red rain.

Lucien gasped, as red tears hit his face with a sickening splat, and slid sadly down his cheeks.

The giant put his maw of a mouth to the unfortunate neck, and began noisily slurping and sucking at any of the red delight he could get his mouth to.

Blood dripped from his mouth, thickening and clotting in his unkempt auburn beard. Some of it slid to his thick neck and barrel chest, staining them red.

Madame Dagger cackled and clapped her hands, her eyes crinkling with merriment, as she enjoyed the morbid spectacle.

Ivy watched beside her, head tilted strangely, a detached look of curiosity on her face, as if she were watching a scene from a play.

The Marquis looked shocked, his mouth had fallen open like a trap door, and it hung ponderously.

His shock soon turned to amusement, though, and he burst out laughing. "Hadur, you crazed lunatic! You should have told me! I would have had them bring out appetisers!" He slapped the giant good naturedly on the back.

Hadur sucked the last remaining sustenance from his meal, then tossed the dry husk carelessly to one side, where it hit the wall with a squelch and a thud.

"Sorry, monseigneur". He belched coarsely.

The Marquis grimaced and waved his hand in front of his nose. "Mon dieu".

Hadur grinned stupidly, then wiped the back of his hand across his mouth and beard. Seeing his hand slick with blood, he shook the excess from his fingers to the floor with a sickening splat.

The remaining servants sat, paralyzed, scared to so much as breathe, their eyes fixed on the remains of their colleague.

"Don't you worry jeune homme! I've not an appetite for more!" Hadur roared suddenly at the servant closest to him, a particularly ashen faced man.

Hearing this, the man shook so violently his bones rattled, and he fell from his kneeling position, banging his head against the floor.

Hadur roared with laughter.

"Quite the bunch, monseigneur", he said to The Marquis.

Still chuckling to himself, he started licking and sucking his fingers loudly, the way one might after a particularly tasty roast chicken.

"Perhaps just a **mite** peckish", he said thoughtfully, eyeing the ashen faced servant longingly.

Suddenly, he slapped his over-large hand down on the table and leant forward, exclaiming loudly, "Marquis, monseigneur". He bowed his head. "I apologise for this...indiscretion...please, forgive me". He lowered his eyes.

The Marquis grinned imperiously. "Hadur, all is forgiven, of course... whatever am I to do with you?" His grin curled fiendishly, as if he had plenty of idea what he intended for Hadur.

The room went quiet then in anticipation.

Marceau rubbed at his neck, adjusting the neckline of his robe.

"Marceau, approach". The Marquis beckoned.

Marceau rose, and The Marquis led him to the end of the room, next to the hidden entrance.

There was a thin table there, and a fireplace, though the fireplace looked like it had not been used for a very long time.

On the table, was a dagger with an embellished hilt, adorned with rubies.

The Marquis picked up the dagger and ran his hands over it reverently. Marceau sank to his knees and bowed his head.

"Repeat after me", The Marquis said solemnly.

"Omitto lucem", The Marquis began.

"Amplector tenebris".

"Ego ad mensam".

"Iusiurandum et brachium meum".

"Per sanguinem ligati sumus".

The Marquis spoke, and Marceau repeated, unsure of the words he spoke, yet bound to say them.

"By blood we are bound", The Marquis said gravely, repeating the last sentence, this time in the common tongue.

Marceau's eyes widened, as if fully appreciating the gravity of his situation. "By blood we are bound", he said hesitantly.

Madame Dagger watched with eyes wide and excited, locked to the blade in The Marquis hand.

Ivy watched beside her, curious in her own fae way.

Even the haughty dandy Pavo had dropped his bored pretence and watched in silence, his face serious.

Don't do it you fool, Lucien thought desperately.

You don't really know what evil is.

And you do not wish to find out.

The Marquis grinned demonically. His face was barely visible, as there were no torches by the fireplace and the entire area was overcome by shadow.

He turned the blade over in his hands, admiring it, the way one might a work of art.

As he moved, he cast a large shadow on the wall behind that loomed large over Marceau, knelt on the floor.

Marceau looked up at his soon to be master.

Am I making the right decision?

Of course you are!

It is immortality!

Is there anything you would not give?

His stomach churned uncomfortably at that. However, the time for thinking was past.

Fate was here, and held Marceau firmly in its grasp.

Suddenly, The Marquis ripped the sleeve of his robe up to the elbow, exposing his lower arm.

He met Marceau's eyes and stared at him for uncountable moments.

The room was completely still, completely silent.

Then, in a quick, efficient flick, The Marquis opened the vein in his arm with the blade, and blood sprayed out.

"You would be of the Tableau Haute?" The Marquis asked, his face feral.

"Then drink!" he roared, thrusting his arm into Marceau's face, as blood pumped all over him.

Marceau hesitated a moment, then closed his eyes and placed his mouth to the vein, imbibing the lifeblood of his new master.

The Marquis moaned, as if deriving some sick pleasure from the act.

"Enough", he said huskily, after a few moments, satisfied the ceremony was complete. He tensed, his eyes glowed red, and the wound on his arm stopped leaking blood.

The tableau watched, some in awe, others more guardedly.

Marceau opened his eyes, slowly, as if in the midst of an awakening. His robe was red now, clotted in blood.

The Marquis growled.

It was a harsh sound, and his eyes grew redder.

And then, the wound disappeared completely from his arm.

"Is it...done?" Marceau asked.

The Marquis gingerly rolled down the sleeve of his robe. "Not quite", he said quietly.

"You have relinquished the light...now...you must embrace the dark", The Marquis said coldly.

"But I thought...that was...you said that was...all that would be required?" Marceau mumbled, his eyes darting around the room as if trying to figure out what could possibly be next.

He had just drunk the blood of a man! What more could be expected?

"Well, usually, yes...but in your case...I think we are all keen for a little more...**reassurance**", The Marquis clarified.

Madame Dagger chuckled throatily. "Yes dear, you are committed to us aren't you?" she purred.

Marceau reddened, turning the same colour as his robe.

"Don't antagonise the poor dear, can't you see he is already frightened out of his skin?" a friendly looking older woman in a red robe said.

"I am **sure** he is committed to us, aren't you, monsieur Marceau?" she asked.

Madame Dagger pouted, upset at the interruption of her fun.

Marceau remained silent, unsure what to say.

"There is one final undertaking, before we can welcome you into our ranks", The Marquis continued. "A poetic undertaking, given you were the one who orchestrated its circumstance".

He can't be serious.

Expecting a newtooth to... Lucien pondered the situation silently from his seat, still shrouded in darkness.

"We must see you feed, of course. And what finer feeding for your first meal, than that you have brought before us today." The Marquis gestured to the boy by the door, who stood in a daze, forgotten up until this point.

Marceau swallowed audibly.

"Can't I...I have to... the boy?" Marceau said, searching carefully for each word, as if he said the right thing he might worm his way out of this one.

"Indeed", The Marquis said, his eyes narrowing.

"I guess... if its ceremony... the only way", Marceau mumbled, seemingly a little numb at this.

Do something! Lucien's better nature screamed.

"Come Marceau, tis only a little blood", The Marquis said, placing his hand on Marceau's back and steering him gently toward the boy. "Is it really any different from when you humans eat veal, or lamb?"

Lucien gripped the arms of his chair tightly at this.

"Well, I suppose...when you put it like that..." Marceau continued to mumble quietly, as The Marquis steered him across the room to the boy.

They'd arrived in front of the boy now. A servant stood dutifully behind the boy, one hand resting softly on his shoulder. The boy stared sightlessly into the distance.

"Now, just as you did with me, except this time...here", The Marquis pointed at the boy's neck.

Marceau said nothing.

Silent now, his mumbling had stopped.

He hung his head in resignation, only looking up slowly after a reassuring squeeze of The Marquis' hand on his shoulder.

I'm so sorry. Please forgive me.

Please forgive me for what I'm about to do.

Feeling the eyes of the room on him, he stepped forward and placed both hands on the boy's shoulders, trying to look anywhere but his face.

He raised his hand and placed it on the boy's neck, softly, slowly turning his head up and to the side, exposing his throat.

"I am sorry", Marceau said quietly.

As Marceau began to lean toward the boy's neck, a strong gust of wind swept through the room, and the door behind the boy slammed shut with a bang that reverberated throughout the room.

At this, the boy seemed to awaken, as if from a spell.

He took in the room, and the sights in front of him, and screamed. He backed away quickly until his back was against the closed door.

"Enough of this, do it, it's now or never!" The Marquis snarled, grabbing the boy and placing his arm around his neck, pulling his head to the side and exposing his neck for Marceau.

The boy continued to scream and squirm frantically, fighting the powerful arm holding him.

He kicked out with his legs and crashed his fists into the legs of The Marquis behind him.

Something inside Lucien snapped.

Hadur, who had been watching the boy, turned to look at Lucien. He felt the change in Lucien and sensed something was about to unfold.

As he considered whether or not he should do something, Lucien disappeared in a blur of black.

His red robe fluttered, discarded to the floor, as he flew across the room, seemingly in his chair one second, at the door the next.

With a stupendous thunderclap of force, The Marquis hit the wall next to the door, and slid slowly down it in a daze, blood dripping from his nose to his lip.

Lucien stood over him shaking, a terrible anger on his face.

"Get out of here boy, while you still can!" he shouted, pointing through the now open door, which had been shaken off its hinges.

Madame Dagger growled savagely, rising from her seat with a snap.

The others around the table also snapped to their feet, and began to advance slowly on Lucien.

The boy sprinted through the open door and out of sight.

Lucien paused, listening for a moment. Hearing the heavy thud of the grand entrance door opening and closing, he seemed to relax slightly.

He turned back to face The Marquis, who was now propped up against the wall, breathing heavily.

The Marquis dabbed his finger into the blood dripping down his chin.

He put the finger slowly into his mouth, and sucked the blood from it savouring the taste, and what was to come next.

He looked up at Lucien.

"You've really done it this time", he said, a glacial expression on his face.

A Hangover Of Sorts

"How do you know Lucien?" Gabriel asked suddenly.

"What do you mean?" Duphan replied sharply, looking down his glasses in what could only be described as a librarian-esque manner.

"I mean, how do you know him?" Gabriel repeated, frowning.

Duphan considered the question, scratching the bald spot at the back of his head. He tried vainly to disguise it by coming over it with what remained of his hair, but it was too big to hide.

"Well, I met him many years ago…and not long after I started to work for him… much as you are now", he answered.

"Yes I could guess that much, but **how** did you meet him?" Gabriel pressed.

Duphan busied himself at his desk.

For a while, Gabriel thought he was ignoring him.

"I cannot entirely remember…it was so long ago now", he finally admitted.

"I see", Gabriel responded sceptically.

Duphan did not see, for he had already returned his attention to the stack of papers on his desk.

Not as memorable as my first meeting with him then, Gabriel thought.

"Why did he hire me?" Gabriel asked.

Duphan looked at him appraisingly.

"Lucien, why did he hire me?" Gabriel repeated.

"Beats me. Lucien is a strange man", Duphan surmised.

"Oh", Gabriel said, crestfallen.

"Come here", Duphan beckoned.

"What?" Gabriel asked.

"Here", Duphan repeated insistently.

Who is he to speak to me like that? Gabriel thought angrily.

Duphan jerked his head impatiently.

Gabriel bristled, but obeyed.

"What is this?" Duphan asked, producing a small bronze trinket in the shape of a whale.

"Sailor bait?" Gabriel replied insolently.

To his surprise, Duphan laughed.

"Very good", he admitted, like a teacher praising a student.

Gabriel smiled in spite of himself. He was arrogant for an antique's man, but the praise made him feel good.

"You are right...it is...gauche", Duphan said distastefully, examining the whale as if it were a rat. "But it has sentimental value. And there are sailors who would pay well for it. Lucien is shrewd". He nodded.

Gabriel watched quietly, not sure what to make of this.

"Sentimental?" Gabriel asked.

Duphan waved his hand dismissively.

How rude.

"Now, what would you say is the most valuable item in DuPassé?" Duphan asked suddenly.

"It's a difficult question", Gabriel ventured.

"And yet it requires an answer", Duphan replied.

Gabriel scowled.

"Well", he sighed, trying to rationalise an answer.

"Don't think, tell", Duphan snapped.

Gabriel reddened and stormed away.

Before he knew it, he was standing in front of the wooden

display cabinet with the silver ring in.

The same ring he had been so enamoured with...the day he met Lucien.

It sat alone, as always, comfortably nestled on a patch of dark red cloth.

It looked lonely.

"This?" Duphan asked, watching him closely.

"Yes", Gabriel replied dreamily.

"Why?" Duphan asked, joining him at the cabinet.

"I...couldn't tell you. Just a feeling", Gabriel replied lamely. "I don't think I have much of a head for this".

Duphan stared at him intently.

It made Gabriel feel uncomfortable, exposed.

"It's a good choice", Duphan admitted.

"It is?" Gabriel asked, surprised.

"Yes. In fact, Lucien reckoned the value of this ring incalculable", Duphan said quietly.

"What?" Gabriel panicked. "Then why is it here, in the store? Should it not be squirrelled away in a vault underground somewhere, tended by goblin and guarded by dragon?"

Duphan grinned, and his face changed. He did not look the ascetic librarian for a moment. The grin faded as fast as it flowered, and the scholar returned.

"Not a lot of people know of this ring, or its history, so it is quite safe here. Best not to draw attention to it. Hiding in plain sight, Lucien calls it", Duphan said.

"History? What history?" Gabriel looked concerned.

"You'd better ask Lucien". Duphan smirked. "He might not be best pleased if I tell you and scare you off".

"Scare me off?" Gabriel's eyes widened. "What kind of ring do we keep?"

Duphan just shrugged and winked, before sauntering back to his desk and his beloved chair.

"So dramatic", Gabriel grumbled, watching Duphan, who

was already engrossed in his newspaper and leant back contentedly in his chair.

A brass bell rang, as the door to DuPassé swung open.

A horribly overgrown specimen of a man stepped ponderously through into the shop.

He was so large that he filled the doorway, blocking the sunlight from behind, and casting a huge shadow on the floor in front of him.

His scruffy auburn hair hung to his shoulders like red brown reeds. His ill-fitting grey suit looked as though it was struggling to contain him, and he seemed out of place wearing it.

He stepped into the shop and looked around.

"So", he said, his voice rumbling deeply. "This is Lucien's little shop, is it".

He scratched at his belly like a bear, his fingernails scratching loudly.

"Figured it'd be bigger". He sniffed.

"Umm...may I help you, monsieur?" Gabriel asked.

The giant ignored him.

"Excuse me, can I help you?" Gabriel repeated.

No response.

"Do you know Lucien perhaps?" Gabriel asked louder this time, asserting himself.

The giant turned his eyes on Gabriel, surprised, as if seeing him for the first time.

He appraised him silently for a moment.

Then, he gave a booming laugh, throwing his head back as he laughed. "Friend of his", he said slowly. "Yes, you could say that". He seemed to find this amusing for some reason Gabriel could not fathom.

Duphan rose from his chair and leant silently against the back wall, arms crossed.

The giant grinned stupidly, his beetle brown eyes crawling with humour, as he considered Gabriel.

"Well..." Gabriel started, unsure of how much to divulge to this coarse stranger. "Unfortunately, Monsieur Lucien is not here. I am not sure when he will be back", he said cagily.

"Ohhh, **Monsieur** Lucien is it", the giant mocked.

"Yes", Gabriel replied, irritated. "I'm sorry, but we cannot help you, perhaps you could come back. I'll be sure to let him know you stopped by", he said tightly.

Gabriel felt embarrassed. He did not know why the giant mocked him. He felt it was only polite to refer to Lucien as monsieur.

"I don't think that's necessary", the giant said bluntly. "I have a feelin he'll be here soon". He grinned smugly.

What is the oaf smiling at? Gabriel thought, agitated.

Gabriel stood silently. He did not know what to say, or how to act.

He did not want to be rude if this was a customer, but equally, the man unsettled him, and he wasn't sure if he knew Lucien, or if it was just some ruse.

Fortunately, he did not have to fret long, for a few minutes later, Lucien could be seen walking down the street toward the store.

As he drew closer, it appeared he was limping, favouring his right leg.

He looked, as always, impeccable, that was of course, if you ignored his face, which was covered in cuts and bruises.

What the hell has happened to him? Gabriel thought, a jolt of panic running through him.

"Lucien, my boy, you look a little worse for wear!" the giant boomed loudly, striding forward to slap a meaty hand on his back, the moment the door closed behind him.

Lucien snarled.

The proprietor of DuPassé looked up at the giant, his expression deadly. The giant dropped his hand and stepped back quickly, his smile fading.

Gabriel didn't blame him, Lucien looked terrifying. He had not seen him like this before, even the night at De Lune.

Gone was the charm and the impish smile, in its place, was something dark.

"I told you **never** to come here", Lucien threatened.

The giant crossed his arms, no mean feat, considering how large they were. "You are in no position to tell us anything", he countered warily.

Lucien said nothing, he just stared, stared at the giant until he shifted uncomfortably on his feet.

"He's a job for you...do not disappoint him", the giant said mysteriously, handing Lucien an envelope.

For a moment, it seemed as though Lucien would not take it, or perhaps strike the giant, but then he took it, snatching it quickly and turning his back on him.

Lucien nodded stiffly in assent.

"Now leave my store", he ordered, and without another word, he walked away to the back of the store.

The giant breathed deeply and clenched his fists.

Gabriel worried the giant might attack Lucien, but he seemed to think better of it, and instead snorted, as a horse might.

"Some welcome", the giant grumbled, turning to Gabriel, the merest hint of a smile scuttling in his eyes. "Be seeing you... Gabriel", he said with a knowing smile.

Before Gabriel could think of a response, the giant turned away to leave.

He ducked his head and shuffled under the door frame out into the street.

He shook his head, and cracked his neck to both sides, using both hands to do so.

Seemingly relieved at this release of tension, he turned and grinned at Gabriel, before strolling away, the people in the street parting like the sea around him.

Who Are You?

The sky darkened and rain fell heavily to the roof of DuPassé.

Pitter patter, pitter patter.

Lucien was ignoring them, or so it seemed, professing great interest in a paper he'd taken from the front desk.

Gabriel could still feel the anger from him, though it seemed to simmer rather than boil now.

Duphan sighed, and sank to his chair, snapping his newspaper up in front of his face and disappearing behind it.

Gabriel stood awkwardly watching Lucien. After a moment, he looked to Duphan for help.

As if feeling the eyes upon him, Duphan lowered the newspaper slightly, and rolled his eyes at Gabriel, before disappearing behind his paper again.

Great.

What should I do?

How do I unpick this?

What has happened to him?

And who was that man?

Am I supposed to act as if nothing has happened, and this is all completely normal?

He watched the rain for a while, gathering his thoughts, and taking some solace in the gentle sounds of the rain.

Outside, a young father tried in vain to shield his wife and child from the rain.

The little boy cackled with glee, as he made every effort to jump in as many puddles as he could, much to the dismay of his mother.

Gabriel smiled, as the family shuffled awkwardly together down the street to try and find shelter.

How beautiful.

He made up his mind.

Well, best be on with it.

Gabriel approached Lucien at the back of the store. It was darker here, for there were only small panel windows at the top of the walls, not like the big full-length windows at the front of the store. Some small rays of sunlight had managed to filter through though.

He found it peaceful. A twilight solace.

"Lucien", Gabriel asked softly. "What has happened to you?"

Lucien turned slowly, without his usual energy.

As he turned, his face came into profile, and Gabriel winced at the bruises on it.

"Nothing", he said dully.

"What do you mean, **nothing?**" Gabriel said, incredulous. "You look as though you've picked a fight with a mountain, and the mountain won. And who was that man? What on earth was that about? I've never seen you like that...apart from...but this was...different".

"It was nothing, you needn't worry", Lucien responded with a pained expression on his face.

"Needn't worry?" Gabriel could not believe it.

They stood awkwardly in silence for a moment.

"The problem is, that I do worry", Gabriel said quietly, his eyes on Lucien. "Much as I wish that I did not".

Duphan coughed softly behind his newspaper, perhaps trying to inject some levity into the situation.

"Like I said, it is nothing". Lucien waved his hand weakly.

"Do not take me for a fool", Gabriel said quietly, but intensely.

Duphan slowly lowered his newspaper, eyebrows raised.

Lucien's mouth twitched.

Well, aren't you full of surprises? Lucien thought.

"Do not feed me this...nonsense...now that you have brought me into your life and...confided in me. Tell me what has happened, now", Gabriel demanded.

Lucien smiled. "Come then", he said wearily, walking toward the front desk.

When he realised that Gabriel would not follow his instruction, he turned, and gestured that Gabriel should follow.

It was a little imperious. But Gabriel sensed he was trying.

Gabriel made a 'tsk' sound, then strode across, flashing Lucien a withering look as he went.

"I will tell you, but not here", Lucien said, as Gabriel came to a stop.

"Then where?" Gabriel frowned. His patience was wearing thin.

Duphan's paper rustled.

"Where?" Gabriel repeated, looking around confused.

Lucien turned, and walked past Duphan's desk. He walked about ten paces, then stopped, coming face to face with the wall.

Gabriel's frown intensified, and his eyebrows reached for the sky.

What on earth is he doing?

Those blows have addled his brain.

Lucien raised his hand and pushed hard on the wall.

With a click, the wall swung inwards, to reveal what appeared to be a study, with a spiral stone staircase at the back. Where it led, was anyone's guess.

"Really?" Gabriel asked in disbelief. "A **secret room**? Whatever next".

Gabriel's eyebrows zigged and zagged up and down like a rollercoaster.

Lucien watched in quiet amusement, his eyebrows giving their own performance. "Well?"

Gabriel sighed, as if he'd had more than enough of this, and strode into the room.

Inside, he was taken aback, the room was a wonder.

The walls were covered with bookcases, and antiques of all shapes and sizes.

"Is that a...sword?" Gabriel wondered, his eyes on the wall. "Why do you have a **sword**?" he said, reaching for it immediately.

Lucien pushed his hand aside gently, giving it a little swat.

Gabriel glared at him.

There were swords and shields, knives and daggers, and even a complete suit of golden plate armour stood hanging on a frame in a corner.

Gabriel marvelled at them in spite of himself, though damned would he be if he'd let Lucien know that he was impressed right now.

Of course, there were paintings too, though not many. His favourite was a still lake, surrounded by green forest. A lone man sat before it.

A wooden desk sat to one side, with two comfortable looking chairs, one in front, one behind, perhaps to suggest a power dynamic of some kind, perhaps just to entertain.

The desk was messy, with stacks of papers, fountain pens, and a stone paper weight.

Lucien leaned against the wall watching Gabriel.

"Well, does it pass muster?" he asked.

"It's...wonderful", Gabriel admitted grudgingly.

"I like it", Lucien agreed. "It helps me relax...it's very quiet...and I am surrounded by history". He studied the contents of the room, pausing here and there.

"Sometimes, I sit, and I daydream, and I wonder...who wore this armour? Who wielded this sword?" he said.

"You mean you don't know?" Gabriel asked, surprised.

"No, not all of it", Lucien admitted. "The armour is

a…mystery to me. As for the sword?" Lucien trailed off, grinning mysteriously.

"Oh psht", Gabriel scoffed, irritated.

"Others might see a sword, I see a story", Lucien said. "And a gateway to the past. To…simpler times".

"Simpler, but not necessarily better", Gabriel cautioned.

"Yes", Lucien conceded sadly. "Perhaps".

Gabriel watched him, conflicted. He did not know what to make of Lucien. He could be so charming, so warm, yet he had also displayed fearsome anger, and a…darker side.

And vulnerability, Gabriel thought suddenly.

He has displayed vulnerability.

And that is…encouraging.

Who was he, really? Angry, fearful and brooding? Or charming, energetic and caring?

"So", Gabriel said finally, breaking the silence that had developed. "Who are you, really?"

Lucien squirmed. Without dropping his eyes, he pushed a recessed button under his desk, and the wall door swung shut.

"Oh really", Gabriel muttered. "You are too much".

Lucien chuckled.

"I am glad you amuse yourself", Gabriel said.

Lucien smiled sadly, then sadness was all that was left.

"There are some things I can tell you", he said. "And some things I cannot. I'll do my best to answer your questions, but please understand that if I choose not to answer a question, there is a good reason for it".

Gabriel frowned, but accepted what he said after seeing the grave expression on his face.

"Who did this to you?" Gabriel started.

"A very powerful man…a man I've known for a very long time", Lucien responded carefully.

"Powerful? Powerful how? Physically?" Gabriel asked sceptically, wondering what sort of man would be able to cause such injury to him. Then he remembered the giant and winced.

"Yes, you could certainly say that, and in other ways", Lucien said vaguely.

"Other ways? Stop being evasive", Gabriel said shortly.

"This man has great influence in France, more than you could possibly imagine. It is for the best that you do not know too much about him. I put you at risk merely by talking to you about him", Lucien said.

"How cliche", Gabriel quipped cynically. "You make it sound as if this man is some puppet master, and the people of France on his strings".

"Were it only the people of France", Lucien responded wistfully.

Gabriels's mouth dropped open, not sure what to make of this. He couldn't tell if this was some ruse to throw him off the scent, but Lucien seemed serious, and he had not lied to him...yet.

"Why did he do this to you, this puppet master?" Gabriel asked.

"We had a difference of opinion", Lucien said wryly.

"A difference of opinion", Gabriel repeated testily.

"Yes", Lucien replied

"About what?" Gabriel pressed.

"What is right, and what is wrong", Lucien said tight lipped.

Gabriel rolled his eyes.

"He was set on a course of action that was wrong...unjust...so I fought him on it", Lucien elaborated, choosing his words carefully.

"And for this he beat you so savagely?" Gabriel asked. "He must have some strange conceptions of right and wrong indeed. I must ask, why do you associate with a person like this at all, in any capacity? Why not simply cut all ties with him".

"Were it that simple", Lucien said tiredly.

"Why isn't it?" Gabriel said challengingly. "This man could

be the death of you. You should have no part of him!"

Lucien stared at Gabriel, wondering how much to tell him.

Why do I feel the need to explain myself to you?

I have never wanted to before.

Explain myself. Never felt the need.

Never felt...comfortable enough.

Is it a comfort I feel with you, then? I suppose that it must be.

Lucien rubbed his finger over his lip.

Gabriel pursed his lips to stop himself from smiling.

I find that I...know you, Gabriel thought.

I find myself...anticipating you...already.

Isn't that strange.

After so short a time.

"It's complicated", Lucien said.

Gabriel gave him a look that dispelled any notion of this inadequate response being tolerated.

"It is complicated", Lucien repeated. "Were I to try and leave, they would not let me, least of all him".

"**They?**" Gabriel fired back quickly.

Lucien sighed deeply.

"Yes, they, but that is all I will say about it for now". He fixed Gabriel with a stare that signalled he would not elaborate further.

"Well, Lucien, quite the friends you have". Gabriel grimaced. "Might I suggest finding some new ones?"

A pained, uncomfortable expression crossed Lucien's face. It was an unsure thing, and Gabriel felt sorry for him at that moment.

"I need some time to think", Gabriel said suddenly.

Something flashed behind Lucien's eyes, was it panic?

"But tell me one thing, that...big man...who was here earlier. How did he know my name? I have never seen him before. Did you tell him about me?" Gabriel asked.

"What do you mean?" Lucien responded sharply.

"He knew my name. He called me by it before he left, did you not hear?" Gabriel asked, a little unsettled by Lucien's reaction.

"He called you Gabriel?" Lucien asked as he leaned forward in his chair, alert now.

"Well yes..." Gabriel responded. "Have you told him about me?"

"You're certain he called you Gabriel?" Lucien repeated, agitated now.

Gabriel nodded, frowning.

Lucien sprang to his feet and began pacing once more. "I'm sorry, but I must go", he said abruptly, reaching under the desk and popping the door wall open.

"Wait, what do you mean? Are you not going to tell me the significance of this?" Gabriel railed.

"It would be for the best if you did not come here for a while", Lucien said.

"And how will that work?" Gabriel asked, nonplussed.

"I will ensure you are still paid, of course, but please, do not visit DuPassé again until I contact you", Lucien pleaded, his eyes wide and frightened.

"Wait! Tell me what's going on, now!" Gabriel shouted, surprising himself.

Lucien looked as if he desperately wanted to. "I am sorry, but I cannot, not now".

Gabriel's mouth dropped open angrily.

"I will tell you all, soon, I promise you", Lucien said, gripping his hands. "Please, just trust me, were I to tell you, it would only endanger you. And I don't want to put you in danger. It is the...last thing...the last thing I would want", he repeated, confirming this with himself.

Gabriel stared back at Lucien for a long moment, his feelings conflicted.

On the one hand he wanted to rail at Lucien for yet again keeping him in the dark, on the other he was intrigued by the sincerity of his response, and worried by the urgency behind it.

Eventually, he nodded.

As Lucien walked him to the entrance of the shop, Gabriel stopped, and touched his arm fleetingly. "Be careful", he warned.

Their eyes met briefly, and Lucien nodded.

"And I expect you to tell me what on earth that staircase is when you return" Gabriel said matter of factly, gesturing behind him. "And where it leads for that matter".

Lucien chuckled. "We'll see about that". He winked.

Gabriel frowned. Now that he was here, at the door, he did not want to leave.

"I shall see you soon", Lucien promised. "I should hope", Gabriel replied.

And with that, they both left.

They turned in harmony, outside in the street, to look at one another a moment longer.

Then, they went their separate ways.

Alone in DuPassé, Duphan lowered his newspaper.

L'enfants Parisienne

"Give me that Max!" piped a little blonde girl in a hand me down pinafore, as she tried in vain to grab something from behind a boy's back.

"No, it's mine, I found it!" shouted back a scrawny boy with a dirty face.

"Both of you stop it!" commanded a serious looking boy. He only looked to be ten or eleven but was tall for his age. His demeanour was dark and brooding, like his hair.

"I found it, Luca. You saw me!" the scrawny boy continued, looking to the taller boy to arbitrate the quarrel.

"Yes, I know", replied the older boy tiredly. "But you're a big boy ain't ya? Remember what papa said. Big boys share. Especially with their little sister".

The younger boy stood silently for a moment with his arms crossed, seemingly deep in thought. "Am I really a big boy, like you Luca?"

"Course you are. It's what I said ain't it?" replied the older boy, looking around the large hall they were in, his thoughts elsewhere.

Looking down at the younger boy, he smiled wearily and ruffled his hair.

"Go on, big boy", Luca said paternally, giving Max a gentle push.

Max paused for a moment, looking down at his feet, then

passed the little gold anchor he'd been hoarding to his sister. "Here go Mar", he said quietly.

The girl's eyes lit up. "Thanks Max". She took the anchor and leaned forward on one leg to give Max a hug, and then a small kiss on the cheek.

Max grinned. "It's alright, we can share. Maybe I can find more".

The girl beamed at her brother, obviously impressed at his ingenuity.

"Now, where is this food?" Luca muttered to himself.

The two smaller children were huddled together on a small bed, in the back corner of a large room.

The room had a high sloping ceiling, like a church, and light flooded in through large windows on either side of the ceiling.

On both sides of the room makeshift beds had been hastily assembled and laid in rows against the walls.

In the middle of the room, a few children played quietly on the floor, more still sat disconsolately on their beds staring into space.

A long table with a white tablecloth lay empty at the front of the room. Two open doors stood either side of the table leading to hallways.

A rumbling noise punctuated the thoughts of the older boy.

"Luca, I'm hungry", the little girl whined sadly.

"I know sis. Not long now. I promise", Luca replied, bending down and giving the girl a hug.

How can I promise that to her? I don't even know where we are.

Or if they'll feed us.

I wish papa was here. He'd know what to do. I'm just a boy.

Don't think like that! They need you.

You're all they have now.

Looking up with grim resolve, Luca stood and straightened himself, determined to find answers.

Time to find out what's going on.

If they weren't going to tell him willingly, he'd make them. He strode purposefully toward the table and the open doors.

As he went, a group of people appeared in the hallway to the right, walking toward the room, carrying something large in their hands.

Luca faltered, and slowed.

What is this?

He couldn't make them out clearly as the light was not good in the hallway, so he waited cautiously.

Finally.

He breathed a sigh of relief as he spied the large metal pots in their hands, his shoulders slumped, relaxed, for the first time in hours.

Well, no point standing here like a crow.

I should help.

The sooner this food is served, the better.

Luca walked forward tentatively, and greeted the group with a weary smile, watching as they set down their pots. His stomach cramped painfully as the smell of boiling meat and vegetables reached his nostrils.

Pot-au-feu.

It was not his favourite, but at this point, he would eat anything.

He turned, and caught a golden haired man frowning at him strangely.

He must have heard my belly...

The man smiled sympathetically and grabbed a large bowl from a passing adult. He briskly popped the top off one of the pots, and ladled a large serving of meat, vegetables and bouillon into the bowl, passing it to the boy.

"Eat. You must be starving", the man instructed him.

"Thank you, monsieur", Luca said, looking down at the food longingly. "I gotta feed Max and Marie first though". Luca picked up two spoons from the table and walked dutifully away.

The man watched as the young boy walked over to what must be his brother and sister with the food. The boy gave them both spoons then sat back tiredly, watching them as they ate.

How terribly sad, the man thought.

Orphaned at such a young age.

And already he wears the world on his shoulders.

Ladling another generous serving of pot-au-feu into a bowl, the man walked over to the boy and his siblings.

By now, the other children had realised what was happening, and a chaotic queue had formed in front of the food table, with children pulling and shoving in a bid to quiet their belly first.

Order was restored, as one of the volunteers calmed them with a stern word.

Luca felt a tap on his shoulder, and rose to his feet sharply, ready to defend his siblings if necessary.

Seeing it was the man from the food table, he slumped back down wearily.

"Sorry, you scared me", the boy said tiredly, seeing the expression on the man's face.

"No, no, I'm sorry. I didn't mean to scare you..." the man said apologetically, his face concerned.

"I just wanted to bring you this", he said, holding the bowl of food out. "You'll struggle to get a bowl, now that the secrets' out". He smiled mischievously and gestured behind to the chaos at the food table.

"Thanks", the boy sighed, taking the bowl and starting to eat rapidly, too hungry for words.

The man sat down quietly on the end of the bed and watched them eat. Luca seemed a little unsure at this, but he was too tired and too hungry to give it much thought.

When Luca had finished eating, which did not take long at all, he put the empty bowl down in front of him, and turned to face the man.

He stared seriously at him, considering him, man to man.

"I'm Luca", he said quietly after a while, offering his hand.

"Gabriel", the man replied warmly, covering the boy's hand with his own.

"Gabriel", the little girl chimed curiously, a thoughtful expression on her face. "That's a pretty name. I like it".

"It ain't a pretty name Mar, it's a boy's name!" the younger boy said.

"Is so!" the little girl fired back angrily.

"It's quite alright, I think it's a pretty name too". Gabriel smiled at the girl. "But I can see how you might think otherwise", Gabriel added diplomatically to Max.

Max watched Gabriel, unsure of how to respond. He felt like there was a lesson to be had here, but he wasn't sure what. Unable to figure it out, he grinned.

Luca watched quietly. He was just glad of a chance to rest, and some quiet. If this man Gabriel wanted to help him with Max and Marie for a bit that was fine by him. As long as he was nice.

"Was the food good?" Gabriel asked the children.

"Yummy", the girl responded, rubbing her stomach appreciatively.

"I'm glad you liked it... Mar, is it?" Gabriel asked.

"My name's Marie... but you can call me Mar", Marie said seriously.

"Why thank you. It's a very pretty name. Even prettier than mine". Gabriel beamed, his eyes shining good naturedly.

"Thank you", Marie replied shyly.

Max looked back and forth between the two of them silently, taking it all in, still not sure, but piecing it together slowly.

It would be good for him to spend some time around some nice adults,

Luca thought, watching Max.

He's certainly seen enough of the bad sort lately.

"How long have you been here", Gabriel said to no one in

particular, taking in the condition of the children.

The children sat quietly, waiting for Luca to respond. "Not long, we got here today", he said finally.

"Before that, we was on the streets for a while… but that was… bad", Luca finished lamely.

Max looked away nervously at this, swinging his feet back and forth under the bed and watching them swing.

Marie said nothing, her childlike curiosity had taken hold now she'd been fed, and she was gazing around the room with interest.

"I can imagine", Gabriel said sadly, turning back to look at Luca. His grey eyes shone dully, old before their time.

Luca looked away, pretending to focus on the hustle and bustle of the room.

It's alright. You're safe now, Gabriel thought.

I will make sure of it.

Gabriel brushed himself down briskly, then smacked his legs, before rising to his feet. "Don't worry, I'll make sure that they take good care of you here. I promise".

"I know you will monsieur", Marie said immediately, her trust in him complete. She smiled innocently, and it hurt Gabriel, deep in his heart.

So resilient, and so trusting, even after everything you've been through.

"I just wish Lainy was here too", Marie continued sadly.

Max sniffed at this, and turned away from them, swinging his legs over the other side of the bed.

"Lainy? Is that your… father?" Gabriel said, a little unsure of himself, and not wanting to upset the children further.

"Brother", Luca answered quietly, with a faraway look in his eyes. "Lainy's my brother and I miss him. So do Max and Luca", Marie explained.

At this, Max jumped up. "I don't miss him, he left us, just like papa!" he stormed, before running off.

"Don't go too far Max!" Luca shouted immediately, as if from reflex.

Max hesitated, then threw himself brashly onto an empty bed near the entrance. He turned his back to them and pulled his legs up to his chest.

Luca watched him closely, like a parent checking to see if their child had really decided to do what they were told, or if more disobedience was yet to come.

Marie watched curiously, her eyes drifting dreamily from Max, to Luca, to Gabriel.

"Who was...Lainy...Luca?" Gabriel asked quietly.

"Alain was...is... our brother", Luca replied sombrely.

"He..." Luca paused, looking at Marie who was watching him closely. "We haven't seen him for a while...I don't know where he is".

"He's in the cattycombs, silly", Marie said matter of factly, playing fondly with a small golden anchor that she was bobbing up and down on the bed beside her.

"We don't know that", Luca replied carefully.

"Yes, we do. Lainy was always talking about the cattycombs. He said we'd be safe there", Marie declared. "And we wouldn't have to go to any more horrible homes or shelters", she added as an afterthought.

"Lainy told me he was gonna go look at the cattycombs. Lainy's in the catcombs", Marie finished, as if the matter was settled.

"The Catacombs?" Gabriel frowned.

"Cattycombs yes", Marie said, without raising her eyes from her anchor.

What would he be doing down there?

Have things really been that bad for you? Gabriel thought sadly.

Marie nodded. "They're und...undergwound", she said seriously, pointing beneath her feet.

Gabriel chuckled. "Yes, I'd heard", he replied, smiling happily at her.

"I don't think he's there..." Luca said quietly to Gabriel, so Marie would not hear. "Even so, I'd go and look for myself, but I can't leave Max and Marie", he finished dejectedly.

Gabriel sat in silence, thinking about what the children had said.

Marie quietly played with her anchor, while Luca leant back tiredly against the bed frame, one of his legs dangling off the bed as he stared off into space.

It's possible he's down there... They seem rather adamant about it.

Perhaps he was merely saying it to interject some hope.

*But what if he **is** telling the truth?*

*What if he **is** down there, could you live with yourself, if you didn't at least look?*

"Marie", Gabriel said suddenly, breaking the silence.

"Yes..." she replied, without taking her eyes off her toy.

"Where were you when you last saw... Lainy?" Gabriel asked.

"Umm...it was someplace nice, I forget", Marie responded.

"Montparnasse", Luca said quietly. "Is where we last saw Alain".

*Montparnasse...*Gabriel thought.

Makes sense.

There's rumoured to be several entrances to the catacombs there.

I know but one of them.

But which did he take?

I pray it is one of the...safer.

"It certainly is nice, Miss Marie", Gabriel agreed, smiling warmly

Marie paused for a moment, and looked up shyly, blushing a little. She gave Gabriel a shy smile of her own then returned her attention to her toy.

"Why do you ask?" Luca asked curiously.

"I have always wanted to visit the catacombs..." Gabriel responded. "What better time than now?"

"You're gonna look for Lainy?" Luca said quickly.

"Yes. I couldn't live with myself if I didn't at least try", Gabriel said.

"You're gonna find Lainy?" Marie repeated excitedly, abandoning her toy.

Across the room, Max looked up curiously.

"I'm going to try. I'll do my best to help you find your brother", Gabriel responded seriously.

Marie jumped off the bed and threw herself at Gabriel, wrapping her little arms around his neck. He embraced her gently, patting her back.

Overcome by curiosity, Max ran across the room, and threw himself down on the bed, before promptly folding his legs under him.

"Gabwiel is gonna find Lainy, Max!" Marie promptly informed her brother.

"Really monsieur?" Max looked up at Gabriel hopefully, his acquired cynicism for the moment overridden by childlike optimism.

"I'll do my best... I promise", Gabriel said, watching the children each in turn, a sense of wellbeing flooding him as he cherished the smiles on their faces.

"Wow. You're the best!" Max blurted out in awe.

Luca watched his little brother quietly.

Maybe there are good adults.

Maybe there's adults like ma and pa.

Maybe...

"I know what it's like...to be like you", Gabriel said in an undertone to Luca, as the children celebrated. They wrestled playfully on the bed, tickling one another and giggling loudly.

Luca didn't know what to say. He stared back at Gabriel, stared deep into his eyes, for confirmation that this friendly stranger knew. For confirmation that he really understood.

After a minute, Luca nodded.

Just then, a burly man with a white chef's apron called from the front of the room. "Gabriel, we need you".

"I need to go, but I'll be back", Gabriel promised, as the children started to protest. "Look after your brother and sister, Luca. You are doing admirably, and you should be proud of yourself. You're going to be a fine man one day".

Luca blushed but nodded sombrely.

"Bye Max, Bye Marie". Gabriel waved at them with a smile.

And with that, he walked away to the front of the room, where he joined the adults cleaning up after the meal.

Luca watched him for a long time, as Max and Marie started playing hide and seek, taking it in turns to hide under the bed, or behind the wardrobes dotted along the walls.

Don't let me down, monsieur.

You're all I got, Luca thought to himself bleakly.

The Dark Side Of The Moon

In a different part of Paris, a different sort of meeting was taking place, and there was nothing bleak about it.

It was a meeting of the Parisian elite, and to Luca and his little family, they may as well have been a different species, for they were so removed in understanding and experience, as to be totally and abjectly alien. They had never known a dirty face, a cold night, or a hungry belly.

There were actors and musicians, politicians and businessmen, and socialites and climbers. All of them dressed in their finest finery, flashing and fluttering their feathers at one another, like rival peacocks.

The room was full, with a hundred or so hounds, each hungry for their fill, licking their lips greedily as they eyed the prize. All were there for something, something for themselves, something to further their station, fatten their pomp, weigh their purse.

And all could be granted. By one man.

A king. Or so you would think. But we do not call one 'king'. Not now. Not anymore. It is not proper, you see. And it is far easier to swallow, to call him a prettier thing. A softer thing. And a softer thing, has softer edges, edges that easily blur, and shift, and change. Edges that give the pretext of decision, the pretext of freedom, the pretext of choice.

All that we really care, is that the 'king' is grand, and that the things he says are grander. And more importantly, that the grand things he says, are the **right grand things.**

The kings of old had jagged edges that hurt to look upon. The kings of new have no edges to speak of, and shift with the wind.

But their lies are so sweet, that the medicine tastes bitter not at all.

Perhaps it is better this way. A palatable lie. A palatable story. There is no king in this story, you see. And no serf.

And is that not all the people want? To tell themselves things are different, that things are better. To desperately believe the new story is different to the old one.

We chose him! He is us, and we are he! And he is grand, and so must we be.

A grand man sat upon a grand throne. A throne of husks. The husks of poor men. The husks of common men. Exploited men. Bled dry. Their backs, as broken as their dreams.

But remember, he is not a king.

He is a President.

Or a Prime Minister. Premier. Viceroy. Marquis. Grand Wizard. Duly ordained. Honoured. Revered.

The titles change, the story stays the same.

Chosen by god, or chosen by man, what difference? One man and his court rules.

The room was beautiful and grand, steeped in elegance, as befitted a throne room.

The grandest, goldest framed paintings hung from the walls, depicting grander scenes, from grander days.

Regal red drapes hung tightly closed, barring access to the room, to those not of the court.

The carpet was also red, and of course, grand. It was intricately patterned with gold and cream squares, running perpendicular so as to look like diamonds.

Glimmering gold pillars stood strong, holding a muraled

ceiling upon their shoulders, a ceiling dripping with majestic crystal chandeliers, each groaning under their obnoxious load of candles.

The clinking of glasses can be heard, and the smacking of lips, wet with champagne, and anticipation, as the courtiers discuss their latest gossip, scheme or conquest.

The room reeked of privilege and abundance.

The very walls groaned and stretched in an effort to contain it.

Lucien hated it.

That he was here by duress, did nothing to honey the medicine. But consequence hung heavy upon him.

He stood at the edge of the room, leant against one of the grandly golden pillars. He cut a striking figure and had caught the eye of more than one already, in his ruby red jacket and waistcoat.

Taking a sip from his drink, his lip curled.

It wasn't to his taste, nor was anything about this.

A woman walked past him, dressed in an expensive emerald flapper dress. She was deep in conversation with another similarly dressed moth, this one in shades of lilac.

Lucien turned to watch her, narrowing his eyes as she moved into the throng of people.

"So, I said to François, I do not care what the foreman has said to you, any delay to the schedule is simply unacceptable. This is a business, not some sort of **charitable endeavour**". The moth in the emerald dress wrinkled her nose at this, as if the very taste of it passing her lips was unpleasant.

The lilac moth nodded empathetically at her friend's plight, as if this was the greatest inconvenience one could bear. "Of course, Adri, it is just simply **not acceptable**. These **people...** simply do not understand responsibility. They just expect everything to be given to them, on a platter. Well, I am afraid to say, that is simply not the way of things. If you desire something in life, you should darn well work for it!"

"Mm-hmm. Yes. Yes, exactly", queen moth Adri replied. "So anyway...I told Fran, I do not care a whit if those **people** are still there in two weeks, the demolition shall take place regardless. If they remain, on their heads be it. We have given them ample notice, a whole month in fact, to vacate, which we need not have done. I could have had François simply bring in the clearers".

Lucien turned away.

It was always the same with these people and their never-ending quest for more. There was no limit to their greed, and no answer to their avarice.

Somewhere along the way, they had lost something. Something that made them...human. Something indefinable. But what? And for what? Rich or poor, we all rot the same.

He moved away, walking slowly, keeping to the edges of the room, where it was quieter and shaded. As he walked, he watched the guests mingle, his face seemingly relaxed.

His eyes fell upon an extravagantly dressed lady, surrounded by moths. She wore a beautiful dress, scandalously cut a few inches shy of her knees. It was deeply darkly red, and she wore a glittering headband and gloves of the same colour.

By her side, as always, stood the waif.

He watched, as the waif soothed the lady, running her hand softly up and down her arm, as the lady entertained the moths.

The darkly red lady, as though feeling his eyes upon her, looked up. Her eyes met his, and she flashed him daggers, her jaw jutting forward aggressively, before returning her attention to the moths.

Lucien grimaced.

Of course you would be here.

Madame Dagger.

Turning away, he continued his prowl of the perimeter.

There.

The king.

The king was in late middle age, with smartly parted grey hair, and a thin moustache that curved ever so slightly downward.

He was also surrounded, but these were no moths. They were jackals. Desperate for any strip of flesh they could rend.

He had a hearty, booming laugh that made his ample stomach shake and wobble. Although he was round, the king was strong, with a broad back and sturdy shoulders.

Timing his moment, Lucien glided from the shadows, extending his hand fluidly as the king finished his conversation with one of the nipping jackals.

"Monsieur President, it is an honour", Lucien said respectfully, bowing his head.

The president turned, surprised to find he had been caught unawares. "Please, call me Renard", he said warmly, recovering his poise instantly and taking Lucien's hand in both of his own.

"I would speak with you, in private if I may?" Lucien said.

"What's that?" Renard replied distractedly, smiling like a cheshire cat at those vying for his attention from all sides.

"The Marquis sent me", Lucien said quietly, leaning in close.

Renard's face stilled, and he turned his full attention to Lucien. "Perhaps in private?" he suggested tightly.

"Perhaps yes", Lucien agreed graciously.

"This way". Renard gestured for Lucien to follow and began detracting himself from his hangers on.

"Yes, yes, I know, I know, I shall be right back, do not worry", Renard soothed, as the jackals howled in protest.

Renard led Lucien through to an adjoining room, with a high, curved, glass roof. He nodded to a man who stood guard at the door as he passed.

It was sparsely furnished in comparison to the ballroom. A few chandeliers hung from the ceiling, and a single red and gold oil painting dominated the wall at the far end of the room.

Though there was only a half-moon in the sky, it shone

brightly, bathing the room in an eerie glow. Lucien smiled, and looked up, admiring the night sky through the glass. It made him feel calm, and his mind drifted to calmer places.

He loved walking alone, on cold winter's nights, just him and the night. Tonight reminded him of such nights. He could almost feel the chill, winter air biting into his lungs and face. It made him feel alive. The low moans and howls of the wind, and its refreshing kiss. The rustle of the leaves, as they danced across the cobbles, their gentle scratching contributing beautiful music to the melody of the night. And the soft glow of the stars, and their lights in the sky, promising mystery and adventure.

Everything seemed more romantic, in the quiet and solitude of the night. Mysterious, and full of opportunity. In the night, things could be whatever you wanted them to be. The mundane became intriguing, and the stress and pressures of the world seemed far away.

"Ahem", Renard cleared his throat pointedly, fidgeting with his shirt sleeve.

"My apologies", Lucien said quickly, embarrassed.

Pay attention man.

Now is not the time to go walking in the moonlight.

It was Lucien's turn to clear his throat. "Yes, well, as I said, The Marquis sent me".

Renard nodded curtly. "And as I have already said to this...**Marquis**, I have no intention of resigning from office, no matter how many threats he makes, or however many coquettes he deigns to dangle". Renard spoke strongly, and with no sign of fear, which Lucien found admirable.

Admirable, but foolish.

Lucien sighed.

"I do not think you understand the position you're in", he said quietly.

"And what position is that?" Renard's eyes narrowed dangerously.

"This is not someone you can refuse, man", Lucien started to explain.

"Not someone I can refuse? I am the **President** of France! I can refuse whoever I damn well choose!" Renard reddened.

"Lower your voice", Lucien ordered, an angry undercurrent sparking in his voice.

"Lower my voice? Whoever do you think you are speaking to?" Renard seethed.

"Lower your voice", Lucien repeated, through gritted teeth this time.

"Lower my voice! Why, I...I have spent longer than you have stood on this earth, climbing, clawing and fighting my way through the ranks, to stand in this position, as I do before you today. I have fought treachery and intimidation from all sides, and seen off opponents far more formidable than you and your little **Marquis**". He took a deep breath, readying himself for more. "Now I don't want to hear another word from you-".

His words were cut off, for Lucien had pinned him against the wall.

"Now shut up and listen", he hissed, easily dangling Renard in his hand.

Renard recoiled, terrified, and unable to speak for a change.

"I do not have the patience for this", Lucien growled. "Your life is in danger, you pompous idiot. I've tried to be nice with you, but my patience is done. You have no idea how powerful these people are. You think you know power, because you bark, and those pathetic pups roll over? The Marquis is a different beast. He will kill you!"

"Th-these people?" Renard stammered, attempting to regain some of his composure, as sweat dripped from his forehead to his moustache.

"These people", Lucien repeated disbelievingly. "So that you listen to?"

Renard narrowed his eyes, some of his earlier haughtiness

returning.

Lucien shook him aggressively against the wall.

"Listen!" Lucien seethed. "This isn't some game you play in the assembly. This is life, or this is death. The choice is yours. You have not the power nor the wit to survive these people. Believe me".

Renard seemed subdued by the intensity of Lucien's words, but it was short lived, for scepticism soon took over his face.

"I...won't be intimidated", Renard said quietly, meeting Lucien's gaze now. "No matter how powerful you say these people are", he said, slightly more confidently.

Never have I seen such a brave fool, Lucien thought to himself sadly.

"No, you won't", Lucien said sadly. "You'll be dead".

Lucien dropped him to his feet.

Renard eyed him suspiciously, then drew himself up straight. "I do not think so. And your threats frighten me not at all".

Lucien's mouth fell open, unbelieving.

"And I've had about enough of this", Renard interrupted, before Lucien could retort. "Serge! Serge!" he shouted suddenly, turning and running toward the door.

The door burst open immediately, and a powerfully built man with a handlebar moustache and a tightly fitted suit ran through.

"Monsieur, what is it?" the man asked quickly.

"Detain this man and remove him from the premises at once-" Renard turned as he spoke, gesturing to where he had been standing with Lucien.

"Monsieur?" Serge asked, looking to the blank space where Renard had gestured.

"He's...he's", Renard trailed off. "Here somewhere".

"Monsieur?" Serge repeated, frowning.

"Ah, perhaps it was the brandy". Renard turned and grinned sheepishly. "Or the absinthe..."

Serge arched his eyebrows but said nothing.

Renard had a strange, pained look on his face, as if he could not accept what he had witnessed.

"Monsieur president, the people, they ask for you", Serge said, eager to break this strange silence that had developed.

Renard licked his lips, then drew them back, gnashing his teeth together nervously.

Serge cleared his throat pointedly. "And, there's more brandy...and the aperitifs...they are ready".

At this, Renard stilled, and looked straight ahead. "Aperitifs you say", he said quietly.

Renard turned, and smiled weakly, his head hung oddly low.

"Yes indeed, better to tolerate the interminable sycophants", he muttered distractedly.

Serge's eyes widened in surprise.

"Aheh, strictly in jest, of course", Renard assured Serge. He gave him a look reminiscent of a pleading schoolmaster now.

"I thought it was to better tolerate Madame President, monsieur". Serge's face was deadly serious.

Renards eyes popped. "Good lord man, don't let anyone catch you saying that", he replied nervously. "My life would not be worth living".

After scanning the room quickly to make sure they were not overheard, Renard grinned wickedly, then chuckled.

Serges mouth twitched.

"Come, man, back to the sycophants!" Renard grabbed Serge around the shoulder and steered him through the open door.

As he pushed Serge through the door, he paused, and looked back over his shoulder into the empty room. With a rather worried frown, he stepped through, and closed the door behind with a click.

Later that evening, when questioned about it, nobody could recall seeing a man in a ruby jacket.

Lucien stood atop the rooftop, arms clasped behind his back, listening to the sounds of the party gradually fade. His thoughts were maudlin and far from present, as they so often were.

This isn't what I wanted for my life.

Yet it's what you chose.

I didn't have a choice.

We all have a choice.

Quit your whining, or I'll give you something to whine about, his father's voice echoed aggressively in his head.

Are you man, or mouse? his mother's voice joined in scornfully. *The Tableau Haute would laugh you from the room if they heard you crying about how hard your life is. You do not know what hard is!*

Lucien shook his head agitatedly, as if to escape the memories. Better they remain locked away, where they could do no hurt.

Sighing deeply, he returned his focus to the party below.

He stood, silently, in the black Parisian night, watching as the guests left in various states of disrepair. Invisible as he was, held tight by the night, they could not see him.

As the last of the guests left, he prepared himself, as much as one can prepare oneself for such an undertaking.

*

Below the man with the bitter heart and the thankless task, a light flickered into life, bathing a large room in a gentle golden glow.

Renard looked up from the candle on his fine wooden desk and gazed out of the window, a pensive look on his face.

What a strange night, he thought tiredly.

As he began to take off his jacket and vest, a dark face flashed through his mind.

He paused for a moment, wincing.

"No", he said resolutely. Shaking his head, he tore his

cufflinks angrily from his sleeves, and threw them down on the desk where they clattered loudly.

He snatched up an expensive looking bottle of brandy from the dresser beside him, and threw a generous measure into a squat glass.

"Ah, délicieux", Renard said appreciatively, smacking his lips as he drained the brandy in one gulp, before hastily refilling it.

He sighed, and breathed deeply, as if some of the weight he had been carrying had been mercifully lifted from his shoulders.

Walking to the other side of his grandly proportioned room, he sank down heavily in his comfort chair, dropping his glass onto an ostentatious looking side table.

Leaning forward, he lit the fire that lay ready-made and waiting for him. "Ahh", he moaned appreciatively.

A comfortable warmth bathed the room as the flames started dancing merrily, as if they were glad to have finally been called to duty.

As he sat there, staring into the flames, a loud thud sounded from the hallway outside the room.

Startled, he swung round quickly, looking toward the door, his heart beating wildly in his chest.

"Who...who's there?" he called weakly. "I said who's there!" he shouted, more authoritatively this time.

Rising to his feet, he began to mutter angrily. "If this is the kitchen staff again, there will be trouble".

Storming over to the door, he jerked it open, and stepped out into the hallway, of the mind to give someone a tongue lashing.

He frowned, looking up and down the hallway for the source of the thud. But there was nothing, no one, not even Serge. He spat a few choice swear words into the ether.

Where was Serge?

What do I pay him for?

Probably filling his stomach.

Or trying his hand at one of the serving girls.

He smiled lazily, thinking of the young Portuguese girl, what was her name…Gloria. That was it. Yes Gloria. Marvellous young thing. Gloria. Perhaps he should call on her.

"Hmm", he hummed, his good nature restored. Waltzing back across the room, he sunk contentedly into his comfort chair. He might actually be able to enjoy his drink now.

He watched the shapes in the fire chase each other across the grate.

Relaxed at last, he sipped his drink appreciatively, smacking his lips from time to time, and eyeballing the brandy with adoration as he swilled it around the glass in between slurps.

"J'adore", he moaned.

"Mind that you do not let your colleagues catch you talking to yourself like this", a voice rumbled from behind.

Intent as he'd been on his brandy, he'd failed to notice the giant shadow creeping up on him, that now loomed over him like a mountain.

Jumping up from his seat, he spun wildly, sloshing brandy down his shirt and pants, flinching and cursing as he did.

Before him was a sight that chilled his blood like the winter wind.

A monstrosity of a man stood there, towering over him, grinning malevolently. His face was evilly shaded by the shadows cast by the fire.

"Monsieur president". The monstrous man inclined his head mockingly.

"Who are you?" the president shot back quickly, his face torn between incredulity at the size of the man, and panic at his intrusion. "And how did you get in here? I suggest you leave at once!" Renard's voice was surprisingly strong despite the fear he felt.

The giant man calmly stretched out an arm like a log of oak, and lifted Renard from his feet, holding him by his throat, the way a farmer might dangle a chicken for the block.

"I do not think you are in a position to make any suggestions, monsieur president", the giant rumbled, amused.

Renard gasped, and began to choke, lashing out with his fists, smashing them down on the man's arms and kicking at his midsection.

"Get...off...me" Renard gasped desperately, as his face reddened like a tomato ripe to pop.

The giant laughed sadistically, the wicked grin still on his face. "I think you should learn some manners, rabbit".

The giant placed his other frighteningly large hand atop Renard's head, and started to pull, and twist, ever so slowly, as if he were trying to uncork a particularly delicious bottle of wine.

"Aghhhhh!" Renard let out a strangled scream, as his neck began to stretch and crack.

His eyes rolled back in his head and his legs started to kick and thrash wildly at the torture.

Woosh.

A flash of black and red in the window.

Tumble.

A man vaulted through the window like an acrobat, hitting the floor with a thud and rolling to his feet in one fluid motion.

"Hadur!" the man growled violently. "What the fuck are you doing here?" He advanced menacingly on the giant.

Pausing his uncorking, the giant turned, Renard still dangling helplessly from his hand.

"Ah Lucien, was wonderin when you'd join us", Hadur said amiably.

"What are you talking about?" Lucien demanded.

"We had some...concerns...you might not be...up to the task". Hadur waggled Renard, as a child might their favourite toy.

"Put him down. Now!" Lucien spat, pointing commandingly at Hadur.

"As you wish". The giant dropped the dishevelled president

to the floor in a heap.

Renard lay on the floor gasping, too tired to move, his chest rising and falling in great heaves as he struggled to fill his lungs through his bruised windpipe.

"If you've been watching me, as it is clear you have, you know full well I intend to see this through". Lucien ground the words out, the muscles in his cheeks working furiously. "There is no need for this...**torture**". He hissed the last word, narrowing his eyes threateningly as he did so.

"Who said anything about need, Lucien, my soft stomached friend?" Hadur gave Lucien another of his simple smiles, made all the more horrifying by the genuine good humour and lack of emotion behind it.

"I want to," Hadur admitted, his smile darkening malevolently.

"He's a human being!" Lucien seethed. "As you are". He winced, as if the words cost him.

"I am no human!" Hadur roared suddenly, affronted at this slight. "How dare you liken me to this rabbit! I am an Ekur! A god! And these weaklings are to me, as hare to the hunter! To be coursed and consumed whenever I choose!" His voice boomed loudly around the room.

Lucien looked around nervously as the giant shouted, listening for any sound in the corridor.

Hadur laughed harshly. "Calm yourself Lucien, no one is coming".

Renard's breathing had slowed now, and he rubbed at his neck weakly, as he tried to pull himself up against the back of his chair.

Chuckling, as if the whole thing were highly amusing again, Hadur picked Renard up, and held him against the wall by the scruff of his neck.

His head lolled tiredly to one side.

Breathing shallowly, Renard turned to face the newcomer

and stared at him through bleary eyes.

"Y-You…" he said after a moment. "From the party".

Lucien stared wearily, his face before like stone, now crumbling sadly.

"Yes", Lucien admitted.

"So…I'm not mad…after all", Renard said slowly.

Lucien frowned, unsure what to make of this.

"I grow tired of this", Hadur interjected, rolling his head impatiently around his overly thick neck.

"If you don't have the stomach for it, I'm happy to oblige". Hadur tightened his grip on Renard's throat, who choked in pain, contorting his head wildly in an effort to escape the pain.

"No!" Lucien shouted desperately. "Stop…I'll do it".

Lowering his eyes, he walked over slowly to the two men.

If it must be, let it be me, let it be painless.

He deserves that at least.

The man is no coward.

He has borne this bravely.

And coward or not, no man deserves this.

Renard looked pleadingly at Lucien, the fear in his eyes cutting Lucien worse than any dagger ever could. "Please", he moaned.

"I'm sorry", Lucien said sadly, stepping forward and drawing Renard to him.

The Sohei

The room is small, and dimly lit, but not dark. It is tranquil. Peaceful. In the room is a man. He sits, legs crossed, eyes closed. His face is peaceful. His jet-black hair is pulled back tightly from his face, tied tightly at the nape of his neck.

The kimono he wears is black, near as black as his hair, and is cut at the elbows, revealing powerful forearms, taut with muscle.

The room he inhabits does not seem Parisian. Everything about it is... different. The floor is covered in beige mats and the walls are wood, adorned with red and white panels.

His golden skin glistens with perspiration, as if he has just exercised. A single candle on a low table casts an ethereal glow around him.

His features are strong and severe, with a hint of something else, perhaps humour, perhaps compassion. Brooding brows sit atop flat cheeks, and a strong jaw can be imagined beneath a thick, but well groomed, beard.

Breathing deeply, the man slowly pushes his hands out from him, then back, over and over.

Another slighter man, also wearing a kimono, stands silently watching, waiting.

As the seated man's movements come to an end, he smiles, and opens his eyes. "Kenshin, do you bring me good news?"

Kenshin stepped forward and bowed reverently, holding the movement for several seconds, before raising his head and responding.

"That depends", Kenshin said cagily.

"On?" the seated man asked.

Kenshin walked forward and dropped to his knees beside the man, handing him a newspaper as he did so.

On the front page was the headline: "Renard Assassinated, Marceau To Succeed". Beneath the headline was a black and white picture of President Renard smiling and laughing happily.

The man sat silently for a moment, staring at the paper, considering the news. "This is...unexpected", he said flatly.

"Indeed", Kenshin said grimly, moving away to prepare a pot of tea. "What does this mean for us, sensei Hiro?" He looked up eagerly.

"Hiro", Hiro said tiredly, correcting Kenshin for using the honorific.

"Hiro", Kenshin said, frowning, as if the word sounded foreign to his ears.

"And that remains to be seen...but it is not good...not good at all". Hiro spoke quietly, his brow furrowed deep in thought. "Of one thing, I am sure. I sense the Haitēburu in this".

"The Haitēburu!" Kenshin exclaimed. "Hir-" Kenshin stopped, licking his lips. "Sensei", he continued, seemingly calmer with this compromise.

Hiro closed his eyes, exasperated.

"You cannot be serious!" Kenshin resumed his bluster. He pulled his kimono down nervously before continuing. "What makes you think they have a hand in this?" he asked conspiratorially.

"The president of France, killed in the dead of night, no sign of forced entry, and no witnesses", Hiro said drily, waiting for Kenshin to catch on.

Kenshin blushed. He was still young, and often spoke before he thought.

"And with no hint as to who, or why?" Hiro continued, turning his attention back to the newspaper, snapping it crisply flat as he scanned the page for clarification.

"This is not...natural", Hiro said, the words leaving a sour taste in his mouth. "Renard was well liked. He had enemies, undoubtedly, but..."

Kenshin sat patiently, as his sensei drew his conclusions, the tea forgotten for the moment.

"This..." Hiro gestured at the headline of the paper. "Is not their way. They do not use dagger or blade. They use their tongue".

Setting the paper to one side, he looked at Kenshin contemplatively.

I hate it when he does this, Kenshin thought uncomfortably.

Just as Kenshin was about to rise and fetch the tea, glad for an excuse to flee, Hiro smiled warmly.

"Do not fret, Kenshin", Hiro said, in his usual calm, self-assured manner. "I have a plan".

He petted Kenshin companionably on the shoulder, then rose to his feet, perfectly in balance.

"Where are you going?" Kenshin asked quickly. "Do you require my assistance?" He deepened his voice in an attempt to hide his fear.

"To the Catacombs", Hiro replied cryptically. "There is someone I must see".

Kenshin smiled weakly.

"Do not worry", Hiro added, after seeing the look on his student's face. "Look after the temple", he said reverently.

Kenshin looked appraisingly around the small, sparsely furnished room that would not have passed muster as a broom cupboard in their native land.

Their eyes met, and Kenshin's mouth twitched. They both burst into good-hearted laughter.

It was the laughter of two companions who had shared both trial and tribulation before...and would again.

*

Hiro stood silently in the rain outside the children's shelter, his face a mask, his hands clasped comfortably behind his back.

He cut a striking figure in his handsome black robe, with his hair blowing dramatically in the wind, and his wooden tachi scabbard hanging loosely across his back.

Pray that I have no use for you, Saisei, he thought to himself, fingering the scabbard comfortingly. As his finger touched the wood, a memory sang through his mind.

*

A man, sitting upon a high ledge.

In front of him, a waterfall. The man wears a grey robe, dripping wet from the heavy rain that falls relentlessly upon him from above.

Despite this, the man sits, contemplatively, with eyes closed, legs crossed, the expression on his face serene.

In front of him, the waterfall gushes down, and down, a sheer mountain face, the water roaring deafeningly.

Across his lap lies an empty scabbard. A scabbard of plain wood, without adornment.

Beneath him, two red and white pagodas sit at either end of a beautiful red bridge that arches in front of the waterfall.

A scratching noise from behind distracts the man from his reverie. Opening his eyes in irritation, he waits.

A man in a black robe eventually pulls himself over the edge. As the man in the grey robe closes his eyes once more, the newcomer sits down beside him, crossing his legs and closing his eyes in the same fashion.

"Did I disturb you?" the man in black enquired, without opening his eyes.

"...No..." the man in grey responded after a moment.

Grinning smugly, the man in black replied. "Then why were your eyes open?"

"How did you even..." Stopping himself, the man in grey breathed deeply, attempting to compose himself.

"You see all, sensei", the man in grey grudgingly conceded.

"I **feel** all, little hare", Sensei retorted pompously, raising his chin and running his fingers through his drooping white moustache and beard, as was his way when lecturing the little hare.

"I **hate** when you call me that", Little Hare bristled, spitting the words out, his jaw clenched in displeasure.

"I know...it gives me power over you", Sensei replied.

"Then why do it?" Little Hare asked, still chafing at the embarrassing nickname Sensei had chosen for him when he'd donned the grey robe.

"To give you power" Sensei replied cryptically, watching the waterfall, wrapping his beard around his finger.

"That doesn't make any sense. How can it give me power, if it gives you power over me?" Little Hare had abandoned all pretence of contemplation now, and sat watching Sensei intently.

"When you understand the tortoise, you'll understand the answer to your question". Rising to his feet, Sensei brushed down his robe and gave Little Hare one of his maddeningly, infuriatingly smug smiles, before climbing down from the ledge without another word.

"What the..." Little Hare started aggressively, then caught himself.

If I hear one more mention of this fucking turtle... tortoise... whatever! Little Hare thought to himself savagely.

I will stamp the bastard thing out of existence.

With great effort, he attempted to calm himself.

Closing his eyes, he took deep breaths, focusing on the sound of his breath, the sound of the wind, the rain. Anything but his own anger.

One day I will show you...sensei...what the tortoise knows. What the 'Little Hare' knows.

And you shall rue that day.

*

Opening his eyes outside the children's shelter, Hiro grinned wistfully. "You were ever the hare", he said to himself.

The rain had stopped, and with it the wind. Above, a sea blue sky had chased the clouds away.

Hiro didn't have to wait much longer before the door to the shelter opened, and a group of people exited the building.

They must be the volunteers... and yes, there he is.

Spotting a young man with hair golder than his skin, he unfurled his hands from behind his back and crossed the street to approach him.

As he approached the group, he caught some of their discussion.

"I'll have you know my pot-au-feu is very highly regarded, actually!" The golden-haired man shot at a tall, portly man with a friendly, cherub shaped face.

"Regarded? Regarded by who? Your grand-mere?" the portly man responded drily.

"Well, yes alright... she is partial to it, now that you mention it. But she's not the only one! The children love it too!" The golden-haired man exclaimed indignantly; his brows furrowed. His cheeks reddened, as he bristled at the indignity of his famous pot-au-feu being so publicly denounced.

The group laughed good naturedly, smiling warmly at the golden-haired man. That they were fond of him was clear, and they enjoyed teasing him too apparently.

As the laughter died down, the chef of the pot-au-feu included, the group's attention shifted to the oddly dressed man standing silently a few feet away.

"Can we help you, monsieur?" the portly man asked gruffly, taking a challenging step forward, placing himself between the man and the group.

"Yes", the stranger replied simply. "I would like to speak to Gabriel in private, if that is permissible".

"About what?" The portly man crossed his thick arms across

216

his chest.

"Do I know you, monsieur?" Gabriel chimed from the back of the group.

Stepping forward, Gabriel placed a reassuring hand on his friend's shoulder. "It's alright, Hubert, I don't sense that this man has any bad intentions".

Hubert shifted on his feet, cocking his head from side to side as if to assess if the stranger was a threat.

"Besides, you're all just over here, should he try to capture and make off with me", Gabriel joked. Sensing his joke was not enough to dissipate the tension, Gabriel continued, "Perhaps he's heard stories of my cooking prowess from the children and wishes to hire me as his private chef".

The group laughed and Hubert's face softened, a cheeky boyish grin sneaking through his gruff pretence, transforming his features from intimidating, to loveable and soft.

"Alright", Hubert said gruffly, his mind not made up about the stranger, but his doubts for now, on ice. "We'll wait for you over here if you need us".

Quietly watching the dynamic of the group, Hiro smiled.

"So, what is it you wanted to talk to me about? Err...sorry I didn't catch your name?" Gabriel steered Hiro a short distance away from the group.

Too beautiful to be handsome, and too caring to be conceited, Hiro thought as he studied Gabriel.

"Hiro", Hiro responded, dropping his eyes and bowing his head.

"Hiro...what an interesting name", Gabriel frowned and cocked his head to one side. "How marvellous!" His face broke into a child-like grin.

"It is my name", Hiro said simply, his eyes twinkling with amusement.

"So, you mentioned you were looking for me?" Gabriel said.

"You walk a dangerous path", Hiro said suddenly. "You

should walk another, lest it be your last".

"My path? Whatever do you mean?" Gabriel's face creased sceptically.

"The man. Lucien. He is not as he seems". Hiro watched Gabriel carefully, studying his reaction before continuing. "Your path has joined with his now, whether you like it or not. And that path only leads one place".

"And where might that be?" Gabriel said coldly, folding his arms self-consciously, his expression hostile now. He'd had his fill of these men and their doomsaying.

"Ashes", Hiro said gravely.

"Ashes? Whatever do you mean ashes?" Gabriel snapped, angry now. When no answer was forthcoming, he continued. "Stop being so damn cryptic! Lucien is fine, and so am I. If you don't have anything of worth to tell me, then say nothing at all and leave me alone, because I've had my fill of this nonsense!"

Pushing past him, Gabriel stormed off into the distance, away from the strange man.

"Gabriel!" Hubert shouted, running forward, unsure of whether to chase after him or not.

"What did you say to him, eh?" Hubert rounded aggressively on Hiro, prodding him accusingly in the chest.

Hiro stood silently, hands clasped calmly behind his back.

"I said, what did you say!" Hubert shouted, his demeanour once more challenging and protective. It put Hiro in the mind of a mother bear protecting her cub.

"Bah!" Hubert raised his hands dismissively, as if to wash them of the situation.

He returned to the group who immediately put their heads together and started muttering, questioning Hubert, whilst glancing at Hiro distrustingly through gaps in the group of bodies packed together.

Ah, Little Hare, that could have gone better.

What would the tortoise have done, in such a circumstance? A maddeningly smug voice rang through his mind.

"To hell with the tortoise", Hiro grumbled to himself quietly.

Humble Beginnings

Rudra had always been headstrong. Little Think First Rudy her mother had called her, in what she thought was a cute joke, and a play on the fact that she never in fact, thought first before acting.

Although she was headstrong, she wore her heart on her sleeve. With Rudra, what you saw was what you got. She was quick to anger, and quick to forget.

And as quick as she was to lose her temper, she was quicker to make it up to you later with a thoughtful gesture, or a joke and a smile.

She was a big girl for thirteen, already tall and showing signs of the beautiful woman she would one day become. Though she wasn't quite there yet, with her over-long arms that hung down to her knees, and her girlish features.

Where she got her athletic frame from, no one knows. It wasn't from her mother, who was a fragile wisp of a woman. And her mother wouldn't tell her much about her father, who she'd never met.

She was really quite an admirable young woman, given the circumstances. Which makes her story all the more upsetting.

Rudra's story begins years ago in her family "home", if you could call it that.

It begins at a crossroads. A crossroads not of her making, that shapes who she becomes and colours her life irreparably for evermore.

The catalyst for this crossroad...her stepfather.

A foul man, in every sense of the word. A man who took every lemon life gave him and spat back sour pips. A man who thrived on the misery of others and seemingly lived to inflict it.

A man who lived for the warped and twisted sense of power he gained by abusing and preying upon the weak and the vulnerable.

He was only happy, when others were not.

A bully. A drunk. A child abuser.

What chance did little Rudra have, with such a thing for her "father"? Bear this in mind as you think of her.

Not all evil comes from the same place.

*

It was a beautifully sunny day. Peeking through the bleary eyes of the just awoken, Rudra could already see the golden rays of sun sparkling prettily through the curtains of her little room, and she cherished them.

Summer was her favourite time of year. She couldn't explain why entirely, but it made her happy. Everything was easier when the sun was shining, and the sky was blue.

Yawning deeply she stretched, her long arms contorting outwards at strange angles, as she blinked hard to clear the sleep from her eyes.

"Mmm", she mumbled softly.

"It's summer, Alleycat!" she exclaimed excitedly, a little louder this time.

She rolled over and cuddled a rather well-fed ginger and white striped cat that was sharing the bed with her. Burying her head in his fur she rubbed her face against his, purring softly as he did so.

Alleycat glared at her appraisingly with his one good eye, but tolerated the invasion of his personal space. Unfortunately, his other eye had been lost in one of his many fights with the other feral cats who lived in the alleys behind her house.

He was covered in scars, had patches missing from his fur and was generally rather anti-social, hissing at almost anyone who tried to approach him. Almost anyone. Rudra loved him.

She'd been feeding him generous portions of just about anything she could find, since deciding to adopt him, and rescue him from the alleys behind her house he lived in. He had thickened around the midsection rather noticeably since his change in circumstance.

He wasn't much of a morning person, and was probably expecting food.

She didn't blame him. It was time for breakfast after all, and Alleycat did not take such matters lightly.

"Alright alright", she grumbled. "I swear cat, I am the pet, and you my master".

Alleycat stared at her appraisingly, as if he concurred wholly.

Although she grumbled, she didn't mean it. She loved Alleycat, more than perhaps anything in the world. Well, almost anything.

Alleycat was simple. If he was annoyed, you knew about it. You didn't have to play games or try and decipher weird behaviour to know if it was safe to approach him. He just hissed. Rudra liked that, she felt safe around Alleycat.

He liked her too, sensing a kindred sadness, and a deep longing to be loved, beneath layers of distrust.

Creeping quietly from her room so as not to wake her mother or Beni, she padded along the narrow hallway to the small kitchen area of their apartment.

She began to make some breakfast for her and Alleycat, who had immediately sprung into action and followed her out of the room with the prospect of food on the horizon.

Benoni said they were lucky to have this place, but she wasn't so sure. Monsieur Jean-Baptiste on the radio called it apache town, where they lived.

But Benoni didn't like him, Monsieur Jean-Baptiste, and he didn't like any mention of their living in the "apache town" for that matter either. Benoni said he was a useless old fool and nothing like Monsieur Claudius, the old president.

The kids in the neighbourhood just laughed and called them pauvre maison, and made fun of her, singing rhymes where they always inevitably rhymed words like poor and slum into the rhyme. They weren't particularly good rhymes, but it hurt anyway.

Rudra always rose to their bait and had got into more than one fight about it, flying at the bigger girls with her fists swinging, wild black hair whipping around behind her as her eyes filled with angry tears.

She didn't know why it made her so mad, they were just words, and not even very good words. The rhymes were terrible after all! But she was always mad lately.

"There. Isn't that nice, Monsieur Alleycat?" Beaming down at Alleycat, she petted his head softly, her eyes filled with pure and unconditional love.

Alleycat gave a noncommittal shake of his head then returned to his food, which for Alleycat was thanks indeed. The last cat who tried to interfere with him while he was eating...well, suffice to say he only did it once.

"Now, for moi?" Rudra muttered quietly while sifting through the cupboards. "Mmm, lovely". Finding some leftover baguette from the day before, she contended herself with a little bread, jam and butter.

The fact that there was butter cheered her even more, usually there was not a lot to eat in the mornings. Benoni was not an early riser, and her mother left early for work.

She supposed it was because it was the weekend, her mother would have wanted to make sure there was a baguette and croissant for breakfast, for when Beni woke up. She knew better than to touch the croissant though.

Shuddering, she shook her head vigorously from side to side, a pained expression on her face, as if trying to forget a particularly painful and unpleasant memory.

"I didn't touch your croissant. I didn't touch your croissant. I didn't touch your croissant", she mumbled to herself quietly in a sickly mantra as she clenched her fists.

For a second, the sun didn't seem so bright.

She closed her eyes tightly and held them closed for several seconds. When she opened them, the frown lines disappeared from around her eyes.

"That was stupid of me, wasn't it Alleycat", Rudra asked desperately, rubbing Alleycat up and down his back in a frenzied manner. "I shouldn't have taken his croissant! Beni provides for us after all. He works hard to put food on the table and..." She faded off quietly. Her eyes wore a faraway look, her thick brows creased, half up, half down, torn between confusion and self-pity.

Alleycat, who since finishing his own breakfast, had been sitting silently on the table beside her and eyeing her jam with interest, gave her a brief nuzzle, rubbing his furry ginger head across her face.

Without thinking, she began running her hand along his back, taking comfort in the soft feel of his fur, and the gentle purring he offered her as his way of soothing her emotional turmoil.

Her bread and jam half eaten, she rose suddenly from the table and took her dish to the sink to wash it, moving without thought. For some reason she'd lost her appetite, which was a shame, but the sun was shining, and she would beg for some food later with Nico and the others.

She began cleaning the dish in the sink, and thought about putting her leftover breakfast in the poubelle, then thought better of it.

"On second thought..." She wrapped the bread in a sheaf of

old newspaper and placed it to one side. She'd take it out with her and eat it later. That was smarter. Less likely to wake the beast.

"Alright, all done Monsieur Alley-".

Crash. **Bang**. **Clatter**. **Hiss**.

"Oh no! Oh no no no...look what I've done Alley", she moaned frantically from the floor. She'd fallen over Alleycat as she turned around too quickly without looking.

While falling, she had knocked over the chair she was sitting on, and somehow taken the pan from the top of the kitchen counter with her too, which accounted for all of the clattering. It wobbled loudly to a stop after seven or eight loud wobbles.

Alleycat hissed once angrily, then pitter pattered back over to her and sat a few feet away watching her dubiously.

"I'm sorry! I'm sorry! I didn't mean to hurt ya Alley!" she stammered.

"Cette foutue fille", an angry voice came from the bedroom at the end of the hallway outside the kitchen. The voice was muffled, but she'd heard it enough before to know exactly what was being said. "Je vais la tuer!"

"Merde merde merde..." Rudra said to herself under her breath, her eyes darting around the room like a doe deciding where best to run from the hounds.

Making up her mind, she picked up Alleycat and made a dash for the front door. Patting the pockets of her homespun trousers wildly, she cursed again under her breath.

"Putain, putain de merde!" She stamped her foot in exasperation, before turning and bolting down the hall to the room she shared with Alleycat.

She could hear Benoni stirring now in earnest, and the creak of the bed he shared with her mother as he rolled himself out of it.

"Where did I put it, where where where!" Her mother was always telling her to be more organised with her things, but like most teenagers, it fell on deaf ears.

After a few fraught seconds that felt like a lifetime, she found the key to her escape, and ran back out of her room and down the narrow hallway toward the front door.

Unfortunately, as she made it halfway down the hallway, the door to her mother and Beni's room crashed open and Beni burst out.

He looked terrifying standing there outlined in the darkness of the hallway. She could only see his eyes, glittering malevolently, and a small part of his nose and mouth, where some light from the bedroom behind was filtering through. It was enough.

She turned and ran to the door palming her key smoothly into the lock.

She felt a surge of relief as the key turned and the lock clicked open, not this time! She whipped the door open and light from the corridor outside flooded in, blinding her temporarily.

Run run run, was all she could think, before her world turned upside down.

She felt a strong hand grip her upper arm and pull hard. The next thing she knew, she was lying on her back looking up at the ceiling.

She felt as if someone had knocked all the air out of her. She lay panting, wheezing badly, desperately trying to suck in gulps of air.

A bloodshot pair of eyes appeared on top of her, and a pair of thick hands gripped her by the scruff of her shirt. The hands lifted her up and dangled her helplessly just above the floor.

She felt, if not saw, Beni's leg kick out from behind him and the front door slam shut.

Just then, she heard Alleycat hiss wildly, and saw a flash of fur move across the room as quick as the wind howling through a cold winter's night.

"Arghhhh! Fucking cat!" Beni lashed out hard with his

forearm catching Alleycat in the face, as he unleashed a hailstorm of claws, fur and teeth on Beni in a noble attempt to protect his human from the much larger threat.

"Alley no!" Rudra cried out in anguish, as she heard Alley hit the kitchen table and cry out weakly. He tried vainly to raise himself to his feet for another attack, then slumped back down with a feeble cry.

Turning his attention back to his beloved stepdaughter, Beni shook her hard then slammed her down against the floor.

"Bitch", he snarled aggressively in her face, spraying her with tiny drops of spittle as he did. "You never learn. It's time to fucking teach you the hard way..."

Rudra lay stunned. Unable to speak or move. The familiar paralysing terror had crept back upon her, seizing her in its icy grasp, as it always did.

It felt as though invisible tentacles had spread throughout her body, wrapping around all of her muscles and squeezing them in place.

Unfortunately for her, Beni was doing all of the moving. He struck her hard in the face with an open palm and bright lights flashed in front of her eyes.

"How many times do I have to tell you!" he screamed, shaking her, as he slapped her again and again. "No". **Slap**. "Noise". **Slap**. "In". "**The fucking mornings!**"

He finished with a particularly brutal slap that caught her hard across the nose and mouth.

She groaned weakly, all the strength gone from her.

The room had started to darken, the walls pressing in and closing around her, when she heard a horrible scream that cut her to the core of her being.

It was like a tiny pocket knife slicing into her heart just enough to make her bleed, but not deep enough to mercifully end her torment.

It was pitiful. Pleading. Desperate. And completely

powerless.

"Noooooo! Beni no! Get away from her!" She watched as her mother ran from the bedroom and leapt at Beni, flailing at him feebly with her fists, hitting, scratching and clawing in an attempt to dislodge him.

"Fuck off!" Beni turned and pivoted, hitting her with the back of his closed fist with the weight of his hips behind it. The sound of his fist connecting was sickening, and rang out with a horrible crunch.

Her mother hit the wall hard, and slumped down like a marionette cut from her strings, eyes closed and blood running from her nose.

Rudra felt a rage course through her then. Her blood boiled as her face heated up like a furnace. Screaming in fear, frustration and something more primal, she rolled to her knees and punched Beni as hard as she could between his legs.

She wasn't entirely sure why she did it, but she heard Nico's cocky voice course through her mind vividly straight after, as she pictured him swaggering across the park in front of her, throwing punches and feints at the air.

"Guys are easy Rudy. I'll tell you why. I'll tell ya the secret. It don't matter how big they are. How scary they seem. Fastest way to take em down. You just hit em straight in the plums. Down they'll go. Like a vagrant kicked out inta the street at closing time. My cousin told me that, when he come back from overseas", Nico said impressively.

Seemingly Nico wasn't full of hot air this time, as Beni groaned pitifully and fell to the floor clutching his lower abdomen, rocking back and forth in pain.

He cursed and glared at her, a look of purest loathing.

Wasting no time, Rudra dragged herself to her feet and stumbled over to her mother. She was unsteady on her feet, and her vision was still badly blurred.

"Mama! Mama! Wake up!" Shaking her, Rudra buried her

head in her chest. The scent of her mother's lavender hair soap filled her nostrils, as her thick, white blonde hair fell across her face. Just for a moment, she felt safe, and forgot the horror of her circumstance.

Her mother moaned, slowly opening her eyes.

"Rudy..." She turned her head, which had been resting peacefully on her shoulder. "Get out of here". She pushed at Rudra weakly.

"Mama..." Rudra pleaded softly.

"Go!" Her mother said more insistently, pushing her harder this time.

"You better go bitch before I get my hands on you!" Benoni snarled ferally from the floor a few feet away, before continuing to writhe in pain.

He appeared to be getting his breath. Rudra didn't want to risk it. Her mama was alright for now.

Stepping to her feet, she took a deep breath, then hopped nimbly past Beni and opened the door.

She made to leave, then turned back, looking down at Beni, then through the wall to the kitchen, a tortured expression on her face.

I'm not leaving him. I'll never leave fucking leave him! Her mind exploded abruptly, drowning the terror threatening to engulf her.

The ferocity of her feelings shook her.

Making up her mind, she braced herself then dashed past Beni, who pawed at her weakly from the floor, into the kitchen. Stooping down, she picked up Alleycat.

"It's alright Alley", she murmured softly to him, kissing him gently on the back of the head.

A tired meow was all he could manage in reply.

Time to go Rudy.

She braced herself once more, and hopped over Beni, who had rolled himself to block her path out of the kitchen into the hallway.

He grabbed at her with his free hand, as she jumped nimbly past. Unfortunately, he managed to get a grip on her ankle with the tips of his fingers as she landed. He frantically scratched and clawed his way to a firmer grip.

Panicking, Rudra gave a primal shriek. "No!"

Alleycat hissed feebly from her arms, wriggling as if to unleash another barrage of claws on Beni, but not quite having the energy to manage more than a feeble wave of his paw.

"Got you now, bitch". Beni grinned up at her evilly, the light from the hallway throwing his hard face into profile.

She hated everything about his face. The fast-fading circle of wispy, straw coloured hair that sat atop his head like the twisted imitation of a halo. His square, flat nose that had been broken twice, with its ugly bumps.

But it was his eyes that she detested the most. They were small and beetle brown, and in their depths, she saw nothing. Nothing at all. And that scared her greatly.

She felt like breaking down and crying, like she always did. But today something was different. She wouldn't be his victim again. Not today.

"NO!" Kicking out hard with her foot, she caught him hard in the jaw, just as he was reaching across for her with his other hand, using his hatred of her as fuel to overcome his gut-wrenching pain.

Thunk.

The sound of her shoe catching him rang out smoothly. To Rudra it was the most satisfying thing she had ever heard, it sounded sweeter than any song she'd ever heard.

Sweeter than her mama's voice, sweeter than Alleycat's purs. It was the sound of victory. Victory over Beni, but most importantly, victory over self.

She had caught him well, and he fell backwards with a grunt and a thud, and lay still on the floor, mercifully moving no more.

She ran back into the hallway and knelt down, kissing her mama lovingly on the cheek, before turning and leaving.

She didn't look back.

Humbler Middles

"He can't keep getting away with this Rud!" Nico raged, throwing his hands up in exasperation, then punching the wall without thinking.

Dust and debris from the crumbling wall immediately exploded outward like a beige coloured mushroom cloud into his face and lungs.

He started to cough and splutter in an effort to clear his airway. "Cazzo bastardo!....d..a..m..n...poor houses!"

He looked funny standing there, like a ghost. Caked in a cloak of soot, dust and grime covering his usually handsome olive skin.

Rudra didn't laugh as she might have on any other day, she simply sat quietly staring at the far wall, her eyes faraway. Poking fun of Nico was usually one of her favourite pastimes, but today she didn't quite feel like it.

Nico was her closest friend, after Alleycat of course, and she spent a lot of time with him. He was just a little bit older than her, but the same height. Nico said that's because she was real tall, and "they don't make em big as you back in the ol country, they make em reaaal wide".

He'd then slapped his stomach and made that stupid face he was so fond of making, where he puffed his cheeks out like a pufferfish and pushed his ears forward so they looked like miniature sails.

It always made her smile. His stomach had started to become a little more noticeable under his shirts as of late when she thought about it.

Rudra didn't mind though. Thick or thin, rich or poor, as long as he was nice to her, that was all that mattered.

She'd wandered for hours after she left home, aimlessly through the streets of Paris. She didn't know how long for exactly, but her feet were sore, and her legs were protesting too by the time she stopped.

Nico had found her as the sun was setting, casting a warm, dark orange glow over the dusty and disrepaired streets of Paris they knew as home.

It was almost as if the sun understood what had happened, and was shining in a particularly beautiful and calming manner, in an effort to comfort her. As if to say, I saw, I understood, and everything will be alright.

He steered her off the street and up into the little safe haven they'd built for themselves.

It wasn't much, Safe Place, but it was theirs.

They called it their 'Safe Place', but it wasn't actually all that safe. At least not in the literal sense of the word. It was a little room on the top floor of a rundown 'poor house' that had been condemned and would likely be knocked down at some point.

It was accessible only via a damaged fire escape at the back side of the building. The lower levels were unstable, so they didn't hang out there anymore, not after Nico fell through the second floor and cut his leg open.

It was safe, because there were no adults there.

"Back home, he'd **never** get away with it Rud, I tell ya!" Nico paced backwards and forwards in front of her angrily, shaking his head every now and then and cursing quietly under his breath in Italian. "You know what they do to guys like this back home?" He spat on the floor and drew his finger under his neck in a semi-circular motion, like the slashing of a knife.

Nico's family had moved to Paris for a fresh start, but so far all they'd found was pain and suffering.

Nico's dad had died the same year they moved here from the

'old country'. Whatever that was, she wasn't quite sure, but Nico said it a lot. She'd asked Nico, but he just laughed at her and started speaking rapidly in Italian, and making animated gestures with his hands. It looked like he was describing a beautiful landscape and scenery, but she couldn't be sure.

He was pretty animated most of the time, even about food. She found this strange, but her diet consisted mostly of stale bread and leftover pot-au- feu that she wolfed down when she could find it to keep the hunger pains at bay. It sounded like Nico's mother still found it in her to cook him hearty meals from their homeland.

She was grateful that Nico cared about her. He always cared about her. But she couldn't bring herself to relive the events of the morning by speaking about it.

Better to bury it deep, where it couldn't hurt her.

She'd tried to come to terms with the reality of her situation before, but she just couldn't. It was if there was a mental, or rather emotional, block preventing her. Like a huge slab of granite stood gatekeeper to her emotions, and she didn't have the tools to pierce through it.

"Thanks Nico", she forced a grin.

Nico looked at her with a worried expression on his face. Her pretend everything is alright smile obviously hadn't fooled him, as he stepped quickly over to her and knelt down in front of her, wrapping his arms around her and pulling her to him.

He held her there tightly for a long time, with her head on his shoulder, as her eyes filled quietly with tears.

She let them fall freely but uttered not a sound. She didn't know how to be vulnerable with anyone else, and letting Nico hear her cry was not something that she knew how to do.

It was enough, though. As her tears continued to fall, she shook softly. So softly that Nico wouldn't feel it, and she'd be safe.

Nico felt it and said nothing. He knew better.

One day I'll end that bastard, Nico thought to himself darkly, his leopard brown eyes sparkling brightly in the darkness.

Struggling with the depth of his feelings, Nico empathised with Rudra. If he found consoling her this difficult, he couldn't comprehend how she must be feeling.

Nico had a rough start in life, but he had his ma, and she loved him. Rudy still had her ma too, but she may as well have not one.

What kind of a ma would bring a man like Beni into their little girl's life? He couldn't reconcile how a woman like Rudy's ma, who was soft as down and wouldn't hurt a fly, could marry such a cold and heartless bastard, and allow him to abuse her and her girl in such a way.

He didn't understand it. But there was so much he didn't understand about the world still. Like how a man as strong and full of life as his pop could make it back to them from all the dangerous places he'd been in the army, then get got by some sickness that they couldn't even see.

He hoped one day it would make more sense, but he doubted it, cynical and world weary even at his young age.

Unfortunately, he'd seen enough of life already and lived beyond his years, his worldview irreparably warped and twisted by the sharp edges of the world pressing in around him.

He didn't care, he'd live a good life anyway, "la bella vita", just like his pop used to say. And if life tried to stab him with its sharp edges, well he'd kick it straight back in the balls.

Unbeknownst to either of them, Nico had begun to rock Rudy back and forth as she sobbed silently. Lost as they both were in their thoughts, neither of them were really conscious of it, but both took from it in their own way.

Rudy took from Nico some semblance of the love and safety one feels when they are protected, something she needed sorely. And Nico took from Rudy the deep need to feel as though he could protect the ones he loved, a feeling he'd had since his pop had passed, and life had stabbed them deep.

Feeling Rudra go still in his arms, Nico came to, his mind brought back to the present. He pet her hair softly and marvelled at it. It never ceased to amaze him. He'd never seen hair so black.

It reminded him of some of the wild cat pelts his pop had taken him to see back home. There was one in particular he remembered, a large black cat with eyes like yellow gemstones.

The panther! That was it. Rudy kind of reminded him of that panther.

She was wild, and fierce, and had a stare that could pierce right through you like a knife when she was mad, though she didn't always know it.

When Benoni wasn't around, Nico saw the panther Rudy, the true Rudy he called it. When Beni had been wailing on her or her mom, she was more like a tiger with a broken leg. But instead of hiding herself away to heal like a tiger might, she hid inside herself, hiding her true self.

Nico didn't like seeing her like that, it was like…a crime of nature or something, to see someone like Rudy wounded in such a way, forced to hide her light and pad softly around like a kitten after her ma. She was born to prowl, born to strut.

"You alright Rud?" Nico asked quietly

"Yeh…" she responded shyly, but more truthfully this time. They lay there quietly a moment before Rudy looked up at him and said, "Kinda hungry".

Nico stared blankly at her, his mouth hanging slightly open, like a fish sucking in air underwater.

Finding this amusing, she opened her mouth in imitation of him, then started opening and closing it in an exaggerated 'o' shape.

"What the-". Before he could say another word, Rudra started laughing. Lightly at first, then she started to laugh in earnest. It was infectious, and Nico broke into a warm smile and started laughing too, unable to resist her contagious joy.

He loved that she didn't let life shape her the way it wanted. She took her cuts, then got right back at it, just like him. Sure the scars were there, but we all got scars. She didn't let them define her.

"I shoulda know better than to bring you up here without some grub", he teased.

"You shoulda", she replied, rising to her feet and brushing herself down.

"C'mon", Nico threw his arm around her lovingly, and led her out of Safe Place, into the night.

*

She felt better after some food. Nico had spent the whole time talking to her in an exaggerated Italian 'tough guy' accent, imitating Big Tony, the owner of the pizza parlour. That helped too. Her cheeks were a little sore from all the laughing in fact.

She'd almost forgotten what had happened that morning. Almost.

It was dark now, fully dark, and a horrible feeling appeared in the pit of her stomach, like lukewarm lava roiling around uncomfortably. It threw her into a state of uneasy equilibrium.

She'd have to go back soon. And she was dreading it. Nico had offered to let her stay at the apartment he shared with his mother, but she said no. She wanted to see how her mama was. Beni hit her pretty hard and she worried.

After looping around the streets in front of the place she lived three times, she sighed with resignation and looked up at the building they were supposed to call home.

Alleycat had limped off earlier, probably to sleep in his favourite spot beneath the bar in the alley behind their house. He usually did this when things were bad at home. She hoped the other cats would be nice to him, and give him clemency for the night.

Traipsing up the stairs, she was outside the door before she knew it, her journey cruelly short.

237

Placing her key in the lock, she opened the door and pushed it open cautiously, looking before she lept.

*

Immediately, she knew something was wrong. Badly wrong. How she knew she couldn't say, but the feel of it in the air was cloying and she almost gagged.

Her heart began to beat like a drum, and she felt the familiar icy feeling begin in her veins, a premonition of what she did not know.

Stepping in and closing the door behind her, she called for her mama.

Her mama didn't call back, but she could hear a horrible sound coming from behind the closed bedroom door, like a butcher pounding some meat with his fists to tenderise it. And something else. A low cry.

Breathing rapidly, she started to feel dizzy, her breaths coming in shorter and sharper gasps as she began to hyperventilate.

She walked slowly toward the door, looking around the apartment, noting the empty bottle of absinthe and the empty spirit glass on the kitchen table.

She swallowed deeply and clenched her jaw tightly to stop her lip from quivering.

She heard it then once more, the low cry, louder now. Her mothers cry.

No no no, her mind wailed in protest. *Not again. Not today. I can't. Please no.*

Smack, smack. That horrible sound again.

"If you can't teach the pup, teach the bitch!" Beni growled beastily.

She was at the door now, her hand raising and reaching toward the handle, pulled as if by fate, every instinct screaming at her, every nerve ending on fire.

"After everything I do for you. Taking you in and providing

238

for you and that bitch. I didn't have to do it, not a lot of men would. And this is how you repay me?" Beni spat, as her mother sobbed weakly, moaning 'please no' over and over again, as if the mantra would somehow protect her from his fists.

"What's a good man got to do to get a little peace and quiet in his own home? Attacking me and defending her after she pisses all over everything I do for both of yous. Do I ask you for much? All I ask for is a little respect. But do I get it? No!" Beni screamed suddenly, the wrath and rage in his voice reaching a crescendo.

Then, **smack**.

A smack so loud it made Rudy jump backwards in shock.

Then, silence.

Rudy stood rooted to the spot, too scared to move, before she realised she couldn't hear her mama any more.

"Mama?" She called quietly through the door.

Nothing.

She licked her lips. Her upper lip started to twitch strangely, in strange spasms.

Why can't I hear mama.

As if in a trance, she saw her hand reach for the door again. She turned the handle, and it opened with a click, swinging open slowly.

The room was dark. Not completely dark, but the only light was coming from a single candle burning softly at the side of the bed. The light was enough to illuminate the bed partially in a ghostly pallor.

On the bed were her mother and Benoni.

Or rather, her mother, or what was left of her, was on the bed, and Benoni was on top of her, his legs straddling either side of her, as she lay lifeless and still.

Red.

Everything was red.

The sheets, her mother's face, Beni's fists as they hung replete at his side.

Mama's face was all swollen and looked weird.

Why wasn't she moving? And why was Beni crying?

"No, no, no I didn't mean to...wake up...wake up damnit!" Beni sobbed pitifully, shaking her mother by the shoulders.

Her mother wobbled in his arms like a doll, then hung there, still as the wind on a perfectly still autumn morning.

He ceased his shaking.

"Mama?" Rudra asked again, walking further into the room.

"Get back", Beni spluttered, pushing at her ineffectually through his self-pitying tears.

She ignored him, and walked around him out of reach so she could wake mama.

Reaching the bed, she stared down at her mama's face. Though it was swollen and disfigured, she still looked like the most beautiful woman she'd ever seen.

Beni pawed at her weakly again, but she simply brushed his arm away and started to run her hand through her mama's white as snow hair. Had it always been so white?

Rubbing mama's face with the back of her hand, Rudra cooed softly. "Mama it's alright, you just sleep. You must be tired".

"T-tired?" Beni ceased his sobbing for a moment. "Are you broken, child?"

Rudra turned and frowned at him. "What do you mean? She just needs her sleep, you've been hurting her again. She always sleeps when you hurt her".

"S-sleep?" Beni blustered, seemingly, unable or unwilling, to spare Rudra even this small mercy. "She's **dead** you fool!" he blurted out bluntly, his grief for the moment forgotten.

Rudra looked at him blankly. "Dead?" she mused, a strange look on her face as she continued to stroke her mother's hair.

It was eerie, and Beni found it unsettling.

"She's not dead. Just sleeping", Rudra said with a chilling

finality.

"Fucking sleeping..." Beni scoffed. "She's dead! See? Does this look like sleep to you girl!" He callously shook her mother like a child might a ragdoll.

Rudra watched silently, her mind unable to comprehend.

"Dead", she repeated softly, questioningly, as if the words were foreign to her.

"Yes, dead!" Beni wailed, giving her mother another shake. At this, her head rolled to one side, and her beautiful blue eyes found Rudra's own.

Rudra stared into her mama's eyes, and saw nothing staring back at her. No pretty sparkle, no warmth, no mama. It was like staring into an abyss.

And like a piece of glass, Rudra shattered.

She felt it, very faintly at first. A warmth, deep inside her. Like a tiny spark simmering in the ashes of a fire. And then, all at once, it was a blaze, an inferno raging inside her. The heat was maddening. Her teeth ground against each other harshly. She clenched her fists and let it wash over her, as the old Rudra burned away, lost to the flames. Her eyes burned, and in them Beni saw a fire that could not be doused, the fire of insanity.

Without warning, she snatched the razor that Beni shaved with from the bedside table and leapt upon him.

The ferocity of her leap knocked the wind from him, and before he could even draw breath, she drew the blade across his throat with as much force as she could muster, ripping it open from end to end.

She screamed as his blood sprayed out at her, exploding in a bloody fountain. It covered her face, and began to drip slowly down her cheeks in a tragic imitation of tears.

She continued slashing and stabbing in a maddening frenzy, again and again and again, screaming all the while, as the fire raged inside her.

When she was finished, she was bathed in blood, and the fire was done.

From its ashes, a new Rudra emerged, like a twisted phoenix, born in fire and blood.

And from that day, Little Think First Rudy was never to be seen again.

I Must Be Dreaming

He gripped the basin tightly, and raised his head slowly.

He looked into the mirror, and liked not what looked back.

His hair was lank with sweat, and hung raggedly to his shoulders. It clung to his scalp in untidy clumps.

His eyes were a nightmare. The whites were horribly bloodshot. It looked like tiny red fingers were clawing their way across them, desperate to pollute the pupils, which had turned a stale mustard yellow.

What manner of man was he becoming?

"Uagh!" He grimaced painfully, doubled over in pain. Another intense pang of pain and hunger that he knew not how to satisfy. It ripped through his body, like a cramp, but worse. A cramp with teeth, teeth that he felt gnawing away inside of him.

Falling to his knees, he cradled himself tightly, waiting for the pain to subside.

The cramps had been increasing of late, and he was worried. Terrified in fact, that if he didn't find a way to eat soon, he would perish.

Wiping the sweat from his brow, with his now very dirty handkerchief, he rose unsteadily to his feet, one hand still on his abdomen, as if he feared another cramp.

He eyed the chicken that Adairis had left for him last night, and his stomach heaved.

Gripping the wall he gagged and retched painfully, spitting

up only bile.

His stomach had nothing left to send back at this point.

"NO!" he screamed despairingly.

Grabbing the plate of chicken, he threw it viciously against the wall, where it smashed into pieces.

He started to cry, sobbing feebly as the enormity of his situation overwhelmed him.

What is happening to me!

What is happening!

Please god, help me.

This can't be happening.

I must be dreaming.

Please lord.

He turned to his reflection and could not bear it.

He fell to his knees, crying pitifully, deep sobs bursting from his mouth.

And then, he felt it. The panic again. Bubbling within him. First, in his stomach, and then in his chest. His breathing stuttered, as his chest constricted. So dizzy. Everything felt so dizzy. He wheezed, trying to catch his breath, as the panic consumed him.

He gasped, and sucked and wheezed, desperate to take in air and fill his lungs.

Breathe, a voice rang out in his head.

Breathe.

Breathe.

"Ughhhh", he exhaled savagely, clutching and clawing at his throat.

Breathing through his nose, he felt his breathing slow, and the dizziness started to recede.

Finally, he brought his breathing under control, and pulled himself against the wall, where he lay feebly with his back against it.

I cannot give in to despair.

I must endure this.

And return to Amerie.

His stomach clenched uncomfortably, as he thought of his wife. Another face, darkly beautiful, flashed into his mind, and he grimaced, screwing his face up tightly in a bid to forget it.

Outside the room, a woman waited. She had heard Henré's cries and did not want to intrude. At least that's what she told herself. The truth was, she was scared.

She knew what was happening. She had lived in the Under for many years. He was not the first she had seen…with the sickness. But he was the worst, and she prayed for him.

Prayers were all she could offer. For he did not want to hear. Did not want to speak of the changes happening within him. She wasn't sure she blamed him. Would she be any different?

She shuddered and closed her eyes.

Henré was sitting quietly when she entered, staring disconsolately at the floor.

"Henré, how are you feeling this morning?" she asked tentatively. "I brought you some water".

He met her eyes bravely. "Well enough", he said quietly.

"Did you get any sleep?" she enquired.

"A little", he replied.

The hollows under his eyes belied his brave face.

She frowned. "Drink". She knelt and passed him a cup of water.

He took the water gingerly, looking at it with great suspicion. Taking a tentative gulp, he waited, a strange look on his face.

After a few moments, he smiled with relief, and raised the cup, draining it.

"Thank you", he said, a little more warmly now. "I needed that-". He trailed off mid-sentence.

His eyes widened, and his face took on a panicked expression.

He swallowed again, though he had no liquid in his mouth, and his hand fell to his stomach.

"Henré?" Adair made to rise, but Henré threw out his hand, firmly gesturing no.

"Shall I fetch the healer?" Adair asked.

Henré said nothing. He looked like he was going to be sick.

"I won't be but a moment-" Adair said quickly, her eyes frightened.

Before she could rise, Henré rolled to his knees and retched violently, the water he had drunk spilling out onto the floor, along with some other foul effluent.

Adair jumped back and grimaced, the smell was foul.

He began to weep in earnest this time, first on hands and knees, then he fell forward dejectedly, lying flat on his face, his mouth squashed against the dusty floor of the Under, tears staining his cheeks.

She felt no shame for him. This was...terrifying.

"There, there, Monsieur Henré", she cooed softly, lowering herself to the ground beside him and rubbing his back and face in a motherly manner.

His cries continued, so she lowered herself flat beside him, and wrapped him in her arms as best she could.

"Mama Adair got you know", she murmured, wiping his hair from his face, and lending him what comfort she could.

"I can't do this anymore", he whispered weakly, looking at her with his hellish red eyes.

"Certainly you can, Monsieur", she encouraged, meeting his eyes, seemingly unfazed.

He looked at her with hope. The helpless hope of a child.

"Just...tell me what to do", he begged. "Whatever it is...I'll do it".

"Well...you're gonna have to trust me", she said.

*

They walked along a gloomy corridor, Adair leading, Henré following tentatively behind.

He had not been this far into the Under before, refusing to

show his face, confined to a prison of his own making in his dingy little room.

He couldn't bear the looks. The frightened eyes. And then the pitying smiles.

He was scared, and he despised himself for it. What would Amerie think of him? She needed him.

A low hum of conversation drifted toward them, and he began to sweat, rubbing his hands nervously up and down his shirt.

Adair stopped and turned to him just before a bend in the passage.

"Here we are, Monsieur Henré", she said gently, taking his hand in hers.

Seeing his sweat and his restless eyes, she squeezed his hand. "If you feel lost, think of Amerie. She is your light, as you are hers. Right now, she is lost too. She needs you, as you need her. Think of her. Hold to that thought".

Henré took a deep calming breath. "You are right", he said, with a modicum of composure.

He turned to look at her. It was a studying look, and his eyes bored into her own, as if seeing her truly for the first time in a moment of clarity. "You are very wise, Adair". He smiled innocently.

She smiled back in earnest. She'd never seen Henré smile before. "Wisdom hard earnt", she said tiredly.

Before he could respond, she continued. "Now come". Placing her hand in the small of his back, she pushed him forward around the bend, guiding him out of the passage and into the common room she occupied with her fellows.

"Gain your bearings, I will be back shortly". She touched his arm reassuringly.

The first thing that struck him was how low the ceiling was. Although the room was large, it had an oppressive, claustrophobic feel to it. He started to feel dizzy again.

Be strong Henré.

For Amerie.

And the baby.

He felt another pang of guilt shoot through him. He'd been so consumed with his own predicament, he'd not given a thought to his baby since fleeing to this...place.

What sort of man am I? Focus!

Now is not the time for self-pity.

He set his jaw and returned his attention to studying his surroundings.

He noticed that some of the walls were stone...and some bone.

Of course, he had expected this, it was the catacombs after all, but seeing it for himself, he could not help but consider his own mortality. He turned away from a particularly frightening looking skull with large looming eye sockets.

There were torches on the walls, the stone walls at least, casting a yellow orange glow over the room. Even though there was light, it felt... dark. As if the torches only served to remind how far underground they were, in this dimly lit graveyard of bone and dust. He liked it not at all.

"Is this your first time in the Under?" a sing-song voice asked him.

He turned and stared at the speaker.

The man stared back curiously, frowning.

Remembering his manners, Henré jolted. "Yes, sorry, that's right", he admitted. He turned his face away shyly, hiding his eyes lest the man think him some sort of demon.

The man arched an eyebrow. "Me too. It's quite wonderful, isn't it?" he asked, looking around. "Sinister mind, but wonderful".

Henré said nothing.

"These skulls give me the chills", the man continued, turning a rather large skull away from them, so that it would watch them no longer.

Henré smiled suddenly. He decided he liked the man. The man smiled back at him warmly, and all of a sudden, he didn't feel so helpless.

Bracing himself, Henré turned to look the man in the eye. "Are you a healer?" he asked hopefully.

The man's eyes widened slightly, but he made no comment on Henré's condition. "What? Healer? No", he replied sadly. "Would that I were".

Henré's face fell.

"But there are plenty here", the man quickly added. "Or so I am told. You are in good hands, friend, do not fear". He grabbed Henré's shoulder consolingly.

All of a sudden, Henré felt like crying again. Not from fear, or from hopelessness. But from gratitude. And hope. Overwhelming hope and gratitude. He allowed himself to hope.

"They say Old Anne is a skilled healer", the man said sympathetically, watching the emotions play across Henré's face.

"Old Anne?" Henré enquired.

His new friend pointed to an ancient woman with hair as white as bone. She was talking quietly with Adair.

"How old is she?" Henré asked incredulously, forgetting himself. "She seems truly ancient".

"Old", the man agreed. "But I am told, a great beauty in her day".

Henré furrowed his brows and his eyes widened in disbelief. He looked at the man to see if he was jesting. Seeing that he was not, his eyebrows arched in surprise.

He turned to study Old Anne more closely. He noted a garden of freckles, bedded prettily across her nose and cheeks. He squinted, like a merchant of fine gemstones, deep in his assessment of a particularly intriguing gem. And the closer he looked, the more he saw.

Her mouth was finely proportioned, her lips full, their colour a muted red. At one time, they must have been quite alluring.

He blinked, and squinted harder, frowning. He closed his eyes and pictured her as she must have been in her youth. He smiled dreamily.

"I can see it", he said, opening his eyes and grinning at the man. The man winked knowingly.

It had always been so. The young look upon the old and find it inconceivable that one day, they too will age. They cannot fathom that one day they too will sport white hair and tired eyes. One day, their youthful looks will fade, and they will no longer draw looks of envy and lust. One day, their vigour will wane, and they will no longer dance the night through. And so they look, with blinders, to protect themselves from this terrifying certainty, until such a time as they are ready to accept it. To confront it with the wisdom and bravery gained from a life well lived.

Adair beckoned to Henré from across the room.

"Good luck, friend", the man said, extending his hand. "Old Anne will take care of you". He reassuringly covered Henré's hand with his own.

"Thank you", Henré said nervously. He turned to leave, then stopped. "I'm sorry…I didn't even ask your name".

"Gabriel", the man said with a smile.

*

In another part of the Under, there is another path, weaving its way toward the other.

"This is unnatural", Amerie said distastefully, shivering in the cold.

"Indeed", La Meme agreed seriously. "I never liked it down here", she said quietly.

"You have been here before? Whatever for!" Amerie asked, aghast.

"Once or twice", La Meme replied.

"But...why!" Amerie stopped, and her mouth fell open. "Why ever would you come to such a...ghastly place", she wailed.

La Meme grinned, her eyes twinkling mischievously. "I was young once too, you know".

Amerie giggled. La Meme was still a mystery to her, but they had become fast friends, and she was eternally grateful for her confidence and poise. She wasn't sure how she would have coped without her, given the circumstance.

"I think this is it", La Meme said, stopping at a crossroads.

I pray he's here, Amerie thought, rubbing her stomach self-consciously.

Do you?

Of course I do! What a thought.

But what if he's one of those...things?

He's not!

But why else would he be down here in this...dark place?

Shut up! Just shut up! Shut up!

"Is everything alright?" Amerie felt La Meme's arm around her, and jumped a little.

"Yes...I'm sorry", Amerie said weakly, turning to throw La Meme an apologetic look.

"You have nothing to apologise for", La Meme said firmly.

Amerie sniffed and rubbed at her eye. "I'm just so scared", she said suddenly. "What if he's not down here?"

She began to pace, rubbing worriedly at her face. "Or worse, what if he has become like one of those...people...we came across? I don't think I could stand it...I really don't". Her voice broke, and La Meme cuddled her.

"He won't be", La Meme said certainly. "And if he is, I will clout him with my shoe".

Amerie turned to look at her over her shoulder. "Your...shoe?" she said incredulously, eyes wide with surprise.

La Meme nodded sagely. "Wack!" With a showman-like-flourish, she whacked Amerie across the rump with her shoe, then leapt nimbly back, holding the shoe en garde, like a fencer with a rapier.

"Wha...what?" Amerie stuttered, a look of complete disbelief on her face.

La Meme held her pose, glaring seriously at her.

Amerie stared back.

Then, she released a long peal of laughter.

And like the floodgates of a dam, her grief gave way to mirth, and she couldn't stop laughing.

The image of La Meme standing en garde with her dress hitched up in one hand and her shoe dangling menacingly in the other was too much for her.

"If he is wise, he will not anger me so", La Meme said sagely, her face set like stone, which only made Amerie laugh more.

It was just the release she needed.

When she had finished laughing, she straightened herself dutifully. It was time to find her husband.

"Let's go D'artagnan", Amerie teased, linking arms with La Meme, who led her down the crossroads toward a large room.

The room was a bustle of activity. It surprised her how organised everything was. It was like a village, but on a smaller scale. Everyone seemed to have their own assignment, and like cogs in a wheel, they all turned together.

She did not like the skulls and bones in the walls though. She shuddered. It was very morbid. But she was here, and she had to find her husband.

The "Dwellers" of the Under, as they called themselves, were friendly and open, and seemed happy to speak with her. This surprised her, and her respect for them grew. Perhaps she had misjudged them.

But she was still young, and her life had been sheltered to this point. She had not yet learned to look beyond appearances, but she was learning.

She began to feel more confident. They all spoke highly of a woman called Old Anne. They told her, with great enthusiasm, that if her husband was here and needed healing, Old Anne would surely cure him of his ails.

A small flower of hope bloomed inside her.

"La Meme!" she called across the room enthusiastically.

"What is it, mon jolie renarde?" La Meme approached Amerie, a curious look on her face. "Will I need my shoe?" She mimed a clubbing motion, her face serious now.

"No", Amerie giggled excitedly. "The man I just spoke with, he says that a person matching Henré's description was brought here!"

"Wonderful!" La Meme gushed.

"And, he believes that he is still in fact here, in the Under!" Amerie blurted.

"Such beautiful news". La Meme beamed. "And it could have come no sooner. My shoe really is starting to wear thin", she added devilishly, frowning down at her feet.

Amerie beamed. Her heart was so full, she thought it might burst.

"So, where is this roguish husband of yours. I would have words with him". La Meme peered speculatively around the chamber.

"He is just going to look for him. The dweller I spoke with", Amerie said, her eyes bouncing around the chamber in search like a pup after a ball.

"Magnifique" La Meme stated. She looked around the chamber, taking in the people, and the bones, and felt a strange mix of emotions. Her eyes stopped, and narrowed.

Is that? It cannot be.

What are you doing here? she thought, a panic bolting through her.

"La Meme?" Amerie enquired, her excitement forgotten, as

she wondered at the serious turn in her mood.

Before La Meme could respond, a chilling scream rang out. The Dwellers looked frantically for the source of the noise.

A scraping sound from the back of the chamber drew every eye at once. A scraping, and, a shuffling.

A figure...a woman from the looks of it.

There were no torches at the back, so all they could see was an outline, hobbling ever so slowly forward in the shadow.

She seemed unsteady on her feet, staggering slightly from side to side, as she dragged herself forward, step by tiny step.

As she shuffled, her bare feet made a scratching noise against the ground, like sand being crushed against stone.

Shuffle, shuffle, shuffle.

The chamber watched silently, frozen in grim paralysis.

As she moved out of the dark recess at the back of the chamber, the light from the torches hit her feet first. They were weathered, the skin stretched and cracked.

Shuffle, shuffle, shuffle.

The light slowly, sickeningly, crawled upwards, revealing a faded, worn dress. Red, flecked with red.

Shuffle, shuffle, shuffle.

Up, ever up, the light reached, desperate to illuminate her. And then, it reached her face, and Amerie gasped, clutching at her chest.

It was not her age, or her frailness, that shocked Amerie.

It was the bite marks on her neck, pumping blood out sporadically, like a hose with a hole.

The blood was spitting to her dress, and Amerie noticed, dripping down her legs, where it was trying to pool at her feet. But her shuffling legs would not let it.

"Help!" a voice shouted from the other side of the chamber.

A man ran toward the woman, catching her in his arms as she began to fall forward, keeling over ominously like a felled tree.

"Gabriel" La Meme screamed from beside Amerie, running

after the man.

As she ran, a pair of red eyes appeared in the darkness behind Anne and her hero. An unnatural growl rumbled in the darkness, and the room fell silent.

In a heartbeat, the red eyes burst forth, as a feverish looking man sprung forward at Gabriel and Anne. Knocking Gabriel aside, he mounted Anne and pinned her to the floor, rending and tearing viciously at her neck.

The sound of his teeth, and what looked like...claws...ripping into her, rang out horribly for all to hear.

Gabriel had hit the floor hard and moaned weakly. He tried to raise himself onto his elbows, but failed, and fell back groaning.

His eyes rolled back in his head, and he lay still.

The beast raised its head from Anne, its eyes blood filled pools, brimming with hate, heat and hunger in equal measure.

Amerie shook uncontrollably, her face white.

As if scenting her fear, the beast turned its eyes upon her, and made a horrible growling sound from the back of its throat. It was like the growl of a wolf, but sounded infinitely worse, coming as it did from a man.

Before Amerie could muster so much as a scream, the beast sank to its haunches menacingly, then sprang to its feet, rushing at her wildly. It was fast, unnaturally so, and she barely had time to register it.

At the last moment she screamed and raised her arms across her face, squeezing her eyes shut, accepting her fate.

If this is it, Henré, know that I love you, she thought sadly.

She heard a fearsome howl and a thud, but curiously she felt nothing. She stood a moment longer, eyes scrunched shut, before opening her eyes.

When she did, she saw La Meme and the beast on the floor. The beast was atop La Meme, trying viciously for her neck, as she desperately held it off with her elbow at its throat. The beast snarled and spat, gnashing its teeth hungrily as it pulled itself inexorably closer to her neck.

She stared back resolvedly, sweat dripping down her face, as she struggled to keep it from ripping her to shreds.

In that moment, like a spell lifting, the chamber reanimated, and the Dwellers sprang into action, shouting and sprinting across to wrest the beast from La Meme. With great effort, they managed to rip it from her, and three of them threw it to the cold stone floor, where it rolled quickly to its feet.

La Meme staggered to her feet, panting. "Begone from here!" she commanded.

As if against its will, the beast threw its head back and screamed in frustration, before turning and fleeing the chamber.

La Meme's shoulders slumped wearily, and she watched the beast leave.

"Amerie", she said suddenly, turning to her. "Are you injured?"

"N-no", Amerie replied dumbly, still in shock from the attack. "A-are you?"

She did not hear her reply, for satisfied that her friend was safe, La Meme immediately ran across the chamber to the man who had gone to Anne's aid.

Amerie watched as La Meme cradled the man in her lap, inspecting him for injury, tenderly running her hands over his face and neck. She did the same with his arms and legs, then, seemingly satisfied he was uninjured, relaxed.

The man stirred and moaned.

"Petit soleil", La Meme murmured tenderly.

"La Meme?" Gabriel rasped.

"Yes", La Meme purred. "I am here, and you are well".

"What are you doing here?" he asked blearily, opening his eyes and squinting at the light, which stung.

"I think the better question would be, what are **you** doing here?" she retorted sternly.

"Why I...I fancied a stroll", he replied, seeking the words.

"Fancied a stroll?" she repeated, her face darkening. "Fool boy!" she hissed.

He grinned boyishly up at her, his eyes still squinting painfully.

"Petit soleil", she griped. "Petit sotte more like!"

"La Meme, really, you musn't. It's really very unladylike", he admonished her seriously, attempting to stare at her down the bridge of his nose. An act made more amusing by the fact he could scarcely lift his head a few inches from her lap.

La Meme stared daggers at him.

The Dwellers gathered in a circle around them.

"Is he well?" one of the elders asked worriedly.

"Unfortunately, not", La Meme replied.

The Dwellers gasped collectively.

"He has suffered irreparable damage...to his wits", she said gravely, smacking him lightly on the head.

"Oww", Gabriel exclaimed theatrically, before wincing as real pain bit him.

"It is your own damn fault", La Meme said sternly, though her eyes had lost their hard edge, and her mouth appeared to be struggling not to twitch.

She pulled him to her suddenly in a fierce hug.

The Dwellers watched, strange looks on their faces.

"Overworlders", one of them muttered, as the others rolled their eyes and the group dispersed.

The enquiring dweller remained, and knelt down, helping La Meme slowly pull Gabriel to his feet. Between them, they carried him to a padded bench in a quiet corner where the light was low.

Satisfied that they were safe for the time being, the dweller bobbed his head at them politely and left.

La Meme sat quietly with Gabriel, as he lay tiredly on the

bench. She took his hand in hers. His eyes drooped closed and snapped open from time to time, as he fought the urge to drift off to sleep.

She watched as the Dwellers covered Anne gently with a blanket, and felt a deep pang of sadness as her face disappeared from sight.

Her eyes watered, and she turned away.

"You're very beautiful, do you know that?" Gabriel mumbled groggily.

She sniffed, and wiped her eyes on the arm of her dress. "Flattery will get you nowhere", she said, smiling through the tears.

"I know", Gabriel agreed.

Amerie watched them from afar, hid in the shadows of the passage out of the room.

She watched impassively, as the Dwellers solemnly lifted Anne to their shoulders, and led her from the room.

Leaving La Meme to her petit soleil, she turned and walked away quietly, down the long passage, until she was swallowed by the darkness of the Under.

A Bitter Taste

Lucien's thoughts were grim as he brooded over his drink. He didn't know he had ended up in one of these accursed bourge bars, but he was too tired and too maudlin to move now.

Taking in the flamboyant outfits and the seeping excess, his lip curled. He felt the urge to spit.

It was dark, but for some strategically placed lighting, and there were young Parisians draped without care across the sofas and booths.

Like all the bars in this part of Paris, it was glamorous, or so they said, with lots of crystal and gold throwing reflections around the room, bouncing from the large glass backboard behind the bar.

He'd chosen the most secluded corner he could find for his brooding, sitting on one of the little stools at the bar itself. But even here, the entitlement followed him. Like a smog, it hung thick in the air.

Behind him, a group of young sociopaths in training were harassing one of the serving girls, a pretty young thing with carrot coloured hair and a fair complexion. She couldn't have been more than fifteen or sixteen, Lucien thought sadly.

It's nothing to do with you.

Just drink your drink, and go home.

You've shed enough blood for one lifetime.

He pondered his drink and grimaced.

I needn't shed any blood for these privileged pisswits, he thought savagely.

Raising his glass, he drained it in one large swallow.

"Another", he beckoned with his glass to the waiter behind the bar. The waiter looked at him, as if to say something, then thought better of it.

"Monsieur". A large glass of deep red wine appeared on the counter. It disappeared with alarming speed.

Lucien raised his glass once more at the bartender who hadn't moved.

The waiter frowned. "Monsieur..." he began.

Lucien cut him off. "Another", he said firmly.

The waiter paused, and glanced at a heavyset man in a grey suit standing at the entrance.

Before he could reach a decision, Lucien leaned across the bar and pulled him close by his arm.

"I said, another. Don't make me ask again, friend", Lucien said menacingly.

The waiter struggled, his eyes scared and darting to the big man at the entrance.

"I'm sorry", Lucien said suddenly, releasing him. "Please, just bring me another", he pleaded wearily.

The waiter stared into Lucien's eyes, and seeing something there, took pity on him.

"Just don't give me any trouble man, or I'll be for it... you have the look about you, and you've already drunk enough to down a horse", the waiter retorted warily.

Lucien inclined his head gracefully. "I'll not give you any trouble... though I can't promise it won't find me", he finished grimly.

The waiter winced, and swore under his breath, as he walked away to serve a richly dressed young couple.

The woman looked very pretty, Lucien thought to himself, watching them. She wore a sky-blue dress and headband, and she carried herself well. Not with the typical arrogance and disdain. The look under her nose like she'd just walked past a large pile of cow dung, and a demeanour that would sour milk. The glint of a huge gleaming diamond on her finger caught his eye, and he turned away bitterly.

"Come on…just a little kiss", a voice behind him purred, accompanied by some low chuckling.

"I can't, I'm working…" a pained female voice responded.

"I won't keep you long, mon coeur…" the male voice continued.

"I can't, I'm sorry… no, please stop" the female voice pleaded, an edge of panic to it now.

"Do not fret mon coeur…if you had any idea who my father was…you would beg for this…we'll make it worth your while", the man pressed, the sound of his lips touching her neck followed his words.

It's none of your concern.

Just drink your fucking drink.

And leave, Lucien instructed himself.

He looked around, intending to alert the waiter.

Villain.

The waiter now studiously avoided meeting his eyes, though every now and then, he cast a glance at the girl and group of men, before looking away quickly.

Perhaps this lump will see justice done then, if you've not the stomach.

Turning in his seat, Lucien stared at the doorman, who was standing with his arms crossed and his attention on anything but ensuring the safety of the patrons.

He seemed engrossed in two pretty young things who were giggling outlandishly and caressing his thickly muscled arms.

Tiredly setting his glass down, Lucien slid from his stool, and slouched over to the doorman.

Mustering some politeness despite his mood, he interjected, "Monsieur, there is a lady who needs your assistance. She is being accosted…by a group of villains…over there. Just by the bar".

"What's that?" the doorman said absentmindedly.

"I said, a lady needs your help", Lucien repeated insistently, pointing to the damsel.

"Lady? What, where?" The doorman turned and followed Lucien's finger with his eyes. Seeing the girl and the men, he whitened, as if he'd eaten some bad seafood.

"Oh that? It's fine, do not worry yourself", he said quickly, turning away.

Do not worry myself? Lucien felt his temper rising dangerously.

Lucien gripped the doorman by the shoulder, and turned him with ease. "It doesn't look fine to me. I suggest you look again", he ground into the surprised face of the doorman.

The doorman looked Lucien up and down. The women watched excitedly as he scowled aggressively. Their faces flushed. It sickened Lucien.

"I said, it's **fine**, now fuck off before I hurt you little man", the doorman spat, as he gave Lucien a hard push with both hands that would have staggered most men.

Absorbing the force of it, it moved Lucien not at all. Standing deathly quiet, he gave the doorman a look that drew the blood from his face.

The women had quietened now, confused. This wasn't how it was supposed to go.

As the doorman stood, unsure, trying to rebuild his bluster for another attempt at intimidating him, Lucien's hand found his throat.

Without pretence, Lucien flung the man ruthlessly at the hard wooden door behind.

He hit hard, and slumped down immediately, unconscious, his head lolling to one side.

Behind the bar, the waiter ran out of sight.

Before the women could so much as scream, Lucien snarled at them and pushed them both out of the door, kicking the doorman out of the way in the process.

Like a sack of potatoes, the doorman slid comically across the floor, before coming to rest arms and legs akimbo under a small table by the bar.

Lucien stared at the unconscious doorman, his face vengeful. The women were no better, he thought to himself suddenly. They didn't even have the good grace to pretend to be concerned for the serving girl.

Turning to the damsel, he panicked.

She had vanished! Along with the group of villains.

He tensed, and disappeared, shifting through the air like an ill formed shadow.

He moved quickly, down a dimly lit corridor to the left of the bar.

Hearing soft cries through the door at the end of the corridor, he burst through it, his form coalescing as he came to a halt.

The girl was atop a table in the centre of the room, weeping softly, her legs spread, straddling a young man's hips.

Her head lay stiffly to one side, rocking horribly with each of his thrusts.

The others watched lustily.

Her eyes met Lucien's.

Help me, they pleaded.

He felt it boiling within him, as it always did, and his face flushed.

Another face rushed through his mind, contorted with spite.

What are you gonna do about it! The voice snarled.

His rage exploded, and all was red.

He flew across the room, hitting the rapist with enough force to shatter him. The rapist sailed through the air weightlessly, hitting the wall with a nauseating crunch, staining it an unhealthy red.

The rapist fell to the floor, lifeless.

Snarling savagely, he turned on the others, his fist dripping wet with blood as red as his eyes.

One of them, a gangly young man, started shaking violently, as his trousers stained dark with shame and fear.

Lucien ignored him.

The other two stepped forward menacingly, alcohol having made them brave.

Lucien put the first down with a merciless strike from his elbow that split his skull, and advanced on the second.

The remaining man faltered, stepping back slowly, feeling the wall pressing in on him behind. Sweat dripped from his face, and his eyes darted around wildly.

"Aloyse! Help me, you cowardly dog!" the man spat at his comrade-in- folly.

The gangly man stood silently; his eyes sad. "We should never have done this Luc…it turns my stomach".

"It didn't turn it a minute ago, you wretch! You wanted the bitch just as much as we did, and you'd have been rutting away like a dog if you'd had your chance", Luc spat venomously.

Lucien stood in front of Luc, his face cold and unforgiving.

The girl, who had ceased her crying, and had been watching the violence with a grim satisfaction, rolled to her feet, pushing herself off the table.

"This one's mine", she said quietly, advancing on the would-be rapist.

She stood next to Lucien, staring pitilessly at the remaining wastrel who would defile her.

"And just what are you going to do, bitch!" Luc sneered. "Get back on that fucking table-". He did not get a chance to finish his foulness, for the girl lunged forward viciously, burying a small knife in his throat.

"Pour Madame Dagger!" she hissed, stepping close and pushing the blade in right to the hilt.

Madame Dagger? Lucien thought, bewildered, his rage for

the moment forgotten.

What part does she play in this?

The girl watched steely eyed as Aloyse choked on his blood, sliding to the floor, writhing and gasping desperately for breath.

"Rot", she said, spitting on him.

Lucien stepped back and looked at the girl with new eyes. "Remind me never to cross you", he said quietly.

She smiled weakly, then started to sob, as the reality of the situation set in.

Lucien said nothing, taking her in his arms and holding her. Sometimes there were no words that were sufficient.

What could he possibly say to take away the hurt? Her world had just been ripped apart in the most brutal way, and it would never be the same again.

After a while her sobbing subsided and she wiped her eyes.

"Thank you, monsieur". She looked at him seriously. "I will never forget what you did for me here".

He looked at her. She looked different. She was still pretty, but sharp. Like broken crystal.

Lucien touched her face softly. "Do not let this define you", he said, hating himself for how trite it sounded.

She smiled tiredly.

Lucien tensed, and turned, as if listening to something.

The girl frowned, then she too heard it.

Shouting, men shouting, from outside the bar. And, something else. A lower, coarser voice. A man's voice. But it sounded damaged. Like somebody who'd swallowed gravel, and was now struggling to speak through a bloody, ripped throat, but miraculously, making a good go of it.

She dreaded to think what manner of man this was.

Before she could assuage her curiosity, she felt a strong arm around her waist, and the room disappeared in a blur. She caught flashes of Romain, the barman, and what looked like Yuri, the doorman, as the bar passed her by in a matter of heartbeats.

And then, they were outside and into the night, moving through the streets at an otherworldly speed.

"Ugh", she moaned, as her stomach lurched, and her head wobbled on her neck.

Lucien pulled her head close to his chest, cradling it with his hand.

I must be dreaming.

For it feels like I am flying, she thought hazily, as they flew up the side of a tenement building.

The world stopped spinning, as they came to a stop.

She felt herself lowered gently to her feet. She staggered, swaying wildly from side to side, dizzy as if she'd just run in circles for an hour.

Lucien steadied her, then drew her to him once more as she swayed dangerously on her feet.

"I'm sorry...it was the only way", Lucien said.

"What do you mean?" she asked.

"You can never go back there now", Lucien said gravely.

"I-I know", she said, still unsteady on her feet. "I would never go back after what they let happen to me".

"No, I don't think you understand". He watched her, his eyes shining brightly. "If they find you now...they'll kill you".

"K-kill me?" Her mouth dropped open in shock. "They were just a bunch of...a bunch of...bourge bastards...looking to stick their meat somewhere it didn't belong". She was angry now. "The city is teeming with them. They won't be missed". She spat on the floor.

"I think not. The man you heard, the one with a voice like the baying of the hounds of hell...is known to me", Lucien said.

"So what, he's a politician or something?" she asked brashly.

Lucien laughed, long and loud. Suddenly, he did not look so dark, the difference was startling. Gone was the brooding demeanour and the undercurrent of violence. He looked friendly, jovial even.

"What did I say?" she asked, her cheeks colouring.

"I'm sorry. It was nothing you said", Lucien said.

"So he's not a politician then?" she pressed.

"No". Lucien grinned. "Perhaps it was a missed calling of his".

"Stop teasing", the girl demanded.

"I'm sorry", Lucien said seriously. "The truth is". He paused.

"Out with it", the girl said impatiently.

"The truth is... he's a psychotic, murderous bastard, who has likely killed more men than the plague...and he likely wants to kill you now too", Lucien said.

She blanched at this. "Wonderful".

"But do not fear... he has a memory like a pig's arsehole", Lucien said.

The girl's mouth dropped open again, though this time not from fear.

"He'll soon forget all about you. It's likely me he wants", Lucien assured her.

"But, why?" she asked.

"The man I killed, the one who...attacked you". Lucien frowned. "His father is the murderous bastard's...employer".

"What?" The girl blanched.

"Yes..." Lucien nodded gravely. "I didn't realise until after it was... done. I've only seen the boy once in passing, but I would not mistake him. I looked upon him briefly before you...dealt with the last of them".

The girl licked her lips, and looked around the rooftop, as if desperate for a way out of this situation. Then, she looked back to Lucien, clenching her jaw.

"I'm sorry monsieur..." she said slowly. "Sorry that I've put you in this situation...truth is...I'm a little scared...this is..."

"A lot", Lucien interjected.

She nodded. "But I won't be cowed by the likes of them", she said suddenly.

Lucien smiled; he found her bravery admirable.

"What can we do? What do we do now?" she asked eagerly.

"You can stay here...for a few weeks...and stay out of sight", Lucien said.

She opened her mouth to object, but Lucien continued. "The people who live here are good people, and they'll look after you, I'll make sure of it".

"Please monsieur", she gushed suddenly, her eyes blazing. "You say this man wants to kill you, well I want to **kill him!**" she spat. "And every last one of those animals!"

She swung her fists violently, then turned to pace up and down the rooftop, fists clenched tightly at her side.

She paused and faced him. "You...saved me. No one ever stands up to Janver...but you did. And it wouldn't have just been...him...doin...you understand?" She dropped her eyes, ashamed.

The muscles in Lucien's cheeks twitched angrily.

Rot indeed.

"There may well come a time for that", he said, calming himself. "But for now...please...stay here".

She opened her mouth to protest but closed it at the look in his eyes. It wasn't commanding, it was pleading, worried. She didn't see that much from men.

Lucien walked toward the edge of the rooftop, his back to her. "You can get in through the hatch behind you. When they ask, tell them Lucien sent you".

She turned to look for the hatch. "Lucien, that's your name then?"

When she turned back, he'd gone.

*

Back at the bar, a colossus of a man stood glowering, taking in the scene.

He towered over the ragtag group of cutthroats and bandits

who stood nervously behind him.

The doorman approached him. He was large himself, but seemingly insignificant next to this monstrosity of a man.

Nursing his head, the doorman mumbled. "This is where they were, monsieur".

"I can see that, boy", the giant replied without turning.

The doorman's eyes narrowed, but he said nothing in spite of the slight. He'd had his fill for one night.

He walked away, muttering under his breath once out of earshot.

The giant's ears twitched, and he smiled.

"Quite the party you've had here tonight, Lucien my boy!" he boomed suddenly, laughing merrily. "And I do love a party..."

The men behind him laughed, shifting nervously on their feet, trying to avoid standing in any of the blood or viscera.

"Bring me the boy!" the giant boomed suddenly.

Two of the men disappeared from the room, returning a few moments later leading Aloyse between them.

Aloyse looked pale. Taking in the giant, he grew paler still.

"You were party to this, boy?" the giant enquired, still looking around the room for clues.

"Not willingly...but yes, it shames me to say", Aloyse admitted.

"Tsk tsk tsk". The giant made a series of disapproving noises with his tongue and teeth. "This is a bad business boy", he lectured. His face wore the disapproving frown of a parent.

Placing a large mitt of a hand on the boy's back, he continued. "If you want a skirt and tits, there are plenty of whores, boy! And in this part of town, they won't make your meat fall off!" He burst out laughing once more, his voice echoing loudly through the bar.

His men laughed perfunctorily, as expected.

Aloyse smiled shyly, looking up at the giant like a dog who'd been shooed from the table. "I'm ashamed...it was stupid".

"Indeed it was, my boy!" the giant agreed, throwing back his chest and slapping Aloyse magnanimously on the back, a huge grin on his face.

Aloyse's legs buckled under him, and he caught the wall with his hand to steady himself.

"Ah well...all's fair in love and war eh?" the giant mused, beaming down at the boy.

Aloyse smiled up at him, still embarrassed, arching his eyebrows endearingly. Then, he felt the giant's hand tighten painfully on his shoulder. The pressure was immense. The last thing he saw was the giant grinning down at him maniacally.

With a huge roar, the giant ripped him in two down the middle, and he split asunder, his blood and innards showering the room and his men.

As his guts fell out from him to the floor, the giant put one half of the boy to his mouth and began suckling madly like a calf at its mother's teat. He looked like a nobleman eating a rack of ribs, if the nobleman were an insane mountain of a man dripping in viscera, and the ribs of the human variety.

"Raaaaaaaaaaaah!" The giant smacked his lips appreciatively, having finished with one half in a sickeningly short amount of time. "But so nice of you to leave me a **snack** Lucien! I guess you didn't get all the fun after all!" He broke off into his mad laughter.

His men backed away in terrified silence, leaving him to his feast.

An Ekur Queen

Beautiful and frightening in equal measure, is how you or I might describe her. Right now, she leaned toward the latter.

Her eyes glittered like blue crystals, with little sparks of electricity bouncing around inside. The question was, who and when, would the lightning strike?

She lazily drummed her prettily painted, bejewelled fingers against the side of her face, her chin cupped in her hand. This was never a good sign.

Sat upon a throne fit for a king. She wore a queen's crown. Thin and silver, and more of a headband than a crown, it had a marvellous sapphire embedded in the middle, that caught the light and further accentuated her eyes.

Her deep blue gown rested lazily just above her knees, riding up ever so slightly.

A handsome, strongly built man approached the throne, and knelt before her. Bowing his head, he offered her an ancient looking goblet, adorned with garnets the size of plums.

"My queen", he said reverently.

She smiled down at him fondly. "Ah, Zephirin. What do you bring me?"

"The sweetest of nectars, my queen", he replied proudly, raising his eyes tentatively.

Her eyes widened in child-like excitement. "Ambrosia? My, Zephirin... you honour me". She fluttered her eyes prettily at him like a maiden.

Rising daintily to her feet, she curtseyed, a graceful movement, then fluttered down the steps of the throne.

She knelt down right in front of him, so that she could meet his eyes, as she liked to.

He saw an insatiable thirst there, in those chilling blue eyes, and had to stop himself from shuddering. He held her gaze and waited.

It irked him to be reduced to this, scouring the city procuring blood from young maidens, the queens favourite errand boy. The taste was exquisite, of course, but it did not sit well with him.

There were plenty of rogues and reavers for the taking. He did not know why the queen insisted on feeding herself in the most ungodly way possible. To prey on maidens was... not right. And for what? A more...delicate taste.

But what could he do? To go against her would be to forfeit his life. And not only his own, but Marguerite's and Lucien's also. Or so he convinced himself that was the reason for his lack of action.

She pondered her servant, turning her head slowly to the side, as a cat might look at a mouse. It was as if she couldn't quite figure out what to do with him. Should she play with him? Should she chase him? Or smash him out of existence with one vicious whip of her wrist.

She smiled innocently. Deciding she would play with him further yet, she turned her attention to the goblet. Reaching out delicately, she took the goblet from him and stood.

She raised the goblet to her small, feminine nose, and gave the contents a little sniff.

"Mmm", she purred excitedly.

Liking what she smelt, she buried her face in the goblet, and took a long, deep breath in through her nose, like a sommelier savouring the notes of a particularly fine wine.

When she lifted her face from the goblet, it was different. Gone was any semblance of beauty, or so Zephirin thought. She looked like a feral cat.

Her smile was a snarl.

Her eyes, glittering so prettily before, now sparked and cracked dangerously.

She threw back her head and shook, breathing rapidly, in short, sharp breaths.

She opened her eyes, and they glowed red as coals, the lightning now fire, hissing and spitting wildly.

She grinned, and Zephirin's stomach dropped. It was a horrible thing and put him in the mind of some demonic meerkat.

She turns my stomach.

When she could delay her gratification no longer, she raised the goblet to her lips, and drank it down greedily in one go.

She released the goblet carelessly, and it clattered to the floor, bouncing down the steps to the throne. It rolled loudly across the stone floor, the metal of the goblet ringing jarringly against the stone. It came to a stop a few paces from the table where the others sat.

Then, suddenly, she screamed, long and loud. It was an unnatural, disturbing sound, like the scream of a banshee, and Zephirin stepped back quickly in fear.

Behind him, his brethren tensed, some watching in grim fascination, others staring anywhere but at their queen.

When she was done, she opened her eyes lazily, and drew a deep breath, luxuriating in it, seemingly unaware of her surroundings.

Zephirin licked his lips, eyeing the goblet hungrily. The scent was maddening! Though there were a few scant drops in the goblet, it took all his will to remain where he was, kneeling before his queen.

He fixed his gaze firmly on the throne, attempting to ignore the scent.

Smash.

Roar!

What the hell is that? he thought, panicked.

He turned quickly to see a hulking figure fly across the room, his giant body a smoky blur.

The blur coalesced into a man, who dropped quickly to his knees, snatching at the goblet and greedily raising it to its mouth. He licked, and sucked, the remaining drops of blood from the goblet like a man dying of thirst.

"Aughhh, ohhhh", he moaned, stretching his tongue deep into the goblet, flicking it at the sides, and loudly lapping up any of the liquid he could reach like a starving dog.

"Ahhhh, damnit!" he roared, not satisfied with the meagre feeding.

Springing to his feet, he threw the goblet against the wall, where it smashed. He banged on his chest like an ape, and pulled at his hair agitatedly.

"Fuck! Such hunger! It is **unbearable!**" the man screamed.

A peel of laughter rang out from the throne, as the queen bent over double in silent paroxysms of mirth. She covered her mouth with her hand in an attempt to remain ladylike.

"Oh, my Hadur. Was it too much for you, my love?" she breathed. "Oh, come to me, my dear, I have something for you".

Hadur stormed toward the throne, puffing and panting and twitching, still frenzied as he was. Catching himself in time, he gritted his teeth and fell to his knee, bowing his head before springing back to his feet.

"What is it, my queen!" He ground the words out, baying his head back and forth, like a frightened foal.

"Come to me", she whispered, beckoning alluringly to him with her finger.

Hadur paused for a moment, uncertain, then lunged forward close to her.

Her hand snapped forward viciously, grabbing the back of his head. It seemed feeble in comparison to his oversized skull.

He struggled but could not move. Before he could fear, or

comprehend, she pulled him to her. She began kissing him scandalously, her mouth open, tongue flicking in and out of his mouth, loudly, wetly, indecently.

She draped her arm around his neck like a lover, and her other hand roamed over his body aggressively.

Zephirin turned away, disgusted. The sound of their tongues slobbering, and her low moans, was too much for him.

Ending the kiss with a loud smacking sound, she released her plaything, then pushed him back challengingly a few steps, so that he was no longer level with the throne.

She ran her tongue slowly, tantalisingly across her lips, then stuck it provocatively from her mouth for all to see. Her tongue was thick with blood, her teeth stained red with it.

She had fed him with her own blood!

Zephirin could not believe it. Were there no limits to her depravity? Some things were just not done, even among such as they.

"Delicious", she whispered coyly.

Hadur stood silently, eyes closed, savouring the odd taste of her blood as a welcome desert.

"Indeed...my queen", he said quietly, still in a daze of blood and lust.

At the table, a middle-aged man with closely cropped black hair turning to grey, and a powerful, dominant chin, cleared his throat and leant forward.

"And for us?" he asked. "My queen?" he added, as something of an afterthought.

"In good time, Narcisse", she responded playfully. "Why Hadur here was practically **starving,** and I had to feed him first you see. I could not **bear** to let one of my children go hungry", she said dramatically.

"Yes... of course". Narcisse looked Hadur up and down, raising his eyebrows. "I'd hate to see the boy starve".

"Watch who you're calling, boy, **mortal!**" the big man spat, rounding on him aggressively. "Lest I crush your skull!"

"A slip of the tongue, of course, my apologies dear Hadur". He inclined his head the merest of inches, amusement evident in every line of his face.

Hadur narrowed his eyes and stepped toward him, fists clenched. The queen's laughter peeled out once more, dispelling the tension.

"Boys, boys, boys!" she said jovially. "If there's any sport to be had, it shall be at my command, and my command only. And certainly not until poor Narcisse here has earned his teeth. It simply wouldn't be fair. Or much sport for that matter", she mused, an evil grin on her face.

"Sit down boy, lest I rip that newborn head from your shoulders, your posturing turns my stomach!" barked a grizzled looking man with a face like hardened leather.

His face was covered in cuts and scars to such an extent that it looked like one of the training dummies, that the old warriors used to practise their swordplay on.

Hadur growled but remained where he was.

Clearly something about this old man unsettled him.

"There may come a day you can best me, but that day has not yet dawned. Nor will it while you crawl about on your hands and knees after scraps of blood like some babe scrabbling at her mother's tit. Now be seated, and act like an Ekur, and not some pathetic dribbling moindre!" the grizzled looking man thundered across the room, head high, chest out challengingly.

The queen watched with interest, cheeks flushed, one hand surreptitiously caressing her neck and chest.

Hadur's face twitched, and for a moment, it looked as though he would attack.

He decided against it, unclenched his fists, and narrowed his eyes poisonously, like a snake deciding to circle its prey a little longer.

Zephirin was impressed. He did not know if he would

remain so cool if Hadur were staring at him like that.

But then, Rodolphe had always been slightly less than sane, and an aggressive, cantankerous old bastard. He'd fought in just about every conflict on the continent in the past hundred or so years, and killed immeasurable men and women for the tableau. And to satiate his own lust for blood, of course.

Unfortunately for Zephirin, Rodolphe was his father, and although Rodolphe feared no man, and his outbursts were sometimes warranted, he was also a spiteful, wrathful being with a mean streak that ran right through him. A mean streak that Zephirin drew the ire of more often than not.

If he was honest, his father terrified him, and always had. He didn't know why he could never please him, but no matter what he did, or how hard he tried, nothing he did ever seemed enough. Rodolphe would always find fault somehow, like an overzealous preacher, intent on chastising his subject.

And so Zephirin's childhood had been. A confusing haze of criticism, coldness and unpredictability. And perhaps unwittingly at first, in a desperate bid to win the approval of his father, an approval that would never come, he had begun to subject his son, Lucien, to the same treatment.

If Rodolphe saw that he was a stern disciplinarian with Lucien, and instilling the same hard taught values Rodolphe had tried to instil in him, perhaps he would reconsider his opinion of him. At least, it had perhaps started that way.

He didn't understand it. But the hole in his heart had screamed at him to try anyway.

"Your day will come, old one". Hadur contented himself with the jab for now.

Rodolphe snorted, as if he didn't think much of this. "Zephirin, be seated boy", he barked suddenly at his son.

Dutifully, Zephirin joined his father, seated at the table.

"Finished boys?" the queen chimed cheerfully. "Oh good. Then time for **business** I suppose".

Her face fell and she gestured at the sardonic looking man who had bravely, or perhaps unwisely, riled Hadur previously.

"Narcisse, you were wanting to tell us about some business purchase... acquisition...or some such". She spoke in a bored voice, as if she would rather discuss anything else in the world.

She prowled back to the throne, coiling herself into it languidly.

She began preening herself in a small mirror, scrutinising her nails, her attention anywhere but the business at hand.

"My queen". Narcisse stood and bowed formally. "Yes. As you know, I have been in the process of acquiring various properties and businesses for our... cause". He paused, savouring the last word, rolling it around his mouth, trying the taste of it to see if it fit.

"Yes, yes..." she yawned.

"It may please you to know that after a liberal amount of greasing, and just the right amount of blackmail, I have completed the purchase of a... shelter...for young Parisians, on the outskirts of the 18th arrondissement".

A gasp rang out in the room.

The queen's eyes flicked up instantly, all traces of boredom gone from her face. They flashed with cunning, before lighting up like those of a little girl presented with her first puppy.

She grinned and clapped her hands childishly.

She sprung off the throne, pushing off with her hands, extending her legs ahead of her and landing nimbly on her feet.

She bounced across the room to him, gripping his shoulders excitedly, dangling herself daintily in front of him, her hair smothering his face.

"Mwah". The smack of her kiss on Narcisse's cheek rang out crisply. Narcisse had the good grace to blush and drop his eyes, as he felt Hadur's eyes burning into the back of his skull.

"How **wonderful** Narcisse", the queen exclaimed, beaming, her face scant inches from his own.

Enjoying the jealousy from Hadur, and the embarrassed predicament of Narcisse, she spun around and threw herself across his lap, both arms now firmly wrapped around his neck.

Looking up at him like a little girl, she fluttered her eyelashes prettily. "I knew I was right about you", she said, in a sing-song voice.

Looking about the room from her Narcisse shaped perch, she gave her brethren a solemn stare each in turn, her eyebrows high and accusing. "Not even with **teeth**, and look what he brings me".

She made a tutting, disapproving noise and shook her head sadly.

Suddenly, she sprang to her feet and threw her arms wide like a showman. "And **that** is why, he is to **get them**. **Tonight!**" She twirled around madly in a circle, head thrown back, eyes to the sky, arms trailing out beside her like little kites.

Smacking her lips appreciatively, she ceased her twirling and grinned a toothy grin. The grin faded, as she watched the faces of her servants, seeking any sign of dissent. She didn't tolerate dissent. In any form or fashion.

Rodolphe shook his head.

"Something to say, Rolphy?" she asked in a high, lilting voice.

"I don't trust him, he reeks of duplicity. He wears it like perfume". Rodolphe gave Narcisse a look of disgust, which Narcisse had the good sense to ignore.

The queen seemed to find this amusing, as she giggled girlishly.

"Oh Rolphy". She smiled at him lovingly. "Always looking out for my best interests, aren't you?"

Rodolphe continued to stare at Narcisse grimly.

"Tis a wise decision, my queen", a haughty looking woman to the right of Zephirin said. "Narcisse is well respected in Paris, and a well-connected man". She said it as if this settled the matter.

Hadur chuckled. "**Well connected**", he mimed to himself quietly.

The woman looked uncomfortable but said nothing.

"He **is**, isn't he?" The queen looked at Narcisse appraisingly, as if coming to the same conclusion.

"Indeed, my queen", the woman chimed sycophantically. "You have chosen well".

The queen beamed. "Why thank you Marguerite, my love".

She bounded across the room like a punchdrunk hound, and pecked her affectionately on the cheek. It was a quick peck, with just the slightest hint of force, like a pigeon nibbling up seeds.

Marguerite blushed, adjusting the collar of her dress.

"You are all being **so nice** to me today!" the queen gushed. "And for that, I am feeling generous...generous and **graceful**".

"But before I show my grace..." She snapped from playful to serious in an instant.

They bowed their heads.

"Omitto lucem", she intoned.

"*Omitto lucem*", they dutifully responded.

"Amplector tenebris", as she uttered, so they repeated.

"Ego ad mensam".

"Lusiurandum et brachium meum".

"Per sanguinem ligati sumus".

"By blood we are bound", Narcisse mouthed silently, as the tableau finished their chant. It was not his time yet. But soon, very soon. He wiped his hands on his expensive, well-cut trousers.

He knew what was coming now. It was always the same before they fed. The same chant. The same excited muttering. The same anticipation building palpably in the room. The same feral looks, from the dark wolves.

He found the whole thing rather uncivilised and boorish, if truth be told. He was not one for ceremony, and found all the blood and viscera quite tedious and unnecessary. Immortality was all he cared about, and he didn't care how he achieved it.

When he'd first been invited to dine with the queen, he could not believe his good fortune. He'd schemed for years to gain an introduction to the Tableau Haute, consumed with nothing else since stumbling across mention of them in the Catacombs.

The scrolls spoke of the Ekur, who looked as men, yet lived as gods. Much of it was rather dramatic and elaborate, but the common threads remained throughout each story. Heightened strength, speed, durability and lifespan beyond mortal dreams.

There were some rather outlandish stories, of those with the power to bend the minds of men to their will, or the ability to "fly", but he dismissed these as the exaggerations of over enthusiastic peasant storytellers.

The peasants and their stories. He knew it was their way. They needed their tall tales. To tell around their campfires, and their little fireplaces, to keep the cold from their bones, and reality's unrelenting claws from digging too deep into their limited little minds.

What consumed him most, though, was the tale of Dace, the "first" Ekur. In fact, it kept him awake at night, tossing and turning, as he dissected it in his mind. Picking it apart, he hungrily searched for the grain of truth that must be present. He knew these tales always had their basis in fact.

The tale went something like this.

Dace had been an unassuming and unimportant man, a painter, or a shepherd or some such, he forgot the details. Anyway, he lived in a small village with his wife, and he lived a small life.

One day, Dace was out for a walk in the green valleys near his home, when he came across a small cave on the side of a mountain.

He had passed this mountain many times before, but never before noticed the opening, which could not be seen from the path he took through the valley.

On this day, the sun must have been at the perfect point in the sky, for its rays fell just right on the opening in the mountain, illuminating it to him. Even as he gazed upon it, he saw the opening fading from sight, as the sun crept past.

The window of visibility must be tiny, and scared of losing sight of the opening and not being able to find it again, he squeezed himself through the tiny opening in the rockface, manfully putting his fear of small spaces to the back of his mind as he pushed himself into the cave.

Upon entering the cave, he was presented with a disappointing sight. Where he had been expecting gems, great riches, or treasures from battles past, he found but one torch, burning lonely in the wall, and an old, yellowed book upon a stone altar.

The altar and the torch unsettled him. Dace was a superstitious man, and not wanting to involve himself in any superstitious or religious matters, he turned to leave.

As he approached the rockface where he had entered the cave, he began to panic, for the opening had vanished. Scrabbling frantically at the rock, he spun around the room, looking wildly for an escape.

When he could find no means of escape, he fell to his knees and he wept. His greed had got the better of him, yet again.

He sobbed and smashed his fists up and down like a child, flailing at their newly learned sense of powerlessness against the consequences of the world. He gasped painfully, as the fleshy part of his hand struck a jagged piece of rock sticking up from the ground.

"Arghhhhhh!" he screamed in frustration, as his hand ran red, and drops of blood splattered to the floor.

As Dace lay, bewailing his fate, blood continued to drip from his hand to the floor. Just when he thought he could weep no more, a strong wind blew through the cave, blowing open the book on the altar.

Rising to his feet, grateful and curious for this interruption to his self-pity, he approached the altar and the book upon it.

He gazed upon it hungrily, his superstition forgotten in the face of his circumstance. But he could read nothing, the words were alien in his mind, and his eyes seemed to slide across them, unable to focus.

Realising the book would not save him, he railed once more, crying and raging to the skies above.

He brought his fist down hard on the book. As the blood from his hand touched the book, a fierce gust of wind rushed through the cave, and the pages of the book blew at its touch, falling open on the very first page.

He looked down, but saw the same undecipherable symbols as before, and despaired. He blinked, frantically, desperately, to make sense of the symbols. He continued to stare, glaring and squinting through bloodshot eyes.

Suddenly, the symbols on the page seemed to move, and he blinked hard, clearing his eyes. When he looked again, he found the symbols were no longer alien to him. There were only five lines of text on the page.

Sounding out the words in his mind, he proceeded to read them aloud.

"I relinquish the light", he began uncertainly, reciting the lines one after another.

"By blood we are bound..." he finished the last line, pondering the meaning.

He frowned, mouthing the words silently.

With nothing to lose, he returned to the jagged rock on the ground, and used it to draw a deep cut across his palm, which had now stopped bleeding.

Returning to the book, he held his palm over it, letting the blood spill to the page.

As thick drops of blood fell to the page, staining it red and blotting the text, he felt himself gripped by an unseen force.

He tensed, clenched his jaw painfully, then screamed.

It was as if claws of fire and ice were ripping through his body, clawing, rending, tearing. It felt as if he were being remade from the inside out.

He screamed in agony, his back arching, his neck cracking, his veins pulsing and popping.

And then, it was done.

His eyes were a ravenous red, and his skin a deathly pale, and he felt a great hunger within him.

Turning, he eyed the rockface, and knew what to do. He approached it, and ran his hand along it, and an opening appeared, as if it had been there all along.

Returning home, he fell upon his wife in a great flurry of teeth and claws, and her screams were terrible to behold.

It is said that when they found his wife, she was but an empty sack of skin and bone, and had been drained of every drop of blood.

Of Dace, there was no trace.

His belongings remained, but for a small, crudely done painting of his wife standing among the water lilies, that he'd taken with him.

It is said that Dace fathered all Ekur. That he took his teeth and his hunger and his bitterness, and went forth and fed, and fed, and fed. That he assuaged his hunger and his bitterness, siring many progeny, in many lands, over a thousand and more years.

And it is said that the more he fed, the stronger he grew. And that the stronger he grew, the hungrier he grew. Until eventually, his hunger became insatiable.

Great wars, destruction and misery Dace left in his wake. He drew unto him a band of reavers that he trusted to do his bidding, and imparted to each of them some of his power.

To one, he gave the power of flight.

"Aranare, fly the sky and see for me. See all those who may sustain us, and lead us to them", he instructed.

To another, inhuman strength.

"Lukios, fill the rivers with blood, as far as Aranare can see, and we shall never again know thirst", he told Lukios.

And to his last companion, it is said, he gave the power to bend the will and mind of men.

"Kitarae, what Lukios cannot conquer, you must enthral", he demanded of the third.

And so it was, Dace and his brethren scorched their way across the earth for a millenia and more, until one day, he disappeared suddenly from history's blood-soaked annals, without so much as a bloodstain on the page.

Some say Dace's reavers finally turned on him, sickened by the excess and his insatiable thirst for blood. Others say he returned to the cave to sleep, in wait, to pass his hunger down to the next unsuspecting traveller, and finally be free of it.

Narcisse found it a fanciful tale. But then Narcisse wasn't a particularly imaginative man, and what he couldn't fathom, he rationalised.

He was jerked unpleasantly back to the present by some jibe barked loudly across the table by the elder Ekur warlord, the one they called Rodolphe.

He didn't like the man, but men like him had their uses. Although with the other oaf, Hadur, being cut of the same cloth, he wasn't sure if the balance of "hammers" in their midst was quite right.

He contented himself to remain quiet, and bide his time for the time being.

He watched dispassionately, as a hooded group of men and women with their hands bound, were led into the room by the oaf, who could scarcely contain his excitement.

Things would be different, he thought. Once he had his teeth.

The Sad Face Of Evil

The boy's body hit the floor with a sickening squelch.

Hadur stepped back to give his master some space. He had not relished the task of bringing the offal back, it was beginning to stink, and the blood had stained his favourite shirt. He didn't see the point, the boy was dead and done, Lucien had made sure of that.

The Marquis stared down blankly at his son. He looked so peaceful now, he thought.

"I'm sorry, monseigneur", Hadur mumbled.

"Hmm? What's that?" The Marquis asked. He looked confused.

"I'm sorry, monseigneur", Hadur repeated. "For your son", he added, when The Marquis still seemed bemused.

"My son?" The Marquis asked.

"Janver, monseigneur", Hadur said, speaking slowly. "**Your son**". He nodded his head at the corpse.

"Janver..." The Marquis repeated dumbly. "Such a good boy", he said, nodding.

Janver was a fucking wretch, but Hadur kept his mouth shut. He had not one redeemable quality, probably why he hadn't been given his teeth yet. But he knew grief did funny things to people, and now was not the time to lament the boy's failings.

"Yes, monseigneur. He was a good boy", Hadur agreed, frowning.

"Good boy..." The Marquis repeated.

Hadur stood silently for a few minutes, before he cleared his throat and said, "Monseigneur...what do you want me to do with him?"

The Marquis looked up, the same bemused expression on his face. He looked in a bit of a daze, his eyes lazy, his eyebrows raised. "Do with him?"

"Janver, monseigneur...he cannot stay here. It's not...fitting", Hadur said dumbly, searching for the right word.

Subtlety was not something that came easily to him, but even he knew it was wrong to leave corpses rotting on the living room floor, family or not.

The Marquis swallowed hard but said nothing.

"Shall I prepare a plot for him, monseigneur...in the garden?" Hadur offered helpfully.

This seemed to trigger something in the man, for his face twitched, and something of his usual self returned.

"The garden? No", The Marquis responded curtly. "He shall burn...as is our way".

"As you wish", Hadur accepted.

An uncomfortable silence developed between them, at least it was for Hadur. The Marquis returned to his staring and seemed oblivious to him. Hadur stood unsure of how to broach the topic of Janver's murder.

"Ah...monseigneur?" Hadur asked.

"Yes?" The Marquis replied.

"What of Lucien?" Hadur asked.

The Marquis eyes narrowed. "That wretch?" he spat suddenly. "You dare speak of him to me!"

Hadur bowed his head deferentially, and waited.

He peeked cautiously, snatching glances at his lord, as he waited for his rage to subside. The Marquis' face worked furiously, alternating between rage, grief and...something else. Something unsettling. It worried him.

Taking a deep breath, The Marquis managed to calm himself. "Bring me his fucking head. It will play well with my polo mallet".

Hadur grinned. "As you say, monseigneur".

He liked Lucien, it would be fun to play with him. He was always good sport.

Better bring some of the rogues though, he thought to himself. He didn't fear Lucien, of course, and it wasn't that he couldn't handle him, he reassured himself. It would just be...prudent, that's it!

He congratulated himself on finding such a fitting word. The Marquis would like that one too.

Yes, better to bring backup, just in case. Don't leave it to chance Hadur, my boy.

And besides, he didn't want to be the one looking up at The Marquis' polo mallet if he messed this up.

Woe Woe, Reave, Reave

Gabriel watched sadly as Old Anne burned on the pyre.

They had all helped to build the pyre, and gained some small measure of catharsis in doing so. They'd built it in a large room near the surface that they called The Cross. Gabriel assumed this was due to the three different paths intersecting the room.

It had a high ceiling, and the smoke from the pyre drifted lazily into a chimney the Dwellers had chiselled. Small rays of sunlight filtered down from above through the gaps in the chimney, as if the sun were smiling gently down at Anne as she left on her final journey.

The Dwellers stood together in small groups before the pyre, their grief illuminated by the light of the fire for all to see.

Gabriel watched one family sadly, as the wife nestled her head into her husband's shoulder, eyes closed. A little girl cried into her skirt. The husband watched stoically as the flames carried Anne from the world.

She must have been truly loved. He hoped that when it was his time to leave this world, people would care enough to cry. It would be a sad affair, to have no one cry for you when you died.

Gabriel hoped she was in a better place now. He wasn't sure if he believed in a god, or a higher power, but he felt that a woman like Anne deserved something "after". Some peace.

She'd spent her whole life helping those who needed it. She never asked for anything in return, she simply gave. Gave of herself, until she had no more to give. Anne had no care for fame or fortune. Smiles and thanks were her currency. And by that measure, she was richer than any.

Gabriel had listened quietly to the stories of Anne around the fire the night before. It seemed everyone had a story, and every story had a happy ending, thanks to Anne.

Julot spoke of how she had found him under a bridge, when he was laid off from his job at the factory, and evicted from his home. He was sleeping under his jacket propped up on some sticks, his only protection from the rain and the wind, feverish and close to death.

Anne had taken him in, fed him, and nursed him until his fever passed, then gave him responsibility in the Under, helping him feel like a man again, and part of a community.

The Dwellers nodded sadly at this story. They all remembered the condition Julot was in when he first arrived.

Old Aurelienne, who was almost as old as Anne, spoke of how Anne had helped her and her child, when her husband, Evrard, fell under a horse, and could no longer work. Anne gave them a home and made them feel welcome in the Under.

Aurelienne had learned from Anne, learned to heal, to midwife and to care for children. It had been hard, but even Evrard had found a way to contribute. Anne taught him to sew and weave, and he learned to craft exquisite rugs and tapestries that they sold to the Over, using the money to buy food, clothes and medicine.

There were many such stories. Gabrielle was amazed at the rich and fulfilling life Anne had led, and he hoped to have half as many stories to tell.

He knew not everyone would share his opinion.

By the measure of many in the city above, Anne would be viewed as a failure. A villain or a vagrant they would call her. Because she did not fit in the mould made for her. Anne didn't fit into any mould, and she wouldn't play their game.

The game of the politicians, the businessmen, the foremen, the overseers. Those who viewed people as resources, disposable, and valued others only on what they could extract from them. Whether it be a lusty encounter, a furtherance in one's station, or a bundle of coin.

Anne had no interest in any of it. She cared nothing for status, fancy things or stylish clothes. She forsake all of it, and chose to live here, under it all, so that she could spend her time doing what she loved, helping people. Helping those who needed it most, those rejected and spurned by the world above.

It made Gabriel sad. He wished the world could be less cutthroat, and more selfless. More like Anne. Then people needn't hide underground and live like this. Shunned, spurned and derided by a society that by rights should protect them.

But, they were happy, and he envied them the simplicity of their lives.

Beside him, La Meme cried in silence, tears falling from her pretty blue eyes and sliding down her chin.

Gabriel was surprised at the depth of her feelings. He could not remember seeing her cry like this before.

He'd asked her if she'd known Anne well. She had simply smiled and said, "Once upon a time".

Having to content himself with this, he turned his attention to comforting her. Pulling her head to his shoulder, he petted her gently. Sometimes we all need comforting, children, parents, grandparents, all.

The quiet introspection of the funeral did not last long. The Dwellers started whispering excitedly, and gesturing animatedly in the direction of Gabriel and La Meme.

"What is happening?" Gabriel muttered to La Meme, who didn't seem to hear him.

Turning, he saw the reason for their excitement. Behind them stood Lucien.

"Lucien", he said aloud without thinking. Although he

spoke quietly, Lucien heard, and Gabriel could feel, if not see, his grin.

At this, La Meme took her head off Gabriel's shoulder. Her face was impassive, unreadable, but he thought he saw her eyes narrow for a moment.

Gabriel knew La Meme was not overly fond of Lucien, and grew less fond of him with each passing moment. And, he couldn't say that he blamed her.

Lucien was not perfect. He was...restless. Tormented, even.

And everywhere he went, danger seemed to follow. Dogging him like a trusted hound, you could always count on to be nipping at his heels.

He knew La Meme was just looking out for him, worrying for him... what grandmother would not?

He couldn't help himself though. There was something about Lucien. He'd thought of him often, since their parting, had lain awake at night, thinking of their night together at De Lune, and their embrace by the river. He'd thought of Lucien's anger, of his frustration, of his pain.

At first, it scared him, deterred him. But as he replayed it in his mind, he found himself focusing on the pain in his eyes, and the sadness behind them. And he too felt sadness, and sympathy, and an urge to comfort him.

And a curiosity, he felt. A curiosity as to what gave birth to this pain, what caused this shadow to loom over him.

Lucien was a sad man. He had a deep sadness within him, of that Gabriel was sure. But with Lucien, everything was on the surface, every flaw exposed, every quirk apparent. Gabriel found the transparency refreshing.

He felt a sense of kinship with Lucien, for he too knew sadness, and the loneliness that comes with such sadness. And, dangerous or not, Gabriel found himself drawn to him.

In life, it is rare to find a true kindred, and Gabriel wondered if Lucien was one such.

"Gabriel". Lucien placed a hand on Gabriel's shoulder, meeting his eyes for a long moment. "Are you well?"

"Oh yes, never better", La Meme broke in sarcastically. "Quite the training you provide at DuPassé. Rescuing orphan boys from the depths and battling crazed beasts. What **marvellous** career prospects. Where next? Is there some werebeast he should be battling? Some dragon you'd like him to slay?" Though her voice was thick with sarcasm, her eyes glittered dangerously.

"Orphan boys? Beasts?" Lucien asked, looking at Gabriel.

Gabriel blushed. "Something like that. I felt useless doing nothing, so I took it upon myself to find somewhere I could...help", he said lamely. "That led me here...to the Under...which as it would have it, is not the safest of places...though it is never dull apparently". His mouth twitched.

"You find this funny?" La Meme asked commandingly, her eyes flashing.

Lucien grinned, and she rounded on him. "As for you, do not even start", she warned.

She took a calming breath. "Not everything is a game, Lucien. Gabriel is not like you", La Meme said seriously.

Lucien looked at her strangely, then raised his hands in apology.

"Once again I find myself apologising to you. It was never my intention to endanger Gabriel. It is the...last thing I would want. I promise you that", Lucien said.

"An empty promise. Were that truly the case, you would leave him well enough alone", La Meme replied coolly.

Lucien said nothing. She was right, and he knew it. And yet, he could not simply leave him be.

Though he had only known Gabriel a short while, he felt a connection with him, something missing from the other relationships in his life. It was as if they were cut from the same cloth...no that wasn't quite right. As if they were two sides of the same coin. Yes, that was better.

La Meme shook her head and walked away.

"I'm sorry Gabriel, I didn't mean to get you into any trouble", Lucien said sombrely. He felt ashamed, yet also elated to see him.

"It's not your fault...you didn't tell me to come down here", Gabriel replied empathetically. "La Meme just worries. I'm all she's got".

"I admire her for it", Lucien said. "Loving someone is...difficult. Balancing our need to protect them...to lead them...with their need to find their own path...and accepting them for who they are. As scary and foreign to us as that may sometimes be...cannot be easy".

"You sound as if you speak from experience", Gabriel said.

Lucien's face closed over. "Perhaps", he said tight lipped, forcing a smile.

They stood in silence, watching the pyre, alone with their thoughts.

"Lucien, why are you here?" Gabriel asked suddenly.

Lucien rubbed his jaw tentatively, as if deciding how much he should tell.

Always some smoke with you, Gabriel thought to himself.

"I've done something foolish. It seems to be a habit I am incapable of breaking", Lucien said quietly. "And not the only one", he added, watching Gabriel.

Gabriel wondered at this.

"The powerful man I spoke of to you", Lucien continued. "I have irritated him somewhat".

"What have you done?" Gabriel asked, concerned. "Surely nothing that cannot be undone?"

"Well, I killed his son", Lucien replied, surprising himself at this candid divulgence. "He didn't take it too well". He smiled grimly.

"What! But why? How could you do such a thing!" Gabriel

shouted, horrified. He looked shaken to his core, and was looking at Lucien strangely. "I knew you were...tormented...dangerous even perhaps...and I accepted that as part of you. But this is...**Murder?**"

The way Gabriel looked at him hit him harder than one of Hadur's fists. He was disappointed in him. Worse than that, beneath his disappointment, was pity, as if he had failed at being human in the most fundamental way.

"No, it is not as you think", Lucien began. "There was no murder-".

But Gabriel had heard enough and cut him off. "La Meme was right about you...I am a flawed man to find you so...so..."

Lucien did not hear "what", for Gabriel stormed away from the pyre and into the Under.

He watched as he left, his thoughts bleak.

"Leave him be", La Meme said quietly.

He had not heard her approach, consumed as he was by his self-pity.

Would that I could, Lucien thought.

Things were simpler before I met you.

Back when I only had one person to disappoint.

Myself.

*

Gabriel walked mindlessly, his legs doing his thinking for him. Ignoring the twists and turns of the Under, he kept walking straight. He needed straight right now, a clear path, no twists or turns or shades of grey.

Though he realised after a while, that the path was in fact sloping downwards, and he was moving deeper underground. He hoped this wasn't some kind of ill omen.

He walked until he saw some light appear at the end of the path, still far in the distance. Curious, he pressed on toward it. Faintly it shone at first, then it grew larger and larger in front of him. His interest growing, he picked up his pace.

What is it? Another pyre? A campfire?

No, it's not a fire…it's not bright enough, Gabriel pondered.

Chasing the omen, he stepped into a giant cavern, and his mouth dropped open as he took in the sight before him.

A giant lake! Beneath a ceiling thick with stalactites, that were dripping water slowly into the lake below. Drip, drip, drip, the water trickled, down the icicle shaped fingers, before splashing gently into the water below.

I must be beneath the Seine! he thought, with a shade of apprehension.

The lake was a misty, ethereal blue, with undercurrents of grey and purple. It stretched back into the depths of the cavern. He couldn't tell how far back it went, but it seemed to go on forever. He shuddered to think what lay in its depths.

On either side of the lake cavern were two paths winding up back into the Under. He wondered what mysteries they led to?

Approaching the lake, he marvelled at its beauty. Kneeling down on the soft 'shoreline' of rocks around the edge, he ran his hand through the water. It was cold, but not as cold as he expected.

"The Under truly is a marvellous place", he said to himself.

"I couldn't agree more…you never know what manner of thing you may find down here", a sardonic voice replied.

Gabriel almost jumped out of his skin. Spinning to his feet, he looked around frantically, before spotting the source of the noise. A well-dressed man, with a mocking face, and cold demeanour, leant against the wall with his arms crossed.

He looked as if he didn't have a care in the world and had a palpable air of arrogance about him.

Whereas Lucien exuded self-confidence, this man oozed something else. Something unpleasant.

"Who are you?" Gabriel asked, ashamed that his voice shook a little.

"Who me? Why, I'm just a man, like you", the stranger

responded. "And Lucien", he added with a smirk.

Gabriel found the man's choice of words strange. "Another of his **friends,** are you?" Gabriel shot back, his courage returning. He'd had enough of these bullies.

The man's face hardened. His eyes narrowed, and losing their mocking twinkle, took on a more frightening aspect.

"Friends? No. Once upon a time...perhaps. Once upon a time...more than friends. Brothers", the man said coldly. "Now? He is nothing to me. Nothing but a murderer. And he must be brought to justice".

"And what justice would that be?" Gabriel asked. He was worried now, and determined to keep the man speaking while he thought of the best way to escape.

He thought he knew who this man was. Lucien had warned him of him.

"The only true justice...blood for blood", the man replied, his eyes dark and hooded.

"How can you speak of justice and murder in the same sentence?" Gabriel asked. "If Lucien has truly killed someone, as you say, then he should be brought to trial, and judged by the people, not you".

"The people?" The man laughed loudly. It was a horrible laugh, and to Gabriel's ears, rather unhinged.

"The cattle you mean?" He laughed again wildly. "Do not make me laugh, boy!" he shouted suddenly, his voice cracking like glass, his eyes popping madly in his head.

"I wouldn't trust them with a pissing contest. Lucien is of us. He must face our justice. Not the peasant noose", the man spat.

"Your justice? What do you mean? You speak as if you are above the law", Gabriel asked, confused by the strange way the man spoke.

He knew one thing, he liked him less each passing moment, and the less he liked him, the more his fear of him grew. He had a deranged, feverish look about him, like a fallen king watching his kingdom collapse around him.

"As far as you are concerned, peasant, I am the law. Now come here so we can be done with this. Lucien took from me my son, so I shall take you". He took a menacing step toward Gabriel.

Gabriel took a step back.

The time to act was now!

He braced himself, ready to run.

This cuckoo of a man was approaching him from the eastern entrance, so he'd run west, and not stop until there was some serious distance between them.

However, he made it not a pace, for a strong hand gripped his arm.

Instinctively, he struggled, and tried to pull his arm away, but the grip was iron strong, which was disorienting, given that the hand was stylishly bejewelled, and had prettily painted black fingernails.

He was pulled sharply backwards, into the bosom of a woman. Sweet perfume filled his nostrils, and thick panther black hair fell across his face, as she caressed his face with her other prettily painted hand.

Through the gaps in the hair covering his eyes, he could see the man laughing. What an odd sight.

"Don't make me hurt you, pretty one", the woman whispered in his ear. "Do as he wants, you needn't die...more's the pity", she added wistfully.

He shook the hair out of his eyes. "Why are you doing this? The man is evil. He means to murder me!" Gabriel shouted.

The woman chuckled, a throaty seductive sound. "Really?" she asked, her breath kissing his neck.

"So you're a villain like him, just the same?" Gabriel said, disappointed.

"Do not make the mistake of likening me to one of **you**", she said coldly, her voice losing its charm.

"One of who?" Gabriel asked, confused.

"Enough talk", she replied, hitting him on the back of the neck with the side of her hand.

Elsewhere in the Under.

Hadur bounded along the passage toward the Dwellers, whistling merrily, a huge club in his bear-like paw.

His reavers followed behind silently, their faces grim.

He wasn't initially thrilled The Marquis had given him this task. Clear out a bunch of Dwellers, and absolutely no teeth involved. It seemed like a damned waste of good food, and a test of his self-control that he did not relish.

But when The Marquis had promised him one of the orphan boys that slimy weasel Marceau had procured for them, his objections were quickly forgotten.

As he approached the camp, a dweller appeared, greeting him warmly with hand outstretched and a dumb smile on his stupid face.

Stupid oaf, Hadur thought blithely to himself.

Chuckling loudly, Hadur ceased his bounding. "Why **hello to you too!**"

The dweller's head disappeared in a bloody spray, as Hadur's club swung wildly through the air at the space it used to inhabit.

He seemed to find this incredibly amusing, as he turned to his men with an expectant grin on his face.

"Very funny, boss", one of them chimed from the back.

"Yeah, great boss!" another hurriedly offered, as Hadur looked from face to face hungry for acknowledgement, like a child with its first finger painting.

"The fun doesn't stop there my boys!" he boomed.

Confused, his men paused and looked at each other nervously. They never knew what he had up his sleeve. With Hadur, anything was possible.

"Just...a...moment", he turned his back to them, and fussed

with his jerkin, moving his big arms around clumsily as if searching for something. "Know that I have it here...somewhere...brought it specially...pissing thing!...ahah!" he exclaimed suddenly.

Hadur pulled something from his jerkin, then hastily hid it under his meaty arm before his men could see.

Smartening himself, something hid under his arm, he strode forward into the Dweller camp.

Quietly filing into the chamber behind, his men could see now it was a curved hunting horn he held.

Hadur stopped and raised the horn to his mouth. Tipping his head back, he breathed in hard, his chest expanding like a hot air balloon. Having filled his awesome lungs, he blew long and hard on the horn.

It rang out with a loud **ooh ooh** sound, like a particularly large cow expressing its discontent.

The Dwellers stopped what they were doing and turned to look. The noise had startled them, and somewhere in their midst a child began to cry.

Hadur stood grinning stupidly from dweller to dweller, before looking down with surprise at the club and horn he held, as if not sure why he held them. His smile faltered for a moment.

Sheepishly, he carefully placed the horn back in his jerkin, before looking up again, a tad awkwardly, at the gathered mass.

"What was I...ah yes!" he said to himself. "Woe woe, reave reave... something like that", he uttered half-heartedly.

"It's the damn club...throwing me off", he wailed, swinging the club frustratedly side to side, then up and down, as if it were restricting him in some way and he were trying to rid himself of it.

"Ah, to hell with it! Hunting time!" he boomed, his voice rolling out like thunder.

Grabbing a torch from the wall, as if he felt he needed weapons in both hands for this style of murder, he leapt forward

into their midst, torch in one hand, club in the other, a mad grin
on his face.

A State Of Emergency

The Marquis was furious.

He had been certain to find Lucien with the boy, Gabriel. It had enraged him greatly when he found the boy alone, and Lucien's piss-eaten face nowhere in sight.

Marceau's secretary, Carmen, bit her fingernails nervously, as the scary looking man paced up and down in front of her, relentlessly, pivoting viciously on his feet each time he turned.

It was a truly strange sight. The waiting room outside Marceau's office, that was, and its assortment of oddballs.

The oafish giant sat calmly reading in one of the visitor chairs. His body dwarfed the tiny thing, and she worried it would break under him. Yet another thing for her to worry about.

The woman was a queer thing also. She found her unsettling with her flashing eyes, her black nails and leanly muscled figure.

Very unladylike, she thought to herself pompously.

She didn't carry herself as one should, and her oufit...it was scandalous. Her dress was so short! And, really, a mink coat? Who did she think she was?

Catching the harlot in mink looking, Carmen dropped her eyes quickly, her heart skipping a beat.

What a strange assortment of folk Marceau had begun associating with as of late.

The scary restless man stopped his pacing suddenly, and

whipped a gold pocket watch from the breast pocket of his jacket.

The sudden motion startled Carmen, and she jumped a little in her seat. She hoped they hadn't seen. Rearranging her over large glasses on her face, she continued pretending to work.

"Will you cease your pacing?" the woman drawled in a bored voice.

The man shot her a venomous look, which she returned. The Marquis' attention was elsewhere, else he might have shot her down with a cutting remark. As it was, he resumed his pacing, contenting himself with the look.

The woman curled her lip, and resumed her studied indifference to the whole affair.

Hadur said nothing. He was enjoying his book. Though he couldn't understand all of it, it gave him great joy when he found passages he could understand fully.

Just as Carmen was about to make an excuse and remove herself from the horrible atmosphere of the waiting room, the door opened.

Hadur looked up from his book. Marceau, and another pompous old windbag, he thought. They all look the same, these politicians, like wizened old lizards, their skin stretched out like parchment over frightened eyes and deceitful mouths.

He still didn't know why Marceau had been given his teeth, but he trusted The Marquis with these things.

He liked to kill, always had, even before he'd earned his place in the tableau. But the scheming bored him to tears. As long as they had a hearty supply of food and sport, he was happy, and cared not a jot for any of it.

"Ah, Carmen, why don't you go home for the day?" Marceau said hesitantly. "I have no more need of you, and it's getting dark, you shall be glad to leave I expect".

"Really? Are you sure?" Carmen asked half-heartedly. "What about our...engagement?"

"Another time", Marceau said tightly. "I promise, my dear, I shall think of it constantly until then", he said with a little of his charm, letting fall the pretence of modesty.

Carmen blushed at this, and Hadur laughed. She shot him a filthy look.

Marceau's lips thinned, and he hurriedly ushered her away toward the door as she gathered her jacket.

Carmen seemed unsure. She gave the oaf another withering look but did as Marceau bid. "As you say, monsieur". She curtsied prettily.

Hadur stifled another laugh, as she left with a glare.

"Quite the girl you have there, Marceau". Hadur grinned stupidly, his eyes mocking.

Marceau frowned.

"Come in then", he said wearily, beckoning them into his office. "Madame Dagger". He addressed her slightly more enthusiastically as he noticed her and offered his arm.

She took it and let him lead her to her chair. She allowed him the reward of a sultry smile before seating herself, as he pushed the chair in under her.

He blushed like a schoolboy.

The Marquis swept into the room impatiently, seating himself, Hadur close behind.

"Sit", The Marquis commanded, gesturing to Marceau's desk.

Marceau, remembering himself, tore his eyes from Madame Dagger, and walked behind his desk, seating himself on the other side in a businesslike manner, as if this were any other meeting.

The Marquis liked this not at all.

Realising the faux pas, Marceau rose and bowed quickly. "Monseigneur". He fell back into his chair, embarrassed. "How can I serve your cause?"

"Our cause", Madame Dagger corrected, before The Marquis could respond.

Reddening further Marceau replied. "Of course, a slip of the tongue, my apologies, madame".

Throwing Madame Dagger another poisonous look, The Marquis said. "This is rather urgent".

"Oh, yes?" Marceau asked diplomatically.

"The villain Lucien...has...killed my son", The Marquis replied, the words costing him. He paused, the muscles in his jaw and cheek working. "And he must pay".

"Monseigneur", Marceau bowed his head. "My deepest condolences". After a moment, he continued. "Of course, he shall be brought to justice. For the guillotine, his head".

"Perhaps. But first, he must be found", The Marquis said.

"Are you...ah...unable to find him?" Marceau asked cautiously. Though he had his teeth, he was pink as a babe still, and was loath to offend his new master if he could avoid it.

"You dare question me?" The Marquis asked, rising to his feet, eyes burning.

"Monseigneur...I only mean that if you cannot find him with all of your...powers...what chance would I have? I am but a child compared to you", Marceau grovelled.

It seemed to work, for the anger disappeared from The Marquis' eyes. "As you say I am powerful...yet I cannot find him", The Marquis admitted. A fact that seemed to pain him greatly, from the expression on his face.

Marceau frowned. His lips joined in thin sympathy, and what he supposed was empathy, shone from his eyes. It really was a smug patronising thing, his 'sympathy' face.

"But you can", The Marquis said.

"Monseigneur?" Marceau asked weakly.

"Un état d'urgence", The Marquis said quietly. His eyes had taken on a haunted look and were making Marceau even more nervous than usual.

"Monseigneur, you cannot be serious. I have just taken office, there will be a revolt... how would I ever justify it?"

Marceau said.

"You forget yourself, boy!" The Marquis retorted.

"Monseigneur, respectfully I disagree...I have...am...meeting my end of the bargain with you. But this...you ask too much", Marceau said.

He felt emboldened since gaining his teeth. He knew he was still a... new tooth...but he had a lifetime of these back-office dealings behind him, and understood how and when to play his hand.

The Marquis' eyes simmered, and Marceau could feel heat emanating from him.

Marceau licked his lips. Perhaps he had miscalculated.

The giant, Hadur, stood up ponderously, and walked over to the window by Marceau's desk.

Seemingly admiring the view of the grounds, Hadur spoke without turning. "It would be a shame if they had to find a new president, monseigneur, so soon after the death of the last".

The Marquis looked up, surprised.

"Most tragic it would be. Un...precedented", Hadur said, taking a moment to finish the last word, a satisfied smile on his face.

The Marquis gave an evil smirk, and rose to his feet, approaching Marceau from the side of his desk. Marceau looked rather feeble, sitting there sandwiched between The Marquis and the giant.

Realising the precariousness of his situation, Marceau cleared his throat and hurried to his feet, squeezing past The Marquis and scurrying to the other side of the desk, putting some space between them.

"Ah, yes. Perhaps I have thought this wrong after all", he said hastily. "It will be...as you say, monseigneur".

The Marquis continued to stare that horrible stare. The heat radiating from him was oppressive. After a moment, he said, "See that it is".

Without another word, he turned and left, leaving Marceau with the oaf and Madame Dagger.

"Close one, boy", Hadur said. "Tis not the time to question him".

"Not to question him?" Marceau said incredulously. "I hope the people are so inclined".

*

Outside the palace, The Marquis waited.

Seeing Hadur as he left, he pulled him to one side. "I don't care what he says, see to it that he does as I say. Stay with him until it's done".

"You don't trust him, monseigneur?" Hadur looked genuinely surprised. He had given Marceau his teeth after all.

"Trust a politician?" The Marquis laughed with genuine good humour. It was good to see him smile a little. "Lying to them is as natural as feeding to us, boy".

Hadur nodded dumbly.

The Marquis wasn't sure he'd understood entirely, but he said nothing else.

Good oaf, The Marquis thought to himself absentmindedly.

Were all my servants so unquestioningly obedient.

"What about you, monseigneur?" Hadur asked. "What will you do now to flush Lucien out of his hole?"

"I shall fish", The Marquis replied.

307

Madame Dagger

The voices in her head never stopped, but she didn't let them stop her. They were persistent, the voices, and sometimes they shouted so loud she wanted to scream. But that would just be giving them what they wanted.

She knew they wanted her to scream. Wanted her to lose control, to give in to the pain and the hate. To rend, to tear. To scratch, to bite, to claw.

These were just a few of the things the voices often bayed for.

They hadn't always been with her. The voices. She remembered a time before. But that was long ago, and seemed so alien as to be a different world now.

They weren't all screams and shouts. There were some nice voices. Not many, mind, but some. The nice voices came sometimes when she felt happy, or safe. There weren't many people who made her happy, or places she felt safe...but there were some.

There used to be **people** who made her feel safe, and **places** that made her feel happy. Then things got all muddled up. And then she didn't know what was what anymore.

Now **she** made herself feel safe, for the most part. And she took her happiness where she could find it. She'd never again let someone make her feel scared, feel powerless. She had that much at least. But she didn't think she'd ever be truly happy again, like she once was. But she could hope. It was all she had.

L'aile Cassée made her feel happy. L'aile Cassée made her feel safe. It hadn't always, but it did now. She knew she had to get to L'aile Cassée.

She had made a promise you see, and she never broke a

promise. No matter how long ago it was made, or how heavy the burden upon her. She was many things, Madame Dagger, but she was no liar.

She enjoyed the desiring looks men gave her as she passed. It made her feel powerful, and when she felt powerful, she felt safe.

She knew she could have any of them, if she wanted.

Of course, she didn't, and the thought of letting another man touch her made her skin crawl, and her blood bubble. She would die before she let another wretched man defile her.

But that didn't mean it didn't have its uses, her power over men, and she used it to good effect. And why shouldn't she?

Twas a man's world, and as they used their force to achieve their means, so she used her beauty. One flash of her eyes, one flick of her hair, and they would fall drooling at her feet. Stupid creatures.

As base as dogs, were most of them. All they wanted was to pump madly for a few chance moments, before rolling over and falling asleep. Pah. They all promised her the best lovemaking, assured her of it. But there was no love involved.

At least, not for her. Just blood. Sweet blood soaking her mouth, her lips, her neck. Blood, and the sweet release in her head as the voices left her. But they always returned.

There were some men she despised more than others. Those who sought power. Sought to dominate. Sought to rule over their fellows. Sought to stamp their will upon them with an iron boot.

These were the worst kind. The rutting dogs she could tolerate. The dogs she understood. The would-be-dominants, she could not. And for this, she despised them.

She didn't want to dominate anybody. She just wanted to be left alone, and not have some power hungry man trying to stamp his authority on her or exploit her to his means.

She didn't know what compelled some men to act this way. Everything they saw they tried to conquer, buy or bed. Maybe it was an absence in the trousers.

In her eyes, this very desire made them unfit for the purpose. If they wanted to rule, they should not rule. Greedy, ruthless men were seldom abundant in virtue.

As L'aile Cassée came into view, she smiled a rare smile. It was a beautiful thing, her smile. Not because of her beauty, but because it shone pure and bright as the sun. Not many had seen Madame Dagger smile, and she intended to keep it that way.

She'd been so lost in her thoughts this evening, that she hadn't even stopped to gaze upon the Sacré Coeur on the way.

She chided herself for this. It was one of her favourite things to do. Sometimes she sat outside on the steps for hours, shawl or hood drawn tight about her face.

She dared not go inside, but there was something calming about the place, and the voices in her head quietened a little there. Anything that quietened the voices she tried to make a habit of.

L'aile Cassée was a maison-close. A place where men with the mind to, could pay for the company of women, with the mind to provide it. Madame Dagger preferred the term to "whore house", as some crassly put it.

It was a big place. The largest in the district, in fact. An entire tenement building built to house cocottes. The owner had been an ambitious man, a man of great vision, so they said.

Realising that sex had a far more favourable margin than rentals, he had the foresight and genius to evict poor tenants from his tenement buildings, and fill them to the brim with cocottes, until their ivory legs, and busty dresses, oozed from the very seams.

The only remarkable thing about it was the sign. A snow-white swan with a broken wing, on a brown wooden backboard.

She walked in with a smile. She was home.

Yvon greeted her warmly at the door, taking her jacket and offering her his arm. She liked Yvon, and that was a rare thing, for she liked almost no one. Yvon understood her. He'd never tried to bed her. He was just her friend. Nothing more, nothing less.

She didn't know a lot about Yvon, but then he didn't know much about her either. And in that she felt comfort.

There was no prying, no difficult questions, and no desire to deepen their friendship by baring all. Yvon was warm and kind, and he made her feel safe and familiar, like spending time with a long-lost uncle, or perhaps a grandfather. She wasn't sure which.

He was a big man, with a shining bald pate circled by closely shaved grey hair on the sides, and forearms like boughs of oak. He had a warm friendly smile, and rosy cheeks with high cheekbones. The ladies loved him.

Yvon wasn't always warm and kind, mind. He'd break your skull as good as look at you, if you got out of line, or broke the rules. Madame Dagger liked that about him. She shared his passion for vengeance, particularly when it came to those she loved.

It was Yvon's job to look after the women at L'aile Cassée. She'd met Yvon years ago, at a less than choice bar. Yvon had been working the door, keeping the scoundrels in check. Unfortunately for Yvon, at this particular bar, that included nearly everyone.

She had first seen him, covered in blood, swinging his club like a wrecking ball, powering through a particularly nefarious group of young villains like a thresh through wheat.

When the dust settled, and the scoundrels lay still, he dropped his club, straightened his jacket, and fell to his knees before a young lady who had been the chosen victim of the men.

Offering his hand to her, he pulled to her feet and ushered her to safety, genteel as any courtier she had ever seen. She knew immediately that she liked him then.

Yvon was the perfect man for the job at L'aile Cassée. He could be soft as silk, or hard as rock, which was what the women needed.

They were fragile things, most. Mistreated, exploited and abused by everyone they had made the mistake of trusting. It was a lesson she knew well herself.

The last thing they needed was another macho brute around them with the emotional intelligence of a block of cheese. She had chosen well. Yvon cared as well as he clubbed, and the women flourished, for the most part.

For some of them, this was all they'd ever known. Coerced or lured into the life of a cocotte by gutless sewer rats, bound for the fires below if she ever laid eyes upon them. No swift death for the likes of those, she thought to herself.

There was a market for children, in some circles, and some of the girls had been taken young. Too young. And some particularly unfortunate young boys suffered an even worse fate...

She shuddered.

"Madame?" Yvon asked.

"It's nothing". She waved her hand dismissively but smiled to soften the gesture. "How are things?" she asked, changing the subject.

"Well, for the most part. Rosalie has had some trouble settling...she has run away twice in the past fortnight", Yvon said.

"Twice? She returns?" Madame Dagger asked.

"Yes..." Yvon broke off, unsure.

"Go on", Madame Dagger commanded, her eyes narrowing.

"She has come back...but with fresh bruises each time. The last time she returned... her rib was broken and her eye swole shut", Yvon said.

Her eyes flashed.

Yvon swallowed before continuing. "I believe she visits her old pimp... Clovis".

She turned her back to him, as a face hurtled through her

mind.

Cruel, high cheeks. Sensual, full lips.

A hand stretched out, entreatingly.

Turning back to Yvon, she said, "I will see to it", her voice harsh. Her eyes shone unnaturally and were no longer inviting. Yvon said nothing.

Truth be told, she scared him a little when she was like this.

"Yvon", she said curtly. "There will be a lockdown. Take this and see that everyone is well cared for". She handed him a large sum of money, which he stared at open mouthed.

"Madame…it's too much", Yvon protested.

"I'll decide what is enough", she said coldly, "Now take me to Ivy".

Yvon was hurt, but he did as she bid. He knew he should not take it personally. When these moods came upon her, Ivy was the only one who could calm her turbulent heart. He had known she would not take it well…to hear of Rosalie.

He never thought to think thoughts of sympathy for a pimp, but he thought them now for Clovis. The man was base, and his body should by rights rest at the bottom of the Seine, but the fate now in store for him turned his stomach.

It still made him shudder, some of the stories he had heard about Madame. He tried not to dwell on it. Among other stories, he had heard of her past, enough to understand why.

He felt an outpouring of emotion for her then, and a desire to protect her.

He did not know what had compelled those she trusted to mistreat her in such a way, but he despised them for it. He'd like to crack their skulls with his club, and watch the blood run clear.

Feeling Madame's eyes on him, he cleared his throat. "Sorry Madame. Right this way".

L'aile Cassée was beautifully furnished for a maison-close. But then, Madame was its proprietor. The first thing that struck you as you entered was the plush, lipstick red Savonnerie carpet that covered the floor. It ran through the place but was particularly striking in the main lounge. Expensive artwork covered the deep gold walls, some of it so striking it would not look out of place in the Élysée itself. Madame had spared no expense.

Beautiful women of all sorts and persuasions lazed on cosy red canapés and chaise longues.

Seeing the storm clouds still swirling in her eyes, he led her past the main lounge and up the stairs to Ivy's room. The room she shared with Ivy was at the very top of the building with windows overlooking the district.

Ivy said she liked to watch the sun in the mornings, and as she was well loved in the maison, no one minded much that she had the best room.

As they approached the room, muted voices could be heard within.

Knocking softly, Yvon stepped back and waited.

The voices stopped, and the door opened. Ivy stood there smiling shyly in a white dress. Seeing Madame's face, she stepped forward and embraced her.

"Mon coeur", she purred softly in her ear. "What is the matter?" She kissed Madame softly on her neck, then petted and pulled at her hair in a motherly fashion.

"Nothing", Madame said tight lipped.

Recognising the que, Ivy turned to Yvon. "Merci, Yvon".

Yvon glanced at Madame, then bowed and left, back downstairs to the lounge.

"Who were you talking to?" Madame asked, the clouds in her eyes parting.

"Little Lili", Ivy said.

Madame's face fell. "Désolée", she said sadly. "I didn't mean to interrupt. How is she?"

"It's one of those days", Ivy replied.

"Go to her. I will wait", Madame said.

Ivy cocked her head, and smiled prettily, before throwing her arms around Madame's neck, and kissing her softly on the mouth.

Stepping back into the room and closing the door, Ivy walked back to the bed and lay upon it.

A small girl lay with her on the bed, a dainty thing, and Ivy lay behind her, wrapping her arms around her and pulling her close.

Lili wrapped her arms around Ivy's own, and squeezed her tight. Her eyes were red, and a trail of makeup and tears stained her face in blotchy black streaks.

"Don't cry, pretty", Ivy cooed softly. "You shall ruin your pretty makeup". She wiped Lili's face, her long, delicate fingers gently rubbing the streaks away.

Lili sobbed, then nodded.

Seeing that she was still sad, Ivy began to hum, softly at first, then with more gusto, before breaking softly into song.

"Au clair de la lune, Mon ami Pierrot".

Lili lay quietly, her eyes closed, letting the music wash over her. It soothed her, and after a while, she joined in, first with hums of her own, then with her voice.

"Mais je sais qu'la porte, sur eux se ferma".

They finished the song in unison, and Lili smiled. "By the light of the moon. My mother used to sing it to me".

Ivy smiled and waited, it was good for her to talk.

"One of my favourite memories..." Lili broke off.

Ivy gave her a reassuring squeeze.

"It's hard for me to speak of her", Lili said. "I miss her so much sometimes".

"Go on", Ivy prompted. "Tell me".

"I'd had a nightmare...a man was chasing me through a building, and I couldn't escape. No matter where I went, he followed. I tried climbing, but his head popped out of the floor...grinning. It was dark, but his eyes were glowing yellow...I tried closing the door, but his head came through it, always grinning. I couldn't see his arms or legs. Just his floating head. I don't know why I can remember it so...vividly...but I see it bright as day..." Lili said.

"Sounds scary". Ivy shuddered.

"It was...eventually the man caught me...and his face pressed in on me, so close...all I can see are those bright yellow eyes, like a cat... or a lizard. I woke up screaming, it felt so real, like the man was in the room with me", Lili said.

"I'd scream too", Ivy admitted. "I've had dreams like that too", she said, a fae look on her face. "Go on", Ivy focused, prompting her to continue.

"Well...the man caught me...and I screamed...and then my mother came. She came with me in the bed, like you are now, and drew me to her. I remember telling her about the man, and that I would never sleep a wink ever again", Lili said.

Ivy grinned. Lili was so sweet. "And what did your mother say?"

"She said...she said if the man came back, she'd poke his eyes out. That she'd pop them like balloons". Lili giggled. The laughter was infectious, and Ivy joined her.

"She had a little hair pin with a flower on it she always used to wear, and she gave it to me. She said it was a magic pin, and that if the man came back, I was to poke him in the eyes with it. Said it had been blessed by a king, a priest and a witch, and it would pop his eyes and make him blow away out the window into the night", Lili said.

"How wonderful", Ivy said enthusiastically. "I wish I had such a pin".

Lili couldn't tell if Ivy was humouring her or not. She had a strange way about her sometimes.

"I shall bring you one", Lili said.

"And what about the song?" Ivy asked. She seemed to really want to know. Lili loved her for it.

"Well, after she gave me the pin, I was still a little scared...and I begged her to stay, so she sang for me. She sang me 'By The Light Of The Moon'...like you did Ive", Lili said shyly. "And then she just stayed...she stayed and slept in the bed with me, and didn't go back to my pa the whole night..."

"She must have loved you very much", Ivy said seriously.

"She did", Lili said. "Did..."

They lay entwined together, each lost in their memories.

"It's my favourite song", Lili said, breaking the silence.

"Hmm?" Ivy asked absentmindedly.

"Light of The Moon", Lili mumbled, reddening.

"I like it too", Ivy said.

"Why do you look after me like this?" Lili asked suddenly, her confusion genuine.

"Because I love you, of course", Ivy said automatically.

Lili turned over to face her. "Do you really?" she asked, her eyes full of hope.

"Always", Ivy said. Leaning forward she kissed her forehead softly.

Lili said nothing, but held her tightly. Burying her head in Ivy's dress, she screwed her eyes shut. If she tried hard, she could almost picture herself back in her ma's arms. She didn't think she'd ever feel loved again, after ma went, and she wound up in the maison-close.

"Love you", Lili mumbled quietly.

Ivy said nothing, but smiled sweetly, and continued to stroke her hair.

Her eyes had a distant, faraway look to them, and her stroking seemed bittersweet, almost as if she were unaware of it.

Outside in the hall, Madame cried silently in the darkness, trapped in memories of her own.

Rocking backward and forward on her feet, tears fell down her face like rain.

Who could ever love you?

Who?

Who?

Who?

The voices screamed, over and over. She screwed her eyes shut and clenched her fists. The muscles in her jaw worked furiously as she quietened the voices and forced them from her mind.

She cast her mind back to the day she met Lili.

She remembered it as if it were yesterday.

Innocent, blissfully naive, and bursting at the seams with an insatiable lust for adventure.

She had a smile that could light the darkest night and warm the coldest heart.

She had been Tomas back then, before Joachim and his knife.

And Swallow It You Shall

Garlon cleared his throat, a horrible guttural, gloopy sound. It sounded like he was revving up a snotty motorcar. Rolling his collected phlegm around his mouth, he selected his target, then let fly with his spit.

Shplat.

"Hoho!" he exclaimed, as his phlegm hit the face of one of Marceau's scoundrels. "Take that...vache puante".

The flic dropped his baton in disgust, falling out of line. "Aaaagh", he moaned loudly, wiping his face with his sleeve.

A ruddy-faced man with a thickly curled moustache and a chest full of medals started shouting angrily at the flic, his cavalry sabre bouncing in time to his shouts.

"Good one Garlon". His friend Clet thumped him one on the back. "Marceau thinks he can deploy les flics like they are his personal honour guard. The man has balls like a bull".

"Yeh, and brains like shit", Garlon fired back. "He'll be removed from office before his second month is up. Why go through all the scheming and plotting to get elected, just to throw it all away on some foolishness? It doesn't make any sense".

Marceau's behaviour baffled him. Springing a lockdown on them like this, on some jumped up claim that there'd been...what did they say? An attempted coup?

Apparently, some madman named Lucien and his men had

stormed the Élysée by night and taken a bunch of hostages. Apparently.

Garlon didn't believe a word of it. It smelled like bullshit. And if it smelled like bullshit, and looked like bullshit, it's probably bullshit, his father used to say.

Garlon didn't like when people tried to feed him bullshit. Especially so soon in the day, and in such large quantities.

Thousands of Parisians had gathered at the Élysée to protest the lockdown, and the atmosphere was tense, like a block of dynamite with its wick in, waiting for a spark to ignite it.

Garlon as always, was in the thick of it, standing close to the front of the crowd with Clet.

He was enjoying the righteous discontent of the crowd, and the nervous shifting of the flics trying not to piss their trousers. He grinned at Clet.

"Gar, what's that?" Clet said suddenly, pointing over the crowd.

"What in the..." Garlon exclaimed.

A hulking tree of a man was stomping through the crowd, parting it like water, knocking aside unsuspecting protestors like boules pins.

He was clad in one of the old-style jerkins, and striding head and shoulders above any in the crowd, a surly look on his face.

A small group of men followed hastily behind in the vacuum of his path, avoiding the eyes of the disgruntled protestors turning to curse the giant as he passed.

Quietly they cursed him, mind, and very much under their breath, and very much once he was out of sight.

"Who is that monster?" Garlon muttered incredulously, his eyes on the giant.

Clet whistled admiringly. "He's a big one. Bet he'd sink a few jugs".

Beer was never far from Clet's mind, and his measure of respect for a man was largely determined by how many beers he could sink before falling down, and how much weight he could hoist above his head after imbibing said beers.

They watched together, as the giant approached, leaving a trail of chaos in his wake.

They stepped back quickly to avoid him, and Garlon admired him anew.

He was even bigger up close, his chest and shoulders truly enormous.

He swept past them, pushing his way to the front of the crowd, and stood before the gate of the Élysée, his men huddled close to him. He stood, talking in low tones to his men, his eyes constantly scanning the crowd as he spoke.

He looked very conspiratorial, Garlon thought.

Garlon's curiosity was piqued, and he elbowed his way to the front of the crowd near the gate, so that he could better overhear the giant's conversation.

"Now if you see Lucien, you kill him on sight. No questions asked", the giant said grimly.

"In front of everyone, boss?" a pale man with a pockmarked face asked.

"It's The Marquis' orders", the giant said, as if that explained everything.

"Marquis?" Garlon mouthed, a frown on his face.

"What about them?" a man with a cudgel resting lazily on his shoulder asked, gesturing at the protestors with his head.

"What about em?" the giant growled.

"I mean...what if they try to...intervene?" the man asked.

"Hurt em, but don't kill em", the giant grunted. "It's Lucien we want. We don't want any peasant blood spilled. Yet". He grinned evilly then, his eyes lighting up.

"Lucien", Garlon muttered to himself. "That's the man on the posters".

Picking up a piece of paper from the floor at his feet, he turned it over and studied it. A handsome face stared back at him from beneath the words: "WANTED: Lucien, reward 100,000 francs". There was a brief description, and a warning that the man was highly dangerous. Wanted for conspiracy, kidnap, murder and sedition.

Garlon opened his mouth in disbelief.

100,000 francs!

He frowned, studying the man in the picture.

He don't look so dangerous, Garlon thought.

The murder hungry giant looked far more menacing.

Looking up, he felt his stomach tighten. The giant was watching him, no, glaring at him, as if he had heard him speak Lucien's name. But he can't have.

Don't be stupid man, you barely whispered his name.

The giant pointed at him, and his men began to run toward him.

Maybe not. Merde!

Spinning around, he elbowed his way back into the crowd frantically. Seeing his friend in peril, Clet waded through the crowd to meet him.

"Gar what is it? What's wrong?" Clet shouted over the crowd, who were baying angrily now, and rushing toward the gate.

"Run, run, run!" Garlon shouted back.

Clet grinned, enjoying himself, but he obeyed.

Behind Garlon, the pock faced man who had been speaking with the giant, grabbed at him.

Getting a hold on the back of Garlon's shirt, the pockmarked man whooped happily. "I got him, I got him boss!" he shouted, turning to grin triumphantly back at the giant, who was now rapidly clearing his own path toward them.

"Putain!" the man screamed suddenly, as Garlon's pocketknife whipped out viciously across the side of his face, spraying blood into the crowd.

Not wasting any time, Garlon sprang away into the crowd

and started ducking and weaving, keeping himself low to avoid the prying eyes of the giant and his men.

Hadur leapt to the pockmarked man and roared, knocking a group of men to the floor in the process.

Picking him up as if he were a child, he growled, shaking with anger. It seemed as if Pockmark was done for, but then, the giant took a deep, calming breath, and closed his eyes.

A look of divine contentment appeared on his face, and he grinned stupidly.

Opening his eyes, slowly, he looked at Pockmark. "You know, Gérard, for such a fuck ugly son of a bitch, you surely smell good". Hadur licked his lips and grinned malevolently.

Gérard started to squirm and beat at him wildly with his fists. Wildly but ineffectually. His eyes were wide with horror.

"You are lucky, you troublesome morsel, that I have fed...and that I am trying to improve my...self-control". Hadur nodded sagely.

"You'd surely make a tasty snack. I'd have to do something about that face though...it's enough to put a man from his dinner". He thinned his lips as he smacked them, turning his head from side to side, as if wondering how he'd best go about it.

"Boss...please...I have a family", Gérard begged.

"Oh, a family you say!" Hadur laughed. "And I wonder what they'd make of your raping and reaving!" He chuckled to himself.

"A family, indeed. Ah boy, you do make me laugh". Ogling him like a sweetcake, he growled irritatedly and dropped the man to his feet.

"T'would not please The Marquis", Hadur said, looking terribly disappointed at this fact. He settled for running his finger across the cut on the man's face and licking it clean. "For a sour son of a bitch, you surely taste good. Who'd have guessed?" He smiled.

"Now, where is this pissing peasant!" Hadur boomed, turning from Gérard and scanning the crowd.

Unable to find the peasant, Hadur turned back to stare at Gérard, as if reconsidering eating him to ease the disappointment.

"Damnit all", he muttered after a moment.

*

At the edge of the crowd, a hooded figure watched, and hungered.

Hungry, his mind pulsed.

Bite them. Eat them. Bite them.

Tis a good thing he was hooded, for his face was a nightmare. Bloodshot eyes in a bloodless face. The whites of his eyes were startlingly white. Grey threads of vein throbbed painfully through his face, running rigid as rock.

Beneath the hood, some semblance of Henré remained, struggling deep within the beast.

I won't! he raged.

Bite. Bite. Bite. Thirst. Drink.

He screwed his eyes shut and covered his face with his hand.

How do I wake from this nightmare? he thought in a moment of clarity.

A high-pitched scream rang through his head, and his eyes snapped open.

When he closed his eyes, all that he saw was Anne, covered in blood, staggering away from him.

He could still taste her blood in his mouth. Its warm, rich taste, flooding him with pleasure as it dribbled thickly down his chin.

Her scream never left him, and he heard it ring through his mind again and again, clear as clarion. Sometimes in the night, he would wake, covered in sweat, and hear it as if she were there in the room with him.

He shook his head.

"No", he moaned. "No, no, no, no".

The pain came upon him then, and he doubled over, as a painful cramp ripped through him.

"Are you well, friend?" He felt a comforting hand on his shoulder and closed his eyes. The scent of the man so close was maddening. He could not bear it.

He could not speak through his pain and his hunger, and merely nodded.

The hand remained on his shoulder.

Get off me!

Bite. Bite. Drink!

As the cramp faded, the pain subsided, and he managed to gain control of his senses for a moment.

But then, as if on cue to torment him, a dizzying scent filled his nostrils.

Blood. Fresh blood. His mind went blank.

Screaming.

A delicious, rich taste filled his mouth.

More screaming.

He vaguely felt himself hit the ground, and heard shouting. A group of figures had ringed him and were shouting down at him.

It sounded so muted, as if someone had cut their vocal cords, he could barely make out what they were saying. He found it eerily amusing.

Drink! More! More! More!

His blood felt alight, he could feel it rushing through his veins like hot liquid fire. He felt so disoriented, so confused. Why was he on the floor? It was so hard to think with this fire burning through him!

Breathe.

He listened to the voice, and focused on his breathing, taking deep breaths through his nose. As if he had just surfaced from underwater, the noise of the crowd, and the screaming of the figures around him, rushed back at him.

Blood.

So much blood.

Who's blood?

Looking down at his shirt, drenched in blood, he panicked, and started patting at himself frantically, trying in vain to wipe it clear.

"You've killed him!" a woman screeched.

He winced. The voice sounded so loud, so sharp. It rang out like a bell in his mind.

"You bastard!" she continued to scream.

Looking up, he saw the body. A man. The man lay face down in a pool of blood, his head to one side, his eyes open wide and staring. The ground around him was slick with blood, blood that was slowly spreading toward Henré.

He couldn't control it. Springing to his feet, he fell to the floor hungrily by the body. and began suckling madly at the blood on the ground, like some ravenous dog.

"Noooooooooo!" the voice screamed in anguish.

Through his hunger, he heard the pain in the voice, as the woman cracked and broke.

A booted foot hit him hard in the side, sending him sprawling to his back. Fists and kicks rained down upon him then, as the crowd closed around him. He covered himself, bunching up tightly like a babe.

Through the blows, he closed his eyes and licked his lips appreciatively. He floated on a sea of bliss, lost in his thoughts, numb to the pain raining down on him.

He'd heard tales of the opium dens and the addicts who frequented them. It was said they'd visit day after day, spending every franc they had, and sleep blissful, drug induced dreams all day long.

That they'd beg, borrow and steal to feed their habit and that when the coin ran dry, they'd trade their bodies, even their own wives or mothers for a hit.

It was said that you could do anything to them under the influence of the stuff, the addicts, and that they'd scarcely notice. They'd merely wake up, and hunger for more, wondering when they could dream again.

He'd never tried opium, but he felt sympathy for those under its spell at that moment. He knew he'd do anything for blood, anything it commanded. He knew it was his master, and he its servant.

"Stop it! stop it, stop it, stop it!" a voice screamed. A familiar voice. He knew that voice. Where had he heard that voice before?

A creeping feeling began in the pitt of his stomach and he opened his eyes.

The blows stopped, and he rolled slowly to his knees, probing his injuries gently with his hand. He had several cracked ribs from the feel of it, and his right eye was almost totally swollen shut. But he barely felt a thing, high as he was.

"Henré?" the voice asked in anguish. "Is it you?"

Henré? he thought to himself.

He frowned, thinking, and then, a tidal wave of feeling and memory washed over him.

It felt as if he had been dunked headfirst into a pool of ice water, and as it washed over him, he saw, and he remembered. He saw clearly for the first time since Anne.

He saw a girl. A pretty girl, in a pretty dress, her eyes glittering with promise across the dancefloor.

He saw the girl. Saw a picnic by a lake. A spring meadow. Autumn hay.

A barn in winter. A hand, in his all the while. Her hand. On her finger, a ring.

"Am...Amerie?" Henré rasped.

"Is it you?" she asked again, horrified. "No, no, no...it can't be...it can't".

The small crowd that had gathered around Henré watched, confused, unsure what to do.

The distraught woman broke the spell. "Kill him!" she screeched. "Kill him! He killed my Ivan!"

"NOOOOOOOOOOOOOO!" Amerie shrieked loudly. "Get back!" She stood over Henré protectively, shielding him with her arms and her body. Her eyes darted wildly from person to person.

"Amerie", Henré rasped. "No".

My wife.

The crowd hesitated. The woman was pregnant, but they would not be denied their justice.

I don't have a wife! he thought.

Amerie is your wife.

No!

Henré reeled. It was too much for him to comprehend. Seizing upon the indecision of the crowd, he scrambled to his feet, and fled.

The newly widowed woman grabbed at him desperately as he passed, but he was too quick, and she lost her footing.

"Le pied m'a manqué", she wailed piteously from the floor.

"Henré, no!" Amerie shouted, running after him.

The widows' friends moved to close around Amerie, cutting off her retreat, but at that moment the crowd surged wildly, and they were swept forward in its current.

*

Marceau was worried, and it was making Carmen worried too. She'd never seen him like this before. He was usually so calm, so collected, but now, he looked like a tired father about to hit the bottle.

He paced up and down in front of her desk, glancing out of the window at every turn, which at his current rate of pacing, was alarmingly frequent.

I never should have done this. I've buried myself, he thought.

Of course he meant in the political sense. There would be no rotting in the ground for him now. Not now that he had his teeth.

Death? That was for lesser men. His bones would not turn to dust. He would remain strong and virile for a thousand years!

He allowed himself a small smirk.

"Marceau", Carmen asked, as he stopped his pacing.

"Yes?" he replied, turning to face her.

"Are you well?" she asked.

She looked scared, he thought. He could see it in her eyes, but he could also smell it on her, he realised with surprise.

"All will be well, Carmen, dear, do not fear", he said smoothly. "They will run out of steam soon enough, and this will run its course". He gestured at the mob outside the palace.

"Are you sure?" she asked, frowning.

He strode over to her and took her hands in his own. "I am sure", he said, holding her eyes.

She smiled and breathed a sigh of relief. "I am so glad. I was starting to worry".

Marceau would keep her safe.

Turning back to the window, he resumed his pacing, a little slower, and a little more considered this time.

As he took his steps, he placed his hands behind his back, and his face creased, as he thought the situation through.

The Marquis' men are out there. I am safe.

And besides, I am an Ekur now myself.

He puffed his chest a little at this, raising his head, and jutting his chin out imperiously, as he gazed upon his subjects.

Citizens, he corrected himself.

He'd been having strange dreams since taking his teeth. Very strange.

Dreams of celebrations and parades. Huge affairs, with thousands of people lining the streets of Paris, all screaming his name. Lines of troops, all rallying in his honour. At his back, his enemies lay dead at his feet, their bones crumbling to dust in the wind.

He wasn't sure what to make of the dreams yet, but he found himself longing for sleep, and closing his eyes excitedly each night.

Each night a new dream would take him, each more grand than the last, and as his adventures grew, so too did his legacy. Waking in the morning, he would smile lazily, and lay still, reliving his exploits.

Although he was but a 'newtooth', he could feel his power growing, and with it, a thirst. So far it had not bothered him much, but he could feel it gnawing at him, and he'd caught himself admiring the curve of Carmen's neck from time to time. He supposed he'd have to do something about it sooner or later.

The oaf Hadur spoke of "feeding" as if it were better than sex. He had scoffed at this and wondered what sort of sex he'd been having.

"I hope the men don't encounter any trouble". Carmen bit her lip nervously.

Foolish mortal.

Where did that come from?

Marceau rubbed at his eyes. He was probably just tired. Just tired, that's all it was.

"They'll be fine, Carmen". He smiled his winning smile, and she smiled back.

It didn't take a lot to assure the common folk, Marceau found. A few pleasant words and a smile, and they'd eat it up like pot-au-feu. Easy to assure, easy to sway.

He watched as Hadur spoke in hushed tones with his men below by the gate. The wretch Gérard was asking him something, and Marceau found that if he stared hard, he could read some of the man's words from his lips. Something about the crowd.

His eyesight and hearing had increased dramatically since his rebirth as a newtooth. He found he could hear the faintest whispers now and had overheard some truly choice things. Things that he fully intended to use to his advantage.

"Carmen, I'll take an absinthe, s'il vous plaît", he said, turning on his feet imperiously. "Just the thing to calm the nerves-".

He stopped abruptly, and his mouth fell shut with a pop. "Mmm, yes, just the thing, Carmen. I shall take one also", a commanding voice replied from the door to Marceau's waiting room, which was now open.

Carmen jumped and spun round, her hand on her chest. She was still a little on edge after all.

In the doorway, stood a man.

"Monsieur". Marceau inclined his head, before Carmen could respond. "You are welcome".

The man was The Marquis. He narrowed his eyes but said nothing in response.

Carmen thought this was rather rude.

"I did not expect to see you here", Marceau continued, waving his hand haughtily.

The Marquis arched his eyebrows.

Your pretty palace might make you feel important and safe, but remember, there is nowhere on this earth you are safe from me, boy. The Marquis' voice rang menacingly through Marceau's mind.

Marceau jumped, in a good imitation of Carmen, and threw his hand out to steady himself.

"Monsieur, are you well?" Carmen exclaimed, running over to Marceau and giving his back a little rub.

She was still unsure of the situation. She did not like this "Marquis" and wished he would leave and not come back.

Marceau looked shaken but responded in the affirmative. Carmen didn't look happy with his response, but she accepted it and did as she was bid.

She always did as she was bid.

"Well then, I shall leave you", she said dutifully, scurrying from the room and shutting the door hastily behind her, grateful to put some distance between her and this Marquis.

"I did not know you could do that", Marceau said quietly, in awe. "Monseigneur", he added.

"There is much that I can do, and you know but a fraction of it", The Marquis replied coldly. He had a wild look to him, and he felt...different. More dangerous, Marceau thought. But why?

"Monseigneur", Marceau bowed deeply, happy to debase himself now that Carmen was out of the room. By now, he knew when to keep his mouth shut in front of The Marquis.

"Do you have anything to report to me?" The Marquis chose his words carefully, to remind Marceau of his place. Marceau noticed but made no comment.

"Not yet, monseigneur, but it seemed Hadur may have been on to something..." Marceau said, trailing off. Movement from the crowd below had drawn his attention.

The Marquis noticed it too and strode forward to the window.

Something in the crowd had caught his eye, really caught it.

Staring hard, he muttered. "He couldn't possibly be so bold".

*

He moved through the crowd like a wraith, the hood of his cloak pulled tightly about his face. He could feel eyes on him from above. Raising his eyes ever so slightly, he chanced a look at the upper floor of the palace.

The crowd was rocking back and forth now with a frenetic energy against the front gate of the palace.

The Marquis' men had retreated through the postern doors and stood watching nervously, as the gate groaned with each swell of the crowd.

332

The blood-flecked giant stood, arms crossed, grinning stupidly, watching.

At least someone was enjoying themselves.

He drew his hood closer about him, and continued forward, head down, blending into the crowd.

"Justice pour les enfants de Paris!" a woman to his right shouted. She looked haggard, with haunted eyes, and wore a threadbare dress.

"Pah. Justice, my arse!" a man replied, hawking and spitting at his feet. "You'll see no justice from the likes of these, lest it profit them in some way. There's no election looming, they've no need to lie and pretend that they give a damn about any missing children. You'll get no help here", he finished bitterly.

The woman frowned and hung her head dejectedly.

There you go again with your big mouth, Garlon, the man thought.

"But there's always a chance, Alberta, my dear", Garlon said hurriedly. "I shall tell Marceau and his men the children were last seen making off with a big bag of the taxman's takings, I'm sure they will be found this very day".

Alberta giggled.

Smiling, he threw his arm around her and gave her a peck on the cheek. He had a habit of letting his cynicism and bitterness get the best of him, at the worst of times. He knew it was likely that the children would never be seen again, but he felt awful for upsetting Alberta. He didn't want to kill her hope, it was all she had.

It was hard **not to be** cynical and bitter, when you saw the world as a steaming vat of corruption, overflowing at the brim. Like an overfull pot of soup, sloshing about under the cold metal of the ladle, as the politicians and the money men stirred. And as it spilled, over the sides of the pot, it fell scalding, upon people like Alberta and Garlon, who waited patiently, bowl in hand for whatever meagre offal fell, deemed fit to fill their bellies.

He knew he could be a bitter bastard. But the world had made him that way.

The cloaked man watched the interaction from under his hood. It warmed him a little, though he knew not why. Feeling eyes upon him, he turned his face away quickly, and moved away into the crowd.

Garlon frowned and watched as he passed.

Was that...him from the poster? he thought to himself.

Can't be...he'd have to be mad to show up here.

"Les enfants", a man at the front of the crowd cried suddenly.

"Les enfants", the crowd roared in unison.

"De Paris", the man cried.

"De Paris", the crowd cried back.

There were many children in the crowd, in spirit, if not presence, their faces held high on posters and pictures. Some held above the heads of mothers and fathers. Others waved like flags by what must be siblings and friends.

I had no idea it was this bad, the cloaked man thought.

As he approached the centre of the crowd, he spotted another man in a cloak. He was tall and dark, and lean. As good a doppelganger as any. Walking close behind the doppelganger, the cloaked man whispered. "Now".

True to his word, the doppelganger threw back the hood of his cloak and screamed, "Marquis!" He pointed dramatically at the upper level of the palace. "You want me? Then come for me, coward!"

Marceau's men began gesturing frantically at the doppelganger. Before their giant overseer could respond, one of them whipped open a postern door and ran out blindly.

The crowd roared, and seizing the opportunity, surged forward madly toward the door. One of the protestors dived through the open door, tumbling to the floor and wrestling with one of Marceau's men.

And then, they were through! And flooding through en masse into the courtyard of the palace.

The giant cursed, and began snatching protestors off his men, flinging them back over the wall like bags of flour. Unlike bags of flour, they landed with sickening smacks, rather than soft white puffs.

It was too little, too late, however, as the gate of the palace swung open with a creak, and the Parisians stormed through into the courtyard.

The cloaked man stood watching, grinning grimly beneath his hood. He stood still, as the crowd raged about him, like a rock in a storm as the waves beat upon it.

The giant saw him, and watched, some unfortunate hanging limply in his hand like a slain hare.

As they met one another's eyes, a haughty blonde man came running into sight, a band of cutthroats at his heels.

"The traitor, Lucien", he said severely, coming to a halt before the cloaked man.

"To what end, Pavo?" Lucien replied sadly.

"What end?" Pavo asked, confused. He looked a little unsure of himself.

"To what end, am I a traitor?" Lucien asked slowly.

"You are a traitor to our cause", Pavo replied pompously. "You betray your oath, and your brethren".

Lucien laughed coldly. "Because I stopped that wretch Janver raping his way across Paris?"

Pavo stiffened. Lucien could feel The Marquis' rage even from here.

"You betrayed us, killing one of your own, and you shall be brought to justice", Pavo informed him.

Lucien laughed. "Justice? Come now, Pavo, what do you know of justice?"

"And what **do you** know of justice, Lucien? You are but The Marquis' errand boy", Pavo spat. "His knife in the night", he finished, half smirking, half snarling.

"And what does that make you, Pavo?" Lucien said quietly.

"I am many things, but no traitor", Pavo said after a moment.

"How poetic", Lucien sneered.

Pavo's face flushed. "We'll see how bold you are when we drain every drop of blood from your boy, Gabriel".

Oh boy, that was a mistake, Hadur thought to himself.

But then you've always had piss for brains, Pavo.

Hadur watched the exchange from the courtyard, his face thoughtful. He didn't like Lucien, he could be an arrogant wretch, and he even thought he was a match for **him.**

But he wasn't sure about this. It didn't sit well with him. Battle should be blood and fists, tooth against tooth. It irked him to hold the golden-haired boy over Lucien. But The Marquis willed it, and he had always kept Hadur's teeth bloody.

Lucien turned to look at Hadur, and Hadur felt the hackles on his neck rise.

Damn, he could feel his anger from here.

Then, more anger.

Turning, Hadur glanced up at The Marquis, who was standing wrapped in shadow at the window above.

He wasn't sure who he feared most.

Lucien looked up at The Marquis, and raising his hand, drew his finger slowly across his throat like a knife.

The message was clear, and Hadur couldn't help but laugh. Lucien had balls, he had to admit.

Pavo watched, as Lucien threatened his master, and his face flushed. "You would embarrass me like this in front of him?" he hissed.

Pavo would know no further embarrassment.

Lucian darted forward and slashed his head from his shoulders, in one vicious blow, using his open hand like a blade.

"Putain!" Hadur exclaimed. "The boy is like lightning!"

Lucien caught Pavo's head as it fell and stood holding it by the hair.

Raising the still animated head to his face, he spoke to it, "Bold enough for you, **boy?**" Lucien hissed, knowing The Marquis would hear.

Pavo screamed. The pain must have been intense.

Lucien had heard tales of Ekur beheaded and kept alive for decades by their conquerors, in ages past. Perhaps he'd keep Pavo on his mantle for a few hundred years to stew and learn some humility.

Ignoring his screams, he raised Pavo's head high above his own defiantly, his eyes on the figure above.

Occupational Hazard

Gabriel was cold, miserable, and he ached everywhere.

The woman, Dagger they called her, was stronger than she looked. She'd carried him here from the Under, to this place, and dumped him unceremoniously on the floor to wait. But not before the 'Marquis' had hit him with a few choice blows. Although, for some reason, it felt like he'd been holding back.

Why they'd brought him here, he knew not, but he hoped they didn't find Lucien. Well, part of him did. Part of him hoped Lucien fled far from here so they never found him. Part of him hoped to see him burst through the window and roll across the floor like some acrobatic hero of the night.

They had come up from the Under and emerged into this strange hall.

It scared him. It had a morbid feel to it, and the picture on the wall was grotesque, a cruel looking man standing on his servant, or subject, whatever.

How these people cared to refer to their "lessers" he didn't care to learn.

The man in the painting looked a little like the "Marquis", as his minions called him. It would not surprise him if the man had commissioned the painting himself, to further inflate his already over buoyant ego.

He wondered what manner of man he was, to have his own personal entrance to the Under. But then, Lucien had warned him. He just hadn't listened, intent as he was on his own adventure. And now look where he had ended up. It could be worse, he supposed.

Looking around the room, he called for one of the servants. "Water, please!" he groaned.

He didn't know how long he'd been here, but they'd been none too gentle with him, and he was sore, and tired, and he had a headache. He rubbed at his temples irritatedly.

"Merci", he said gratefully, as a young serving girl bought him a goblet of water. "Please". He grabbed her arm. "Help me".

The girl scurried away, eyes down.

Merde!

The fact that they hadn't even bothered to shackle or chain him, grated on him. Did they hold him in such low regard? Though he probably couldn't have escaped, even if they had walked him to the door and ordered him a carriage, weak as he was.

He supposed the woman, Dagger, was waiting just outside the door. Or perhaps prowling about the place, ready to dismember him should he be stupid enough to try.

She needn't a blade. She could cut you with her eyes.

For some reason, he found her even more frightening than The Marquis. Or the oaf that had visited them at DuPassé. Vladur or something, his name was.

He was starting to feel less fondly of antiques by the minute. As he lay there, propped against the wall too tired to move, contemplating his fate, the door opened. The woman Dagger entered, carrying a silver platter. Upon it was some food, thank the heavens. She brought it to him without a word, then turned to leave.

"Wait! Wait a minute!" Gabriel said.

She turned to face him and raised an eyebrow questioningly.

"Don't go", he said feebly.

She grinned. It was a beautiful smile, but there was

something dangerous about it, and it put him in the mind of a wild cat.

Her eyes fluttered prettily, as she moved toward him. He felt that she could kiss or kill him at her whim, and he wondered if he'd be able to resist either.

She dropped to her knees in front of him and ran the back of her hand across his face.

"Why?" she asked huskily.

"Just...don't", he said, gently pushing her hand away. "Please, tell me why you're keeping me here?"

The smile faded, and the air of danger intensified.

"That's why you want me to stay?" she asked haughtily. She seemed upset, offended even.

"Yes...no..." Gabriel said, confused. He didn't know what he'd said to upset her, but he knew he had to tread carefully. That she was not fond of men she had made clear already.

"If I have offended you, I am sorry, truly", Gabriel said sincerely.

She stood up suddenly and turned her back to him. Had she looked...scared...for a moment?

When she turned back to face him, her face was cool again, her eyes cold. "You haven't offended me, manling".

"Then, can you tell me, what am I doing here?" Gabriel said. "Or what I have done, to earn such treatment?"

"You are here because The Marquis wills it", she replied neutrally.

"Oh, well if The Marquis wills it", Gabriel snapped sarcastically, his hunger getting the best of him. "Let it be so".

Her mouth twitched at this, and she turned away.

She walked to the door and paused. "Watch your mouth...manling", she said, back turned, before closing the door.

Gabriel shook his head.

He couldn't help but admire her a little. That she held court with such as The Marquis and showed no fear impressed him greatly.

Lifting the food to his mouth, he grimaced, as pain lanced through his jaw.

"Merde", he muttered. "I hope Lucien feeds you his fist".

*

Back in the Under, La Meme sat quietly, legs crossed, rocking slowly back and forth.

She was angry. Angrier than she'd been in years. A vein throbbed intensely in her temple.

It was an odd sight. A sight made odder by the carpet of bodies around her.

Hadur had hunted well. The Dwellers had been massacred. Not a man, woman or child remained.

Some of his villains had chased her, and she had fled. She knew the Under, and luckily, she was able to escape, taking older, lesser-known passages. She hated herself for running, but all she could think of was Gabriel.

She had run straight for the lake. She knew Gabriel, knew he would be there, drawn by its beauty.

She had arrived to watch as they led him away. She wanted to scream out, to run to him. To rend and tear and scratch and bite at the reavers taking her Gabriel. But she could not. She was no match for them. What could she do?

If she allowed herself to be captured, what hope would there be for Gabriel? She knew she had to keep a clear head. However, it was proving very, very difficult.

She despaired and put her head in her hands. She had tried hard to keep him safe, and for what? Here he was, deep in the belly of the beast. And she may as well have put him there herself. She had driven him toward Lucien at every opportunity.

"It is not your fault", she said aloud.

Gabriel is a wilful boy.

He always has been.

341

He will walk his own path.

It didn't make her feel any better, or do anything to assuage her guilt.

She could have tried harder to keep him safe.

But you are all he has!

"Yes, I know!" she shouted. "Ahhhh!" She threw her hands up exasperatedly. Searching for an outlet for her frustration, she kicked a large clump of stone and dust aggressively into the wall of the chamber.

"Merde, merde, merde, putain, merde!" she screamed, as her foot connected with the stone, and she began to limp precariously.

"I did not think it proper for a lady to use such language", a soothing voice replied.

She spun quickly at the sound, her eyes wide, her manner alert. Her eyes narrowed as she saw a man.

"Who are you?" she asked immediately.

Hiro was impressed, though he didn't show it, stoic as he was. He had expected panic.

"A friend", he replied cryptically.

"You are no friend of mine", she replied coolly.

He raised his eyebrows, again taken back.

"I mean you no harm", he said, walking forward with arms clasped behind his back.

Unconsciously, his hand inched a little closer to his blade, Saisei.

"Then what do you mean here?" she shot back, inching away from him, as they slowly circled each other.

Hiro frowned at her choice of language. He stopped. "I mean to help, madame...no more, no less".

He watched her closely, tensely, before bowing stiffly, his eyes on her all the while.

She looked merely sceptical now, which was an improvement on open hostility, he supposed.

"Help me how?" she asked.

"Gabriel", he replied.

"What about him?" she asked, her response swift and sharp as a whip.

"I know where he is...and more importantly, how we can free him", Hiro said.

Back Under

Amerie walked numbly through the Under, turning left and right, as she trudged deeper, and deeper.

She was still reeling from what she had seen at the palace. Even now she struggled to believe it. Henré, yet not Henré. What manner of affliction was he cursed with?

She stopped, as her eyes filled with tears.

Do not give up! a fierce voice inside her cried.

Never give up.

She rubbed her eyes and carried on down the path. She knew she was close. She had taken the same paths that La Meme had led her down previously.

Luckily, she had a good memory for places, and once she had been somewhere once, she could usually find her way back.

It was made easier by the blood in the path, which she followed like a compass, and the heavy booted footprints.

It looked like some manner of giant had been this way recently, for his footprints dwarfed those of the others. She stopped to marvel at the size of them for a moment.

She knew she should be scared by this omen. Ordinarily she would. But she was too numb to care now. She'd spent too long worrying for her husband, lost too much sleep and shed too many tears. It ended now.

"Yes", she said aloud, reassuring herself of her course of action.

Approaching the Dweller camp, she increased her pace, then broke into a run. As she entered the camp, she stopped, uncertain once more.

The ground was slick with blood and there were bodies everywhere.

Men, women and...children...lay slain throughout the chamber.

She tore her eyes away from a little girl in a frilly dress. She was so small, so fragile. And like a candle, her life had been snuffed out, her flame mercilessly short lived.

There was a bloody stain on the wall above her. She didn't need to be a man of violence herself, to realise how the girl had been slain.

Walking to the girl, she turned her to her back, and gently closed her eyes. Spotting a worn teddy bear with a missing eye nearby, she picked it up and put it in the girl's arms. She looked almost peaceful now.

"Sleep now", Amerie whispered, brushing the little girl's hair from her face.

She cried then, her tears coming hard and fast, and she fell to the floor and wept. Her cries came in deep, heavy sobs, racking her body as she struggled to draw breath through the grief and panic threatening to overwhelm her.

This was more than she could take, and she felt dizzy, her head spinning as her emotions spun out of control. She cried until no more tears would come, then cried some more.

When the crying was done, she rose silently to her feet. She knew what she had to do now. Turning from the bodies, she walked to a room at the back of the chamber and paused before it.

Are you sure you want to know? a little voice in her head asked.

The truth was, she wasn't. At least now, she still had some modicum of hope left. Once she entered that room, there was no turning back. She wasn't sure she wanted to know what it contained.

Why did this have to happen to her? How was she supposed to take care of herself and the baby alone? That would be hard enough, but this as well? She felt like breaking down again, as the enormity of the situation threatened to overwhelm her.

Think of the baby.

She placed her hands protectively across her belly. She loved her, more than anything in this world. She knew it was a little girl that she carried within her, she didn't know how, but somehow, she just knew.

But this was all too much. She missed Henré so much, and she felt so alone. She had never felt so alone in her life, nor so frightened.

Catacombs...murder...whatever affliction plagued Henré. It was like a bad dream that she knew not how to wake from.

Henré had always been there for her, and before Henré, her mother and father. This felt like a different world to her, a world that she was ill equipped to traverse by herself.

But you'll have to, the voice in her head chimed persistently. She hung her head and screwed her face up, distraught.

"Damn it all!" she screamed.

Channelling her anger and frustration, she stormed into the room. She was taken aback.

This was Anne's room? She didn't know exactly what she had expected, but certainly not this.

Anne's room was meticulously clean, but for a dull red stain on the ground in front of a small bed. By the bed there was a dresser and a bookshelf.

On the wall hung a painting of a pretty red-haired lady, with her arm around a rather striking woman with brilliant blue eyes.

She looked closer. Was it Anne? Perhaps. She didn't know who the other woman was, but her eyes sparkled vividly. They felt familiar to her somehow.

She had expected altars, scrolls, ancient chests and meaty magic tomes. Anne was a revered healer, and it was rumoured some manner of witch, so they said.

Amerie wasn't so sure; she knew people were prone to

exaggerate. But she had no other option, she had to put her cynicism to the side.

She began opening books and flicking through them, seeking any sign or portent to aid her. Placing the first book back, she opened a second. Nothing. She put this back too, then opened a third.

"Sacré bleu!" she exclaimed.

Snapping the book shut, she angrily shoved it back onto the bookcase. She was beginning to lose patience, and a dull panic began within her.

Fourth book. Nothing. Fifth book. Nothing. Snap. Working her way through the books with increasing frustration she stopped. The last book. And it looked not at all like the kind of book to detail whatever sorcery or witchcraft Henré had been so accursed by. It looked as though it had previously been a rather majestic silver but was now more of a withered yellow colour.

She took a deep, steadying breath, then opened the book. She stopped at the first page. There was an illustration of a man, his face contorted with rage, grappling with another man. His victim?

His arms were wrapped tightly around the other man, who appeared to be struggling to push him off. It looked as though they were locked in some deathly lovers embrace.

It was the angry man's teeth that her eyes were drawn to, though. They were sunk deep into the other man's neck.

'Of Ekur and Moindre' the title read.

Furrowing her brow, she turned to the next page and read. As she read, she felt an apprehension growing in her. It worsened with each turn of the page.

"The Ekur have been known by many different names throughout the ages. But one thing is certain. As long as there have been men, there have been Ekur. In Albania, they fear the Shtriga, come to devour their children in the night. The Greeks, they bolt their doors against the Vrykolakas, came to feast on both blood and flesh. And in Romania, they patrol the graveyards, lest a Strigoi rise to feed upon them".

"Ekur...Vrykolaka". She struggled to pronounce the second word, unsure if she was saying it correctly.

She did not like this book, it was horrid. The illustrations were all of truly fearsome creatures. Some looked manlike, others like animals, with claws and fangs and eyes like cats.

Turning the page, her stomach tightened.

"The Moindre. Akin to the Ekur, and yet not. The moindre is a creature born of the Ekur, but not its true progeny. Put simply, the moindre is a bastard, the bastard child of a careless Ekur, too blithe to kill its food after feeding.

The Ekur has no intention of making the moindre its progeny, for to do so, it must feed it of its own blood, and such a thing is not done lightly.

The moindre is the aftermath of an incomplete feeding. A human that did not have the good grace to die, left to suffer a half-life, a cursed life.

Forever will the moindre crave blood and need it to sustain them. If they do not drink blood, they will die.

However, the moindre is often imbued with some of the Ekur's powers. Increased strength, durability and longevity, the extent of this seeming to differ from case to case".

Her eyes flicked to the bottom of the page, and her heart started beating hard in her chest.

Snapping shut the book, she began to hyperventilate, finding it harder and harder to breathe.

It's not Henré.

It's not Henré.

It's not Henré, she chanted like a mantra in her head, eyes closed.

Opening the book again quickly, she returned to the page and the troubling image.

It was a man with bloodshot eyes and veins popping out of

his face. He looked truly distraught, knelt as he was on the ground, with his head and hands raised to the sky above entreatingly. He looked as if he were begging for help, from anyone who cared to listen.

The man looked like Henré had at the palace.

She pictured Henré's face, and screwed her eyes shut.

No, no, no, no, no.

Her chest felt so tight. Why was it so hard to breathe?

Steeling herself, she forced her eyes open and continued to read, consuming every word painfully as though it were poison.

"Vampyric Rejection", this title read. "The most accursed of fates".

She swallowed hard. She'd started to sweat and rubbed her brow with the back of her hand.

"Of this, not much is known. It is said that in some cases, the host (human) does not take to the vampyric infection, and becomes crazed, with an uncontrollable lust for blood.

In these cases, the infected human exists as neither moindre nor human, and as a result, can sustain themselves on neither blood or meat.

Though they crave blood, and will seek it at all costs, they can take no sustenance from it. As such, the unfortunate victim is doomed to starve, unable to feed as man or beast. The kindest thing in such a case, would be to end their suffering".

End their suffering, the words echoed in her head.

She stepped back slowly, and the book fell from her hands to the floor with a thud.

Try Not To Lose Your Head

Marceau was sweating, profusely.

Carmen looked at him appraisingly. The back of his shirt was wet through, and it made him look a bit like some of the men she saw at night in the street, drinking and hollering loudly.

She wondered if he'd also pass out in a stupor when this, whatever this was, was done, or stumble home, crawl into her bed and grope at her in the dark again.

Carmen, really! She flushed, pulling at her neckline.

Thankfully, he hadn't noticed, intent as he was on the...riot outside.

There was really no other word for it, it had long since passed the point of 'protest' she felt.

The tension was worsened by his incessant pacing, back and forth, back and forth, in front of the window. Carmen **really** wished he'd stop pacing.

And to make matters worse, that **Marquis** was still here. He was so uncouth. Uncultured, really. Carmen felt that he had no business in such a sacred place as the Élysée, but she daren't say anything. The man was unhinged, who knew what he'd do.

Though Marceau's nerves were making Carmen on edge, it was nothing to the manic energy now oozing from The Marquis.

He stood deadly silent; hands clasped behind his back like some mad scientist. Every muscle in his body was taut. He hadn't said a word in some time now. It was disquieting.

She really wished he'd say something. Anything. Even some of his uncouth foulness would be a welcome interruption to this horrid mood.

She had tried to leave, really, she had. Unfortunately, she didn't make it very far. When faced with the angry mob outside in the courtyard, she'd turned around and ran back into the vestibule, as fast as she could manage with her dress hitched up about her knees.

"What should we do?" Marceau asked nervously, still pacing.

Silence.

"Should we gather the rest of the tableau?" Marceau continued. "I cannot see Madame Dagger, is she here?" He looked around shiftily.

What I would give to see her face at this moment, he kept the thought to himself.

Still nothing.

"Say something man!" Marceau snapped.

The Marquis remained silent; his eyes fixed on the courtyard. "The time for talking is done, boy", he said finally.

Boy?! Carmen bristled.

Marceau flashed Carmen a warning look. He looked uncomfortable.

"What are you talking about?" Marceau asked

"The people have spoken", The Marquis replied. "They have spoken and found you wanting. I fear that a change in the presidentship, is what they desire now".

Marceau paled. "B-but I did what you asked of me".

Carmen frowned. Why was Marceau talking like this? Debasing himself before this man.

"Well, it didn't work!" The Marquis snarled suddenly, pinning Marceau against the wall by the window.

Marceau hung uselessly for a moment, his face terrified, then a change came over him. He grinned an evil smile. A smile that would be better worn by The Marquis, Carmen thought.

There was a loud bang, and the next thing she knew, The Marquis was on the floor and Marceau was standing over him snarling. He looked ghastly, like a pit dog, his lips pulled back, and teeth bared. Had his teeth always been so unnaturally long and sharp?

The Marquis lay silently, then propped himself up on one arm. He looked like a replete lover, lying in bed, satisfied with his performance for the night, she thought.

What has gotten into you?

She fanned her face with her hand, watching the scene play out before her with morbid fascination. She wondered why he just lay there, The Marquis, shouldn't he do something? Fight back?

She had no idea that Marceau had it in him. Sudden violence was the last thing she would expect from him.

His fighting was done with his tongue. His arena, the assembly and the house. Yet here he was, like a man of action. It was a side to him she'd never seen before, and it excited her. She hoped that wasn't all of it.

Carmen's hopes were not unanswered, for Marceau suddenly cried out in pain, rubbing at his head and temples madly, as if he were trying to put out some unseen fire in his mind.

Why was he crying like this?

She looked down at The Marquis, still laying on the floor, and she saw that his eyes were glowing red. But that couldn't be. People's eyes didn't just glow red. They didn't glow at all. Was he sick?

He didn't look sick, in fact his face was contorted in a twisted, hateful expression. He looked like he was trying to cook Marceau alive, or maybe just his brain, fry his brain like an omelette.

She stifled a giggle, as an image of Marceau's head basting in a pan popped into her mind.

Good lord, woman.

The stress was getting to her.

Marceau was rolling around on the floor now, writhing in pain, apparently too intense for words, for he didn't seem able to draw breath to scream.

The Marquis rose slowly to his feet, and advanced on Marceau. He loomed over him, his eyes burning madly in his head, like someone had pulled them out and replaced them with eye shaped rubies, then set those rubies on fire.

Finally, it stopped, and air exploded from Marceau's lungs like he'd been punched in the stomach.

He moaned, long and low. It was a pitiful sound. Like that of a hound, mauled half to death by a lion, waiting for the mercy of its owner to end its suffering.

He lay, gasping, on the exquisite Savonnerie carpet, covered in sweat, his shirt horribly creased and bunched. His normally carefully groomed and oiled hair was splayed madly across his face.

Carmen grimaced. He used to be like the carpet, she thought. Exquisite. Now, he reminded her of the peasants who fitted it. It wasn't nice watching him unravel before her, like an old rug.

"But a fraction of it, boy", The Marquis growled fiercely at Marceau.

Carmen looked at The Marquis with a newfound respect. This was a style of dominance she wasn't used to. It was so...masculine. So raw. There was something intoxicating about it.

She had always been attracted to powerful men, which is what led her to Marceau's office in the first place, but this was a different kind of power. It was raw, unfiltered, and virulent.

Not like the ineffectual effete's she was used to. Constantly bickering like children and playing their back-room games, stabbing each other in the back over and over.

She wondered how they had the gall to look each other in the eye, conspiring in the dark as they did, professing friendship one day, then publicly tearing one another apart the next.

She had never thought about it like that before. She'd always thought it was rather genteel, and civilised. Settling arguments through debate. Great minds battling it out. But suddenly it didn't seem so genteel. In fact, it seemed rather gauche.

She wondered how The Marquis would fare in the house? Or the assembly for that matter. The thought excited her, and she stored it away safely in her mind, now was not the time. She was looking forward to giving it a more thorough examination later. Perhaps before she slept.

Marceau panted like a dog. He'd managed to pull himself up to his hands and knees now. He was so exhausted from whatever The Marquis had done to him, he could barely lift his head, and it hung low brushing the carpet.

How...did...he...do...that, Marceau thought.

Never...felt...such...pain.

He felt humiliated. He didn't like to be humiliated. He was used to doing the humiliating. Used to lashing his opponents with his tongue. Used to dismantling them handily with his sharp rhetoric, his peers watching admiringly, Carmen often among them.

She'd always cheer for him and celebrate his victories. It made him feel good. It made him feel powerful. But now, he felt as far from powerful as possible.

Glancing at Carmen, his face fell. She looked as though she admired **him**. She was running her hand absentmindedly across her neck.

Marceau turned away, disgusted. The slut was preening herself in front of him. Would she let him mount her, on the floor, like a dog?

As you mounted her?

So much for loyalty, he thought savagely.

The bitch will mate with any dog that will have her.

Not that he cared, he had his wife. And there'd be other secretaries. He had found Carmen's performance most unsatisfactory as of late, and felt it was overdue time to tell her, after he'd gotten out of this mess of course.

The Marquis had returned to staring silently out of the window, ignoring him.

The fact that he didn't even consider him a credible threat anymore stung his pride even more.

All he had to do was glare at him, with his fucking red eyes, and he was laid low like a whore by her pimp's hand. No, worse than that, he thought painfully. Far worse than that.

What the fuck was he staring at?

A Queen's Prerogative

Régine was well on her way to being drunk. Drunk on a heady combination of wine, blood and lust.

Extending her long leg languidly from under her expensive silks, she smirked lasciviously at the large man next to her.

He groaned wantingly.

Perhaps, if he was well behaved, she would let him take her once more later. For now, she felt a desire to stretch her legs, the night was still young. Besides, he had already given her what she needed, and admirably so.

It amused her, the power she held over him. She found him more entertaining than her other lovers. Perhaps it was his fierceness. Perhaps his simple nature.

It was certainly more enjoyable wrapping a man like Hadur around her finger, than some of the fine haired dandies in the city.

To have such a savage, beast of man do exactly as she bid. To have him beg, to plead, just to taste her.

She shuddered with pleasure.

There was something so incredibly, raw, about him. And he shared her insatiable bloodlust. She found this extremely desirable.

It aroused her to watch him feed. She had shared many a divine evening with him, as they lay together, bathed in blood, hungrily licking and sucking the crimson delight off one other.

Bodies writhing. Tightly intertwined. Hands pulling desperately in a scarlet frenzy.

She closed her eyes as her face flushed.

Biting her lip, she touched herself.

She was wet.

There was nothing else for it.

The night was still young, she reasoned.

Turning to the giant, she pulled him to her.

When her passion had been spent, she lay replete, wonderfully relaxed. "Délicieux", she moaned throatily.

Hadur grinned at her proudly.

"And now I must go". She rose suddenly from the bed and began to dress herself.

"Don't", Hadur grunted, reaching for her from the bed.

She side-stepped his hand nimbly and flashed him a licentious pout. He panted from the bed and began to pleasure himself.

Enjoying the attention, she exposed her leg from under her dress, leaning forward to tease him with her bust.

His breathing grew quick, and he pulled at himself harder and faster. Finally, she let drop the dress and bared all for him.

He finished quickly, then lay back, smiling at her lazily from the bed.

She prowled over to him, her movements slow and sensual. Leaning forward ever so slowly, she kissed him on the lips.

"What a filthy beast you are, Hadur", she said.

He grinned wickedly. "That was good", he admitted.

"Of course it was", she purred, walking away. "Never forget how **divine** I can make you feel". She pouted.

He moaned, and her face flashed from coquettish to murderous in an instant.

She disappeared in a haze of smoke and shadow, then reappeared before him.

Her hand shot out, gripping his chin tightly and raising it

toward her. "And **never**, think to cross me", she warned.

Hadur was torn between fear and arousal. He settled somewhere in between and merely nodded.

Why would he seek to cross her? She pleasured him as no other woman ever had, and under her reign, he was drunk on blood more often than not. He was no fool.

"Where are you going?" he asked.

"Out", she teased.

She looked most alluring, in her lightning blue dress, her face expertly made up to further accentuate her striking eyes and beautiful features.

He watched, punch-drunk, as she pulled her shoes on, and wondered if there was a finer woman anywhere.

She turned to blow a kiss at him, and was gone, into the night.

*

She swept through the doors of Sous Les Étoiles as a queen might.

She smiled prettily at the doorman and handed him her coat, into his already outstretched hand.

Leaning forward she kissed him softly on the cheek, running her gloved hand up his arm as she did so.

She saw desire kindle in his eyes.

Perhaps I shall take him in front of Hadur and watch as he is ripped limb from limb.

What a delicious thought.

She turned from the doorman and walked into the dancehall, glancing back over her shoulder to pout at him, enjoying the disappointment on his face as she moved away.

Sous Les Étoiles was her favourite place to let off steam. It was dark, mysterious, and exclusive. She loved it. Only the finest Parisiens were lucky enough to be admitted, and every person had a story to tell, whether from the dancefloor or one of the stylishly lit tables.

It wasn't just politicians, or money men, like some of the more bouge establishments. In fact, they were a rare sight, thankfully, for they bored her to tears. There were actors, musicians, activists and men of action.

It was an architectural wonder, modelled after the Jardin d'Hiver, of the Élysée Palace. It was unique, even for Montmartre, with its curved greenhouse style glass roof stained a deep crimson colour.

The effect of the starlight above filtering down through the red glass was enchanting. She loved dancing under the stars until the sun rose, her body moving rhythmically in time with the music, her worries forgotten.

She adored the dance halls. The music, the dancing, the cabaret. And although they were still few in number, and viewed as scandalous by some, they were a welcome addition.

She felt Paris had been enriched by them and expected them to become hugely popular. She had a canny way of always being a step ahead of the trend. And it was very different to what she was used to.

Régine appreciated variety. Twas the spice of life, after all. She found the stuffy ballrooms tedious, and they bored her to tears. And they were always dripping with pompous men, oversure of themselves and their station. And quite frankly, their appeal.

They were better served in the whorehouses. There were special establishments for wooden bores like them, where the women were specially trained to feign enjoyment, which was clever business, as the chances of it happening organically were slim to none.

Not only was Sous Les Étoiles a source of constant pleasure to her, carnal and otherwise, it was also largely responsible for her meteoric rise to power within the tableau, and for cementing her place as their self-anointed queen.

A chance meeting with a small-time villain had yielded more

than just flesh and blood. Twas here she had met the fool who sat wearing treasure beyond measure upon his dirt riddled finger, waving it around as if it were the poxy signet ring of some inconsequential bouge family.

Amusingly, he had one of those too on his smallest finger. Of course he did, they always did. He took great joy in telling her the story of his lineage. Some mind numbingly boring story of shipping merchants and wool. Or was it linen?

She had stopped listening early into his tale, adopting an expression of rapt wonder, as she plied him with wine after wine, until he was unsteady on his feet.

The Soif De Sang! And the fool had no idea. How in the world had he stumbled upon the bloodlust ring? She expected it was at least partly to blame for his murderous nature.

Having listened to his endless stories, it seemed he had not always not been a true villain, having diversified of sorts from racketeering and gambling, to extortion, blackmail, murder and worse.

Of course it was all very mundane to her, but she didn't let on to the fellow, gazing at him wide eyed in wonder, and nodding encouragingly as he spoke, giving his hand a little squeeze now and then across the table.

He couldn't hide his lust, it shone forth bright from his eyes like a lantern. She knew she had him. She had hatched the plan almost immediately, but it was difficult. She could scarcely contain the hunger in her eyes as she gazed upon the ring and had to force herself to be patient. With it, she would be invincible. No Ekur in all the world would be able to challenge her.

Eventually, mercifully, the fool had his fill of flapping his gums, and clumsily invited her for a nightcap. She thought if he drank anything more he might collapse where he stood, but she said nothing, glad of an excuse to end his babbling and bring the evening to a close.

She had gone back with him, to his apartment.

It wasn't in Montmartre, as he had promised, but in Saint-Ouen-sur- Seine. Thankfully, he hailed a carriage, grinning self-importantly at her as he did so.

Unfortunately, it still meant more choice time listening to him boast and brag of his business empire and how feared he was in the district. What she truly found fearful was his breath.

As they arrived, she considered gutting him and watching him bleed out over the carpet. She watched the scene play out with interest in her head.

At the third mention of the carpet being Savonnerie, she had to restrain herself from whipping her knife out.

Mercifully, he wasted no time in making his move, pulling her to him and sticking his disgusting tongue in her mouth.

She almost slew him then, but then he stopped, and dropped his trousers, standing bold as brass in front of her, a libidinous grin on his face.

She arched her eyebrows, surprised.

What the hell, she thought.

*

She hungered now. Not for a man, but for blood. The dawn was close, but she cared not. She would feed regardless.

She prowled near the basilica, keeping to the shadows, wearing them as comfortably as any dress. She knew the peasants revered it, sacré they called it. Perhaps that was why she enjoyed feeding there, taking some kind of perverse pleasure from it.

Régine was far from sacré.

It was beautiful, the Sacré Coeur, but it made her feel vulnerable. It made her consider her **own** mortality, which she did not like. Twas her prey who should be savouring their final moments.

Scowling up at it, she continued her search.

Just as she thought her hunt fruitless, a rich, warm sound filled her ears. It was so innocent, so pure. She hated it. It grated, like that fool villain and his endless stories.

She moved quickly toward the sound, shifting formlessly toward the steps in front of the basilica.

There. A couple. Stood with their backs to the basilica. The man had his arm around the woman and was gesturing expansively with his arm out toward Paris. The woman stood with her head resting lovingly on his shoulder, her arm wrapped around his waist.

Perfect, she thought greedily.

I shall dine well this night.

Wasting no time, she flew at them like a gale.

The woman was knocked down the steps by the force of her attack, and rolled uselessly to a stop a short way away.

The man fell hard in front of her, the wind knocked out of him, as Régine landed atop him.

He had beautiful hair, she thought, cocking her head. Like spun gold. She ran her fingers through it, brushing some dirt from it that had kicked up from the floor.

The man moaned, and opened his eyes, gazing blearily up at her. It was the last thing he saw.

She smiled malevolently and sunk her teeth deep into his neck. She was so hungry that she drained him of his lifeblood in moments.

It was mercifully quick for the man, and as his face turned grey, she drew her teeth from him and sprung to her feet, turning greedily on the woman.

The woman was regaining her senses now, and Régine's heart started beating faster. She preferred her prey to be present during the act, she took no pleasure in feasting on zombies.

Unfortunately, sometimes, she was over-hasty, using more force than was necessary to subdue her victims. And then they just lay there uselessly, too stunned or hurt to cry out. She hated that, but she would enjoy this.

It had been months now, since she had slain the villain and

taken his ring. Since taking it, her thirst had steadily grown. It had become... overpowering.

She had found the need to feed increasing, until it reached the point that she had to feed every single day, and sometimes, more than once.

Not only that, but she found that when fed, she was scarcely aware of the world around her, so frenzied she became.

So it was that she saw now, through a red haze, her vision clouded, blood pumping loudly in her ears.

The ring burned, ruthlessly red upon her finger.

The woman stared, horror struck, at the remains of her husband and his killer. Comprehension started to dawn on her face, and she screamed.

At least Régine thought that was what she was doing.

Her mouth was open in the familiar gape of terror. The sound was so muted though. Everything was muted, she realised.

She didn't care. Snarling, she sprung at the woman.

The woman turned from her, so that her back was to her, and she couldn't reach her throat.

Régine cackled. It would not stop her. But she'd play the game. Landing on the woman hard, she grabbed a handful of her hair, and pulled her head back. She turned the woman's neck toward her with her other hand, slowly, tantalisingly.

Surprising herself at her self-control, for everything in her screamed at her to drain this woman as she had her husband, Régine ran her tongue slowly along her neck. The taste of her fear was exquisite, and she shuddered in pleasure.

The woman, blasted thing she was, kept contorting her body strangely, hunching over as if she had been hit in the stomach, all the while trying to free herself from Régine's grasp.

It irritated her, and she decided she had played enough. She pulled the woman's head to the side, and sank her teeth in deep, drinking of her as if her blood were the finest wine.

When she was done, she threw the husk to one side carelessly.

A sound.

She stopped in surprise.

A baby.

Squalling on the ground.

The cow must have been protecting it, shielding it with her body. It must have been why she was writhing around like a contortionist. Perhaps she didn't fear her fate as Régine had originally thought.

A truly abhorrent thought came to her then and she picked the thing up, pondering it. Why shouldn't she? She was a queen, after all.

A hand gripped her then, the grip was firm, but frantic, and more screaming came. She could hear it faintly, the muted buzzing in her ear.

Reacting instinctively, she pulled away. As she pulled, the hand pulled too, but she was the stronger, and broke free of the grip.

As she did so, a disorienting feeling came upon her.

She heard a clattering sound.

The ring! The Soif De Sang!

It was bouncing down the steps of the Sacré Coeur away from her.

The cow must have pulled it from her finger. Wet as it was with blood, it must have slid off as she pulled at her.

She moved as if to run after it, but the hand gripped her once more.

Crying. So much crying. Why was it so loud? It hurt her ears and she moaned. Why did it hurt so much! She couldn't think.

She snarled at the woman holding her. She was ready to lash out and separate her head from her shoulders.

Why? A voice rang out in her head.

What do you mean, why?

Because I will it!

But she wasn't so sure. She was so confused. Everything felt wrong. Like a bad hangover, but worse. Like waking from a dream, a long dream, a lucid dream. What was she even doing here?

She looked down at the baby squalling, and something in her broke.

"Stop! Madame, stop!" the woman screamed, still pulling ineffectually at her arm.

"What am I doing?" Régine asked pitifully.

Looking down at the baby, she felt a panic rise deep from the depths of her stomach.

As if she were watching the story of someone else's life, she replayed the events of the past months in her mind.

Memories flashed through her mind. The giant, Hadur, sweating above her. A handsome dandy kissing at her neck. The villain. The ring. A vast, vast, river of blood.

She glanced down at the baby.

Remembering her intentions, her stomach heaved.

She passed the baby quickly to the woman, before emptying her stomach on the steps.

No, I wouldn't have.

I would never!

Another memory came to her then. A throne. A room with a long table.

The Tableau Haute. A jewelled goblet. A slick, sweet, heady taste on her tongue, dripping warmly down her chin. The giant's tongue, covering her own, as she shamelessly fed him before her brethren.

Yes...I am...ruthless.

But I would never stoop so low as this!

This is...abhorrent.

Wouldn't you?

You are Régine, the Ekur queen!

And you have drunk of the maiden.

What have I become?

Her stomach heaved, and she retched hard, vomiting again.

The baby was still crying, oh how she wished it would stop crying.

The woman was crying too, whilst gently bouncing the baby up and down in the crook of her arm, cooing at it to try and soothe it.

"Don't look, little one, don't look", she muttered desperately, as she turned the baby away from its parents.

"What are you still doing here?" she screamed suddenly at Régine, her eyes wild. "Get out of here, foul creature!" she spat.

Régine jerked as if stung. Who was this mortal to speak to her so?

"Go!" the woman screamed again. "Go! go, go, go!" She pushed and slapped at Régine to no effect.

For some reason it hurt Régine, not physically, but mentally, emotionally.

She felt defiled. She felt ashamed.

Backing away from the woman, she turned to leave. She couldn't deal with this right now. Her head throbbed and pounded awfully, and she needed solitude.

Stealing one last look at the baby over her shoulder, she fled.

The last thing she saw before she left, was the baby wailing pitifully in the woman's arms.

C'est La Vie

It soon became apparent what The Marquis had been staring at. The gate to the palace had proved pitiful protection against the angry mass of Parisians, who had long since taken control of the courtyard and lower level of the palace.

They were building something in the courtyard, but what?

Marceau sat huddled against the door to his office in a vain effort to barricade it, should the protestors reach it.

Carmen sat quietly at her desk, biting her nails.

Marceau watched her, an odd look on his face. It was a testament to the gravity of the situation that she was being so quiet. Usually, she had something to say about everything.

But he had no time now to think of Carmen, for another vision came upon him then. He closed his eyes gratefully, willing it to flow through him, willing it to revitalise him in this trying time.

The citizens of France roared his name loudly.

Oh, how loudly they roared! And with such fervour!

Marceau! Marceau! Marceau!

He shivered in ecstasy as their voices roared through his mind.

Carmen gave him a withering look, an expression bordering disgust. The man is deranged, she thought. How could she have ever held him in such high regard? The peasants hunt us through the palace, and he sits eyes closed, dreaming of lord knows what.

A hundred thousand strong, they thronged the courtyard of the palace, swamping the surrounding streets for miles, desperate to catch a glance of their hero, Marceau.

For only he could lead them, and France, into a new era of wealth and prosperity. An era born of blood. The blood of their enemies. France would grow fat on the spoils of war once more and the world would fear it, and him, as no other.

Heady thoughts of empire filled his brain, and he imbibed them greedily, drunk on the heady taste of his own prophetic legacy.

He would be a new Napoleon. No, more than that! He would go further than the man could ever dream! He would bring glory back to France and sit upon a throne of skulls. No. An entire palace of skulls! So many enemies would he slay, in France's name.

He would grip the world in an iron fist, and squeeze. Squeeze until it bowed before him. Wept before him. Crawled before him. And paid him his due. Paid him obeisance. Take the knee or die. Yes. That was it.

He would. He knew it! He felt it so strongly! He'd never felt anything so strongly! How could he have ever doubted himself?

The world over, they would speak the name Marceau in hushed whispers. In their cafes, in their bars, in their factories, in the streets! With respect. Yes, undoubtedly. The men would fear him, and the women, well...

He shot Carmen a poisonous look.

Luckily, she wasn't watching, distracted as she still was by The Marquis, watching him coquettishly from the corner of her eye.

*The women, they would desire him, lust for him, pant for him. There would be no place for the likes of **she** in **the new** France. Craven bitch. Perhaps she can serve my men. That's probably what the bitch really wanted anyway, to be passed around, like a camp whore.*

He saw Carmen in a different light now.

He wondered how he had ever been taken in by her before. She was nothing more than a common strumpet, parading as a lady of breeding. A lady of breeding, he scoffed. **Certainly not**.

She had betrayed her allegiance to him, in his time of greatest need, and he would not forget.

She would rue this day.

A noise distracted him then from his mad machinations, and he frowned, narrowing his eyes in concentration.

It couldn't be. Could it? Not now. He hadn't brought them glory and victory, yet. Had he?

"Marceau! Marceau! Marceau!" a group of voices chanted angrily from below.

Yes! He heard it now, clearer this time.

"La tête", he mumbled. "La tête!" he exclaimed louder this time.

"They come for me!" he shouted ecstatically. "My people!" he shouted

back, running to the balcony.

"What are you doing?" Carmen cried, petrified.

The Marquis turned from the window as Marceau rushed past him, his face impassive.

He said nothing, simply stood with his arms clasped behind his back. His face was so dark. So chill. He watched Marceau, a strange look on his face.

"Do not worry, Carmen", Marceau gushed, as he ran back from the balcony and threw his arms around her. "All is well!"

"All is well?" she repeated, incredulous, as she brushed his arms away.

His touch made her skin crawl. She glanced across at The Marquis, shamefaced, but he was still watching Marceau.

"What are you talking about?" she continued, disheartened.

She was so worried. Do not worry? He might as well ask her not to breathe. It was all she could do not to break down or jump from the window. It wasn't supposed to turn out like this.

Mother had told her that taking office with Marceau would make her career. That she'd be well respected and climb the ranks. Within ten years you'll be a made woman, her mother's voice chimed pompously in her head. That man is going places, and he'll take you with him, if you let him. He likes you, dear, you know that. Use that.

"Everything will be well", Marceau repeated happily, a dumb look on his face.

He looked even crazier now, she thought. His eyes were so wide and staring, and sickly bright with fanaticism. She had seen this look before but couldn't place where.

"I am coming, my people! I shall lead you through this!" He pushed Carmen to the side and went to his mirror.

Him and that damn mirror she thought. Ever the popinjay. Even with an angry mob about to kick down the door, all he could think of was petting his hair into place and running that horrible little comb through his eyebrows.

Boom.

The room shook, and Carmen screamed. The Marquis simply arched an eyebrow. Another boom.

Carmen ran for cover under her desk.

"Yes! Yes!" Marceau turned, madly, and opened his arms in embrace.

Carmen watched and wailed. He had lost his mind!

She looked to The Marquis for help, but he had...gone? Where had he gone? Why had he not taken her with him? She'd always liked him. She had made that clear, hadn't she?

"Oh, no, no, no", she mumbled despairingly, her mumbles muffled by the wood of her desk. So much shouting. So much noise. She placed her hands over her ears and sat rocking back and forth beneath the desk.

Smash!

She heard, if not saw, the door explode inwards, and the shards of wood splinter everywhere across the floor.

"Hurah!" the crowd screamed wildly.

"My people!" Marceau screamed back. "You have come for

me!"

And come for him they had.

The crowd surged forward and grabbed him, hoisting him atop their shoulders and carrying him from the room.

She waited a few moments until she was sure they had left the office, then when she was sure she was alone, scrambled out from under the desk. She ran to the window to look down onto the courtyard.

"Oh my!" she exclaimed, clapping her hand over her mouth.

*

They carried him atop their shoulders, like a hero of old.

It is symbolic, he thought. To show that they revere me. That I am above them. Their true lord and master. Not the damned assembly. Not the blasted house. There will be no need for them now, not in my new world, in my new France.

He would forge his own path now, like Napoleon before him. He saw it clear before him, his path. It would be difficult, challenging certainly, but he would persevere, he would win through. He had to. For the glory of France. His people need him.

Emperor Marceau. It sounded so fitting. They were wrong to abolish the monarchy. They'd grown weak and decadent ever since. And with the power now imbued upon him by The Marquis...he would reign for a thousand years. No, for eternity!

Foolish man. To have such power, and to squander it so. He was stupid to think he could play Marceau, play him at his own game. To control him.

Control such as he? It was laughable. He was of the blood of emperors, of kings. The Marquis was some...common businessman. He would find it hard to swallow, his place in the new order of things, but swallow it he shall.

He would have his uses though, surely. He was devious and cunning and had acquired power of sorts. He would be useful in commerce, and in logistics, and more importantly, in war.

He would profit well, in the supply of his armies, provided he learned his station, and how to serve his betters.

Thousands screamed his name now, as they carried him outside, triumphant.

They thronged the courtyard excitedly. Laughing and smiling up at him.

Look! Even the children of Paris had come to honour him.

He smiled dumbly, his eyes glazed and faraway, as they dropped him to his feet and marched him forward, two strong men gripping him under either arm.

My throne! And such a throne!

But why is it shaped so?

And wood? Surely this does not befit an emperor.

He frowned, his eyes still unseeing, as the men pushed him to his knees, one of them kicking him gruffly in the back of his legs when he would not cooperate.

My knees? But why?

This is not how one sits a throne...

Perhaps it is a new honour. A special honour, for a special man. Perhaps they wish to crown me...yes!

Crown me! That's it. An emperor cannot rule without his crown. I hope it's flattering to my hair.

These brutish peasants are not the most stylish bunch.

"My crown!" he mumbled madly. The crowd laughed and jeered.

"His crown!" a burly man standing by Marceau shouted. "He wants his crown; shall we give it to him?"

"Give him his crown, Rémond!" a thickset woman with a hard face shouted back.

"Emperor", Marceau mumbled.

"What's that?" Rémond leaned in close to Marceau.

"Emperor Marceau!" Marceau said excitedly.

"EMPEROR MARCEAU IS IT?" Rémond boomed loudly for the crowd to hear.

A small boy ran from the crowd and threw an egg.

It hit Marceau square in the face, the crack reverberating through the courtyard. The yolk dripped slowly down his eyelids, nose and chin.

It was a pitiful sight, the president of France grinning blissfully on his knees, yellow yolky comeuppance staining his handsome face.

The crowd laughed, but a middle-aged woman grabbed the boy tightly by the arm and whisked him away, admonishing him as she carried him kicking and screaming further back into the crowd.

"Well, there's your crown!" Rémond leaned down and cruelly smeared the yolk around Marceau's head so that it resembled a yolky crown.

"You've got your crown, what now?" Rémond asked the crowd, who tittered and jeered.

"Be done with it", a voice said quietly, but audibly, from the front.

"Oh, you're never any fun Garlon", Rémond griped.

"Lui couper la tête!" someone shouted.

"Lui couper la tête!" another voice called. And then another. And another.

"Are you sure?" Rémond shouted back, cupping his hand to his ear and turning himself side on to the crowd, playing his role to perfection, as host of this sickly pantomime.

"Lui couper la tête!" they roared, again and again, louder and louder.

The whole crowd was chanting loudly now, the sound of it thundering through the courtyard and likely echoing for miles.

"Oui, oui, oui", Rémond mouthed noiselessly, raising his hands, and bouncing them softly up and down, to calm the crowd.

He motioned to the two men standing silently either side of Marceau, and they forced his head forward into a crudely cut head shaped hole.

Marceau was silent now, but still gazing vacantly into the distance.

My people...

My people...

Rémond raised his hand, then lowered it sharply.

There was a great whooshing sound, followed by the sound of metal hitting wood, with a satisfying thud.

The crowd roared their approval, as Marceau's head hit the ground.

"Vive la France", Rémond said.

My people?

My people?

Why have you abandoned me so?

My people?

BANG BANG BANG!

A high-pitched scream rang out from the crowd, as gunshots thundered from the palace walls!

"Les flics! Les flics!" a man shouted.

"Disperser! Disperser! Disperser!" a heavyset man screamed in a gravelly voice.

"S'enfuir, s'enfuir!" another voice shouted from further back.

More gunshots rolled out, and panic spread like wildfire in the crowd. The people in the crowd pushed and pulled one another frantically in an effort to flee the gunfire.

It wasn't long before chaos ensued.

Men and women fell under the weight of the crowd, where they were trampled by the unending mass of fleeing Parisians.

Gunshots?

It has begun!

Marceau grinned.

Or rather, Macrceau's head did from the ground, now very separate from the rest of him.

*

Night had fallen and things had quietened down now, thanks to the flics, soldiers, and an odd assortment of characters, who neither flic nor soldier trusted, nor in fact knew anything about.

"Who are they again?" a fresh-faced young recruit asked.

"Beats me", a grizzled looking veteran replied.

"They don't look like soldiers..." the recruit said.

"No shit", the veteran said grimly.

Clément blushed. He hadn't meant to embarrass himself, but it seemed every time he opened his mouth, he succeeded in doing so.

He looked up to Constant. In fact, he was in awe of him, if truth be told.

Constant was a war hero. A real hero! He'd been in the thick of it and survived to tell the tale. He'd fought his enemies and slain them in combat. Constant had fought for the Republic all over, for twenty years. From West Africa to Madagascar and Ouaddai, he'd battled the enemies of France all over the world, and emerged victorious every time.

And he'd come home a celebrated hero from Ambiliony, having daringly routed a group of rebels who had led a devastating counter offensive on the French guns. Had the rebels succeeded, they surely would have been massacred.

Constant made him feel useless, and that made him feel insecure. But he was still young, barely eighteen and still tugging at the hems of his mother. Too young to know what lay in store for him. And too naive to be scared.

Young he may be, but he was ecstatic to have been selected for this duty.

He knew Clément had vouched for him with the colonel. He was by rights probably still too inexperienced for such a delicate assignment.

But he didn't care, he would show the boys back at the barracks. Him! Clément Aguillon! Guarding the Élysée.

Standing before it like a soldier of old, stoically deterring anyone stupid enough to approach.

He'd guard the palace with his life, if he had to.

He glanced nervously at the body on the floor, by the impromptu guillotine the protestors had built.

He hoped his bravery wasn't put to the test.

"I don't like them", Clément said, glancing at the oddballs, his face still red.

Constant grinned at him.

"Sacré bleu", he muttered suddenly.

Clément watched him, confused, then saw the reason for his curse.

A man was approaching them, and what a man. He'd seen some big men since enlisting, and Clément was no mite himself, but this man took the cake.

He had a chest like a barrel of ale, and arms that looked as though they were cut from grandfather oak. He could probably club you to death with them, as good as any flic stick.

Clément felt his stomach roll like the sea as the man looked right at him.

"He's coming over here!" Clément whispered frantically.

Constant said nothing, he merely stood to attention, his face set. The only indication Clément could see of any nerves on his friend was the fact that he had gone deadly still, and his eyes were fixed straight ahead. Usually, they would be watchful.

Clément prayed the man was not coming to speak with them. But his prayers were unanswered, for the giant swaggered over to them, and stopped in front of them.

"I'll take it from here, boys", he rumbled.

Boy? Clément bristled.

He was no boy.

And Constant certainly wasn't either!

Clement looked to Constant, but he showed no reaction to the slight. "We have been ordered to guard access to the courtyard", Constant replied robotically.

"Well, orders have changed", the giant replied.

Constant looked uncomfortable. "My orders come from the colonel", he replied in the same robotic voice.

"Well, boy, my orders come from that man over there", the giant replied, pointing at a heavily decorated iron haired man, standing by the postern gate.

He had so many medals on his jacket Clément wondered how he managed to stand under the weight of them.

"You see him?" the giant asked, with a mocking smile on his face. Leaning in close, the giant draped his arm around Constant's shoulders.

"This is above your paygrade, boy, so unless you fancy butting heads with old iron balls over there, I suggest you just let me through. Post haste!" he shouted suddenly in a booming voice.

Clément jumped.

The giant laughed hysterically, as if he had told the greatest of jokes, slapping his leg with his meaty paw.

Constant said nothing, but glanced across at the general, who was watching the interaction.

The general nodded stiffly, then returned his attention to a nervous looking aide taking orders from him, as they flew out of his mouth at a rapid pace.

"Clock off for the night, jeunes hommes!" the giant ordered. "The night is but young. There might even be a buxom lass or two waiting for you out there. Even you, pimple britches!" He rounded on Clément, smacking him happily on the back.

This seemed to amuse him even more, and he started laughing obnoxiously loudly again.

Clément stumbled under the force of the smack, his eyes wide and startled. He opened his mouth to say something, but no words would come.

Embarrassed, he returned sharply to attention, eyes down,

blushing several shades of scarlet.

"Let's go", Constant said suddenly, dragging Clément by the arm.

"Good boy!" the giant said amiably.

Clément allowed Constant to lead him away from the gate.

Glancing back, he saw the giant speaking to a group of flics guarding the other postern gate. He was dismissing all the soldiers and flics! Why?

"C'mon", Constant grunted, giving his arm a pull.

"But he's dismissing all the guards!" Clément exclaimed. "Who is he to do such a thing? What about protocol? The colonel will be furious!"

"I don't think so", Constant replied.

Turning back to look at the courtyard one last time as Constant pulled him away, Clément frowned.

This wasn't right. He thought back to the oath he swore. Honoré and fatherland. That was what he had been taught. They had drummed it into him, until it was all he could think of. There was no honor in this. The whole thing stank.

*

Hadur looked down at Marceau and stifled a laugh.

Damnit if the man didn't look ridiculous. His pompous head lying there, mouthing soundlessly, like a fish snatching at food. And what was that he was muttering? Something about empire. Or was it emperor?

He didn't know, it was all he could do not to break down and laugh his guts out.

Marceau's presidentially attired body hung limply in the guillotine behind, which didn't help.

Damn but it was funny.

"It looks like the shoe is on the other foot now, eh Marceau", Hadur jibed.

He couldn't help himself, and giggled into the back of his hand like a maiden merry on mead.

378

"Hadur? Is that you?" Marceau asked desperately. "You have come for me! My loyal servant! I knew you would".

Loyal servant?

The man is unhinged.

Hadur frowned.

This was spoiling his fun. He had expected the man to plead, to cajole, to beg to bribe. Anything to save his skin.

He'd expected him to try and feed him some of his politicians' horseshit. Promises of future wealth and power and bla de bla de bla. All backed by lies and empty promises.

But not this.

This was just weird, quite frankly.

"It is I", Hadur said simply.

"I knew it!" Marceau exclaimed. "I knew The Marquis would send someone for me. He knows of the glory I shall bring to France!"

What the hell was he talking about? Glory? France? Last he remembered; the whelp had been a piss scared new tooth bringing The Marquis his food like a pliant serving girl.

Now he was talking as if he were emperor of France.

"Hurry, my boy, my faithful servant", Marceau said. "Before my enemies return. I thought they were allies of the great emperor, but no, no no, they have betrayed me".

Hadur narrowed his eyes. He'd seen this before, but not to such an extent. The delusions of grandeur and the prophetic visions.

It happened sometimes, when egotistical men got their teeth. He remembered The Marquis, my what an annoying son of a bitch he'd been for a while. Flapping his gums constantly about his great plans, and the prosperity he'd bring to the tableau.

To be fair, things had been good under The Marquis, and he was never without a soft neck to sink his teeth into.

But this was worse, much worse.

What a bore. He'd been looking forward to having his fun

with the man. He'd never liked him. Slimy little eel. But this was no sport at all. It felt like tormenting a child, and it did not please him in the slightest.

Why drag it out?

The whelp had reaped what he sown. But he didn't deserve this. No-one deserved this.

"Vive la France", Hadur said softly, before stepping down hard on Marceau's head.

Henré, Mon Coeur

She couldn't stop the tears. She wasn't sure she wanted to. All she wanted was to cry. To sob and weep and shake with sadness. To let the despair wash over her and carry her away, far from here.

It hurt so deep, and she felt it so heavy upon her. It felt like someone had punched a hole in her chest and crushed her heart to pieces while it still beat.

She kept picturing Henré. But her Henré, as she knew him. Not what he had become.

She lay sobbing on her bed, thinking back on their time together. It all ran through her mind in a blur.

She saw his beautifully innocent face smiling at her across the room, gesturing invitingly to her with his hand.

She had caught his eye early on, and they had played that game of glances for a while, while he worked up his courage.

She was so nervous, but he didn't care that her parents watched on disapprovingly. He had no care for anyone else in the room but her. And she loved him for it.

When she finally took his hand, the feel of his hand in hers was electric, and such a thrill went through her. She'd never felt so alive. From then, she only had eyes for him.

They danced together the entire night, oblivious to their surroundings, the music serenading them as they swayed together in a lover's embrace.

She loved Henré. She knew that from the moment she saw him.

Something about him called to her. And something in her called back.

There was a sameness in him. And he knew that. Though she tried to hide it, for fear the world would reject it, scorn it, shame it, Henré saw it anyway, and in seeing it, accepted it, embraced it.

His eyes screamed to her, I am you, and you are me, and we are one. Cool as he tried to play it, his eyes gave the game away. She would never forget his eyes. She saw herself mirrored in them, and more, she saw her future.

Now that was all gone. All for nothing. She'd never see those eyes again. And she despaired. It hurt so bad she could barely bear it. She just wanted the pain to end. Anything to numb this hurt, end this hurt. How could it hurt so bad?

She had mourned before, but this hurt so much worse. It felt like she'd lost a part of herself, and she didn't know if she wanted to go on without her Henré.

Why did he have to take the job at that cursed club? She hated it, and all the god forsaken rich bastards that inhabited it. She wanted to wipe them all from existence. But her anger was short lived, for another wave of grief hit her hard, washing over her in a grey wave.

"Why does it hurt so bad?" she sobbed.

She couldn't take it anymore. She couldn't. She wouldn't. She wouldn't live without Henré. Her love. Why had he forsaken her like this?

She gripped the dresser by her bed, and stared at herself in the mirror.

Her eyes were bloodshot and swollen. Her face, full of despair.

Henré's face appeared in her mind once more. Cuddling with her on their little sofa this time. Playing lovingly with her hair, and gently rubbing her still small stomach. She'd been newly pregnant and scared at the prospect of childbirth.

Henré had cradled her and assured her that everything would be alright.

It was a simple memory. But it felt like a jagged piece of glass being twisted through her chest.

Painful sobs ripped through her, and she covered her eyes with her hands.

The kindest thing in such a case, would be to end their suffering. The words from that accursed book rang through her mind.

"End their suffering?" she spluttered.

No, it was too much.

She felt a new feeling then. An apprehension. A fear. Her heartbeat quickened and her mouth dried.

Ceasing her crying, she looked into the mirror, then lashed out hard with her fist, smashing the glass.

She went still then. Stiller than she'd ever been.

Then, she started to shake and tremble, unable to catch her breath.

I love you Henré.

Picking up a shard of glass from the dresser, she pictured Henré as he was, and held him in her mind.

Closing her eyes, she saw him, clear as day. Standing there, smiling invitingly. He was gesturing to her, beckoning, and she started to smile. He was walking over to her now, across the floor of the dancehall.

She glanced at her father, his face was thunderous. She grinned, her smile exploding across her face. The pain had stopped. It no longer hurt!

He was almost there now, striding so confidently toward her. Her heart was beating like a drum in her chest. Almost there! A few more steps! And then, he was before her, and her eyes met his.

"Voulez-vous danser, madame?" Henré asked, extending his hand.

Oh Henré...

She held the shard of glass to her wrist.

Mon coeur.

Everyone's Invited

Hiro trudged wearily through the tunnels of the catacombs. He was worried about La Meme, he had lost her a way back, when they were ambushed by a group of what could only be The Marquis' men. Villains.

He had quickly dispatched two of them before the rest fled. He replayed the encounter in his head. Saisei had left her scabbard almost of her own volition, sliding smoothly into his hand as he dropped into water stance and cleared his mind.

Slashing forward, left then right, in two blisteringly fast motions, he had palmed his cloth and was cleaning the blood from Saisei, even before their heads hit the floor. If only he could have helped La Meme.

Unfortunately, they had been ambushed at a crossroads, the blasted place was full of them, and she had been cut off from him.

He had watched as she fled, but not before turning and raising her knee, hard, into the groin of one of them. He smiled at the memory. He hoped she found her way.

She was full of surprises.

Watch and report back. Keep an eye on the situation in Paris, they had told him at the temple. An eye on what he did not know. He had asked sensei what he should watch for, and he had simply replied, "The situation".

Like a parent, he somehow always found a way to rile him,

even now. He considered asking his sensei's sensei, but the old man scared him. They say he can see into your soul, and having conversed with him a few times, Hiro believed them.

Besides, the last thing he wanted was to agitate sensei by dishonouring him. He knew he'd pay for it later.

All he knew was his mission to watch the activities of the Tableau Haute, and relay anything of importance back to the temple.

In particular, they had told him to watch the man, Lucien.

"The grandmaster says he sees this one in all of his dreams. He will draw the ungodly unto him like a vortex. Watch him. There is another. A boy. Gabriel. He has some role to play in this that is still unclear. Protect him if you can, for he is an innocent, but do not jeopardise the order".

Do not jeopardise the order.

He found these words grating.

They were sworn to protect the world from the Ekur. But sometimes, it seemed hopeless. For every one they killed, another two seemingly crawled out of the sewers. It was like battling blood hungry medusae.

Their numbers were growing.

This Marquis had already given two new wretches their teeth, bringing them into his ungodly order.

It was...disquieting.

The vampyric order in Paris had always been an incestuous affair of closely guarded secrets, and closer guarded teeth.

He knew from his studies that they believed vampirism should be kept to the old bloodlines, and typically only passed down from father to son. Bloodlines that ran back thousands of years, some say to Dace himself.

Hiro wasn't sure about this. They were an arrogant bunch, the tableau, and he thought it was more than likely that one self-important sucker had simply created the rumour to bolster his legend.

But that was how it went with rumours. Once they were spoken, there was no taking them back.

In Paris, they took things particularly seriously, and up until the past few decades, no new Ekur had been created outside of the old bloodlines.

This Marquis didn't seem to share the same philosophy though. Perhaps it was his merchant background. His rise to power and his position as lord of the tableau was something of a mystery.

Though he was certainly preferably to the Mad Queen. Anything would be preferable to seeing another such as her sit the throne.

Here already.

He had expected a grander entrance, from such a man. But the entrance to The Marquis' manor was nondescript, in fact if you didn't know it was there, you probably wouldn't notice it all.

It was the catacombs after all, he supposed.

The "entrance" turned out to be a simple block of stone that was darker than the rest of the wall, with a single symbol on it. A blood red eye, barely visible, etched into the centre.

Perhaps he wasn't as free and loose with his secrets as Hiro thought. Or perhaps he just didn't want the Dwellers stumbling upon it by chance.

He expected the other side of the entrance was secured by some vampyric sorcery. But he was prepared, should it come to that.

Placing his hand on the symbol, he pushed hard against the stone. To his surprise, a doorway opened in the stone and swung inward without resistance.

Hiro frowned.

Was it a trap? It was not like what he had heard of the man. He was not one to leave his drawbridge down.

Shifting Saisei on his back, he stepped through, one hand

trailing his scabbard.

Gabriel was miserable.

He was sick and tired of the oaf's constant farting and this new woman's patronising remarks. So far, she'd called him boy, youth, youngling, stripling, whatever that meant, and most gratingly, enfant.

She was like a more bitter version of La Meme. Not bitter in the sense that she was harbouring some deep resentment, but bitter like wine gone bad.

Where La Meme was warm and sweet, she was cold, and sour. He wasn't sure she intended to be, but it was certainly how she presented.

He had the impression she was used to getting her own way, and had an irritating aura of entitlement, like she expected people to fall to their knees whenever she entered a room.

Gabriel disliked her intensely.

She'd sat with the oaf, watching him, since the other woman, Dagger, had departed. He wished it was still Dagger watching him, not this awful woman.

At least they'd decided he was worthy of being watched after all. It still ruffled his feathers that they hadn't seen fit to chain him, or secure him more thoroughly from the offset. Though he supposed they probably assumed he was still in no state to get very far.

And they had assumed right. How far would he get, beaten, bloody and tired to his bones in the middle of the night? And he didn't even know where he was.

He wished Lucien were here. He would know what to do. He was so decisive, and always seemingly in control of the situation, not controlled by it.

He missed him, he realised.

He resolved to be more decisive. He wouldn't just sit here awaiting The Marquis' pleasure. He might be the king of this castle, but Gabriel didn't care a whit.

He was sick of this charade and had things to do. There were people relying on him.

Like little Luca, he thought guiltily.

But what can I do against such as these?

The oaf's arms are bigger than my legs.

And the woman...Dagger...must be some freak of nature.

Never have I felt such strength.

And she frightens you.

So what if she does?

There is something there...behind those eyes.

Rolling madly, like a ship in a storm.

Something that could tip, at any moment.

Luca needs you!

And Marie.

He saw the little girl's face. Saw her smile. So hopeful, so trusting.

And Max. And...Alain...Lainy.

Do it for them. Who else do they have in this world? And do it for La Meme. It would kill her to lose you.

Steeling himself, he swallowed hard.

"Oaf!" he barked. "I grow tired of this waiting. If your Marquis means to kill me, I would prefer he did it sooner rather than later. I do have things to do, you know", he said, in a manner reminiscent of Madame Dagger.

Hadur growled and leapt to his feet.

He stormed across to Gabriel menacingly, fists bunched by his sides.

"Ah, ah, ah!" Gabriel waggled his finger. "Your lord Marquis won't be best pleased if you kill me and deprive him of the pleasure now, will he?"

"Wretch", Hadur spat, glowering at him.

"Where are your manners, **boy**", Gabriel said with a smirk.

Gabriel thought the oaf would hit him, but then he relaxed,

his face stretching into a smile of its own.

"Very good...boy", Hadur replied. "But watch yourself, for The Marquis will soon tire of this farce...and you".

"I shan't ever sleep again". Gabriel feigned terror, placing his hand over his mouth, aghast.

"I can see why he likes you", Hadur replied.

"Who likes me?" Gabriel asked.

"Not me, you wretch", Hadur shot back.

Gabriel frowned, none the wiser.

The door opened then, and The Marquis swept through, like some sinister butler.

"It is time...bring the boy", he said, gesturing at Gabriel.

"Time? Time for what?" Gabriel asked.

Hadur grunted, then picked him up and threw him over his shoulder. It was humiliating, and an upsetting reminder of just how powerless he was in this situation.

He railed silently.

What would Lucien do?

Or Dagger, he thought with a mischievous grin.

"Quite the bumpy ride, oaf", Gabriel quipped, bouncing against the giants back, as he led him wherever it was The Marquis deigned.

He felt the giant grin. The Marquis shot him a dark look, but otherwise said nothing. He was still in a terrifying mood.

"Set him down here", The Marquis ordered.

'Here', was the cold floor of yet another hall.

The place must be huge, Gabriel thought, as he rubbed at his bruised buttocks.

The hall stretched for a hundred or so feet. At the end there was some kind of...altar? He shuddered to think what that was used for. He hoped he was not here to find out.

Bar a few torches, it was completely absent of light, for there were no windows. It was cold and draughty, and he found it rather unnerving. What was the purpose of this place?

Taking in his new surroundings, his eyes were drawn to a painting hanging on the wall at the opposite end of the hall to the altar.

Two fearsome looking men were duelling, or at least he supposed that's what they were doing, for they were circling each other with murder in their eyes and, strangely, one of the men had blood on his mouth.

But where were their weapons?

Such a strange painting. But then, The Marquis was a strange man. Strange and frightening. Mirrored in his taste in artwork apparently.

At least Dagger had style. He wondered how The Marquis had come to be head of this order of...people, and not her.

She had something of a queenly quality to her. He could see her giving orders, a crown atop her head.

He felt The Marquis was more suited to commerce.

Or at least might have been, before whatever had addled his mind so.

Now he was more suited to a lunatic asylum.

Oh, what have I gotten myself into this time.

*

In the Under, Lucien approached the hidden entrance to The Marquis' manor cautiously, but it was already open!

He looked around sharply. Were they waiting for him? This must be a trap, he thought. Or has someone been here before me?

He didn't like it. His senses screamed at him to turn back, but he had no other choice. It was the only way in. The front gate would be suicide. And he no doubt had men in the grounds patrolling the walls.

Oh, how he'd enjoyed killing the wretch Pavo. He grinned grimly, as he re-lived it in his head. Now it was time to kill his master. First the pup. Now the old dog. The Marquis should have been put down long ago, and this time he had gone too far.

He hoped that Gabriel was alright. The alternative made him queasy, and he pushed such thoughts from his mind.

He expected if he was dead, he'd know about it. There was no way The Marquis would miss an opportunity to punish him, to hurt him, for Janver.

And so, he slid stealthily into the darkness of the entrance, placing one foot in front of the other, as he inched inexorably closer to whatever fate lay in store for him.

*

"I grow tired of this", The Marquis growled. His pacing back and forth was unsettling.

Gabriel was scared, though he did not show it. He wouldn't give him the satisfaction, if he could avoid it.

"Yes, it is quite tiresome, isn't it?" Gabriel replied.

The muscles in The Marquis jaw pulsed angrily.

"Watch yourself, boy, for my patience is not limitless", he replied.

"Neither is your hospitality, apparently". Gabriel made a show of appraising the sparsely furnished hall. "Would a drink kill you?"

The Marquis fumed.

Just when Gabriel thought he had gone too far, a woman's laughter peeled out from the other side of the hall. It was infectious, and full of good humour.

Gabriel looked around for the source of the noise.

It was Dagger!

She'd returned, and was leaning nonchalantly against the wall, near one of the entrances to the hall.

A door was open behind her and he could see light and…was it a dining hall? A living area?

He couldn't make sense of these huge houses. There were too many rooms, and none of their purposes were immediately apparent to him.

He thought a house should have somewhere to live, somewhere to eat, and somewhere to make love, that somewhere not necessarily being a somewhere exclusive from the others.

He didn't understand these 'great halls' and all this pomp. It seemed wonderfully unnecessary to him. But then, he'd always been a man of simple pleasures. It didn't take much to make him happy. His happiness came from people, not things.

He was glad Dagger was here, though he didn't know why, she was just as fearsome as The Marquis. Even so, her presence reassured him.

Hopefully she would do something to diffuse the tension, or at least divert the attention away from him.

He'd noticed she and The Marquis had been butting heads somewhat, and he got the impression she wasn't overly fond of him. Not that The Marquis was a man inviting fondness. He was a cold bastard at that.

"**Madame Dagger**", The Marquis stressed her name through gritted teeth. "How nice of you to join us".

"Nice for you, perhaps". She wrinkled her nose at the scene before her. "How long are you going to play this little game with the manling?"

"As long as I choose!" he thundered.

She straightened against the wall.

Gabriel could feel her anger.

He glanced at the painting, then back to the pair of them. He wondered if he would see such a duel here tonight. It would be nice to witness something of note, before they did away with him.

"Enough!" The Marquis spat suddenly, breaking the tension. "If the coward won't come, I'll bleed his boy, that ought to encourage him to crawl out of whatever hole he hides in".

He strode across the hall, and wrenched Gabriel painfully to his feet.

Madame Dagger stepped forward, as if to stop him, then

hesitated.

"Wise", The Marquis told her.

"Do not bleed him too much, monseigneur", the oaf chimed in.

"And why is that?" The Marquis asked.

"He is already weak. You don't want to kill him before the boy arrives", Hadur replied.

The Marquis gave Gabriel an appraising look, running his eyes over him, like a surgeon, determining if he was fit to survive the surgery.

Muttering inaudibly to himself, he nodded as if reaching a decision. "Yes...just a bit, yes", he said to no one in particular.

Gabriel was terrified now and couldn't help the sheen of sweat that appeared on his brow. He could control his feelings, but not his body, and it was unfortunately betraying his fear.

He felt ashamed. He did not think Lucien would show fear. He'd spit in the bastard's face and bloody his nose.

He was scared to move, as if it would break the spell, and the man would begin his foul torture, whatever he had in mind.

Be strong. Be brave. Do not give him the satisfaction.

He stood silently, braced for attack, wondering if it would be fist or blade.

Suddenly, he was hit with the most excruciating pain he had ever felt in his life, and fell to the floor.

It felt like someone had pumped him full of poison and fire, and he writhed silently on the floor, hands clutching desperately at his head.

The pain stopped, and he found the breath to scream. He hated himself for it.

The Marquis laughed. It was a truly unpleasant sound, and in that moment, Gabriel was glad Lucien had murdered his bastard son.

No.

No, I'm not.

He couldn't believe his thoughts. But the pain was so bad. It had filled him with hate for the man. Hate he didn't know he had him in. Hate he didn't know existed.

"That was just a taste of what I have in store for you, boy", The Marquis sneered. He looked so ugly, his face horribly contorted with hateful spite.

Is that what I'd look like, if I told him my thoughts? Gabriel thought.

"And there'll be even worse for the traitorous turncoat Lucien!" The Marquis screamed. "I'll have him torn limb from limb and set his treacherous head upon my mantle where it shall rest for a thousand years!"

"We shall see about that", a voice responded.

Lucien! Gabriel thought.

He lifted his head weakly from the floor, and there he was. His face was dark with anger. Darker than he'd ever seen it.

The Marquis' eyes burned wildly in his head.

Lucien grunted and grabbed the wall to stop himself from falling. He struggled for a moment, then...disappeared?

A thunderclap of sound rang out, and Gabriel heard someone stumble.

He dragged himself out of harm's way, and slumped down, exhausted against the wall.

Then Lucien was there again, standing over The Marquis who had fallen to his feet.

His wits must have been addled, by whatever manner of tool The Marquis had used to inflict such great pain on him. For it looked like Lucien had **flown** across the room and hit The Marquis, causing that thunderous boom.

The scene now reminded him of another of The Marquis' sick paintings.

The one with the...lord...stood over his subject. Except in this case, it looked as though Lucien were the lord, and The Marquis his subject.

He smiled. It was nice to see the bastard humbled.

Hadur stepped forward to aid his lord, but Dagger stopped him, her arm whipping out to hold him back. He gave her a strange look but relented.

The others watched in silence.

Others? Gabriel realised with a start.

They must have snuck in through the door Dagger came through, whilst The Marquis and Lucien were fighting.

They had quietly formed a circle around Lucien and The Marquis and stood, watching, silent arbiters of whatever was taking place.

The Marquis wore an unpleasant look on his face, like he had swallowed something particularly foul.

He glared up at Lucien, his eyes, thankfully, now back to their usual cold and uninviting selves.

Then he hung his head, perhaps in shame. He started to laugh. Quietly at first, then loudly, ever so loudly.

Raising his head, he smiled at Lucien.

"And so, it comes to this", he said. "You leave me no choice".

He fumbled in his pocket a moment, then paused for effect, grinning at them all in turn, savouring the moment.

"Out with it, man", Lucien said tiredly.

"Certainly", The Marquis replied. He removed his hand from his pocket.

Upon it was a small silver ring.

Lucien stumbled backwards.

The circle gasped collectively.

"The ring!" Lucien exclaimed. "Where did you...how did you?"

"At a loss for words, Lucien?" The Marquis laughed. "I never thought I'd see the day"

Rising to his feet, The Marquis took a step toward him.

Lucien took a step back.

Gabriel liked this not at all. He didn't know what was going on, but Lucien seemed shaken by this ring, and it seemed like The Marquis had gained the upper hand in their...battle.

It looked familiar, the ring, he was sure he had seen it before, but the lighting was poor, and he was too far away to get a good look at it.

The Marquis held his hand up for all to see, as if he were displaying some treasure.

Gabriel saw it then, in the light of the torches. He remembered that ring, he'd recognise it anywhere, the pains he took to acquire it.

It was the Soif De Sang.

Bloodlust

She stumbled through the streets of Paris, her bloodlust still wet upon her.

The Queen.

Queen Régine.

Queen of The Damned.

Queen, no longer.

As the ring had slipped from her finger, she had seen anew, and she hurt. She hadn't really felt for so long, she had forgotten.

Forgotten what it felt like to **feel.** To consider, to care, to love, to... repent.

Forgotten a life beyond blood, beyond lust, beyond desire.

She felt sick. She had to get away from here. Away from this nightmare.

She gazed down at her hands. They were shaking. Her beautiful hands, so finely formed, so beautifully painted. Yet so ugly. So horrifically stained. So irreparably tarnished.

Why wouldn't the blood come off? She scratched at it frantically, until she drew blood. More blood. Now she couldn't tell which blood was hers, and which was not.

Her stomach turned, and she closed her eyes, self-loathing quickly replacing nausea. She felt tears fighting their way through the maze and warren of her stunted spirit.

That awful feeling of repression came upon her as she tried to stop them, as she engaged in an awful attempt to suppress her heart's release. Stop it, in the vain hope that she could bury her feelings deep, deep where she need not face them, feel them, or be hurt by them.

She felt the tears at the corners of her eyes, but they could not come forth, she could not release them. She did not know how. It had been so long.

Like a child, she needed her bed, needed the comforting darkness that only sleep could bring. She was bone weary, but hers was a different kind of weariness. The weariness of the spirit. The weariness of the damned. The weariness of the sinner, confronted with their sins.

Only blissful darkness would give her the release she needed. Only darkness would allow her to escape the sins burning so painfully in her heart, however temporary the release.

She knew she'd have to face her sins. Knew she'd have to walk the path of the damned, but not this night. This night was for sleep. Sweet, blissful sleep.

She would give herself to the darkness of the night. She hoped it took her, cradled her, caressed her and whispered sweet nothings to her, as her mother might.

She knew she did not deserve it. She feared the night. For she knew for her, the night would not be kind.

It would be her friend no longer. It would be her prison. A prison of her own making. Built from the stone of her heart.

And she would be her own gaoler, and she would know no rest, take no leave, allow herself no relief. She could not. Would not. This was her punishment. And her soul would allow no parole.

Mercifully, she arrived swiftly to her den of iniquity, that she had so fondly called home. It stunk, and it reeked, and she grimaced.

She could feel the evil of the place. He had gone. Blissful relief. She could not face him. This night was hers alone.

She lay down and cradled her pillow under her head like a babe. She feared the darkness, but she knew she could not run from it.

She lay there a while, softly rocking, hugging the pillow, her eyes screwed shut. Eventually, when she could fight it no longer, the rocking stopped, and her eyes unscrewed.

The darkness had taken her away to her prison of stone. It would be a long and painful night for her, and she would know no peace, for a very long time. She would make sure of it.

Longue Vie Au Roi

He took his first breath as a god.

For wasn't he, now that he possessed the ring?

Its power rushed through him.

It was...virulent...like bottled fire.

He felt he could erupt at any moment and burn them all to ash. And why should he not? He was a **god,** after all.

His blood coursed angrily, smoking and spitting and snarling. Such anger he had never felt.

Was it anger? Or something else. Something base. It wasn't just anger...no. That was but a part of it.

He looked at Dagger with hungry eyes.

Had her skin always shined so...deliciously. He watched, enthralled, as tiny drops of sweat beaded gently, on her soft as silk skin.

He listened, rapt, to flick of her tongue in her mouth, her perfect mouth, and the thud of her heart in her comely chest.

She looked at him strangely.

"Where did you get that?" a voice called. It hit like a drum, crashing against his ears, and he spun at the sound.

"You", he replied coldly, narrowing his eyes.

Red rage seared his senses, and he felt an uncontrollable urge to sink his teeth into the boy, to rend his flesh until he bled his last drop.

He struggled to speak.

"How I acquired it", he said slowly, his chest rising and falling strangely. "Is none of your concern! Now be silent and know your place".

"I beg to differ. It is not yours. I didn't take you for a thief, **Marquis**", Gabriel retorted.

Lucien's mouth dropped open.

Perhaps I am not such a good influence on him after all, he thought wryly.

The Marquis went still.

Lucien braced himself. He did not know what hope he had, now he wore the ring, but he did not care. Gabriel was here because of him, and he would not stand by while The Marquis beat him black and blue. It would not be right.

And, truth be told, he didn't care much about much anymore.

He was sick. Sick of being angry. Sick of being sad. Sick of being lost. Sick of sleepless nights, of meaningless mornings, and colourless days. Sick of being scared.

Scared of being alone. Scared of connection. Scared of loss. Scared of driving away anything good, anyone good. Scared of his anger, scared of his rage, scared of his fear. Scared of becoming his father.

Scared of the dark, scared of the night. Scared, of closing his eyes, scared to dream. Scared that he might see his mother, his father, his family, swirling blue and grey and red.

Scared to relive his mistakes. Scared to meet those he had pushed away. Those he had lost. Those he had driven from him.

And sick of playing errand boy, to this psychopathic narcissus, and his endless scheming.

He was tired, so tired. It was so tiring, to never know stillness, to never know peace.

He stepped forward quietly.

The Marquis turned on him. He had expected anger, violence, wrath, but the fool merely stood there. "How quaint", he mocked.

Lucien said nothing but moved to stand between The Marquis and Gabriel.

The Marquis' eyes filled with red. "Go then", he spat. "Try your strength against me, mortal".

Mortal? Lucien frowned.

Does he think himself a god?

He truly is the most deranged narcissus.

I have had my fill of these bastards.

"Are you a coward?" The Marquis hissed.

Lucien felt his hackles rise but did nothing.

"As I thought", The Marquis sneered. He was a handsome man. But he'd never looked so ugly.

All Lucien could think of was to keep him talking, perhaps he would reveal some weakness with the ring, or something he could use to his advantage.

After all, it was a weakness possessed by every narcissus. A love of one's own voice. A love so strong, that they would speak and speak. Speak when they should not. Speak what they should not.

All so they could listen. Listen to that beautiful, dulcet sound, of their own voice. Speak, just so they could hear one more refrain, of that beautiful poetry. Speak, so they need not listen to the tone-deaf ramblings of their captive listener.

Oh, the injustice. Of being forced to silence oneself, to not spew one's genius, even for a second, to be forced to listen to lesser minds.

And why should they? When they were not in possession of such uniquely novel genius, as the world had never seen?

It was a heavy burden, being the greatest mind in every room. But bear it they did.

"Monseigneur, where did you come upon the ring?" a breathless voice interrupted. Colette.

Lucien thanked the stars silently.

The Marquis looked at her appraisingly.

Has she always been so alluring?

She lusts for you.

He smirked pompously. "Well, twas actually our friend Hadur here, that led me to it", he drawled.

"Monseigneur?" Hadur asked, confused.

The Marquis smiled and said nothing, savouring the suspense.

"Yes, indeed, my boy!" He appeared beside the giant, smacking him jovially on the back.

He's fast, Lucien thought.

Hadur looked uncomfortable but said nothing. He knew not what to make of this. He didn't know if it was good or bad. But something told him bad. He did not like bad. It usually meant less eating.

"Monseigneur?" the giant repeated.

"Yes, it is thanks to you, my loyal servant", The Marquis droned, his gaze intense, his hand still firmly pressing down on Hadur's back.

"You see, I had a task for Lucien here. A simple task, really, for one such as us. You likely know what I speak of. But Lucien is not a simple man. Or so he likes to think. So, I sent Hadur here to watch over him. To make sure Lucien completed the task...without incident". He paused, revelling in the feel of their eyes upon him. It was almost as intoxicating as the inebriating scent of blood.

"Well, he completed the task, but certainly not without incident". He threw Lucien a scornful look before continuing. "But that is by the by. The deed was done, and Lucien did his duty, albeit begrudgingly".

"What has that to do with the ring?" Colette asked excitedly.

It was out of character, she was a laconic woman, usually happy to just sit and listen. It was something The Marquis liked about her greatly. But he would forgive her the interruption.

"Quite the question, my Colette". The Marquis tipped his head at her.

"Oh, for god's sake man, get on with it", Gabriel blurted.

Madame Dagger turned away for a moment, her hand to her mouth. When she turned back, her face was strangely serious.

The Marquis glared at Gabriel, and his eyes began to simmer.

Colette hopped across the room rather coquettishly and grabbed his arm. "Please, monseigneur, the ring". She squeezed his arm softly, looking at the ring greedily.

It had the desired effect, for the glow left The Marquis' eyes, but hunger quickly took its place as he looked down at her.

Lucien caught Gabriel's eye and shook his head at him.

"Yes, the ring..." The Marquis continued, distracted, as if struggling to collect his thoughts.

"Well, Lucien may be a disappointment to us in many ways, but in this, he is an unadulterated genius...though I suppose the glory is not his alone, isn't that right, my boy?" He smiled approvingly at Hadur.

Colette nodded enthusiastically, urging him to continue.

"You see, buried deep in the depths of Lucien's little **shop,** are many things. Most of them are nonsense pieces of memorabilia and overpriced trinkets for the faux rich of course. How they love to show off their **antiques** and impress upon one another just how rich and important they are". He chucked with good humour.

"Can you think of anything more gauche, than to fill your home with musty relics, from **Angleterre,** of all places? Apparently, they are quite popular, these, **English** trinkets, and fill the shop from every corner. There are paintings and books, crystalware and jewellery, even **swords and shields**", he scoffed.

He found this last particularly amusing for some reason, chuckling as he lunged forward at Lucien, mimicking the stab of a rapier. He saw fit to stab at the air ineffectually a few times in Lucien's direction, before letting fall his air blade.

Lucien tensed but held his tongue.

"Quite the D'artagnan", Colette purred sycophantically.

He smiled at her. "Quite".

"Is that where you found the ring, in DuPassé?" Colette asked.

The Marquis looked a little irritated at this, as if she was rushing a story that should not be rushed, and he had still had further satisfaction to squeeze from its telling.

He looked at her, staring at him raptly, and his irritation passed, perhaps massaged away by other wants.

"Why I found nothing, my dear", he said affectionately.

Madame Dagger's lip curled.

Colette looked bemused.

Perhaps just a **tiny bit** more to savour from this, The Marquis thought.

"I don't understand", she replied, spelling it out for him.

The Marquis smirked mysteriously, like a magician preparing for the finale of his show.

"Why it was Hadur here, who found the thing". He inclined his head at the giant. "Not directly, of course, but he gave me the scent".

Deciding the time was right, he pressed his showman's advantage.

"You see, when I had Hadur check up on Lucien at his precious DuPassé, he said something rather interesting to me", The Marquis continued. "Do you remember what you said to me, my boy?"

Hadur shook his head.

"You said 'nothing unusual, monseigneur, full of vieille merde'", The Marquis said. "Quite the poet, aren't you?" he quipped for Colette's ears.

She played her part, giggling girlishly.

"Yes...vieille merde indeed. But you also said something else.

Something that intrigued me. Something that has been playing on my mind ever since. Do you remember what it was that you said?" The Marquis said.

Gabriel rolled his eyes theatrically. Thankfully, The Marquis did not see.

Hadur pursed his lips and shrugged. "I was hungry, monseigneur, I had other things on my mind".

"Other things indeed". The Marquis chuckled. "I shall tell you what you said to me. You said 'lots of rings'. And I must admit, that at first, I thought nothing of it. And why would I? It's how Lucien makes his living, after all, collecting and selling his little trinkets to the nouveau rich".

"But then, he killed my son", The Marquis said suddenly, his voice chilling. "And I have thought of him ever since".

*

She was bleeding badly now, and could feel the strength leaving her body.

She had tried so hard to keep him safe. And for a while, she thought she had.

She'd been too protective of him. Too overbearing. She told herself she would let him find his own path, yet there she'd been, at every turn, every crossroads, a quiet hand on the shoulder, a quieter voice in the ear.

It was her own fault that he'd gravitated to the boy, Lucien. She didn't blame him, truly, how could she. She had walked every path. Taken every turn. Seen every end. Why should he not?

Was he not young? Was it not the domain of youth? To throw caution to the wind, and leap blindly. To dance in the dark, to spin with the wind, to flirt with fire.

Oh, to be young again, every path unwalked, every step untaken. Would she live her life any differently? Almost certainly. But then, perhaps that was hindsight talking. Hindsight gained through wisdom. Wisdom gained through pain.

Would it be the same life, lived over? Would she still dance in the dark?

She had yearned for the unknown, yearned for danger, as she yearned to keep him safe. She could not help it. She knew how cruel and uncaring the world could be, better than most.

Every line on her face told a story, every grey hair an ending. She had earned them. To some, they merely signalled the passing of time. To her, they were the souvenirs of adventure, and each reminded her of another chapter in her story.

But this did not feel like an adventure.

She stopped, and hung her head, defeated, as sadness washed over her in a great wave.

"I thought we'd taken care of you, old one", a voice echoed in the tunnel.

Old one?

Her head perked up angrily.

*

Gabriel knew not what he saw, but he could not turn away.

Lucien had been in battle with The Marquis for what felt like an eternity, but he knew it could only have been minutes. Each blow Lucien bore, Gabriel felt, and his face had turned white.

They both bore wounds from their fight, but Lucien was tiring fast. He was bleeding and sweating, and breathing heavily.

The Marquis seemed to be gathering momentum, like some kind of sadistic steam train. Each blow he landed, his eyes seemed to grow redder, his growls deeper.

He'd seen men fight before, outside the bars, but not like this.

Each blow sought to maim, to kill, to end.

He knew then that they were not human.

That he, Lucien, was not human.

And he realised that he did not care.

Lucien hit The Marquis with such force that Gabriel reeled

back, unsteady on his feet, as a shockwave burst through the hall.

The Marquis groaned and fell to his knees.

Yes! Let that be it, please. Please let that be the end to this twisted man, Gabriel prayed.

In true narcissus fashion, The Marquis began to laugh a loud, mad, obnoxious laugh.

He raised his head, and grinned at Lucien, it was not a pretty sight. A pomegranate smile of blood-stained teeth.

Lucien sagged.

It must have demoralised him, how could it not? He had hit The Marquis with everything he had, and he'd laughed.

The Marquis dragged himself to his feet, and began to walk slowly toward Lucien, grinning his mad grin. And then it faded. The perverse humour left his face, replaced by a darker thing, a more wrathful thing, and Gabriel felt fear creep back into his stomach.

Lucien clenched his jaw hard, and his fists followed. He had more yet to give.

The oaf, Hadur, watched with arms crossed, his face impassive.

Or so he thought. Gabriel was astute enough to see the concern in his eyes. Or was it fear? It was hard to tell. Something about this unsettled him. Nettled him. But what? He was The Marquis' man, was he not? Why should he care?

Why did they not simply all fall upon Lucien, the others, and tear him limb from limb? Whatever the reason, he was glad, for he knew Lucien would stand no chance against them all, and he knew he could offer no help.

He was shocked from his contemplation, as Lucien and The Marquis came together again with an awful crash.

There were no blows this time, for they were locked together, hand in hand, one raised high above the shoulder, the other low by the abdomen.

They stood, shaking, each trying furiously to overpower the other, like vibrating statues of rage.

The Marquis was snarling, his teeth bared.

Lucien snarled back, but there was something else there, beneath the fire, beneath the flames. A more considered thing.

"Useless fucking son of a whore! You are nothing! Just like your father!" The Marquis spat suddenly, as he butted his head viciously into Lucien's face. The vitriol was almost worse than the violence and Gabriel gasped.

Lucien rocked on his feet but kept his grip.

He was tiring fast, Gabriel could see the effort it was taking him to hold The Marquis from him, his arms were shaking hard now. He couldn't hold him for much longer. Gabriel knew it was only a matter of time before he fell and did not rise again.

He had to do something. He could not just sit here and watch as the man he...cared for...died for him.

Before he could act, a sound like hammer striking steel rang out, and Lucien was lifted high from his feet as The Marquis swung ferociously upwards.

Lucien flew through the air, and hit the floor hard, crumpling against the wall where he lay still.

"Lucien!" Gabriel cried out. He ran to him without hesitation and fell to his knees beside him, turning him to his back.

He was alive, but unconscious. Snakes coiled tightly in Gabriel's stomach.

"What have you done, you bastard!" he spat.

The Marquis ignored him, and strode toward Lucien, murder in his eyes. He intended to finish the thing.

Well Gabriel would not let him. He'd sooner die himself. As The Marquis approached, Gabriel timed his moment.

He rose to his feet, and backed away slowly, in apparent fear, allowing The Marquis to approach unhindered.

The Marquis paid him no heed. He stood over Lucien, and

paused, no doubt to savour the moment. He looked to his brethren, each in turn.

"Oh, how the mighty have fallen", he sneered.

It appeared he was done savouring, for the sneer fled, and the snarl returned. He tensed, ready to bring an end to his enemy.

Gabriel swung hard, with all his force, hitting The Marquis hard on the side of the head with a weighty candelabra. He'd snatched it up when The Marquis' back was turned, and used it to good effect, for The Marquis crumpled to the floor immediately.

"Monseigneur!" Colette exclaimed. She moved as if to run to his aid, but Dagger grabbed her by the arm, restraining her easily.

Gabriel flushed with relief, the adrenaline bursting from him. It was done.

Wait, not yet!

With a start, he remembered the others and spun round wildly, the candelabra held tight like a club in his hand.

He was ready to defend Lucien from them. From all of them. From any of them. He would not go gently, should they want to harm him further.

But the others said nothing. Did nothing. They simply watched in silence.

Colette struggled half-heartedly against Dagger's grip.

The giant frowned and took a huge breath, exhaling deeply through his nostrils, and stretched his neck side to side, as if deciding whether or not to enter the fray.

Gabriel held his breath and waited. But the attack never came. He settled back into position, on guard, his expression wary.

He looked down at Lucien and allowed the warm relief he felt to comfort him. He smiled fondly and reached for him.

But he would not reach him.

A sudden movement came from behind him.

He turned, but was not fast enough, and a hand closed

viciously around his throat.

The Marquis' hand.

He lifted Gabriel effortlessly from his feet and began to squeeze hard.

Even as Gabriel felt his windpipe close, and his vision stared to blur, he couldn't fail to notice how ghastly the man looked.

The side of his head was cut and torn open horribly, leaking blood and lord knows what else. Huge folds of skin hung open haphazard across his face and head. Blood had dripped into his eyes, blending with the red that was already there.

He looked like a monster. Not at all like the hero of justice he fancied himself.

Isn't it funny, how our perception of self, can sometimes be the farthest thing from the truth?

Gabriel thought it was fitting.

What an end to my little story, he thought to himself sadly, as the light dimmed around him.

I'm sorry, Lucien.

I did my best.

I think we were kindred spirits, you and I.

I can see that now.

You didn't lessen me.

You weren't a darkness in my life.

You were a torch, burning brightly.

You showed me who I could be.

We showed each other.

Or maybe, we just reminded each other.

Reminded each other what was already there.

What was always there, if we had the courage to seek it.

I'm sorry we didn't get a chance to know one another better.

But, I feel that I know you, perhaps better than you know yourself.

You see yourself, as a dark man, in a dark world.

I do not think that is entirely true.

There is dark in you, certainly, but there is dark in all of us.

You are not just dark.

You are so much more than that.

You are grey, and you are blue. I have seen you sad.

You are red, and you are orange. I have seen you angry.

And you are gold, and you are yellow. I have surely seen you happy.

The dark man does not tread in murky waters.

He knows nothing of sadness, only disappointment.

He knows nothing of anger, only rage.

And happiness, happiness is as alien to him, as love of self is to you.

But you should not hate yourself.

You are a colourful man, full of vibrant hues, passionate strokes and considered touches.

I see it in you, even if you do not see it yourself.

I think you feel more than you know.

And...you make me feel.

Perhaps, in another life, we would feel together.

Goodbye, friend.

As his eyes fluttered their last, softly, gently, like the beat of a butterfly's wings, he smiled.

It hadn't been so bad as he'd feared. Dying, that is.

*

She felt a cold dread come over her, and a panic such as she'd never felt.

Something was wrong, terribly, terribly wrong.

She had never felt so powerless, in all her long life.

She had no choice.

Something broke in her then.

Something long chained shook free its shackles.

And she screamed.

A scream of pure frustration, and then, some other thing.

A powerful thing.

A primal thing.

And they knew fear.

*

As he came to, he was gripped by pain, pain and...fear. His head throbbed, and waves of nausea rocked him.

He moaned weakly.

A sound cut through his pain. It was a retching sound, no, choking. Someone was choking!

Gabriel!

He surged to his feet, and the world spun around him.

He fell fast, headfirst, at the wall.

Frantically he tried to stop his fall, scrabbling and clawing, he managed to contain his fall to his knees.

This was not good. He was injured. Badly. But it didn't matter, it couldn't matter, not now.

Wiping the blood from his eyes, he pushed himself to his feet and threw himself at The Marquis.

A hand shot out and gripped his throat before he could land an effective blow, and he was lifted from his feet, stopped dead in his tracks.

He felt the pain hit him, as The Marquis' eyes turned on him, and burned red in his skull.

He screamed, and started swinging through the pain, smashing blows to The Marquis' head and body, and hitting him again and again on his arm in an attempt to dislodge his grip.

Gabriel looked so grey.

His fear turned to panic, his panic to fury.

*

She moved through the Under, like a bolt of lightning thrown by Fulgora herself.

Their bloodless bodies lay forgotten behind.

Sparks shot from her, crackling wildly as she flew, a tempest, a hurricane, a reckoning.

She was awake.

*

Lucien watched as the light left the eyes of his friend, and screamed.

He struck The Marquis viciously, savagely, again, and again, and again, strikes that would kill a lesser man many times over, crumble him to dust, reduce him to ash, render him undone.

But he could not lay him low. For the bloodlust was upon him.

The Tableau Haute watched, grimly silent.

They knew this had but one ending.

*

She blew through the stone doorway like a tornado, the stone disintegrating into pieces as she passed.

She could feel him, he was close.

The sparks in her eyes danced violently.

They danced a dance of death.

*

The Marquis was afire. Ablaze. Aglow. Incandescent. His form seemed to shift from still to smoke, then back again, over and over.

He pulsed, like a man who had swallowed red lightning. It shone from his eyes. Leaked from his skin, burst from his pores, cracked from his hands.

He possessed the power of the ring. Or rather, the ring possessed him.

He would have to feed it now, lest it consume him.

He cared not, his dawn had come.

He turned his fire upon the traitor Lucien, and let it engulf him. He watched with pleasure, as the traitor blackened, and his skin cracked and popped under the searing heat of it.

He revelled, as the inferno consumed Lucien. The traitor

415

knew justice, at last.

He turned his eyes then upon the boy, Gabriel, hanging limp in his hand, and smiled.

"In sanguine serviunt nobis", he growled.

*

A chilling scream rang out from below. Somewhere close. Very close.

It reverberated from the walls, which recoiled and shuddered in fear.

It was otherworldly. It was terrifying.

And then, a gale hit the room, and all present were thrown from their feet by the force of it.

All but one.

*

Gabriel felt cold stone against his face.

It was uncomfortable, he thought, and he'd much prefer his bed.

He had been having the strangest dream. He'd dreamt he'd been battling vampyres, in a great hall, and that Lucien had been there.

But that was ludicrous. So he thought he'd just go back to sleep. He liked the second part of his dream better.

He'd dreamt of his parents. His parents who he never knew. But somehow, in this dream, he knew. Knew their faces. Knew their spirit. Knew their essence.

He saw his mother, smiling down at him. Saw his father, holding him high. He could picture it, as clear as the painter at his easel. Could hear the sound of their voices, and the happy squeal of his own.

The gentle laughter of his father. The soft cooing of his mother. It was... so soothing. It felt like warm down upon his soul.

He thought he'd sleep some more. He'd rather like to know them better. He'd rather like to see them again.

But he could not, for all the awful racket in the room, and the light.

The blasted light. It was shining like a thousand torches. Even through his eyes scrunched irritably shut, he felt it, seeping under his lids.

He was going to say something. These people had no consideration. He was trying to sleep. It was simply bad manners.

As he opened his mouth to cry out that they keep their racket down, a chill wind went through him, and he shivered.

How odd. The wind had rolled him! It had actually moved him. He rather enjoyed the feel of it, as he slid across the floor.

He felt himself hit the wall with a bump. That rather hurt a little. Really. He was going to say something now.

He opened his eyes, and wished he hadn't. He felt as if he'd held them open against a lantern in the dark for too long. They stung and watered.

He opened his mouth to cry out for some water, but no sound came, just a soundless rasp. His throat hurt. A lot.

He peered blearily through his painful eyes, blinking to clear the moisture gathering in them. It looked like some sort of fight was taking place. How strange. Why would they be fighting here in his bedroom?

And even odder. It looked like a **woman** was fighting a **man**. How untoward. What sort of man would wail upon a woman like that! He **really** must say something.

*

The woman hesitated but a fraction of a second, taking in the scene before her in the hall.

Then, she flew at him, her face contorted so terribly with rage.

*

Gabriel watched from his pillow of stone, as the woman flew at the man.

417

He really wished they wouldn't fight in his bedroom.

He'd just got it looking nice.

Oh look. A head.

Bounce, bounce, bounce.

The head is bouncing.

The man's head is bouncing on the floor.

I must be dreaming again.

This is turning into a very strange dream.

And now the head is rolling.

Oh no, it's stopped.

And the head is facing me.

It's not a very nice head. Horrible in fact.

It's all cut, and leaky.

The woman must be strong indeed.

To defeat a man so quickly.

Strong and beautiful.

My, she is beautiful.

A regal beauty. Her features, fine indeed.

But bloody. She should see to that.

And she shouldn't snarl so.

It is not befitting for one so beautiful.

So beautiful.

And her hair, my it is like spun gold.

But why does she look at me so?

With those eyes. So striking. So piercing. So blue.

I feel I know those eyes.

That I've looked upon them before.

Surely I have.

Many a time.

I've seen them dance.

I...love those eyes.

But they are not right.

They are not your eyes to dance with.

You have stolen them.
They are not yours.
They are...
He frowned, searching his mind.
For the face.
For the owner of those eyes.
The true owner.
Not this pretender.
Ahah!
Of course.
He smiled dopily.
"La Meme", he purred.
And the last thing he saw before the darkness took him, was her tear-filled eyes, staring prettily back at him.

*

She blinked the tears from her eyes, but they continued to come.
She turned to the ring upon the floor.
Gabriel was gone.
There was nothing more for her now.
Kneeling, she picked the ring up, and held it high for all to see, admiring its beauty.
She had no more fight in her.
Nothing left to give.
She had tried.
Truly she had.
Perhaps this was simply her fate.
We cannot all escape the ever-raging winds of the tempest.
Try as we might.
A still came upon the room as they watched her.
It hurt so much.
Too much.
She lowered the ring toward her finger.

419

Felt her finger stretch, impatiently, towards it.
It called to her.
It knew her.
She hesitated, breathing deeply, closing her eyes.
Then, she slid the ring slowly onto her finger.
It was always for her.
Always hers.
It had come home.
Finally.
She opened her eyes.
The eyes of a queen.
She held them in her gaze.
And smiled.
A bittersweet thing.
And then.
A sweet thing.
And finally.
A lusty thing.
She twirled.
The ring, twirling with her.
She threw her arms out wide to stop her spin.
The ring shone red.
Red as her lips, flush with life.
She stopped and stood, perfectly still.
At peace with her tempest.
At one with it.
She was La Meme no more.
There was no need for her.
Not anymore.
La Meme was dead.
She...
She was Régine.
And she would hide no longer.

"Long live the Queen", Régine said sombrely.

After a moment, she smiled prettily at the assembled Tableau Haute.

When they did not respond, she narrowed her eyes, and placed her hands haughtily on her hips.

"Well? Did you miss me?" she asked.

Humblest Endings

She'd walked for what felt like forever. Until her feet bled, and then stopped bleeding, and then bled again some more.

She didn't know where she was. She vaguely recalled the sun rising, and then falling, as she trod on, ever onward, unable to stop, unable to look back.

All she knew was that she had to keep walking. Had to keep moving. She couldn't stop. If she stopped, she would have to think. And if she had to think, then she would have to see. See the things she did not want to see.

And so she walked, and walked, and walked. Faces and places passed, their aspect blurred, their finer details lost to her.

She felt a hand upon her once, and heard a voice. A familiar voice, perhaps, but she simply shrugged it off, and kept on walking.

Sometimes, she didn't even know why she walked, numb as she was. Everything was out of place in her head. Everything was blurry. Nothing seemed to fit. The edges didn't line up right. Like a broken jigsaw puzzle. She didn't know how to put them together again.

Didn't know if she wanted to even, for to do that, she'd have to consider each piece, and the picture it made.

Confused and tired, little Rudra plodded on, her fragile little mind reeling.

She paused for a moment, tiredness getting the better of her.

"Hello", a shy voice said quietly.

She blinked and rubbed her eyes. She thought she'd heard something. She had probably imagined it. She'd been hearing things all day...and night.

She made to press on, when the voice spoke again.

"I'm over here, silly", the voice said.

Again the voice! She shook her head and covered her eyes with her hands. The voices were becoming more persistent. She had to keep moving. She was foolish to stop.

"Are you blind?" the voice asked in a matter-of-fact kind of way.

She started walking. Just keep walking. But she made it not a few paces, before a soft hand found her arm, and a fae face appeared in front of hers.

Mama?

Rudra jumped backwards, her face ghostly pale.

"Are you well?" the voice asked. "Sometimes I'm not well. It's fine if you're not well too, you know".

Was she now seeing things as well?

At first she had thought it was her mother, but she saw now it was a girl. A thin waif of a thing with white, blonde hair down to the back of her legs.

The girl stood, looking at her strangely. Looking at her up and down as if considering her. Strangely, she did not feel judged.

It was not the kind of look boys gave her. It was appraising, but in a curious way, as if simply for curiosity's sake, and no other sake. And it was not the kind of look...papa.

She stopped and screwed her eyes shut.

"Hey", the voice said. "It's alright". She felt a hand on her arm once more. It was very soft, and she started to shake and rock back and forth.

"Got to keep walking", Rudra muttered.

"What did you say?" the voice asked.

"Gotta keep walking", Rudra repeated. "Gotta keep walking…"

"You want to walk?" the girl asked. "You must really love to walk!"

Rudra paused.

The girl giggled.

"So let's walk!" the girl said. And with that, she laced her arm through Rudra's, and began to pull her gently down the street.

At first Rudra resisted, but then, she started to walk. Slowly at first. One slow step. Then another.

The girl pulled her all the while, and spoke excitedly about something or other. Rudra did not hear her. The girl's touch frightened her. But at the same time, she took some comfort in it.

Part of her wanted to lash out and throw the girl from her. To scream at her, to rail at her, to run and never look back. Part of her wanted to be led by the girl. To listen to her. To be with her.

She did not know. So she walked. She knew to walk. There was no thinking to be done. And the girl led her, so the walking was easier, which was a good thing, because her feet really were rather sore. And she really was rather tired, she began to realise.

They walked for a while, Rudra and the girl.

The girl spoke, and Rudra listened. At first, she didn't hear much, didn't make much sense of what was being said, but as they walked further and further, more of the words got through to her, and she knew more of the girl.

After a while, they came to a stop, in front of an old building in quite the state of disrepair. Rudra squinted her eyes in the dark.

Safe Place?

It can't be…

"It's in here", the girl said with a smile.

Rudra wanted to reply, but she could not yet. She opened her mouth, then closed it. The girl said nothing, she simply turned and led her to the side of the building, where there was a boarded-up entrance.

The girl nimbly crouched, and squeezed herself through a girl sized opening in the bottom of the entrance.

Rudra stood and watched. She didn't know what to do. Part of her wanted to keep walking. But she was so tired. And the girl did not frighten her anymore.

She turned, looking back at the street, as if considering, when a small face popped through the gap in the entrance and grinned up at her with innocent enthusiasm.

"Are you coming?" the girl asked sweetly.

It was enough to sway her, and Rudra dropped to her knees slowly, and pulled herself through into the building.

It was dark and dusty.

She saw now it was not Safe Place, but it reminded her of it greatly. It had the same air of neglect. The same feeling of empty. But also a feeling of safety. A feeling that no one else knew about it, or cared to, so she would not be bothered, or sought, or chased.

A hand grabbed her own, and she jumped wildly, her senses firing.

"I'm sorry, I'm sorry!" the girl exclaimed, her face falling sadly.

Rudra's heart beat in her chest and she placed her hand on it as she began to hyperventilate. She stepped backwards, until her back was against the entrance to the building. She watched the girl frantically, her eyes shining vulnerably, like those of a doe.

The girl started to cry. "I'm sorry, honest I am, I didn't mean to scare you".

Rudra tried to control her breathing. She felt bad. And realised with a start that she had felt something. She hadn't felt anything since...

She breathed deeply, and as her breathing slowed, she took a step forward. "I'm sorry".

The girl stopped crying, and looked at Rudra, peeking at her through delicate hands. She grinned suddenly, and Rudra felt a little better, a little less guilty. Her smile was like the sun after the rain.

"Me too", the girl said. "I really didn't mean to scare you. I get scared too sometimes..." she trailed off and looked out one of the windows.

Rudra hesitated, then stepped closer to the girl. "Thank you", she said.

"For what?" the girl asked, cocking her head, that curious look about her once more.

"I don't know", Rudra said lamely. "For taking me here. I...used to come somewhere like this".

"Used to?" the girl asked.

Rudra stiffened and turned away, her thoughts tumbling madly through her head. She buried her head in her hands.

The girl approached her cautiously. She did not want to startle her or scare her again. She watched for a moment, then made up her mind. Softly, ever so softly, she wrapped her arms around Rudra, and gently rested her face on her back.

Rudra tensed. Every muscle urged flight. Every impulse screamed flee. But she did not. Something in her told her to stay. And so she stayed.

And after a while, she relaxed. Her muscles unknotted, and after a while longer, her feelings did too. Her defences stood down and rested, their need, for the time being, not required.

She didn't know how long she stood there, with the beautiful girl cradling her. She didn't know when she started to rock, or when the girl started rocking with her. And she didn't know when she started to cry, or sob, or wail piteously.

She did not know at what point she fell to the floor, or when the girl started running her hands through her hair, and across her face, and under her chin.

In her mind, she was with her mama again. Her mama's beautiful white blonde hair gently caressed her face, and she buried her head in her chest. She loved to cuddle with mama like this, she had ever since she was a little girl. Mama didn't cuddle her like this much anymore, Beni didn't like it.

He shouted at her and said that she didn't deserve it, that she was always cuddling her and not Beni. And then he'd drag her away from her into their bedroom, and she wouldn't get to cuddle her mama anymore.

But not now. Now she was all hers.

Mama's hair smelled so nice, so comforting, so safe. Mama would keep her safe while she cried.

And so, she cried. And cried. And cried. And mourned her mother lost. Lost to her heart. Not yet lost to her mind. Her mind that clung on desperately. Unable to comprehend. Unwilling to accept.

She clutched at mama and pulled her closer. Pulled her tight. She would never let her go. Never ever.

The girl lay there with her, and the girl cried too. She felt the grief. It reminded her of her own.

And so they lay together, each lost in their grief, each taking from another, a small solace, a small comfort, on a dark, dark night.

*

They cried until their grief was spent, and their tears would come no more.

The two girls, companions in grief, bonded by trauma.

It creates a special bond, such a thing, and Rudra knew this girl would be no fleeting friend. She knew not how, but she felt it.

Sometimes, our feelings know better than our thoughts. And in some matters, we should defer to our feelings, for they have authority over our thoughts in certain domains. And friendship is such a domain. It is the domain of the heart. And it is our hearts that sing that song of friendship, our feelings, the strings it plucks to create the melody.

We cannot always choose our friends, with thought and logic and reason. Sometimes, they choose us. Sometimes, they are chosen for us. By our hearts. For they know better. Better than we.

It was such a matter with Rudra and her new friend. She did not know it yet. But their friendship would define her. Shape her. Tether her and anchor her. It would be her shelter in the storm. Her harbour from dark and murky waters. And it would serve as her compass, it would help her point true north, and find her way, when she could find no way.

For now, it was shelter, and it was shade. And it would suffice to keep her tethered to this dark and cold world, so that her feet did not lose the path, did not tread paths untreadable, paths with no return.

For some paths once walked, cannot be unwalked.

It is a tight rope she walks, our Rudra. To tip, to lose her balance, surely she could, and could we think poorly of her, could we condemn her? How could we?

How would we fare, forced to walk the same rope as she, lashed by strong winds, assaulted by stronger feelings, lulled by darker demons. Harsh voices, wilting whispers, maddening screams.

It will be a long and lonely path she walks. A hard road. With many a twist and turn. Be thankful of her friend. Of her friendship. For it will give her some measure of light, some measure of hope, in the face of darkness, in the face of hopelessness.

And sometimes, that is all one can hope to ask for.

On some level, she knows this. Perhaps it is why she gravitates to the girl. Perhaps it is why she lets her in. Into her world of grief. Grief too strong to endure alone. Grief that would consume her alone.

And so she went with the girl. Went with her from her Safer Place. Back into the world. Into the city. The city of romance. The city of love. Where iniquity and loss were the most common bedfellows, for girls such as she, as they smile coquettishly from every corner, and beckon invitingly from every window.

*

"This is Mama Magda", the girl said happily, gesturing at a matronly woman of middle age.

"Hello", Rudra said meekly, glancing at the woman behind the counter.

The woman wore a stained white apron over a flowery dress. It was pink like fuschia and green like olives and white like milk.

Her skin was beautifully tanned and complimented her curly black hair that sat prettily just below her neckline.

Rudra found her not at all threatening, and found herself smiling a little in spite of herself.

"Why hello, my beautiful, and what might your name be?" the woman asked, looking up from her cleaning.

Her eyes twinkled mischievously from behind a glass pastry case. Her mouth curved insolently into a little smile, beneath her finely designed cheeks.

"Have you come to take years from my life, or pastries from my case?" Magda asked suddenly before Rudra could respond, fixing her with a piercing stare.

Rudra froze.

Magda laughed, breaking the tension. "This one". She gestured at Rudra's friend. "She comes for my life. She **liiives** to age me. To wrinkle my beautiful face. To turn my **glorious** midnight black hair to grey. Oh it's a tragedy!" She pouted and pawed dramatically at her face with her hands, before resting them prettily under her chin and gazing at Rudra like a little puppy.

Rudra found her wonderful. How fascinating.

Never had she met such a woman who acted in such a way,

429

and she quickly forgot herself, watching raptly as the woman swept about the room, cleaning and tidying, sorting and sweeping, talking animatedly all the while.

It was a blissful change of pace. And the voices in her head quietened. They liked her too. They were glad for the peace. This woman worried them not at all.

"Mama, do you have any food?" the fae girl asked quietly, breaking the comfortable silence that had developed as the woman finished off the last of her chores and came to a halt.

"Oh, of course! How could I forget myself? Bad Mama Magda", Magda muttered, shaking her head as if she couldn't believe herself. "Yes, yes, yes", she continued to mutter, as she slid open the back of a glass case and pulled out a selection of pastries.

"Here you are, my dear". Magda placed a selection of pastries in front of the girl on a pretty little plate. She turned to Rudra. "And you, my dear, what is your heart's desire?"

The girl nudged Rudra.

"Who, me?" Rudra asked dumbly.

"Is there another beautifully underfed girl that I do not see?" Magda peered about the room theatrically. "Yes you!"

"Uh..." Rudra said. She was terribly hungry, now that she thought about it. She couldn't remember when she last ate. Her stomach growled loudly. It punctuated the silence and brought a smile to Magda's face.

Magda laughed. It was a loud laugh. On another person you might have said it was haughty, the way she cackled, and threw her hand in the air above her head. But on Magda, it was warm, and entertaining.

"For you, ze works!" She spun and snapped her fingers, then wiggled her hips immodestly.

"It's fine", Rudra started. But Magda cut her off, shaking her head and wagging her finger at her, as she busied herself in the kitchen.

"Isn't Mama Magda great?" the girl asked dreamily. She watched Magda with her head cupped in her hands from the little table they'd seated themselves at.

"She is certainly something", Rudra agreed, grinning. "Is she...your mother?"

The girl's face fell. "No", she replied simply, in a high voice.

"Oh, I'm sorry... I didn't mean", Rudra said.

"It's fine", the girl said, forcing a smile.

"Mama mia!" Magda exclaimed suddenly in a funny voice, tossing something high into the air, before spinning and catching it in a worn pan.

The girl giggled, her eyes on Magda once more. Rudra watched the girl quietly. The girl jumped suddenly, and spun to face Rudra.

"I just realised. I didn't even tell you my name! Mama Magda says it's very rude", the girl said seriously.

Rudra smiled. "If Mama Magda says it".

The girl reached for Rudra's hand, and this time, Rudra shied away only a little, before reaching out to take it in her own.

"I'm Ivy", the girl beamed. "Like the plant!" she added importantly. "Magda says Ivy is important. Says that insects and birds like to eat it. Says that some of them even live in it. Says that it keeps them safe, shelters them. From the dark. And the cold. I don't like the dark. I don't like the cold much either", she finished with a most thoughtful look on her face.

"And you?" Ivy asked.

Rudra froze.

Who am I?

She didn't know. Everything was fuzzy. She felt dizzy and closed her eyes.

"Oh là là!" Magda shouted suddenly. "Ow ow ow". She dropped the pan she was holding and it clattered loudly to the counter top. She scurried away quickly to a sink in the back of the kitchen, exclaiming all the while.

"Mama?" Ivy called. "Are you hurt?" She leapt from her chair and ran to the back of the kitchen where Magda was cooling a burn on her hand.

"My beautiful hand!" Magda moaned. "Such a horrible blemish. Ugh. How ghastly".

"Hold it under the water, mama", Ivy said seriously.

Rudra watched the woman. And something in her warmed to her. She was so caring and...motherly.

"I'll never be beautiful again!" Magda wailed.

"Of course you will, mama", Ivy cooed. "You're the most beautiful woman I ever saw".

"Oh, darn it!" Magda said. She turned the tap off, and whipped her apron off, throwing it unceremoniously on the floor.

"Sorry, dear", she called over the counter to Rudra. "Coming".

Rudra squirmed uncomfortably. She was not used to being the centre of attention. And she was even less used to someone being so nice to her, someone that wasn't...

She pursed her lips and frowned.

"Is something the matter, my dear?" Magda asked, as she placed a large omelette in front of her.

Rudra shook her head. Not wanting to seem ungrateful, she forced a smile. "Thank you, Magda".

Magda beamed at her. "That's quite alright".

Rudra paused. Magda was still staring at her.

"Eat up now", Magda ordered.

Rudra felt nervous and unsure. But she picked the fork up and forked a small amount of omelette onto it. She didn't like the silence, so she stuffed it into her mouth, and began to chew.

She didn't like omelette much, but she forced herself to keep chewing. After a few chews, she swallowed, and felt her stomach cry out with joy. It growled once more, as if to tell her, keep going!

She obliged and forked a larger amount of omelette into her mouth. She swallowed this with gusto, as the juices of the omelette spilled out into her mouth, and she savoured the spices and the small chunks of ham Magda had sprinkled throughout the omelette.

Magda nodded her head and smiled with satisfaction. She returned behind the counter and began cleaning her pan.

"Wow, you must have been **starving!**" Ivy exclaimed, as the omelette disappeared with alarming speed from Rudra's plate.

Rudra smiled embarrassedly. "I guess so", she said in between mouthfuls.

"So, how was it?" Magda asked, returning from the counter and crossing her arms. She narrowed her eyes and started rubbing her bottom lip quickly back and forth. "Well?"

She threw her arms out wide, and Rudra noticed her foot had started to tap quickly. She crossed her arms again and turned dramatically away from Rudra.

"Horrible! I knew it!" she exclaimed. "I knew the ham was a bad idea! Never again!"

Childlike laughter peeled out from the table, and Magda spun back, her mouth wide open, aghast at such treatment. She took a deep breath and made as if to admonish Ivy, but then stopped.

Ivy was sitting quietly, with a bemused expression on her face. For it was her new friend laughing with childlike joy, and not her.

Rudra covered her mouth with her hand, lest she return some of Magda's dreaded ham to her at a pace quite unfavourable to her.

She swallowed hard, finishing the last bite of her omelette, which was just as well, as another laugh burst from her, and she bent double over the table, laughing into her hands.

Magda stood still watching her, quite taken aback. "Well I never".

Rudra leaned back in her chair, laughing hysterically, hands raised in apology to her host. "I'm...so...sorry", she breathed through paroxysms of mirth.

"Hmph", Magda said. But she smiled thinly. She liked to see the girl smile. And laugh. She had sensed a sadness in her since she had arrived. And for the first time, she didn't sense it. If only for the moment perhaps.

Magda liked to make people smile. She liked to make them laugh even more. The truth was, she liked to entertain people. It was the quickest way to smiles, and the quickest way to laughs.

It was part of why she carried herself as she did, why she liked to inject a touch of theatricality into the most mundane of tasks, a flourish of the dramatic to the simplest of things. And if the girl found her ham a source of amusement, well then, she supposed that was alright with her.

She could be a little touchy about her cooking, but some things were more important than ego. And she knew a broken heart when she saw one.

She knew she couldn't mend the girl's heart. Or put it back together again as it once was.

But she could make her smile. She could make her laugh. She could make her forget.

If only for a little while.

*

"I don't think I've ever laughed so hard", Rudra said to Ivy, as they left Magda's little pâtisserie.

Ivy giggled. "Mama is very funny", she agreed. "And she makes the most **delicious** pastries".

"Mmm", she moaned, as she stuffed an unladylike amount of strawberry topped pastry into her mouth.

"Ivy!" Rudra giggled.

Ivy smiled blissfully, her teeth and lips covered in cream.

"You have some on your chin", Rudra said, as she leant forward and delicately removed the cream from her chin with her finger. She hesitated, then licked it clean. "Delicious!"

They both laughed mischievously.

"Oh, isn't it just", Ivy moaned through a mouthful of pastry and cream. She swallowed and grinned. "So good!"

"I always go to mama's when I'm sad", she declared suddenly, her expression serious now.

"Do you get sad a lot?" Rudra asked tentatively.

"Sometimes..." she replied vaguely. "More than I'd like", she admitted, with an astuteness not often found in one so young.

Rudra said nothing. She hoped she would not make Ivy sad.

"Here we are", Ivy said.

Rudra stopped, surprised. Intent as she'd been on Ivy, she had not watched where they'd walked. She'd been here before but couldn't quite place it. Perhaps earlier in the day.

"Where are we?" Rudra asked.

"Here", Ivy repeated simply, as if it were a silly question.

"And where is 'here'?" Rudra asked dumbly.

"It's where I live", Ivy said, looking deep into Rudra's eyes, as if daring her to mock her.

Rudra looked up at the imposing stone building.

Presque à La Maison, a poorly painted red sign read above the door. She shuddered, as a chill of premonition went through her.

"It's big", Rudra said.

Ivy nodded quietly.

"It's where I live", she repeated. "Emmanuel looks after me. He lets me live here".

"Emmanuel?" Rudra asked.

Ivy nodded.

Rudra paused, she was loath to ask the same question twice, but ask it she must.

"Is he your father?" Rudra asked.

"No", Ivy replied, a faraway look in her eye. "But he lets me live here. In the big house. It's a nice house. And I have a nice room. My own room".

"That's nice", Rudra replied uncomfortably.

A silence developed then.

"Well, I guess I should go", Rudra said finally.

"Go where?" Ivy asked.

"H-". Rudra stopped. "I don't know".

"Then how can you go there?" Ivy asked.

"I don't know", Rudra replied lamely. She turned away sadly.

"You don't have somewhere, do you?" Ivy said quietly.

Rudra thought of lying, but she was too tired to spare her pride. "No".

"I didn't have somewhere, once", Ivy said. "And Emmanuel let me live here".

"That's nice of him", Rudra said, still unsure of the relationship between this man and her friend.

Ivy brightened. "You can stay with me!" she cried suddenly. "Oh, you must! I would love you to stay with me!"

She pulled at Rudra's arm like a child eager for the funfair.

"I've never had a friend before! And you are my friend! That's why I took you to meet Mama Magda!" Ivy said quickly, with no trace of embarrassment.

Rudra was moved. Ivy's profession of friendship touched her deeply. She'd had another friend once, though it seemed like a different life now, in a different world.

A boy's face flashed through her mind. She screwed her eyes shut and shook her head rapidly.

"You don't want to be my friend?" Ivy said sadly.

Rudra's eyes snapped open, and she grabbed Ivy's hand with no hesitation this time.

"No, no! It's not that! Of course I want to be your friend!" Rudra said. The look in Ivy's eyes almost broke her. She saw fear, longing, and such pained rejection as she'd never seen.

Ivy smiled with relief, and her eyes took on their childlike innocence once more. Rudra liked those eyes.

"Phew!" Ivy exclaimed. "That was a close one", she said seriously.

"Why, what were you going to do?" Rudra asked.

"Cry", Ivy replied.

"Oh", Rudra said.

Stupid!

She chided herself. It was a tactless question. She would have to be more mindful.

"But I don't have to now", Ivy said with a smile. "We're going to be best friends!" she burst, throwing her arm around Rudra and pushing her face against hers. She was so soft.

"Now, come", Ivy broke their embrace and stepped away from her, beckoning with her fingers, waggling them invitingly. "We must be quiet. For it's late. And we mustn't disturb the guests".

"Guests?" Rudra asked, bemused.

Ivy nodded. "Emmanuel doesn't like it if we disturb the guests. It's not good if Emmanuel doesn't like things, so we mustn't upset him", she warned.

Rudra's sense of foreboding increased, and she felt a voice stir from its slumber at the back of her mind.

Be careful.

Something about this felt familiar to her. And not in a good way. But what choice did she have?

She had walked her feet bloody and could walk no longer. She needed sleep. And she could not go home. She would never go back there. Or anywhere near there.

And so, she walked into the building, from the darkness of the street, to the darkness of the unknown. She didn't know which was preferable right now, but she had Ivy, and her unknown darkness, so that was something.

Perhaps it wasn't bad at all, perhaps she worried for nothing. Not all men were Beni.

The entrance was dark, but for a little table with a candle on it. To the left, she spied a coat room, full of coats, to her right, a closed door. Why were there so many coats?

"This way", Ivy whispered, as she crept up the wooden staircase behind the table. She pulled Rudra gently behind her.

It was hard to see, and Rudra feared she would stumble and make a noise, causing the displeasure of this Emmanuel man.

They climbed several stories, then Ivy reached the top of the stairs ahead of her, and turned to raise her finger seriously to her lip. She giggled silently and Rudra did too.

Ivy pointed to her left and Rudra nodded. Rudra placed her foot on the second to last stair, and as her weight fell upon it, a loud creaking sound rang out in the hallway.

Almost at once, a door flew open to Ivy's right, and a tall thin man burst out of it.

"Ivy!" he hissed. "Where have you been?" He grabbed Ivy firmly by the arm.

Rudra quickly jumped the last step and pushed him backward. Her face was fierce, her eyes aflame.

"And who is this?" the man asked angrily, his pretence at quietness abandoned, as he took a step back and gestured at Rudra, unsure of her.

"She's my friend", Ivy said, rubbing her arm. "I said she could stay with me".

"You did, did you?" the man asked, fixing her with a heavy stare. The man turned his attention to Rudra, scrutinising her.

She felt his eyes roam over her face and body, and her skin crawled. This was the scrutiny she was used to from men. She liked it not all.

"Well", the man said, unsure of how to play the situation. "Perhaps for the night. Perhaps we can discuss it in the morning", he said, watching Rudra all the while, his eyes becoming speculative.

"But there are rules in this house", he said seriously. "And the first rule is".

"Do not disturb the guests", Ivy chimed in dutifully.

The man looked irritated but attempted to hide it. "Yes...and the second rule is".

"Do not disturb the guests", Ivy interrupted him once more.

He narrowed his eyes and forced a laugh. "Always an answer for everything, my little Ivy", the man said, running his hand down Ivy's arm.

Rudra looked away, her stomach churning.

Her eyes fell on a painting behind them on the wall, in the middle of the hallway. She would come to loathe this painting.

It was a sombre scene.

A finely dressed gentleman, a noble from the looks of it, and what must have been his wife, stood with arms outstretched, pointing accusingly at two women.

The women stood with their backs to a cliff.

The sky loomed over them, grey blue as the sea behind them.

One of the women stood protectively in front of the other, a cloak drawn tight about her face, a sharp blade in her hand. A storm raged around her, yet she stood still and firm in its fury, her face set and determined.

Behind the gentlefolk, stood armed men, swords drawn, and behind them, a mob of angry faces.

The gentleman was very handsome, but his beauty was soured by the expression on his face. It was magnanimous, yet Rudra felt there was no glory to it, she felt it was somehow scornful.

She wondered what victory he had won. She wondered what the women had done to draw his wrath.

She liked the woman with the blade. Her face was brave, and her eyes were steely strong, even in the face of such a perilous predicament.

The other woman looked hopefully up at her protector from the ground, where she must have fallen, for her dress was ripped, and her leg bloody.

Rudra studied the blade the brave woman held. It was short, but thick, tapering into a sharp point. It had a simple black hilt, adorned with a gold base and crossguard.

What did you call such a blade?

"I **said,** what is your name?" the man demanded.

She felt a sweaty hand on her arm and jumped back sharply, throwing it off.

"Woah!" the man exclaimed. "I just asked your name! But if you cannot tell me, I cannot let you stay", he declared pompously.

She said nothing.

"I'll have no strangers in this house", he said, taking a step toward her.

She looked around wildly, as if she would spring from the rooftop or the window, desperate for an escape, when she felt another hand on her arm.

This hand was softer. Familiar. And she jumped, but only a little. Ivy.

She took her hand, and Ivy squeezed hard. A squeeze that said, do not be scared, I am here, and I am with you.

Rudra forced herself to relax.

"Well?" the man asked impetuously, arms crossed. He looked irritated at Ivy's intervention. "I don't have all night, you know".

Rudra looked around, at Ivy, at the man, and at the painting again.

The man opened his mouth to speak once more, but she turned her eyes on him, and he paled.

"My name?" she said suddenly, her face cold as the grave. "My name is Dagger".

Thank you Gerry, for reading my book when it was nothing more than ill formed ramblings.

Thank you Eva, Josh, and Clare, for reading my book, and assuring me that ramblings aside, there was also a story, a story worth telling.

Thank you Mina Anguelova for creating a beautiful book cover that encapsulates the essence of my book.

Most of all, thank you mon coeur, for believing in me, supporting me, and convincing me to take a chance.